INVISIBLE: À PERTE de VUE

INVISIBLE:
À PERTE de VUE
Volume One

By P. W. Hand

Edited by Claire L. Hand
Cover illustration by Claire L. Hand

Wilhelm Libertaire series

Invisible: À Perte de Vue

Volume One

Wilhelm Libertaire series

Copyright ©2013 Phillip William Hand

ISBN-13: 978-0-9960673-0-0 (pbk)

ISBN-13: 978-0-9960673-1-7 (eBook)

Editor: Claire L. Hand

Illustrator: Claire L. Hand

Printed in the United States of America.

First Printing, 2013
Second Printing, 2013
Third Printing, 2015

Harvard Bookstore
1256 Massachusetts Avenue
Cambridge, MA 02138
http://www.harvard.com/book/invisible_a_perte_de_vue

First eBook Edition, 2015
Fourth Printing, 2017
https://www.amazon.com/Invislble-Perte-Wilhelm-Libertaire-Book-ebook/dp/B00WJMZ0BQ

Imprint: P. W. Hand

Disclaimer

Any similarities to any person or persons dead or alive are purely coincidental. This story and its characters are fictional.

Acknowledgements

To my wife Claire who is my muse, my editor, and my staunchest supporter. Her patience and attention to detail is a godsend. She believed in this book from the beginning. To Dr. Felicia Campbell who left me to my own devices and vices to write this book. She gave me guidance but did not interfere with the process. To Ms. Bell my high school teacher who encouraged me to write way back then.

Table of Contents

Table of Contents

Preface

This contemporary spy novel is written to point out a shift in the importance of the modern threat to a country's security, not that nuclear weapons and chemical weapons are not important and deadly threats. But new threats command the order of importance and compromise of the world's resources. Whoever can control the freshwater supplies or create these supplies in conjunction with steady food supplies will be as powerful as any nation with nuclear weapons.

Often, modern technology has been shown as a driving force for intelligence gathering and field work. In this modern story, technology is used as a tool but not as a crutch so that the agents do not rely on flash and extremely high-tech gadgets to get their jobs done. Here, the master spy uses a unique blend of Cold War spying methods and modern techniques to accomplish his task with plenty of hands on action.

Most of you will recognize the countries where this story takes place. Current happenings have put these locations in the forefront of our daily readings. Thus, these settings will keep the reader in the here and now. The twist and turns, the masterful use of deception, and the unforeseen betrayals coupled with experienced adversaries who are worthy of the challenges will keep the reader spellbound.

The introduction of diversity into the world of spy novels is presented in a way that will make the reader take serious notice. The members of the teams are as unique as the spy master himself and his nemeses. This element will help this spy novel stand out even more and set a higher bar. I hope to point out that America has an under-utilized resource and that the CIA could make good use of this resource. The spy master himself challenges the status quo as well as old stereotypes of what is acceptable and what a spy master should be.

Reminiscence

Chapter One

As Frank and his assistant, Linda, prepared to leave the company apartment in Charlottesville, Virginia, Frank took a moment to check his Walther PPK. He looked over the fine silver inlay and scroll work that adorned the slide. The silver trigger and hammer reflected the light with a smart sparkle. The grip was made from Thai iron wood and the red grain ran in gentle swirls along the handles.

Frank thought back to the night when he received this pistol; he and his best friend Wilhelm were celebrating the successful completion of a tough assignment when Wilhelm presented the gun to him during dinner that night.

"God!" he thought. "That was twenty-five years ago. Shit! Where did the time go? And how in the hell did I ever end up as an enemy of my best friend in the process?" This job not only sucks the life out of you, but it causes you to make decisions that make enemies out of friends. Frank took a deep breath, holstered the pistol, took one last look in the mirror, turned, and headed towards the living room.

As Frank entered the living room, his assistant Linda was sitting on the couch looking at a file. He hadn't heard her enter the apartment; he must have been deeper in thought than he realized. Frank paused and ran her background through his head as a manner of routine. This was something he did and he couldn't help it. The company psychologist had told him the medical name for it once, but what-the-fuck does he know. His sorry ass actually gets to sleep at night.

"Fuck him!" he thought. Then his thoughts reverted back to Linda's background.

"This has to be the ugliest couch in all of Virginia, and it's not all that comfortable," Linda said critically.

Frank grunted, walked over to the chair where his coat was draped, and said,

"You happen to be sitting on $78,000 worth of ugly sofa. As a matter of fact," Frank continued, "there's about a million dollars' worth of furniture and art work in this place. How about that?" he said sarcastically.

"W-o-w," was Linda's response as she made a funny face. "Somebody sure got taken for a ride if they actually paid that much for this crap," she continued.

Frank ignoring her last comment said,

"Let's go. I don't want to be late for this meeting. By the way," he continued, "this crap, as you put it, is called federalist. It is not only expensive, it's historical." Frank laid his coat over his left arm, picked up his fedora, and headed for the front door with Linda following a few steps behind.

While waiting for the elevator, Linda wondered why this meeting with Wilhelm was making Frank so uneasy. This was not like him; he was usually detached. Not cold, but cool would better describe him.

At the elevator, Linda started to ask Frank about this man they are going to see, but Frank cut her off with a quick,

"Not here!" At that exact moment, a couple came out of the apartment directly across from the elevator. Frank shot her an evil look. Linda looked away; she would hear about this again. "Fuck! Will I ever understand this world?" She thought about it for an instant, and then the elevator arrived.

Linda, Frank, and the other couple all piled in. The other man pushed the lobby button, and the doors closed. On the way down, Linda thought, "Why didn't he ask us what floor? or say, hi?" Her spider sense tingled. When the elevator doors opened, they saw a man standing there. He was nondescript, average height, fit, weighing about 200 lbs., all of it muscle. He was dressed in a light weight pinstriped suit. Hair cut close but very stylish. Linda looked for his gun, but could not locate it. Although, she was sure he was armed. "He looks like he is a company man, probably the driver," she thought.

Linda had stopped wondering what the different drivers' names were a long time ago. They changed so frequently, and Frank never talked to them except to give directions. As they stepped out of the elevator, Frank did something that Linda had never witnessed in all of the five years she has worked for him. If someone had told her about what just happened, she would have called them a liar.

Frank smiled, extended his right hand, and then addressed the man by name.

"Hello, Kevin. It's been awhile. Good to see you," Frank said, as he shook the man's hand. Kevin smiled and replied,

"It's good to see you too, Frank." Then he turned, headed towards the door, paused, looked over his shoulder, and said, "The car's out front." When Linda regained her composer, she found herself standing with her left hand on her left hip with her right leg extended and an OMG look written all over her face. Frank looking over at her shook his head and said,

"I do have some friends." And then, he followed after Kevin, leaving Linda standing there to process what had just happened. In her confusion, Linda had forgotten all about the couple that had ridden down with them.

But as she got into the car, she looked back at the lobby. And there they stood, watching.

As the car pulled off, they headed southeast down Route 64 towards Richmond. Frank said one word to the driver,

"Wilhelm." Kevin looked at Frank in the rear view mirror. Then he punched some numbers into the computer that he had on the seat next to him and stepped on the gas. Linda sat there taking all of this in. Nothing was making sense—the light blue town car instead of the usual black sedan, staying at the company apartment in Charlottesville, and a file that has no pictures in it concerning this Wilhelm fellah or his family. What-the-fuck is Frank up to? And who is this driver? These thoughts and more streamed through Linda's mind as she looked out of the car window.

They had been traveling down Route 64 for about twenty minutes when Linda finally said,

"Okay, what's the story on this Wilhelm guy?" Looking straight ahead, Frank smiled.

"It took you all of twenty minutes," he said, "… must be some kind of new record."

"Stop dancing, Frank!" Linda interjected in an unusually stern voice. "Tell me what's going on."

"Okay, okay!" Frank said. "Don't get your knickers in a bunch; I was going to fill you in."

"Now would be a good time," Linda stated. Frank closed the file he was reading and adjusted his sitting position. He looked straight ahead; and in the rearview mirror, he caught Kevin's eye. Kevin gave him a slight nod and then turned his attention back to the business of driving.

"I first meet Wilhelm in Lebanon in the early 80s," Frank began. "I was sort of, well, trapped in a building by four not too friendly gentlemen.

All I had was a pistol and one extra magazine. I managed to kill two of them before I ran out of bullets. When the remaining two figured out that I was out of bullets, they decided to rush in to finish me off; and they magically turned into four. I was standing there with my hands above my head thinking, 'Shit! I can kiss my poor ass goodbye.'" Frank laughed at the thought, paused, and then continued. "Just about the time they were going to shoot me, four quick shots rang out. Well, I hit the floor. When I looked up, the four men were dead."

"Well, who did it, Frank?" Linda questioned half excited.

"It was Wilhelm. He was standing there about 10 meters from me, and he said, and I quote, 'Get your sorry white ass up.'" Linda let out a laugh. She couldn't imagine anyone saying that to her boss.

"Well what happened next?"

"I got up. It turns out that he had been there all along watching the whole incident unfold."

"You mean he was in the building the whole time, and he didn't help you until then?" Linda blurted out.

"Yep, the whole time …."

"Bastard!" she mumbled.

"Not really."

"How can you say that is beyond me? He almost let you die. And what was he doing there in the first place?" Linda continued.

"Well, he was in the Corp at the time, in the unit they referred to as the suicide squads."

"Suicide squads? Are you fucking kidding me, Frank? Who in their right mind would volunteer for such duty?"

"Do you want to hear the story or not?"

"Yes," replied Linda.

"Then be quiet for a moment, will ya," Frank said with a little annoyance in his voice. "You see, these squads were made up of volunteers from the force reconnaissance units in the Marine Corp at the time. They only went on high risk missions; as you can imagine, not many survived," Frank said in a quiet voice. "After he took a look around outside, he had me help him move his equipment to another position. We moved down two buildings and up to the fourth floor of the third. By this time, I had figured out that he was a Marine scout sniper. And he had a particular target in mind; he wasn't just out hunting." Frank paused for a moment and looked over at Linda. She was looking at him concentrating on what he was saying. But Frank also knew that she was searching for information that was not in the files. In short, she was trying to fill in the gaps. Frank loved this quality about her. It was one of the reasons he had selected her as his assistant, that and those great legs of hers.

"Who was the target?" Linda said impatiently.

"Hold on, there is a little more to this story than who was killed," replied Frank.

"There is? What I'm getting from this so far is one, you messed up. Two, Wilhelm saved your ass. And three, he shot someone, same old story, Frank."

"I know you think that's all there is to it, but you're wrong. You see, once we got settled in, I asked him what his mission was. He didn't answer me. I mean he just ignored me. Then I asked him for the safest route out of the area. Again he ignored me. He just kept looking through his scope."

"That scope," Frank continued, "was unique even for that time, and the rifle was not standard Marine Corp issue either. The barrel was at least four inches shorter than the standard issued 308 caliber sniper system of the time. The stock was made of a synthetic material in black. The rounds he used were shorter and fatter than any I had seen until then. He carried a Browning high power 9 mm pistol as his side arm with a Stykes Fairbanks knife. None of these items are Marine issue. He was dressed in black jeans and wore a mud colored loose fitting shirt, the kind you pull over your head, no buttons. He had on black rubber soled ankle boots, which had no tread on the soles. He carried a black backpack that held everything else that he needed.

"Well, we stayed in that building for two days and nights with Wilhelm rarely taking his eyes away from the spotting scope. Hell, I don't think he slept. At least, I never caught him. He was already awake every time I woke up. Needless to say, we didn't talk much. On the third day around 1100 hours, his body posture suddenly changed. He'd gone on high alert. I quickly looked through the spotting scope, and what I saw were three men standing around carrying AK47s, nothing unusual about that. These same guys had been there off and on for the last couple of days. I wondered what he was looking at.

"Around 1300 hours, four women and six to eight children showed up. The women began to setup two tables with food and drink. Well, the food looked real good. I was kind of hungry for something besides the trail mix that Wilhelm was kind enough to share with me. Anyway, at 1500 hours, four more men showed up. Wilhelm took out a small picture and looked at it. Then he put it back in his pants pocket, adjusted his shooting position, and nothing. This guy was driving me batty. When was he going to shoot? Who was he going to shoot? Shit, if he waited any longer I was going to shoot somebody." Frank looked at Linda. She still had that intense look on her face.

"Why are ya looking at me?" Linda said, "continue, you big boob."

"Alright, you can be a real nuisance sometimes, you know," Frank said.

"And she sure knows how to interrupt a good story," Kevin said from the front seat.

"The hell with both of yous," Linda said.

"Okay, okay, children. Calm down!" Frank chimed in. "Anyway," he continued, "around 1723 hours, Wilhelm readjusted his position a second time. I was looking through the spotting scope watching the children running around. I saw one of the men holding a child when Wilhelm pulled the trigger. The shot startled me, and my eye left the scope for a moment. When I looked back into the scope, it took me a minute to find the target. The men were franticly looking all around. The women were franticly pulling at a body on the ground. When they finally stood up and moved away, I saw they had a child in their arms. It was the little girl that the man was holding a second ago. Shit! I thought. This bastard just killed a little girl. When I took a closer look, I saw the young man who had arrived with the last four men. He had a hole in his chest, the likes I had not seen before. Funny thing is I didn't pay him any attention before. He looked like a common solider, a target of no value. It turned out that the target was the leader of a faction that didn't want to go along with the program. Wilhelm had put a bullet through the girl's shoulder in order to kill his target. This is the man we are going to see." Looking over at Linda, Frank said, "This man doesn't let anything get in the way of a mission."

"You mean to say that this Wilhelm guy is so cold hearted that he would shoot a little girl?" blurted Linda.

"What is he, Frank, one of our special contractors? an independent? How is this guy connected to us, Frank?"

"None of the above, I'm afraid. He's one of us."

"Shit, Frank, what does he do for us? I mean, is it his job to remove personnel or arrange their removal?" Linda asked.

"No, no, my dear," Frank replied placing his hand on her knee. "He is one of our best managers, and I do believe he has given up the removal business, for now." Frank was looking at her now. He was studying her reaction to the story. Sure the story was true enough, even though he had left out a part or two. The main purpose of the account was to get her senses firing on all cylinders. He would need her at her best for today's meeting with Wilhelm. The added touch of removing the pictures and other selected information had the affect he was hoping for. Frank knew that an incomplete file would drive her crazy causing a crack in her mental armor. He knew that Linda was no fool. If he wasn't careful, she might figure out what he was up to. Removing that information combined with the story would allow him to plant whatever information he wanted about Wilhelm, and she would buy it, hook, line, and sinker.

As Frank moved his fingers ever so lightly up and down her thigh, Linda was staring out the window comparing what she had just heard to what she had read in the file. She wondered why key information was missing from the file.

"Frank, you son of a bitch," she thought, "you may fuck me in bed but you won't fuck me on this mission. What are you really up to you crafty old fox?" If there is one rule she understood, it was not to trust anyone and that included Frank.

"Mmmm," Linda moaned. Frank's fingers were starting to feel good. She would think about this later. She had time, lots of time.

Thursday, September 23, 2010

It was 4:30 a.m. Colleen was lying in bed. She stirred, rolled over, and instinctively felt for her husband. When she discovered that he was not in bed, she got up, put on her robe, and headed down stairs. She had a good idea where she would find him at this early hour. At the bottom of the stairs, she turned left and entered the library. There, he sat bathed in the soft light of the desk lamp. Wilhelm looked up from the papers he was reading as she entered the room.

"What has gotten you up so early?" she asked.

"I was about to ask you the same," Wilhelm replied. Then he noticed her robe was open and the night gown she had on wasn't hiding very much. At that moment, Colleen headed towards that overstuffed chair she loved and curled up in it.

"Come on. Tell me what has you up so early," she said.

Wilhelm looked at his wife. From his position behind the desk, he had a perfect view of her curled up in the chair. She was still as beautiful as when he married her, he thought; and she was still a wildcat in bed as that night gown suggested. He looked at the curve of her breast and how her night gown only covered the upper part of her thighs. You couldn't tell by looking at her that she had borne him three children. Wilhelm refocused himself and looking at his wife said,

"The Toad is coming for lunch."

"What! You mean Frank is coming here," she exclaimed.

"I mean just that," said Wilhelm.

"Well? What does he want?" Colleen questioned.

"You know better than to ask me that, Colleen," Wilhelm replied. "It's about time he paid us a visit, don't you think? It's been seven years," Wilhelm continued.

"Has it been that long, Will?" Colleen said in a low voice. "Let's not think about it just now. Come back to bed."

"Okay, you know you're not hiding much under that gown," Wilhelm said with a devilish grin.

"So you noticed."

"How could I not with the way you're sitting in that chair. If you're not careful, a girl could get herself into trouble," Wilhelm said as he started coming around the desk.

"I'm not worried. You're not as fast as you used to be. If you can catch me, I'm yours for the rest of the morning," Colleen said with a sexy smile.

"Slow am I. So you think I'm slow? I'll show you slow, missy," Wilhelm said as he raced from behind his desk towards her. Colleen let out a girlish squeal, popped out of the chair, and headed for the stairs with Wilhelm right behind her. As they ran out of the library and headed for the stairs, they both said good morning to the guard who upon hearing the noise had come out to investigate. He returned the greeting, smiled, shouldered his weapon, and headed for the kitchen.

Wilhelm caught up to his wife at the top of the stairs. After giving her a passionate kiss, he patted her on the ass and said,

"Now let's go and find out how old I really am." Colleen let out a little sigh, turned, and headed for the bedroom. She put a little extra sway in her hips as she walked. It didn't go unnoticed.

It was 8:30 a.m. when Colleen finally came downstairs. She used the backstairs; the one that led directly to the kitchen and to the safe room.

"Well, look at what the cat dragged in or should we say, look at what the tiger released," said a voice within the kitchen.

Colleen blushed and addressed the two ladies in the kitchen, "Don't tell me you two heard."

"How could we not hear," said Afef.

"Yeah!" chimed Afra. "With the two of you running up and down the halls like newlyweds, how could we not hear?" Afra said with a big smile on her face. Colleen poured herself a cup of coffee and asked if the children had left for school and if either of them knew where Wilhelm was this morning. She was now thinking about the visitor they would be receiving for lunch today.

Afef told her that the children had left for school on time and informed Colleen who were the bodyguard and driver for the day.

"Good," Colleen said as she sipped her coffee. "So, where is Wilhelm?"

"He's out at the gun range, I think," said Afra. "He and George left with two shotguns, a little while ago."

"Hmmm," Colleen said into her cup rather than to the two women in the kitchen with her. "We have a lunch guest today, ladies."

"Who could possibly be visiting us on a week day?" interrupted Afra.

"The Toad!" Afef's face turned serious as she looked at Colleen and Afra.

"What? Who is the Toad?" asked Afra.

"He's in the same business as Wilhelm," explained Afef.

"Oh, I understand," replied Afra. "So, why do you refer to him as the Toad?"

"We will fill you in later," said Afef. "Right now, we better get ourselves ready for our lunch guest. Who is he bringing with him?" Afef directed her question towards Colleen.

"A driver and his newest slut who he calls his assistant," Colleen said with particular disgust.

"What do you want me to do?" said Afra.

"You shouldn't worry yourself with this, Afra," said Afef. "You're six months along. It won't do you any good to get involved, and Wilhelm doesn't want you doing any work," she continued as Colleen shot her a look.

"Okay, then. I will stay out of the way," Afra agreed. "You two can handle it all as far as I'm concerned."

"That's the spirit, Afra. You just relax and let me and Colleen handle our guests," Afef stated devilishly as she looked at Colleen.

"We're here, sir," was the announcement from the front seat. This snapped both Frank and Linda out of their moment of pleasure.

"Good!" said Frank. Kevin then made a left turn onto what was obviously a private lane. He drove about 20 meters and stopped at the intercom posted on the left side of the lane. Nothing else was there to let visitors know that they should stop there, no signs, no gate.

"State your business," bellowed a voice from the intercom.

"Mr. Frank DePore to see Mr. Libertaire," Kevin replied.

"Hold station, please," replied the voice. At the same time, sensors rose from the ground as well as from under the car and begun to scan the car and its inhabitants.

"We're being scanned, sir," Kevin said.

"I expected as much," was Frank's reply.

The voice returned,

"You may proceed. Please stay on the lane. Do not exit your vehicle until you have reached the manor."

"Understood," was all that Kevin said. The car proceeded slowly up the lane. Linda sat staring out the window.

"Geez!" said Linda. "Does he own all of this?"

"Yes," said Frank. "He even has property on the other side of the highway." As they drove along the lane, Linda could see pastures filled with different types of horses, quarter horses, Andalusians, and Morgans. Crops and the usual farm animals were visible as well. The lane was lined with oaks, poplars, and maple trees. The grass was so pretty, and it looked like a blue green sea as it stretched across the meadow. She loved this time of year, early fall but still warm, commonly known as Indian summer. Then the house came into view.

"Wow, this is really a manor, isn't it?" said Linda.

"Yeah, it's a real manor with all of the privileges," Frank said sarcastically.

Kevin pulled into the circular driveway and stopped at the front entrance. At the manor's front entrance, a tall man about six-foot-three, well-dressed in linen trousers and an Egyptian cotton shirt and wearing Italian loafers was standing on the top step. He wasn't armed, Linda noticed. At his side were two very large dogs, French mastiffs, the red mask type, one male and one female. Then a man who was working on a jeep wrangler in the driveway appeared from under the hood. He was armed. He had an M&P Smith & Wesson in 40 caliber on his hip. Then another man came into view carrying a Winchester SX semi-automatic shotgun in tactical configuration; he also was carrying a 40 caliber M&P.

"He sure likes his privacy, doesn't he?" stated Linda.

"Yes," replied Kevin, "he's particular that way." Kevin got out of the car, opened the door for Frank, walked around to the other side, and did the same for Linda.

"Hello, George," Frank said. "Hello, Frank." At that precise moment, Colleen stepped out of the house.

"Kevin, you old dog!" Colleen exclaimed. How the hell are you? You don't come by and see me anymore!" she continued as she approached him with a big smile on her face. Kevin opened up his arms and the two of them embraced. When they separated, Colleen looked over at Frank and said, "Welcome, Frank. Wilhelm will receive you in the library. I'm sure you remember where it is. But in case you have forgotten, George will show you the way." Frank nodded his response. He and Linda followed George up the blue marble stairs leading to the house. Linda couldn't help but wonder who could possibly own all of this on a manager's salary. And then she thought, "What a pretty rose that was carved into the marble on the top step." Frank seemed not to notice the rose but he was careful not to step on it, either. As they entered the foyer, her eyes took in the beauty of the rose marble flooring along with the copper cathedral ceiling. In the middle of the foyer was an oversized round table made of mahogany; it looked small compared to the room it was in. In the center of the table lay a handmade Egyptian lace doily. Everything in this room said wealth, and Linda hadn't seen the rest of the house yet. That thought troubled her but she didn't know why. At that moment, George instructed her to place her weapon or weapons on the table. She did as she was asked. Then George patted her down. Next he turned to Frank and asked him if he was armed. Frank opened up his jacket and showed George the Walther PPK.

"Anything else, Frank?" George asked with a questioning look.

"No," was his reply.

Then George led them to the library. As they were entering, Linda looked up. Above the door and carved into the wood was that same rose. When they entered the library, Wilhelm was looking out of one of the many floor-to-ceiling windows that wrapped around the room.

"Mr. DePore and Ms. Banally to see you, sir," announced George. Wilhelm turned around and with a smile on his face said,

"Frank, Linda, nice to see you. I have a fantastic lunch planned for us today. And while we talk shop, I thought Ms. Banally could enjoy the comforts of Libertaire Manor." He said all of this as he approached her and Frank with his right hand extended and a contagious smile on his face. He was dressed in light blue linen trousers with a cream colored Egyptian gauze tunic. Around his neck, he wore a hand braided white gold chain suspending the medallion of his family crest. On his right wrist was a presidential edition Rolex. His stride was confident and easy, and the handmade Spanish leather loafers he wore made his steps silent.

"Good to see you, Wilhelm; it's been awhile," Frank said as he extended his hand to shake Wilhelm's. "That sounds just fine, and I'm sure Ms. Banally will enjoy your hospitality immensely," Frank continued. Linda just stood there listening to every word and not believing any of it. But what was harder to believe was what she was seeing. Wilhelm was nothing like she imagined. He didn't fit the profile. Hell, he didn't look like what she thought he would. If she was confused before, now she really was confused.

Wilhelm directed them to the leather chairs that where in front of his desk. Sitting there, Linda couldn't control her wandering eyes no matter how hard she tried. Her eyes darted all around the room as if she had never been in a private library before.

"Well it's certainly nice of you to visit, Frank, and to bring such a charming assistant with you as well." The sound of Wilhelm's voice brought Linda back into focus; unconsciously she adjusted her skirt and crossed her legs. She was nervous which was totally out of character for her. Linda had met other managers of his status, and she certainly had been in countless meetings with such people before. So why was she so damn nervous? "Ms. Banally, perhaps you would like to look around my modest library since this is your first visit to the manor."

"I'd love to," she replied."

"I have some first editions that may be of interest to you," Wilhelm said as he came from behind his desk.

"As for you, Frank, there's Hendricks at the bar."

"Will you join me?" Frank said as he headed for the hand carved Kona wood bar.

"Maybe, after lunch," replied Wilhelm.

"How about you, Linda?"

"No thank you, Frank," she said sweetly.

Frank walked over to the bar and began pouring himself a double, neat. As he sipped his drink, he watched Linda with Wilhelm who pointed out certain books and answered questions about paintings and sculptures. "Look at them," he thought. "He's being his same suave self. And she's acting like a school girl with a crush on the older boy who just said, hi. Huh, she never wiggled for me like that either. How this bastard gets women to do that is beyond me. Wait a minute. This is the guy with three wives. I don't think I want to know that trick," he thought shaking his head. Frank turned and poured himself another drink. This is an impressive library by anybody's standard he had to admit as he swept the room with his eyes.

The library is two thousand square feet. It is twenty feet high. The shelves are made from oak and popular trees that were grown on the property. The wood stain on the shelves highlights the beauty of their grain. The maple plank flooring with its clear protective finish showcases its beauty and brightens the room just right. The décor creates just the right mix of pictures to statues, and the handmade area rug is a nice touch even if that great big beast of a dog is laying on it at the moment. The shape of the library is not quite circular; it has an oval feel to it. His desk is flanked on each side by four floor to ceiling windows, each wide enough for a person to step through comfortably. The ceiling is covered in pecan wood panels carved with a map of the ancient world, including the sea lanes.

In the center of all of this is that big fucking desk which holds many secrets. If Frank could just get a peek into one of those draws, he would die happy. Frank started walking towards the desk. The French mastiff let out a low growl reminding him that he was being watched.

"Frank, are you trying to look in my desk?" Wilhelm said without turning around.

"If it wasn't for that damn dog, I would have had a chance," he replied as he gave the dog a dirty look.

"That's why I have the dog, Frank," Wilhelm said as he turned to face him laughing just enough to get Frank's goat. Linda also had a smile on her face. She was trying desperately to hold back a giggle with her hand. Her effort was in vain, and she burst out into laughter.

"Okay! So the dog busted me; it's not that funny," Frank said with a slight gin slur.

"Lunch will be served in a few minutes, Frank. With a little food on your stomach, the dog may be the one at the disadvantage." Frank was about to reply when George interrupted.

"Lunch is served, sir, out on the patio."

"Good, it's a beautiful day; we should take full advantage of it. Do you agree, Ms. Banally?" Wilhelm stated.

"Whole heartedly, Mr. Libertaire," was her reply. Wilhelm led them out of the library down a short hallway through white French doors framed in black onto the patio with George bringing up the rear. They walked out onto the Spanish tiled patio where a magnificent white marble table was situated. The table was adorned with silver and crystal cups, goblets, and glasses with Wilhelm's three wives standing on the opposite side. They were stunning. Linda caught her breath at the sight of them. Even Frank paused for a moment. As they approached the table, Linda observed the place settings; the luncheon ware was fine china trimmed in gold. The silverware was not silver but platinum with a small crest on the handles.

Linda turned her attention to the women. Colleen was dressed in a powdered blue silk satin skirt set with a scalloped ruffled edge that stopped just above her knees. Her hair was braided in an intricate pattern that brought out the softness of her face. She wore a large emerald set in platinum around her neck. On her wrist, she wore a charm bracelet that had small emeralds intermixed with platinum charms. Her wedding ring sported yet another large emerald surrounded by diamonds. Afef was dressed in a turquoise dress with fine silver threading around the neck line, hem, and sleeves. She wore a pendant with a very large sapphire set in white gold. Her charm bracelet had little sapphires hanging from it intermixed with other charms made from white gold. Her wedding ring was a large sapphire surrounded by diamonds. Afra was wearing a beautifully embroidered saffron colored raw silk kaftan which concealed her pregnancy well. Around her neck, she wore a large ruby set in white gold. Likewise, she was wearing a charm bracelet that had rubies intermixed with the other gold charms. Her wedding ring was a large ruby surrounded by diamonds. They all wore silk shoes matching their attire.

Colleen smiled to herself. Her plan had the desired effect judging from the facial expressions that Linda and the Toad were exhibiting. She knew all too well about how much Frank resented her husband's wealth and the special privileges he is afford by the agency. That is why she had them dress as if someone important was dinning with them. It was just the opposite, and she didn't understand why her husband hadn't killed him seven years ago. But she had patience and trust in her husband's judgment.

"Frank, if you would, sit next to Colleen. And Linda, would you do me the honor of sitting to my right? Ladies and gentlemen please be seated," Wilhelm instructed. George went around the table helping each lady with their chairs, first Colleen, then Linda, next Afef, and then Afra. Frank and Wilhelm remained standing until the ladies were seated. After they were all seated, George exited through the French doors.

Now Linda was able to get a better look at the table and its settings. The table was more than long enough to seat all six comfortably. As she looked up and down its length, she noticed just how wide and thick the marble actually was. "Wow," she thought, "This is living. No wonder, he has three wives. The jewelry alone would tempt any woman." Next, her eyes caught the family crest; it was inlaid in the center of the table and appeared to be formed from semiprecious stoned. Linda couldn't be sure so she looked down the table at Frank. But he was locked in conversation with Colleen and didn't notice she was staring at him.

"Is everything alright, Linda?" Wilhelm asked.

"Yes, yes, it's just that ..." she stopped short.

"Go on please continue you are my guest; ask what you want," Wilhelm said.

"I was wondering if this is your family crest as she indicated towards the center of the table. And what is it made of?"

"To answer your first question, yes, it is the family crest. As for the second, the crest is made from semiprecious stones. It was a gift from Afra's father. Do you like it?" he asked with a smile. Before Linda could answer, Afra interrupted,

"Do you speak French, Ms. Banally?"

"Yes, I do."

"Then we shall have a fine conversation over lunch," Afra continued. Linda was struggling to remember her name; she was half paying attention when the introductions were going on. She had been distracted by all of those rocks they were wearing.

« Vous pouvez commencer nous servir, maintenant. » ("You may begin to serve us now,") a gentle voice in French commanded from the opposite end of the table. Linda heard Colleen announcing that lunch had begun. Two servers placed fruit on the table and began filling their water goblets.

Linda noticed the lavish variety of fruits displayed. She feasted her eyes on the mangos, kiwi fruit, apples, oranges, bananas, papaya, and pineapple, as well as grapes and cherries. She loved fruit. "This was fantastic," she thought. She could live solely on fruit.

The conversation around the table was light and friendly, but also careful. Linda noticed that Afef and Afra kept in tune with Colleen by using a series of looks and phrases. Linda was having difficulty keeping up with all that was going on; this was made even harder because everyone was speaking French. "Damn you, Frank! You could have warned me," she thought. Her French wasn't that bad but she definitely would have to work harder on it from now on. Frank seemed to be right at home. He and Colleen as well as Afef were talking and laughing. No doubt, Frank was telling one of his many stories.

Wilhelm and Afra were also talking. He was asking her how she was feeling and how the pregnancy was going. He was genuinely concerned; his soft tone reflected this sentiment. Linda was impressed and her impression of him was changing by the minute. He was obviously a very cultured man. This was clearly shown not only by his collection of literature and artwork but also by his mannerisms. "He was a true gentleman," she thought. "So how could he be such a cold and calculating killer as Frank had described earlier in the car? Something was missing here."

The first course was being served. It was a tomato and roasted pepper gazpacho soup served with warm homemade crusty dill bread with their fresh farm butter and extra virgin olive oil. Colleen surveyed the table. After she was sure that everyone had finished their soup, she instructed the servers to remove the bowls and bring out the next course. As she directed the servers in French, they began their work by replacing the soup bowls with footed crystal bowls filled with citrus fruit. Linda sat very still, not talking. She was admiring the precision in which the staff worked. More so, she was amazed by how gracefully Colleen was orchestrating lunch. So far, it was flawless. She could hardly wait for what would happen next.

"If you do not like the fruit, I can have the servers bring you something else if you prefer. The fruit will cleanse your palate," Afra remarked in French.

Linda heard her clearly, but it took a second to process. "Shit, I am looking really stupid about now. Hurry up and answer, you idiot," she thought. « Oui, j'aime bien les fruit. » ("Yes, I like fruit very much,") she finally replied.

« S'il vous préférez, nous pouvons nous parler anglais. » ("If you prefer, we can talk in English,") Afra continued in French.

« Non, ce n'est pas nécessaire; Bien sûr, français est bon. » ("No, that isn't necessary; French is fine,") she replied in sketchy français. "Pull it together, Linda; this is just lunch; you've been to fancy places before. Stop acting like a raw recruit," she thought encouraging herself. She took several deep breaths, composed herself, and let the French fly. It was great; she was speaking French as if she was a native. The seven years of French classes along with the year she lived in France while in college started to come back to her.

Wilhelm sat quietly enjoying the food and observing Ms. Banally. As he listened to her and Afra talk, he was running her background through his head. He would add what he learned about her today to the file that he had in his desk. He needed to know why Frank picked her. Sure she was a looker, but that wouldn't be enough for Frank to make her his assistant. She must have a special skill, but in what area. That is the question he needed answered. He listened closely to her French. It wasn't academic; it was closer to a native speaker. He made a mental note to investigate further. Then he joined the conversation between her and Afra.

The servers came around and took away the fruit bowls. At this point, they started to open up several bottles of a 1998 Fume Blanc, pausing while Colleen inspected each bottle before it was poured. Next they brought out silver serving trays and placed two trays at each end of the table. One tray held fresh lake trout and the other held fresh largemouth bass. Covered silver bowls held vegetables to accompany the fish and fresh baked rolls. After everyone had a full glass of wine, Wilhelm tapped on his crystal water glass getting their attention.

"To sharing a good meal with old and new friends," he said as he raised his glass and took a sip. Everyone at the table followed suit with Afra drinking from her water glass.

The conversations around the table resumed with Linda, Afra, and Wilhelm conversing and occasionally interacting with the others. But it was mostly Afra and Linda that did the talking. Meanwhile, the servers were busy filling and refilling the glasses and plates with delectable main course dishes and wine. Before Linda knew it, they were clearing away the dishes and replacing them with chilled silver bowls filled with raspberry sherbet covered with fresh raspberries and raspberry sauce resting in ice. Linda was stuffed, but she wasn't passing on dessert.

"Did you enjoy lunch, Linda?" Wilhelm asked.

"Yes, very much. Everything was delicious. I'm stuffed. I couldn't eat another bite," she replied.

"Good, I'm pleased that you joined us for lunch and it was to your satisfaction."

"No, no, Wilhelm, I am honored to be your guest. Thank you for your hospitality."

"Everything you have eaten except for some of the fruit was grown and raised right here on the farm; it's all organic," Afra added. "After lunch, I will show you around if you like."

"I'd like that very much. I've been looking at your gardens," said Linda as she looked to her right past Colleen.

"You are correct, Linda. We can start our tour there if you like," Afra replied.

"That sounds like a plan; after a marvelous lunch, a walk will be good."

"Good, then it's settled," Wilhelm interjected. Wilhelm caught the eye of his wife; and without saying a word, she knew just what to do.

« Tout le monde, le déjeuner est terminé! » ("Everyone, lunch is now concluded!") Colleen announced. "I hope it was enjoyable to all as it was for me. I do believe the gentlemen have some business to attend to." Then she instructed the servers to clear the table. « Débarrassez la table, s'il vous plait. » ("Clear the table, please.") The luncheon party stood up and started to leave the table as Frank came around to where Wilhelm was standing. Colleen motioned to Linda to come over to where she and the other wives had gathered.

As Linda reached the ladies, she looked back in time to see Frank and Wilhelm disappear around the corner of the house heading towards the library. At that moment, she noticed the wraparound porch curled around this part of the house and swept down the opposite side of the patio.

"I hope the lunch was to your enjoyment, Linda," said Colleen. "Afef and I have some business of our own to attend to. So Afra will show you around and keep you company while your boss is busy. I'm sure you two will get along just fine," Colleen informed her. Her statement was more of an order than a suggestion. Linda picked up her meaning immediately. She would have to step lightly around this woman from now on.

"That will be just fine; Afra and I have gotten to know each other over lunch. I am looking forward to learning more about her and the farm," Linda replied.

"Very good, then I shall leave you two to it," Colleen stated as she turned and exited through the French doors with Afef. Afra and Linda headed for the gardens. Afra led Linda down a stone path leading to the gardens. When they reached the edge of the lawn, Linda saw the patio situated on the top tier of the west lawn. She could also see that two more levels were below this one. The second level was decorated with wooden lawn chairs and small stone tables. The gardens were positioned on the last level. From this vantage point, Linda could see four interconnected gardens; they were beautiful. Each garden had a different theme, yet they flowed and complemented each other. Behind the gardens was a vast expansion of open lawn.

The two, stood there for a moment taking in this beautiful sight; it was so peaceful and pleasing to the eye. The air was filled with delightful scents wafting from a carpet of flowers planted all around. Indeed, it was a tranquil sight they were enjoying. Linda looked over at Afra, who was gently rubbing her stomach and breathing in slow deep breaths. Linda wondered what it was like to be pregnant, safe, and loved and to have a family looking after her during this special time in a woman's life. Oh well, she would have to wait a while longer before she found out. She had a plan, and she was going to stick to it. When the time was right, she too would have a family to look after her; and she, in turn, would look after them.

"The garden on the far left," Afra began, breaking Linda's thought. "This is the game garden. It is filled with various board game tables. There are eight game tables in all: Chaturanga Indian chess, Shogi Japanese chess, Makruk Thai chess, Weiqi Chinese chess, American chess, Shatranj Persian chess, Backgammon, and Dominos. A card table sits in the middle of a large gazebo in the center of the garden. As you can see, next to it, we have two mazes, one circular and the other square. The children love this garden as you can imagine."

"How many children are there?" Linda asked.

"Eight including this one," Afra said caressing her stomach. "The next garden is the martial arts garden," she continued. "As you can see, it has a large training circle."

Linda focused on the garden. She saw a large white circle with eight symbols in red around it. In the center was a sitting dragon colored in purple, gold, and red. The dragon held a sword in its left hand and a reddish orange fire ball surrounded by those same symbols in its right hand. Under the dragon was something written in Chinese characters. Around the circle were stone benches and weapons-stands. A manicured lawn surrounded the circle. This garden was separated from the other gardens by flowering hedges.

"What are those symbols?"

"Bagua symbols."

"What's Bagua?"

"It represents the eight directions and denotes the circle of life, pre and post heaven," Afra explained. "It is also one of our family fighting arts."

"Oh, how many arts do you and your family practice? Are there any favorite weapons?"

"There are four fighting arts taught to family members, and the weapon of choice is the sword," Afra stated with pride as she started down the steps. "This next garden," she continued, "is the water garden. Would you like to go inside? This one is my favorite." As they approached the garden's entrance, they were joined by a guard. Afra greeted the man and introduced Linda but she did not give his name. Linda took notice. The guard was casually dressed and wore a shoulder holster.

They entered the garden but the guard remained at the entrance.

"This is my favorite place," Afra said with a little excitement. "It has all of the things I like, and the water is so soothing. Listen. Just listen," she continued. They stood there a moment listening to the running water and smelling the perfume emanating from the fragrant blossoms.

"So, this is what they mean by stopping to smell the roses," Linda thought. She liked this; this was something she could get used to. Afra showed her around pointing out the different quiet spaces throughout the garden.

"This is Wilhelm's and my special place. We come here to talk or just to sit." They lingered awhile longer listening to the water. After a moment, they left and headed to the fourth and last garden. The last garden was spectacular and the largest by far. In its center lay a small stone and sand garden. Positioned around the smaller garden were concealed and semi-hidden spaces allowing different levels of privacy. Interestingly though, wherever someone sat or lounged, they could always see the sand and stone garden without being detected, themselves. It was a well-planned landscape. Whoever designed it was very smart and very clever. The garden had a feel of its own. The selected plants stayed green late into winter allowing for its use late in the season and provided excellent cover. This was more than a retreat; it also was a killing ground to the unsuspecting.

"Who designed this garden? It makes you want to either think or sleep."

"Colleen. She designed it for Wilhelm at his request; this is their special place. I am glad you like it; it takes a special eye to appreciate it."

"Thanks."

"Let's start at the east end of the house; then we can look at the farm if you like," Afra continued.

"Great!"

Now the trio headed down the stone path towards the house. As she walked, Linda looked up at the house and spotted Frank and Wilhelm. Frank had his game face on as she called it. His mannerisms told her he was selling something and was working awfully hard at it. Wilhelm was standing there with his arms folded across his chest listening intensely. At that moment, she lost sight of them as the path dipped down and turned to the right.

The two women entered the house through the sunroom that had black and white checkered granite and marble floor tiles and curved windows lightly tinted in yellow. The lounge furniture was made of teak wood which Linda found fitting for such a space. As they left the room, Linda noticed that the guard wasn't with them. She didn't say anything, and Afra acted as if the guard was never there. They exited the sunroom, made a right, and headed down a long hallway. Afra pointed out the family library and entertainment room as they passed them on their right side. Linda was more interested in the layout of the house than the rooms; so she paid particular attention to the angles, widths, and lengths of the hallways and rooms as she passed them. The design of the house's lower level was laid out strategically. She noticed that the angles allowed the defenders to see an intruder and engage them from cover. She was impressed with the amount of thought that went into this design. Before she knew it, they were at the west end of the house; and Afra was asking if she needed anything before they continued the tour.

"No, I'm fine. Let's continue," Linda answered. Afra led her through a set of double doors. Once outside, Linda was directed towards an electric club car.

"I hope you enjoyed the tour of the house but I think the farm will interest you a little more," Afra said while giving her a look that let her know she was aware that Linda wasn't paying her much attention. Linda looked away from Afra as she got into the cart. She noticed that the driver was a different guard. "Stables, please," Afra directed him after they were seated. As they headed towards the stables, she felt an uneasy silence. Linda knew she had insulted her host by not being attentive.

"I'm sorry if I insulted you by paying half attention. I started the day very early and after such a big lunch, well, I'm a little sluggish."

"It's quite okay, Linda. I understand completely. Perhaps a walk in the fresh air will help you," Afra replied as the cart pulled up to the barn. "Here we have three barns that house sixty horses in total. This is barn one; it houses the families' horses. What size shoes do you wear?"

"What? Linda said a little confused at the question."

"You can't walk around a barn with heels," Afra said as she pointed towards her feet.

"Oh! Size eight," replied Linda. Afra told the guard; he reached into the cart and handed her a pair of size eight duckies. While Linda was changing her shoes, Afra changed into her own pair, and then they started towards the barn.

As they walked through the barn, Afra pointed out whose horse was whose and what breed they were. Linda was trying her best to pay attention but what she really wanted to know was what this beautiful, smart, young woman was doing married to a man that already had two wives. Of course he was rich. That was obvious. But didn't she want someone her own age? ... someone of her own? ... not someone shared with two other women? Linda couldn't get these thoughts out of her head. She had to find a way to approach the subject. She just had to. She was dying to know.

As they were leaving the last barn, Afra stopped and asked,

"Would you like to walk a bit? It's a nice afternoon and I could use a little exercise."

"Great! But can we walk on the grass? I'd like to feel the grass on my feet; it looks so soft."

"Of course, we can. The grass is very soft here on the farm," Afra stated with a smile.

"Wait a minute, will ya," Linda said as she ducked quickly into an empty stall. When she returned, her stockings were removed. "Ah, that feels a lot better. Shall we proceed," she said with a big smile. Afra gave the guard instructions in Arabic. And off they went walking across the lawn with their shadow a few paces behind.

They walked for a few minutes in silence. The grass felt as good as it looked under Linda's feet. Linda looked over at Afra watching her mindlessly walk along. Afra knew every inch of this lawn, and it showed as she casually strolled along. Linda turned her attention to the trees that they were walking under and to the unique benches situated under the sprawling branches of some of the trees. The leaves were starting to turn colors, and the view was awesome. She took a deep breath. The country air smelled real good. This definitely was not D.C. or any of its many parks. The air was different here. Somehow it was cleaner, and it made you feel good. Linda looked behind her and smiled at the guard but he just looked at her. She noticed that he was dressed much like the first guard and sported a shoulder holster too. His gun appeared to be the same caliber.

"It must be some kind of uniform," she thought. Personally, she liked it. It made them look less threatening, although she knew he would not hesitate to shoot her if she made a wrong move. "Gee! The countryside is great," she thought sarcastically.

For the next five minutes, they walked and just enjoyed the afternoon.

"Would you like to see anything in particular, Linda?"

"No, but I would like to sit for a moment if you don't mind."

"Will over there do?" Afra asked as she pointed to a canopied glider sitting under a big popular tree.

"Yes, that will do just fine, Afra. While we sit, maybe, we can get to know each other a little better?"

"Alright," Afra said sweetly. Then Afra told the guard something and he started talking into his radio. She then headed towards the glider. Linda followed wondering what she told him. When they reached the glider and sat down, Linda discovered that it swung quietly back and forth.

A moment later, a cart pulled up. A woman got out and started to setup a small table. Upon it, she placed a pitcher of ice tea and designer cupcakes.

"I thought we might get a little thirsty, and cupcakes are always good for any conversation. Don't you agree, Linda?" Afra said as the woman went about her work. The server poured two glasses of ice tea and then placed napkins on their laps. The woman asked Afra if she needed anything else. Afra shook her head no. Then the woman climbed back into the cart and left as quickly as she arrived.

Looking to her left, Linda saw that the guard had posted himself with his back to a tree at a perfect angle facing her about ten meters away. Just then, a gentle breeze blew. Linda stretched her skirt with her legs to feel the breeze upon her upper thighs.

"Oh! That feels *sooo* good on sweaty thighs," Linda exclaimed as she cut her eyes at the guard. "He couldn't have missed that opportunity," she thought. Afra giggled and took a sip of her tea.

"They don't show any emotion," she said. "My husband picks men that have one track minds, and women are not on them."

"I see, but that breeze did feel good." Afra let out another little giggle. "So you do laugh; I was beginning to think you didn't," Linda said looking at Afra with a big smile.

"Oh, I laugh a lot. Depending on whom you ask, I might laugh too much. Although my husband loves my laugh and I love laughing with him," she said. Looking at her face, Linda could see that far off look in her eyes when she talked about Wilhelm. It was clear that she loved him deeply.

"How did you meet your husband if you don't mind me asking?" Linda inquired.

"No, I do not mind. You must be wondering how I got involved with an older man. I am accustomed to the question and more so with the looks I get when we are out or host a gathering with people who are new to our circle," Afra explained as she looked at Linda, all the while gauging her reaction.

"I'm not as interested in the age difference issue as I am in the wife thing. How does that work for you?" Linda said as she looked over her sunglasses at Afra.

"Let me tell you a story," Afra began as she turned her head to look at Linda. "And at the end, you tell me what you think. Okay?"

"Okay, I can do that," Linda replied with a nod.

"My father and Wilhelm have conducted business for many years when I first noticed him. I was a sophomore at the university when I became interested in Wilhelm. He had visited my house many times before. He also attended my sister's and my brother's weddings as a guest of honor. I never really noticed him before because he was usually talking business with my father in his office. Or they were going out to enjoy the city together when he was in town. Anyway, one day my father asked me to bring some coffee to his office. When I entered, Wilhelm was standing there talking to my brother. When he looked at me and spoke, that was when I really noticed him for the first time."

Linda knew exactly what she meant. She just had that same reaction a few hours ago. "He captivates you," she thought.

"Later that night, I asked my father about him. He told me to concentrate on school and that he already had two wives. Basically, forget about it. So I waited for my chance. A few days later, I got it." Linda was listening intensely; she was enjoying the story and found herself really liking Afra. Linda had removed her sunglasses and was giving Afra her full attention. "Well," Afra continued, "Wilhelm was sitting in the courtyard at the house. So I went out, sat down beside him, and said, 'I like you and I want to get to know you.' Well, he just looked at me. So I asked him if he understood me because I said it in Arabic. He answered me, and then he asked me why in Arabic. So I told him why. He listened. And then, he told me that I should finish school first. Then he asked me why I wasn't dating guys my own age. I didn't have an answer for that question. Anyway, I left the garden in shame. For the next few years, I avoided him whenever he came to visit my father."

"So how did you end up a misses if you avoided him for so long?" Linda asked a little puzzled.

"Patience, I'm getting to that. When I was graduating from the university with my masters in mathematics, my father invited Wilhelm to my party. My father thought that I had gotten over my crush on him. At the party, I pulled him aside and reminded him of his question. And then, I answered it. Being a gentleman, Wilhelm pretended to remember the incident. He congratulated me on my degree and then disappeared into the crowd. My next move was to work on my father. So I applied pressure on him to talk to Wilhelm about me. My mother helped me in this area also," Afra said with a grin. "It must have worked because when Wilhelm came back a few months later, he invited me out to dinner. Over dinner, he asked me a lot of questions. I must have answered correctly because afterwards he asked my father for permission to see me. Of course, my mother said, 'yes,' and my father went along with it."

"And then, you were married?" Linda asked.

"No! I came to visit his home here at the farm. My father told me how splendid Wilhelm's farm was. But I did not believe all he had told me. So when I arrived the first time, I discovered that my father was a little modest in his description of the place. My first reaction was WOW! And then, I wondered will they like me? Will I like them? You know, the usual worries." Afra paused and studied Linda's face for a moment then she continued. "Anyway, that first meeting went fine. So over the next year, I made several visits. And with the consent of my father, Colleen, and Afef, we were married. It has been four years now and this is our second child," Afra paused waiting for Linda to say something.

"I have two questions," Linda began. "First, where did you earn your masters? Second, what do you do all day? I'm not saying that relaxing and shopping is a bad thing. Hell, it's every girl's dream mine included. But you have a master's degree. Don't you want to use it?" Linda's face was serious and perplexed at the same time.

Afra laughed and said,

"I wish you could see your face right now. I do not know what to make of that facial expression. Would you like to walk while I answer your questions?" Afra said as she rose from the glider. The bodyguard instantly repositioned himself, and Linda was aware of him again. She had forgotten he was there while she was listening to Afra's story. But now, she was focused and back to taking mental notes of all that she heard and saw. She got up and quickly caught up with Afra. "I earned my master's degree from the University of Aleppo in my home town," Afra stated as Linda caught up to her. "As I stated earlier, it is in mathematics which I use every day in my work here on the farm which leads us to your second question. I would love to shop and relax my days away but sadly this is not the situation here at the manor." Afra stopped, turned to face Linda, and said, "All that you see in front of you," as she pointed her slender finger towards acres of crops and farm animals that were in view, "I alone make the decisions on what is grown, raised, and harvested from the land. It is also my responsibility to decide what is planted and which stock are to be sold or bought. Also I am in charge of the shearing and slaughter houses and all of their operations. I buy all of the farm equipment and hire the farm employees. So Linda I have very little time for shopping and lying around the house not to mention my little one; I'm also a mother." As she said this, Afra was looking at Linda with pride as she informed her of her responsibilities. Linda noticed she had a regal look as she surveyed the land around them.

"I see. I had no idea that you worked so hard. Frankly, I had a totally different notion of what life was like here."

"No problem, most people think just because you live a certain way somehow you do not work for that lifestyle. Here at the farm, we all have our areas of responsibility. My husband insists on this." Then Afra gave Linda a sarcastic little smirk. "Today was a treat to have you and your boss over for lunch on a weekday. The chance to play dress up was a welcomed distraction."

Before Linda could reply, the guard approached them and told Afra something in Arabic. Afra acknowledged him and turned towards Linda. It seems your boss has finished his business and is ready to leave. The guard will take us back to the house now. A moment later, the cart drove them back. They entered the house through one of the side entrances. Afra then led her to the library where Wilhelm and Frank were waiting.

"Ah! There she is," said Frank. "I trust you had a good time."

"Yes, I did," Linda replied. "Thank you again for a most lovely lunch, Mr. Libertaire," she said as she extended her right hand towards him.

"The pleasure is all mine, Ms. Banally. I hope Frank will bring you again when he visits," Wilhelm said as he shook her hand.

"And special thanks to you, Mrs. Libertaire, for putting up with her," Frank added.

"No special thanks needed, Mr. DePore," Afra said in the soft, sweet voice that she reserved just for such occasions. "I think we got along just fine," she added as she looked at Linda.

"Well, it's time we get going. I still have a stop to make and it's getting late," Frank said looking at his watch.

The four of them headed towards the front door. When they reached the foyer, George was waiting with Linda's gun and knife in hand.

"Thank you, George," she said with a smile. "I almost forgot I brought them with me," she said as she holstered her pistol and put away her knife.

"I seriously doubt that, Ms. Banally," was his reply as he escorted her to the front door. When they stepped out onto the front landing, Kevin was standing by the car. Wilhelm and Afra stopped in front of the carved rose as Frank and Linda proceeded down the steps. After they reached the car and Kevin helped Linda into the backseat, Frank turned and said,

"See you soon, Wilhelm, and bring you're A-game." Then he stepped into the sedan. Kevin closed the door, turned to Wilhelm, tipped the brim of his hat, and got in. A moment later, the car was headed down the driveway.

"Did she inquire?" Wilhelm asked Afra.

"Yes."

"Did you tell her what we discussed?"

"Yes, my husband," she said as she looked up at him. "How did you know what she would ask?"

"I'll explain it over ice cream." Then he kissed her lightly on the lips and the three of them headed for the kitchen.

Failure and Revenge

Chapter Two

Monday, September 27, 2010

Frank sat in his office in D.C. The clock on his desk read 9:00 a.m. He was rethinking his decision to work in the city today. Linda was in the outer office talking on the phone. He listened for a moment then swiveled his chair to face the window and started to think about his luncheon with Wilhelm.

"I hope this works," he thought. "Wilhelm is not the fool they think he is. And if they aren't careful, this whole operation is going to blow up in our faces. This was the last phase of the operation and if anything goes wrong, I'm a dead man." Just then, Linda walked in with notepad in hand. "Here's the layout for the day, boss," she said as she began to read from the notepad. Frank was paying half attention to her. He was still deep in thought. But the mention of his two o'clock jarred him back to reality.

"What was that last one?" he said. "Go back, I didn't catch that one."

"It's with a congressman's aid; something about an impending trip."

"Have Robert handle that for me; it's a normal briefing. And cancel everything else after one o'clock, okay." Linda nodded as she wrote on the pad.

"Do you need me for any of these appointments?" she asked.

"No, why?"

"I have that project to complete by Wednesday as well as the extra paperwork you want on Turkey. That's why," she said giving him a strange look in the process. Frank turned to face her.

"Now tell me again what you thought about Afra?" Before answering, Linda walked over to the office door, looked out into the outer office, and made a visual check to make sure the door was fully closed. Then she sat in the chair in front of his desk and began. She knew he might ask her to recite her report two to three more times before he was satisfied. This didn't bother her at all. In fact, she learned something new every time she repeated it. When she finished, she sat there with legs crossed and waited.

"Nice skirt," he began, "Doesn't it strike you a little weird that she knew exactly how to answer you?"

"Thank you and yes, it does. I even twisted some of those questions in such a way that she shouldn't have been able to *not* tell me something. But when she felt trapped she just buttoned up tight as a clam. Did you find any useful info in my report?"

"Yes, I did, especial the layout of the halls. That crafty bastard has redesigned since my last visit. The rest, I'm afraid I can't use any of the information she divulged; it's already in her jacket." Frank leaned forward and handed her a file. Linda quickly thumbed through it. She hadn't seen any of this information before. What she was reading would have been a great help to her on Thursday, she thought.

"Why didn't you share this with me earlier, Frank? Maybe the outcome would have been different."

"No, the outcome would have been the same, I'm afraid," he said as he turned his chair back towards the window. "You see, what I really wanted to know was how much of her husband's work does she know about."

"Well, how much does she know in *your opinion?*" Linda asked sarcastically. Frank smiled ignoring her cynicism and slowly said,

"Since she didn't give you any information, how long would you say it took to train her to evade interview questions as well as she does? Personally, I think it took about a year. What do you think, Ms. Banally?" he said without turning around. He knew when he referred to her in this manner, it pissed her off something fierce. He still hadn't forgotten her little wiggle performance that she put on when she was at Wilhelm's. "Well, no answer."

"Give me a minute, will ya! I would think it was less time."

"Why?"

"Because she would be accustomed to keeping secrets about her father's business; this would be natural I think. Why all of the pussy footing around, Frank? Why don't we send in an agent to map the place out, or at least, turn somebody that works there and get the information we need?"

"Actually, that was tried a few years back and both attempts failed."

"Both attempts, Frank! Which one are you talking about? the mapping? or the asset?"

"I mean both attempts—the turning of an asset and the mapping operation. Both went very wrong, very fast."

"What happened? What went wrong? I haven't come across any reports on any such op."

"It's all in there—right in that file you're holding; it makes for interesting reading."

"You and I both know that everything is not put into the file. Why don't you give me *the Frank version* of events?" When Frank turned around, he saw that Linda had on her *what bullshit is he going to tell me* face. "Don't look at me *that* way."

"You have no idea what went on in this office before you waltzed in. Put that bitch attitude away for a while and learn something for a change!" This outburst caught Linda by surprise. She hadn't experienced this side of Frank before and she didn't like it. She held her tongue for the moment because something was eating at him. They had been sleeping together for two years now, and she knew when he was off balance. But nothing like this ever happened before. His pupils had blackened and he was on edge. She sat back in her chair and stared at him. She wasn't about to get into an argument with him this morning. But she couldn't let this go.

"So, what's the story, Mr. DePore? And this bitch attitude that I have is well earned. Putting up with you for the last five years hasn't been a picnic for me either. So when you think it's okay to kick this dog, remember this dog bites!" she snapped in an angry high pitched voice.

"So, now you bite, do you? You weren't all that toothy when you were wiggling for Wilhelm last Thursday, were you?"

"Wiggling! When did I wiggle for anyone other than you, Frank? When?"

"At Wilhelm's last Thursday! You were shaking that ass of yours, giggling, and smiling at everything he said. And don't deny it either. I was there. I saw it with these two eyes!" Frank exclaimed as he pointed to his reddening face.

Linda sat their quietly remembering the luncheon and her behavior in the library. She had been a little excited and he did make her a little warm. "If Frank hadn't played with her on the way there, maybe she could have controlled herself better," she thought.

"I recall it differently, Frank. If you hadn't been playing with me in the car, I might have had better control of myself and not have been so horny. You shouldn't have started what you couldn't finish."

"So it's my fault that you can't control yourself!" he shot back. "Jeezs! Now I control how horny you get. Come on, Linda; you're a professional."

"Forget about it, Frank. It's water under the bridge. Now tell me about the two failed attempts." She hoped this would end the argument. At that moment, she finally realized how much Frank dislikes Wilhelm.

But this might be just good old fashioned professional jealousy that he's feeling. She would have to be careful from now on concerning matters about Wilhelm.

"Now if you don't mind, I'd like to fill you in on the two operations that I mentioned earlier."

"By all means." It was clear that she was annoyed. If he knew her at all, he knew she would find some way to get back at him for today's slight. As he looked across his desk at her, he saw how much he had hurt her.

"Look, I'm sorry, but you know how I feel about you."

"What do you want me to say?"

"You know how I am." Linda looked at that damn puppy dog face he had on.

She couldn't resist him. Smiling she said,

"Just forget about it, Frank. I'll try harder not to wiggle next time. Now tell me what *wasn't* in the file," she said as she flashed him her signature girlish smile and re-crossed her legs.

"So to get back on track this op took place about five years ago give or take a year. It was conceived by a couple of fellows and a young lady in Department 2. They came up with the same idea as you did; they wanted to map the area around the house and its access routes."

"Sounds okay to me, thus far. What could be silly about that plan?" she said as she shifted in her chair getting comfortable. Frank leaned back in his chair, intertwined his fingers, smiled, and continued.

"Oh, you young, dumb, full of vim and vigor youth. You see, just like you, they underestimated Wilhelm and thought they could out smart him," he said with the biggest smile she had seen on him to date. His expression proclaimed, I know something you don't know.

"Anyway, they outfitted four guys with the latest gear; I mean they had night cameras that were able to take thermal pictures. Their

43

communication gear was internal; they could talk only among themselves. This was done so Wilhelm wouldn't be able to pick up their frequency. To keep in contact with headquarters, they were tracked by GPS software attached to their packs. They decided to go on a moonless night. The team was dropped off three miles from the farm. All members of the team made it to the first check point without any incident. After that was when the mystery began. You see, their GPS signal stopped moving five hundred yards beyond that point and never moved again." Linda sat there wondering how much of this story was bullshit and how much was fact. Oh well, at least she would learn more about Wilhelm. So she sat there quietly listening. "When morning came, there was mass panic. You should have been here. It was comical." Then Frank burst into laughter. "This all happened a few months before you got here. Nobody has ever talked about it to date, not so much for security reasons, you see, but because of the embarrassment factor."

"Embarrassment! Come on, Frank, how embarrassing could it have been? I mean really, we run ops all the time, and they all don't go according to plan."

"Okay, miss-know-it-all. Try this on for size. The team went missing for twenty-four hours. They were finally located in the local jail. You see, the sheriff had picked them up along the side of the road, twenty miles from Wilhelm's farm. The sheriff reported to us that when he found them, they were dazed and confused. The toxicology report showed a large dose of narcotics in each man's system." Linda sat taller in the chair and perked up. Maybe this wasn't just another story after all. She made a mental note to investigate further.

"Well, did they ever find out what happened to them? and why the mission failed?" she asked.

"Yes, they did; but they didn't or wouldn't believe what the men told them. In fact, they sent them for psychological examinations, and still they refused to believe them."

"What did they tell them that was *sooo* remarkable? I mean, that department must hear all kinds of far-out stories."

"Not like this one, Linda. You see, they said they were approached by what they thought were two sheep. Reasonable, since you also saw sheep; it's a farm, right. But what they turned out to be was two sheepdogs, the kind that look like sheep. I don't know if you've ever seen one. But they look like they have dreadlocks, and they are white like the sheep. Anyway, the dogs busted them and started barking and biting the team," he snickered. This alerted the guards and you've seen how efficient and *friendly* they are, especially George."

"Yeah, I know that guy is scary. You can tell he's a stone killer if I ever meet one. And I've meet a few hanging out with you."

"Anyway, they got caught. They reported they were drugged, interrogated, stripped naked, and then dropped off on the side of the road where they were found. Then Frank burst into uncontrollable laughter. His next words were unintelligible breaking through the tears.

"Frank! Frank! Get a hold of yourself. Was it that funny when it happened?"

"Funnier, Linda. It was *way* funnier. Those four young Turks with all of their smarts didn't count on the dogs on the farm. They thought technology would overcome any obstacle."

"Honest mistake, Frank. Anybody could have made that one."

"You mean anybody in your generation would have made that mistake."

"I'm not going to get into that argument again with you. Your generation crept around in the dark ages and mine brought yours the light of technology," she exclaimed with a wave of her hand.

"Very funny, ha-ha. Maybe they should've given them idiots flashlights and a digital picture of a dog. That simple bit of technology might have made a difference. Don't you think?" Frank countered."

"So they got caught; it's not the end of the world. We'll find a way to map the place."

"Maybe, but I recommend that you don't use the same team. Then he broke out into laughter again. He was laughing so hard he started coughing.

Linda sat there watching Frank laugh. She was thinking that this guy was more dangerous than she thought. If he could do that to four agents and cover his tracks, what else could he do? Frank may be right about this one. He and Wilhelm are a lot alike in one way; they don't rely on technology too heavily. Using dogs that look like sheep in the dark is genius, pure genius. She would have never thought of that, not in a million years.

"Are you through yet, Frank? I'd like to hear the next story before I grow old if you don't mind?"

"Alright, uh-hum," he said clearing his throat, and reaching for a tissue to wipe the tears from his eyes. "It's just that…when I think about a highly trained and well equipped team of agents who were caught by dogs that look like sheep, I can't stop laughing." He took a deep breath, tossed the tissue into the trash can.

"*Swishshsh,*" he said as it went in. "All net!" he said with a smile. Then he became serious. "Now this next case is different. I personally knew the agent on this job. He was from this department and was one of my best agents." Frank suddenly had that far off look he gets when he was deadly serious or when he had a vendetta with someone. Linda knew that this story was not just a story. She prepared herself to remember every word.

"This story was important," she thought.

"Tony," he began, "that was his name. He also wanted to find out what was really going on at the farm. He was the first one, as a matter of fact, to start calling Wilhelm's place, *the farm,* by the way. Anyway, he came up with a plan to turn one of Wilhelm's workers. He found a guy who liked to bet on the cockfights. He thought the threat of sending this guy to jail would give him some leverage. So he approached him and gave him the pitch, badge, and all. Tony told the guy that the full weight of the government would come down on his head if he didn't cooperate.

"So when he came back to the office later that day he was high on is success. He had gotten this guy to work for him. I had my reservations, but I keep them to myself. You see, Tony was so delighted that his plan might work. That meant he would be the first one to get the information that all of us wanted but had failed to obtain. He sat in that same chair you're sitting in now when he told me about it. Anyway, this guy starts feeding Tony Intel and some of it was checking out. So Tony and the rest of us were feeling really good about it.

"Then out of the blue, this guy suddenly stopped meeting with Tony. For a week, Tony tried to make contact. He was turning into a wreck trying to figure out why this guy stopped communicating. Then as suddenly as he disappeared, he reappeared. He gave Tony some cock and bull story about being sent on a buying trip for livestock as the reason he was out of touch for so long. I told Tony that the guy was lying and he should end his operation. The Intel that we already had from his contact filled in some of the gaps, and we were more than pleased. So a few days later he told me he was shutting the op down. The information he collected would be presented in his report by the end of the week.

"Needless to say, I was both relieved and elated that he had pulled it off. Frankly, I didn't think he could. Tony was a rank amateur compared to Wilhelm, even though he was a seasoned field agent with ten years of experience." Frank paused and looked at Linda. At that instant, she felt as though he was looking into her soul which caused a shiver up her spine. "Anyway, the next day, he was more than a little nervous. He paced around the office checking his cellphone. When I asked him what was bothering him, he hinted that this guy might not be kosher after all. He worried that this guy might run scared and would tell Wilhelm what he was doing.

"The following day, I received word that Tony was dead. He was killed in his apartment. His throat had been cut. His contact was found two days later, shot in the head. The police said it was over a gambling debt, and they had a suspect in custody. That night the suspect hanged himself in his cell. That's the official story from the sheriffs' office. The investigation into Tony's death revealed that all of Tony's notes and recordings were missing from his safe. All we have on his killer is a shadowy image entering and leaving his apartment. My first and only suspect in his murder is Wilhelm." Linda looked at him closely. The look on his face showed how much he hated Wilhelm.

"What makes you think he had anything to do with it? Is there any special reason that causes you to believe this is true?"

"I know you find it hard to believe that Wilhelm would kill or have any agent killed. But you are wrong, my dear," Frank stated as he pointed his index finger at her. "He is a man of many talents. His best talent is watching out for *Wilhelm* at all cost. I know him better than anyone in the agency. He only has one true enemy and no weaknesses that I have found to date."

"So you actually think he killed Tony or had him killed?" Linda questioned very cautiously while she was watching his body language. She didn't like what she saw.

"As sure as we are sitting in this office. I know he did it but I can never prove it," Frank shot back. "You see, he showed up at Tony's funeral. That bastard had the nerve to tell me that I should keep tighter control on my agents. Then he asked me if Tony was one of my best men. If so, he was deeply sorry for the lost. He understood what it meant to lose highly trained personnel like him. I don't know how he did it but I know he did. And that shadowy figure on the security tape is someone that works for him. I'm sure of it. Attending the funeral was his way of telling me that it was by his command that Tony was killed. Furthermore, that bastard rarely leaves his farm; and when he does, it's for business. Remember, I know this man better than anyone. He is a cold calculating motherfucker so don't take his charm for granted. His niceties are a mask for his treachery. He's a spy like no other we have ever seen or trained. He's not to be taken lightly or underestimated. If you do, it will cost you your life just as it did for Tony." Before she could ask her next question, they heard the outer office door open. She got up to see who it was.

The rest of the morning was uneventful and went by quickly. Before she knew it, Frank was telling her that he was leaving for the day. Linda sat at her desk looking at the door that Frank just walked out of and thinking about what she had just learned. She searched her mind for who she knew in Department 2 who could help her check out his story.

Frank decided to walk the few blocks to the meeting. It was a nice day and the distraction of watching everyday people doing ordinary tasks would be nice. He really didn't want to go to this meeting or hear the bullshit that they would lay on him as if he was an idiot or something. He hated their mightier than thou attitude along with their opinion that any decision he made was usually wrong. Nevertheless, he had to go and pretend to go along with their stupid plan. Those idiots would never trap and kill Wilhelm with what they are planning. He would have to alter their plan, naturally, just to make sure it worked. Once he had Wilhelm out of the way, he would become a member of the Council. Then he would remove those fools.

Frank stopped at the corner facing the W Hotel across the street. He arrived faster than he intended. He checked his watch. He was ten minutes early.

"This won't due," he thought. "You can never be early for this type of meeting." Looking around, he searched for a place to stand and wait. He spotted one and then casually moved into position and waited. He checked his watch again then started across the street. Frank entered the hotel, went straight to the elevator, pushed the up button, stepped in, and pushed the button for the fifteenth floor. A few moments later, the elevator door opened. He stepped out and paused a moment while scanning the hallway. When he was satisfied, he removed his foot that kept the elevator doors from closing. Then he headed down the hall to room 1531. He rang the buzzer and waited. A moment later, the door opened. Frank hesitated before entering, taking one last quick look up and down the hall.

"Hi, Frank," one of the men said as he walked into the sitting room of the suite.

"Hello Number 3," he replied addressing the man at the bar.

"Are you hungry? Have you had lunch yet?" echoed another voice.

"No, I haven't, Number 2," he replied.

"There's a spread over by the bar. Help yourself."

"Thanks, I think I will." Frank walked over to the table and looked at the food. "Hmmm," he murmured. On the table, lay a spread of assorted deli meats and cheeses sliced thin for sandwiches and an assortment of artisan rolls and sliced bread. The spread included potato, macaroni, and shrimp salads, and a few salads that he didn't recognize. "So this is the meal of choice for the good old boys who like to take over countries and kill people," Frank thought as he surveyed the table. Frank began to make a sandwich. As he scooped up some macaroni salad, the one they call Number 5 began to ask him questions.

As Frank sat in an overstuffed chair in the sitting room eating pastrami on rye and drinking several beers, he patiently answered his questions. Sitting there, he wondered who were really under those masks. He often had such thoughts when meeting with the Council of Five. Their manner of concealing their identities was an old one and very clever. He had yet to figure it out. They all wore professionally made masks that allowed them to speak and eat normally. The masks were made from a rubber based material as near as he could tell. It mirrored human skin perfectly. But this was not the genius of the disguise. Its true worth was that the wearer could change appearances at will and often did. At the last meeting, the one called Number 1 was an East Indian man. At another gathering, he was a Swede complete with blond hair. At this meeting, he's a Spaniard. This was the true value of their disguises—their ability to imitate any ethnic group on the planet.

As Frank left the W Hotel, he glanced at his watch; it was 6:00 p.m. The meeting had taken longer than he expected. He took a deep breath looked around and decided to go to his favorite watering hole and have a drink. He flipped up the collar of his overcoat to block the wind, adjusted his fedora, stuffed his hands in his pockets, fingered the revolver he kept in his right pocket, and headed down the street. Tomorrow was a big day, and he still had some details to attend to before tomorrow's meeting with Wilhelm. A drink would help him think. The final phase of the plan that he and the Council have been working on for the last five years was about to begin. There could be no loose ends, no slip ups.

The Meeting

Chapter Three

Tuesday, September 28, 2010

Wilhelm went downstairs. When he reached the landing, he paused, pulled out his pocket watch, and compared the time with that on the grandfather clock that stood in the foyer. The time was correct as always. George saw to that, personally. He loved that old clock. If it wasn't for that fact alone, Wilhelm would have moved it to another room long ago.

"George! George!" he yelled as he headed for the kitchen. "Where the hell are you?"

"Here!" came a voice from his left as George stepped out into the hallway holding a cup of coffee. "What's the matter, boss? Why all of the noise? It's six in the morning. You want to wake up the whole house?"

"Never mind all that; just come with me. I have some changes I want you to make for today's trip into the city." The two men headed to the library. When he reached his desk, Wilhelm pressed a button that connected him to the kitchen.

"Kitchen," sounded a voice.

"Bring me a large cup of strong coffee, Chef," he said and released the button before a reply could be heard. "What's the setup for today's detail?" he said turning his attention back to business.

"There are two men with the car, a driver and a guard. A man will be traveling with you in the chopper. All are armed with pistol and compact sub-machine guns," George said in a flat boring businesslike tone, as he sipped his coffee. "Is there something I should worry about? Do you want me to make any changes?"

"Yes, have an extra man flying along. I want him to stay with the chopper. I want at least one man guarding the chopper at all times besides

53

the pilot. Also, I'll leave a little later than planned. And change the route. I want to arrive at the last minute. Understood."

"I'll get right on it…anything else?"

"No, that's all."

George rose from his chair. As he was leaving the library, he passed the chef carrying a silver tray which held a porcelain cup and saucer, a crystal sugar bowl, and a miniature crystal cream pitcher along with a porcelain decanter full of Rwandan coffee.

"Good morning, sir. I didn't know how large of a cup you required. So I brought you a six-cup decanter of Rwandan coffee since you ordered strong, sir."

"Thank you, Chef. You always know which coffee works best for me."

"Would you like some breakfast, sir? I can whip up something in no time."

"No, Chef, this will be fine. That will be all. Thank you." The chef poured him his first cup, added the required scoops of sugar and cream, stirred the coffee, and then left the room.

As Wilhelm sipped his coffee, he started filling his briefcase with the necessary papers he knew would be needed. In a separate pile on his desk lay the information that he had received from his own sources. This intelligence drew a different picture from the one Frank had framed for him last week. Wilhelm found himself being drawn into a precarious situation. His gut kept telling him this was a trap. "Something was very wrong with this proposed operation," he thought. He finished his coffee and turned his attention to a bit of information which he had become aware of just two days ago. The information suggested that this op was more about the removal of competition and not the information fact-finding trip bullshit that Frank had feed him. He poured himself another cup of coffee and went to the window to watch the sun come up.

As he watched the sun make its appearance, he speculated about who else would be attending this meeting held at Frank's home in Prince George County. Although, he was told it would be held there for security reasons and that this is a sanctioned op, he still felt that something wasn't quite kosher.

"It's time, sir," George said as he entered the library. "The extra precautions have been taken care of. We're ready when you are."

"Thank you, George. I'm ready. Let's go." Wilhelm checked his pocket watch; it was 7:00 a.m. If they left now, he would get to the meeting a little late but only by a few minutes. He knew all too well what a few minutes late could do to an operation. He put down his cup, closed his briefcase, and checked his sidearm. Then he and George headed for the jeep that would take him to the helipad. When they arrived at the helipad, Wilhelm found two armed guards waiting. The pilot had the chopper revved up and ready to fly. George stood by as the men boarded and the helicopter took off. He stayed and watched until the chopper was out of sight. Then he got back into the jeep and told the driver to take him to the stables.

Wilhelm and his two bodyguards settled into their seats on the bell helicopter. It sat six people very comfortably, and the pressurized cabin kept the inside temperature perfect and the cabin quiet. Wilhelm turned on Prince and settled back letting his thoughts wander. When what seemed like a few minutes later, the pilot spoke over the speaker and announced their arrival at the PGC heliport. Wilhelm checked his watch. "Damn, that was a fast forty-minute ride," he thought. The helicopter landed and shut down. The guards disembarked and posted themselves one at each end of the aircraft.

At this time, a midnight blue Lincoln Escalade hybrid pulled up. The guard who was riding in the front passenger's side got out and approached the chopper. Wilhelm stepped out, put on his suit jacket, and picked up his briefcase, as he watched the man approach.

"Mr. Libertaire, George contacted me and instructed me to add extra precautions. So I brought the Escalade instead of the usual SUV."

"Fine, let's get moving." Wilhelm with one of his security men headed towards the car and got into the backseat, leaving the other man guarding the helicopter along with the pilot. The guard who greeted him got back into the front passenger seat. The driver headed out of the airport.

"We will be at Mr. DePore's in fifteen minutes, sir," the driver informed him. Wilhelm didn't answer. Instead, he pushed a button on the console located in the center of the backseat, and Miles Davis began to softly blow his horn.

Earlier that morning

"Ring! Ring!"

"Hel-lo," said a sleepy voice into the blackberry.

"Wake up, Linda! It's Frank," a loud voice shouted into her ear.

"Frank? What is it? What's the matter?" she said still not fully awake.

"Nothing, it's just that I won't be in the office until early afternoon today. So you don't have to be there until 1300 hours, okay, Linda. Did you hear me?" he continued.

"Yes, I heard you, Frank," she replied as she looked at the clock on the nightstand. "It's five in the morning, Frank. Couldn't this have waited a couple of hours?" she said sluggishly.

"I guess so, but it was on my mind. I was up anyway, so I just called without thinking."

"Thanks, Frank. Now I am going to hang up without thinking. Goodbye, or should I say good morning." She hung up the phone and stared at the ceiling trying to go back to sleep.

It was no use; she couldn't go back to sleep. Frank had ruined that dream and at the best part. "Isn't that always the way it happens," she thought. She sat up, stretched, and got out of bed. As she headed for the bathroom, she took off her nightshirt and threw it in the corner. She turned on the shower and sat down on the toilet to pee. When she was done, she stepped into the shower and let the warm water run over her head. As she enjoyed the sensation of the water running all over her body, she began to think about her breakfast meeting with Sally. After Frank left the office yesterday, she went to work trying to find a friendly contact in Department 2 when she remembered Sally. She was glad that she had not erased her info out of her phone.

She and Sally had gone through training at Langley together. After graduation, they had partied together a few times before they received different assignments. Over the next few years, they bumped into each other a few times and even had drinks on a few occasions. She knew that Sally had the information or could get the information she needed. But would she be willing to share it? And at what cost...? Linda rinsed off, turned off the shower, and on her way out of the bathroom flushed the toilet. As she wrapped her hair in a towel, she thought about what to wear to this meeting. She didn't want to attract attention but she had to look like she belonged.

"Damn you, Sally, for picking a place where so many government workers ate and flirted with each other," she thought as she looked through her closet. She finally settled on a red, cream, and black plaid wrapped skirt, a cream colored blouse, black tights, and black Mary Janes. She looked at herself in the full length mirror and thought, "This will do just fine." She looked like any other administrative assistant having breakfast and looking for love in this outfit. She put on her coat, checked her revolver, slung her pocketbook over her shoulder, and with keys in hand headed out the door.

Prince George Meeting

"We're here, sir," the guard announced from the front seat.

"Thank you." Wilhelm turned off the music and looked out of the front window as the Escalade pulled into Frank's driveway. He surveyed the three cars that were already parked and the four security agents who were standing nearby. Two of the cars were definitely agency issue. The third had to belong to the two Stanleys. Instantly, he knew that he had made the right decision to change his routine at the last moment.

The Escalade pulled up into the middle of the driveway and stopped. The guard riding in the front got out and took up a defensive posture with sub-machinegun at the ready. The guard riding in the back got out, walked around the rear of the vehicle, and opened the door for his boss. His sub-machinegun also was at the ready position. Wilhelm stepped out, paused, and looking at his reflection in the car window, straightened his tie, and smoothed out his suit coat. He reached back into the Escalade and retrieved his briefcase.

"Wait by the car," he said to the two guards. "This may take a while." Then he started towards the house.

The four guards standing in the driveway assumed defensive postures placing their hands inside their suit coats as they tried to identify who was approaching them. As Wilhelm got closer one of the guards whispered,

"It's Libertaire."

At that realization, they relaxed their postures and removed their hands from their suit coats. They all knew who Wilhelm was; he was a living legend among the field forces of the CIA. He was what they aspired to be. He came through the ranks, participated in and even planned some of the agency's toughest ops, and *survived*. As Wilhelm approached each guard, he heard a heartfelt,

"Good morning, Mr. Libertaire," and he responded in kind. He walked up to the front entrance of the house. The man guarding the door greeted him in the same manner.

"Good morning, Mr. Libertaire. Are you armed, sir?" Wilhelm opened his suit coat and showed the guard his gun; the guard looked but made no attempt to remove it. "Thank you, sir. You may go in," the guard said as he opened the front door and stepped aside. Wilhelm walked into the house and was greeted by Frank's house manager.

"Good morning, sir. They are out in the sunroom. Please follow me." He turned and led Wilhelm to the sunroom where the others were waiting.

As he entered the room, he paused at the entrance and surveyed the room. He knew everyone there. In attendance was Wendy Liang, section chief in charge of the Stan's as they were referred too. Her domain included Kurdistan, Uzbekistan, Turkmenistan, Tajikistan, Kyrgyzstan and the border region adjoining the Xinjiang Province of China. Wilhelm always thought this was a good post for Wendy since her ancestral home is in Urumqi, the province's capital. Next was Susan Dorffman, section chief in charge of Eastern Europe. And finally, sat the two Stanleys, all 640 pounds of them. They really weren't that big. But at five feet five inches tall and 275 pounds each, they sure looked like they weighed 640 pounds combined. The Stanleys never went anywhere alone. Where one was, you were sure to find the other close by. The Stanleys, as they were known, had been a fixture in the intelligence community for 50 years. They were rumored to have information on or access to information on everyone that was considered important, past and present, in the intelligence world. Now retired, they were freelance consultants and information brokers and were employed by the agency for certain cases. One thing Wilhelm knew for certain was that they had an impressive network and their Intel was usually correct.

"Wilhelm, come in," Frank said as he made his way across the room to greet him. "You know everyone here. You haven't seen my new sunroom. What do you think?" At that moment, Frank reached Wilhelm and started pointing out some of the room's features. The room was very large and rectangular in shape. The floors were covered in hand-painted Spanish floor tiles, and tall large glass windows afforded a spectacular view of the pool and lawn. In the center of the room stood a glass table with a hand-shaped wrought iron base. Around the table sat six well cushioned chairs that had the same iron design. In the corners of the room and under a large picture window, he noticed a variety of ferns and orchids growing.

"I see you still have your love for plants."

"Yes, they are the only living things I truly trust," replied Frank as he looked Wilhelm in the eyes. "Come; have a cup of coffee; it's Jamaican Blue Mountain. I know how particular you are about coffee," he added. "And let's get this meeting started," Frank said as they walked towards the table where the others were seated.

Downtown Washington, DC Meeting

Linda arrived an hour early at the location where she would meet Sally. She circled the block twice before selecting a parking spot that would give her a good view of the entrance. *Sam's Cafeteria*, the sign read above the big picture window. Linda sat and watched as the cafeteria started to fill up with government workers. Now she understood why Sally picked this place. The number of people showing up for breakfast was staggering, and no one was paying any attention to anyone else. The patrons seemed only interested in eating and flirting with the opposite sex. "Sally may be smarter than I give her credit for," Linda thought as she sat and waited. Just then, she spotted Sally who was casually walking down the street towards the eatery. Linda watched Sally check to see if she was being followed by using the reflection of the windows across the street and those of the parked cars that she passed. She paused so often that it took her twenty minutes to cover the one block distance to the cafeteria. Linda waited until she entered the cafeteria, paid for her breakfast, and sat down at a table where she could see the door and look out the window. Then Linda got out of her car, crossed the street, and entered the cafeteria. Upon entering, Linda went straight to the serving line, ordered breakfast, paid for it, casually walked over to the table where Sally was, and sat down.

"Hi, Sal, nice to see you; thanks for the meet," said Linda.

"No problem, Lin. Glad to help, nice outfit." Linda noticed that Sally was dressed in a similar manner; she was wearing a chocolate wool pencil skirt, cream blouse with matching sweater, brown tights, and brown pumps. She also noticed that Sally had a big breakfast in front of her consisting of six scrambled eggs with cheese grits, sausage links, toast, coffee, and juice. This made Linda feel better about her own plate which boasted a four-egg western omelet, a stack of pancakes, sausage links, coffee, and juice.

"I see you still can put it away," Linda said with a smile.

"Yeah, a girl gotcha eat," replied Sally as she ate some grits mixed with eggs and then washed it down with a sip of coffee. So what can I do for you, Lin?"

"I need all the information you have on a guy named Tony and how he died. Also anything you have on Wilhelm Libertaire, my boss, and their relationship," Linda replied in between mouthfuls of pancake.

"You don't ask for much; do you, Lin. Then again, you always pushed the envelope," Sally said. "I brought the file on Tony's death, but you have to have it back to me in the morning. Understand?" Sally slid the file under the table and placed it on Linda's lap. "Remember, in the morning," Sally repeated with a serious expression on her face.

"Don't worry, Sal. I'll have it back in time. Now what's the true story, the one that's not in the file?"

"I'll start with the file you have; it's the shorter of the two. Your boss was right on one part. Tony was the first person to get any type of creditable Intel on the farm. Maybe he could've been right on how and why the asset was killed." Sally paused and looked around for the coffee girl.

"What are you looking for, Sal?" Linda asked looking a little puzzled.

"The coffee girl; my cup's empty," she replied. She spotted her and waved her over. After her mug was refilled, she continued. "Anyway, as for the death of said agent, we found no evidence that Libertaire had anything to do with it. We don't think he even knew an op like that was in play."

"Hmmm, what about that team that got caught trying to infiltrate his property?" Sally smiled and giggled.

"So you heard about that, did you?" she said as she glanced at Linda over her coffee mug.

"Yes, I heard about that." Is it true? Did they really get caught by sheepdogs and later found drugged and naked on the side of the road?"

"Yes, it's true; and I wouldn't let it be known that I knew about it either. Some people in the department are still a little sore about that issue."

"I understand, now what about the hit?"

"You'll find the details in the file I gave you. But the short story is that no evidence was found that linked anybody to the murder. The only evidence found was a miniature Greek statute."

"A mini-statue? What did it look like *exactly*, Sally?" Linda inquired trying to conceal her excitement.

"Well, it's a man kneeling with a sword in his hand. All I can tell you is it was really cute. They said it was handmade. Some guys in *your* department came by and picked it up, and I haven't seen it since. Why, is it important?"

"Yeah, it could be. You think you could find out more for me. I have an idea but I'm not sure yet."

"Okay, I'll see what I can find out on the mini-Greek. As I was saying," Sally continued, "there was nothing on the security films. All we saw was a dark figure. No prints were found either. But there was one unexplained clue." Sally paused and acted like she was trying to remember.

"Well, what was it? Don't hold back, now."

"Gotcha!" Sally said laughing. "Lighten up, Lin; you're way too tense." Sally was right. Linda took a deep breath and ate some more from her plate. "Well, what they found were two sets of footprints which headed in opposite directions. The guys upstairs wrote it off but it was something that has stuck in my mind all of this time. I mean if there were two of them, then why would they leave by two different directions once outside. It just doesn't sit right with me," Sally surmised.

"I see. You mean if there were two assailants, then why wouldn't they leave together."

"Exactly!" exclaimed Sally. The two of them sat there in silence finishing their breakfast. As Linda put the last pieces of pancakes in her mouth, she started to speak.

"So you think there were two different assassins and that's why the footprints went in opposite direction, Sal?"

"Yeah, but when I suggested that scenario, it was shot down viciously by the all-knowing in *your* department." Linda knew who Sally was referring to.

"Sorry about that, Sal. I go through the same thing on a regular basis. Is there anything else about the case you can think of?"

"Nothing, except that your boss charged Libertaire with the crime. Imagine that; he just came right out and accused the man of having that agent killed. I had never experienced anything like that before." Then Sally flagged down the coffee girl and got another refill. All the while, Linda sat there going over what she had just learned. So far, the information jibed with the information Frank told her yesterday and what she had just learned today confirmed it. Frank might not be as crazy as she thought and might be right about Wilhelm after all. Her curiosity was peaked. She could hardly wait to read what was inside of the file that Sally had slipped her. "Are you ready for the next bit of news?" Sally said peering over her coffee mug. Not waiting for Linda to reply, she continued, "Your boss and Libertaire had the exact same instructors at the farm—I mean our farm, not his. The only difference is that your boss started two years before he did."

"So that's nothing. You and I had some of the same instructors when we went through training," Linda retorted.

"No, this is different," Sally said as she leaned forward on the table. "Your boss and Libertaire are the last two field operatives left alive—I mean out of those two classes. You don't understand; they were trained in both the old ways of spying and the new way—you know the tech age. Well, some of their early assignments were to gather up technological information and eliminate all those who didn't take the deal, if you know what I mean."

"That would explain why my boss doesn't trust technology," Linda concluded as she sat back in her chair, rubbed her stomach, and burped. "Excuse me, Sally," she said as she wiped her mouth with her napkin. "I don't quite get what you're getting at. So what, they were trained at a time the agency was making the switch to tech surveillance."

"No, no. Look, I talked to some of the old timers. They told me that during the time your boss and Libertaire were trained, it was something special. It seems that they were trained in that cold war shit, and they also were privy to all of the new stuff coming in. It gave those guys an edge over the later classes and a step up on the older guys as well. How do you think they get to live and act the way they do and get away with it, huh? And another thing, that Libertaire guy is one scary dude and very secretive living out there on his farm doing god-knows-what. But I'll tell you this; the bosses upstairs don't want him disturbed."

"I think I'm beginning to understand now, Sal. And by the way, how did you come by this bit of info?" Linda inquired with a sly smile.

"Oh, the usual way, I just showed them some leg, a little tit; and the old geysers couldn't stop talking."

"Same old Sal, still using sex to get your way," Linda commented.

"And, why not? It still works. While a girl has it, she might as well use it," Sally said in her best imitation of Mae West. "So how are the sleeping arrangements going with your boss, Lin?" she added.

"Touché, Sal. I deserved that. But seriously, I owe you big time, girl."

"Oh, I know; and I won't forget it. You owe me *sooo* big right now, and it feels so good. You bet your ass, I won't forget." Linda glanced at her watch; she and Sally had been there over an hour.

"Oh, Sal, look at the time! I've got to get going."

"Me, too," Sal chimed, "and Lin, be careful. I am afraid you are getting in over your head on this one," she continued with a genuine look of concern on her face. Linda reached across the table and squeezed her hand.

"Thanks, Sal; I'll be careful. Don't worry; I know when to jump ship, girl."

"Well, who leaves first?"

"I will." At that moment, Linda placed her coat over her lap, placed the file into the inside pocket, got up, and headed for the door. She didn't look back. She knew Sal was watching her and she was safe until she reached the street. Sally sat there watching Linda as she headed to her car down the street. Then she got up and left.

Wilhelm took his seat at the table across from Susan and Wendy with the Stanleys on his left and Frank to his right. The house manager went around the table refilling everyone's coffee cup. He set a full decanter on the table and then left the room closing the glass doors behind him.

"Let's get this meeting started. Stanley, I think you have some information for us," Frank said in a matter-of-fact tone.

"Yes, we do," said the Stanley to Wilhelm's left. Then the other Stanley produced four files and passed them out. "In the files in front of you," he began, "is the Intel on seven targets that will be in the Turkish-Syrian area for fourteen days in the month of December for a meeting that we do not know the subject or who will be attending as of yet. What we do know is that all of the participants are independents. They will work for any organization or government if the pay is good. What we haven't figured out is why they are gathering together in this region. But you can bet it isn't a mass vacation on the Mediterranean Sea. Wherever, one of these people show up, something special is being planned. And here, we have seven." The Stanley speaking paused and took a few sips of his coffee. "Our operatives are actively working to find out who is behind this gathering of the most brilliant strategists, intelligence operatives, financial and scientific minds, and killers in that part of the world."

"So it's safe to assume they are all Middle Eastern," said Susan as she read through the file.

"Yes and no."

"And their nationalities are?" she continued.

"That information is being withheld for the moment," Frank chimed in. "This mission will run a little differently than you are accustomed to. Anything else to add, Stanley?"

"No, all of the available up-to-date information is in the file."

"Then thank you, gentlemen; that will be all. You will receive your payment in the usual manner." The two Stanleys got up, said,

"Good day" to all, and then left the sunroom without another word. Frank waited until they had cleared the room before he began to hand out a new set of folders.

"In each of your folders are specific orders and an outline of the part that each of you will be playing in this op. I'll give you a moment to look over the information before I continue."

Wilhelm removed the top secret band that assured that it hadn't been opened and thumbed through the contents. He found seven photographs— four men, three women. He took his time looking at each one studying their features; he didn't recognize any of them. Next he looked at a map with specific cities circled on it; some were in Syria, others in Turkey. He *did* recognize these locales and knew their importance. Then he read the short paragraph on the translucent paper with the official CIA seal. It simply read:

Terminate or capture all targets as you deem necessary. No evidence of your presence or those of your team are to be found. Remove and / or dispose of all identities and bodies including those of your team. Treat all targets with extreme prejudice.

Wilhelm closed the file and took a sip of his coffee as he looked crossed the table at Wendy and Susan reading their files. The look on their faces was disbelief and puzzlement. Wilhelm wondered what their orders were and what part they would play in this deadly game.

"You have to be kidding, Frank. This is a job for a junior or mid-level agent, not a section chief," Susan said.

"I have to agree with Susan. Why am I tasked with this?" Wendy added.

"Anything you want to add, Wilhelm?" Frank said.

"No, Frank; I think I'll wait for more details first, if you don't mind."

"I understand how you ladies feel, but the rest of your orders will be verbal," Frank stated as he refilled his cup. "As you all are aware, the agency has not had a good 2010. Somehow, we failed to prevent the killing that took place in the UAE (United Arab Emirates) by Mossad on neutral ground and in a hotel that has the sign of the rose. Also, we failed to pick up on the double agent that killed seven of our fellow agents in Afghanistan. For this and a few more reasons I can think of, you're receiving your orders verbally. Now if there are no more complaints, I will continue.

"Susan, you will be handling all of the funds for this op. You will also be in charge of the relay communication network. You and only you will handle this task. It is not to be delegated to your most trusted people. In addition, you will not fill out the usual forms that are associated with the handling of op funds. Instead, you will encrypt all transactions and transmit them in that manner. You will be supplied with the codes at the beginning of the operation.

"Wendy, you will be the resource officer for this op. You're duties are to provide any and all resources that are requested. This will include resources needed during the planning and execution phases of the operation. You will communicate in the same manner as Susan and report in the same manner. Here are the codes to be used in phase one. I will provide you with the other codes you will be using as the operation proceeds. And Wendy, if the need arises that extra personnel are to be used, you are to use contractors and only contractors, *no* company employees."

Then Frank turned his attention to Wilhelm and with a sly smile said,

"You, *sir*, have the honor of running this operation. You have full control over every aspect of this op. Susan and Wendy will take their orders directly from you on this one. You can pick your own team; you will have access to any resources that you need. Also, your budget is unlimited. There's one catch, and that is you will have fourteen days to complete this op once it begins. Your files have all of the information you need to conduct this mission. Also, each file contains only the information that you need to do this job. This approach was deemed best by the higher-ups in light of the recent issues facing the agency in this theater of operation. Now are there any questions?" Frank asked as he poured himself another cup of coffee and lit a cigar.

"Yes, what am I supposed to do while I wait for this op to jump off?" asked Susan.

"You will stay in town for a few days, so that you can become familiar with some new communication equipment. Then you will return to Germany and conduct business as usual until you are contacted," replied Frank. Susan didn't respond instead she opened her file and read it in earnest, paying close attention to the information in it.

Wilhelm sat there not thinking at all; he was busy reading Wendy's body language. He could guess what she was thinking. Why is Wilhelm's file so thick? And why does he have three files? But most importantly, what kind of op is this? This had to be a special mission, one of high priority for them to have Wilhelm running it. Wilhelm also knew that Wendy wouldn't ask any questions. She never did. For that reason, he was glad she was part of his team.

"Are there any more questions?" Frank asked. He waited a moment. When he heard no reply, he got up from the table and announced the meeting was concluded. As Susan and Wendy were gathering their things, Frank called Wilhelm over to where he was standing by the big picture window.

"What's on your mind, Frank?"

"I need you to do that *invisible act* of yours on this op and you can use any field agents you want. No matter what's their assignment, I will pull them off it for this op." Frank turned and faced him and said with a worried look, "There's a leak. I need you to be extra diligent and ruthless on this mission. There's a lot riding on this one."

"I understand, Frank. I'll take care of it. Whoever it is, I'll find out. We've been down this road before." Wilhelm turned and with briefcase in hand headed out of the room without another word.

Frank stood there looking out of the window listening to Wilhelm's footsteps fade as he left. He thought to himself, "Yes, we have been here before, Wilhelm; but it won't turn out as before."

Wendy and Susan were waiting for Wilhelm in the driveway. As he approached them, he saw the concern on their faces.

"What seems to be the hold-up ladies? Is my car blocking your way?"

"Very funny, Wilhelm. We were just discussing how hungry we are since the Toad didn't have the decency to provide breakfast," Wendy stated.

"You are right about that, ladies. He might have done you a favor by not providing breakfast, Wen. Since he has dumped this op into my lap, I will buy you, two, dinner. How about it? At the usual place, then? I bet you two haven't had a good meal since you hit town. Dinner will be served at six don't be late."

Wilhelm walked to his car and got in. After his guards were satisfied that the street was clear, they too got in.

"To the heliport," he instructed the driver as the SUV winded its way out of the circular driveway. He sat back, opened his briefcase, and took out the file containing the photographs and bios of the intended targets. He found himself staring at one photo. "I know this face," he thought. Something about the eyes caught his attention. Then a buzzing sound came from the center console. He opened it and answered.

"Good morning, Rodney."

"I need you to stop by the office before you return home. You've been cleared for landing on Pad 3," Rodney said.

"I understand," was all he said before he hung up the phone. Then he went back to studying the face in front of him.

The SUV made its way through traffic with ease; after all, it was mid-morning. This was the best time to be on the road if you had to be. As the SUV entered the heliport, Wilhelm was giving his guards new instructions. The car pulled up next to the helicopter and parked. He got out, walked the short distant to the chopper, and got in.

"Langley, Pad 3."

"Yes, sir," came the pilot's reply as he began his check list while warming up the helicopter. "E.T.A. 12 mics, sir."

"Very well, the code for the day is *visitor*."

"Roger, sir."

Wilhelm resumed examining the photo. He was sure he knew this man. He closed the file and looked out of the window watching the clouds and thinking.

Rodney Daniel...born 1941 Boston, Massachusetts, graduated from Harvard 1963, entered CIA same year, 10 years field work, station chief—East Asia, became CIA director 2007.

Rodney rarely called him in. But when he did, it was always serious business. Wilhelm knew this meeting would be about the upcoming mission. "But what ... ?" He had to wait a little while for that answer.

"Langley, sir, Pad 3." The helicopter landed. Wilhelm got out, got into a waiting golf cart, and headed towards the building.

Langley Meeting

"Hello, sir," he said has he entered the office.

"Wilhelm, how are you doing this fine morning? he said from behind his desk. "Sit down, take the load off. I know you're wondering why I sent for you."

"I bet it has something to do with this mission."

"Correct, but here is something I bet you don't know." Rodney handed him an envelope.

"Does Frank know about this?" Wilhelm inquired after he finished reading.

"I'll handle Mr. DePore. The question here is can I count on *you*."

"Yes, completely."

"Good, I hoped that would be your answer." With that, he handed Wilhelm a file. "In here, you will find all of the information you need. Who is the communications officer on this one?"

"Susan."

"And who is handling resources?"

"Wendy."

"Can you trust them?"

"I will know that answer tonight."

"Good, I see you're ahead of the curve as usual. Now are there any other questions?"

"No, sir."

"Good, so how are those beautiful wives of yours?"

"Fine, sir. I'll tell them you asked."

"That will be all for now, Wilhelm." Wilhelm stashed the file into his briefcase, rose from his seat, and headed for the door. Before he could get to the door, Rodney called to him, "We need you to keep this quiet and I need you to do this in ten days. There are to be *no* reports filed without going through *me*, understood."

"Yes sir, understood." Wilhelm went straight to his office located two floors below. As he exited the elevator and started down the hall, he saw Gladys, his AA, talking with two other AAs.

"Isn't that your boss?" one of the women said to Gladys.

"No, it probably isn't; he doesn't come into the office all that much."

"I think this *is* your boss, girl. You should take a look," she continued. "I'm telling you it's … ." The AA didn't finish her sentence because as Gladys turned to look, she realized it was her boss. Without warning, she took off down the hall to her office.

"Hello ladies," Wilhelm said with his famous smile as he passed the two AAs standing there.

"Good morning," they replied in unison.

"Damn, that's a fine black man," said one of the ladies.

"Uh huh, yeah, girl," the other one added. He walked to his office and went straight to his inner office with Gladys hot on his heels.

"Good morning, sir," she half stammered.

"Good morning, Gladys. Could you get me a cup of coffee, please?"

"Yes, sir, right away, sir." Then she turned and headed out.

Wilhelm turned his attention to the safe that sat directly behind his desk. He knelt down, placed his eye to the retinal reader, paused, placed his hand on the palm reader, paused, and then punched in the code. The safe door automatically opened with a slow purposeful swing. He reached in, pulled out a thick worn file, and placed it on his desk. Then he took off his suit coat, hung it up in the closet, sat down, and opened the file.

"Here's your coffee, sir," Gladys said as she placed it on his desk. "Will there be anything else?"

"No, that will be all for now. And close the door, please."

"Yes, sir," she replied as she left. He waited until he was sure she was gone before he opened his briefcase and took out that picture. Then he opened the file that he had taken from his safe and browsed through the photographs. One by one, very slowly he compared each one to the photograph of the man in his briefcase.

"Gotcha, you son-of-a-bitch," he said under his breath. "I thought you had retired. It seems like you just decided to change your look. Gladys!" he yelled, "come in here, please."

"Yes, sir," she said with a slightly nervous smile.

"Do you know anyone that works in personnel over at the farm?"

75

"Yes, sir, I do."

"Well, who is it?"

"It's my friend's friend down the hall, sir," she said with a worried look on her face.

"You think she would do you a favor?"

"Yes, sir."

"Good, now do you think you could scoot yourself down to her office as fast as you did a minute ago?"

"Yes, sir. I think I can do that. And it's the shoes I'm wearing that causes me to scoot, sir," she said with a bright smile as she left the office. Wilhelm sat back in his chair and took another look at the two pictures as his finished his coffee. A moment later, he heard soft whispers and footsteps entering the office. "This is my friend Karen," Gladys said as they stood in front of his desk. "This is my boss Mr. Libertaire."

"Pleased to meet you, sir."

"Thank you, Gladys. That will be all for now," he said waiting for her to leave. "Please, have a seat, Karen. Did Gladys explain why I wanted to see you?"

"No, sir, she didn't. She only told me that you had something to ask me."

"It has come to my attention that you have a friend in personnel over at the farm."

"Yes, I do." Now Karen was becoming a little nervous at what she thought he may ask her to do.

"Is she a good friend?" he continued.

"Yes, she is. Umm, may I ask what this is about, sir?"

"Yes, of course," Wilhelm said leaning back in his chair, "how rude of me for not explaining. It has come to my attention that you have applied for a position in Department 2. I might be able to help you with this matter. I just thought that being close to Michael would make you happy."

"You know about Michael and me?" she said in a low voice. Her face was starting to show her fear. She knew the rules against fraternizing across department lines, and she was genuinely worried, right now. Wilhelm leaned forward placing his elbows on his desk and gave her a stern look. He had achieved the response he wanted. Now he would make his pitch.

"Look Karen, I would like to see you and Michael together. I can make that happen. In fact, I can arrange for you to become his new AA."

"What would I have to do?" she asked in a shaky voice.

"I need copies of the files on all of the female graduates for this upcoming class. If you could get your friend to provide me with this … well … I see a very happy Karen with a new position."

"I don't want any problems, Mr. Libertaire; I really like working here."

"I understand, Karen," he said in his best sympathetic voice. "What if I could guarantee that you will not get into trouble nor will your friend."

"So you're telling me that if I get my friend to help you, she and I won't get into any trouble."

"Yes, Karen, that's what I'm telling you. Then you and Michael can be together, and nobody will be the wiser." Then he flashed her his famous smile as he sat back in his chair.

"Okay, I'll do it. And you can trust my friend. We both know who you are, Mr. Libertaire; it will be an honor to help. But how will we get the information to you?"

"Listen carefully, Karen. This is what I want you to do." He handed her a small flash drive and explained what he wanted her to do. When he finished, she got up and left the office.

Wilhelm knew she would not betray him. She was not the sharpest knife in the drawer, but she was the horniest. In addition to that, she was truly in love with Michael. He could see why he wanted her as she was five feet eleven inches tall in those three-inch heels and form-fitting skirt that showcased that beautifully rounded ass with just the right length of split in the rear to showcase the seamed stockings she was wearing. Her blouse was tailored to show of those perfect tits and all of this sex appeal was incased in beautiful mocha skin all weighting about 120 lbs. Yeah, he could see why Michael was interested in Karen. But what she saw in a balding 48-year-old senior analyst was beyond him. What he did know was she wouldn't betray him and she would do exactly as she was told.

Wilhelm placed the file back into his safe and locked it. Then he put on his suite coat, closed and locked his briefcase, and checked his watch. Barely an hour had passed since he stepped off the helicopter. As he was leaving, he stopped by Gladys' desk.

"Your friend will contact you sometime tomorrow afternoon. Meet her and bring what she gives you to my home right away. Understand?"

"Yes, sir. I understand." Wilhelm exited through the door without saying another word. Gladys sat there for a moment. Then she got up, looked down the hall, and watched her boss walk nonchalantly down the hallway and turn the corner. "Shit, what just happened?" she thought as she stood there. "Have Karen and I just been recruited as spies? Oh boy, I can never tell my husband about this part of my day. She went back to her desk and just sat there thinking.

Wilhelm boarded his helicopter and instructed the pilot to return to the heliport.

"Roger, sir."

A moment later, the chopper took off swinging low over the trees before gaining altitude. Wilhelm put on a set of earphones and made a call.

"Yes, sir," a voice said on the other end.

"I'm staying in town tonight; please make the necessary arrangements."

"Yes, sir." Wilhelm pressed the button breaking the connection, sat back, and began thinking about all that had transpired this morning.

The helicopter touched down; his SUV sat waiting for him. He quickly made the transition, and they were off.

"Is everything ready?" he asked the guard sitting in the rear seat with him.

"Yes, sir. George gave me the necessary information. I've taken care of all the requirements that he specified."

"Good, I'm expecting a gentleman caller later this evening. Please see to it."

"Yes, sir. I will make sure you are not disturbed."

Wilhelm spent the remainder of the trip in silence listening to jazz. The vehicle made its way along the tranquil tree lined streets of Georgetown. Wilhelm liked this part of town. Maybe it was the college town atmosphere but he wasn't quite sure. He bought a townhouse here ten years ago. It had turned out to be a better investment than he could have imagined. As one of the first people to move here after the area had been renovated, he had the opportunity to be acquainted with each and every one within a three block radius. This assured him that no unfamiliar persons showed up without being noticed.

The SUV made a right and headed down the street. Midway down the block, it made another right and pulled into the driveway. A guard posted at the front rose from his chair, placed his newspaper in it, and advanced to the curb to check if they had been followed. Then the SUV pulled into the garage. Wilhelm waited until the garage doors closed before exiting.

Entering through a doorway to his immediate right, he went up the stairs and emerged into a modern furnished living room, a striking difference from his home at the farm. Here, the furnishings were modern which was in vogue for the moment, not that he paid that much attention to it. He changed the décor regularly to keep up with the ever-changing trends. He didn't do this because he followed such things; instead, it served a purpose. From time to time, he housed assets and other guests here.

He took off his suit coat and laid it on the sofa as he made his way to the wet bar. He poured himself a double Glenfiddich Single Cask, vintage 1976, and headed for the bathroom. After his shower, he dressed in blue silk loungewear, stuck his feet into lambskin slippers, and headed for the bar for a refill and a cigar. Then he went out onto his back patio, sat down, and waited. A few minutes later, he heard a low baritone voice from behind him.

"Good afternoon, sir."

"Good afternoon. Come and sit with me awhile." A tall, slim, well-muscled, young man dressed casually appeared surreptitiously from behind him and sat down. "You look well; how have you been?"

"Very well, sir; I've kept up with my studies and my fighting ability has greatly improved."

"That's good because I have an assignment for you. I need you to find out all you can about what part the Stanleys are playing in Syria and Turkey. In addition, I want to know their every move until further notification. Do you understand your mission? Do you have any questions?"

"Yes, sir, what are my parameters?"

"You may remove any obstacles in your way except the Stanleys. You're authorized to use deadly force if necessary," Wilhelm said looking directly into the young man's eyes.

"Very well, sir; anything else?"

"Yes, I need you to escort me to *Cee's*; be in the area at 1715 hours, this evening."

"Will you need me on the return trip as well?" "No, that has already been taken care of."

"Very well," the young man said. Then he rose from his seat and left as silently as he had arrived.

Wilhelm sat there sipping his scotch and enjoying his cigar as he listened to the sounds of the neighborhood and his guards making their rounds. Just as he was getting lost in his thoughts, a soft voice, distinctively female, greeted him.

"Nin hao, Shifu." ("Hello, teacher.")

"Nin hao, Xiao yi," ("Hello, Little one,") he responded. "How have you been? And congratulations on your successful mission."

"Thank you, Shifu; I am here to serve you. How may I do this," she asked as she lowered her head in respect?"

"I need you to find out all you can on a Linda Banally. Get close to her if you can. But beware, she is a capable agent and not to be taken lightly. You're not to interfere in any way with her movements. Nor are you to save her or render any assistance. Do you understand your orders?"

"I understand; is there anything else Shifu?"

"Yes, I will need you to escort me from dinner tonight. I am dining at *Cee's* until 2000 hours."

"I will be there, Shifu," she said as she bowed once more. Then she too left as clandestinely as she arrived.

Wilhelm got up, stepped back into the townhouse, and looked at the crystal clock resting on the bar.

"Good, its only 1:00 p.m. I have time for a light lunch and some paperwork before dinner," he thought. He summoned a guard and told him what he wanted for lunch. Then he went to his office to work. He took out the three dossiers he was given and began to study them in earnest. Of course, his focus returned to the man with those eyes. Somehow he was a key player in this operation. With that level of talent hanging around, there couldn't be anything but trouble. This whole op was starting to stink to high heaven, and he feared that this may be just another bait mission for a bigger fish. If he was going to survive, he'd have to figure out who and what and fast. At that thought, he decided to take a nap; it wouldn't do to be tried for dinner. He'll have to stay on top of his game from now on and that meant rest. He locked the files in the safe and went to his bedroom for a nap.

He awoke at 4:00 p.m. sharp without the aid of an alarm. Then he freshened up and got dressed. He chose black Dockers with a gray cashmere sweater, black rubber-soled Rockports, a silver pocket watch, and a compact 9mm pocket pistol with a black windbreaker that completed his outfit. He checked the time; it was 1700 hours. He jogged down the stairs, gave the head guard instructions, and left the house at precisely 1715 hours headed for *Cee's*.

Cee's

The restaurant was only a block and a half from his townhouse. With an easy stride, he would be there in fifteen minutes, a full half hour before his guests would arrive. Strolling along, he looked at the trees admiring their changing colors and was glad he decided to walk. He didn't bother looking for his shadow; he knew he was there. With that assurance, he turned his thoughts to *Cee's* and dinner.

Clarence L. Walker, retired information officer, 22 years with the agency, graduated from Dartmouth with a master's degree in mathematics. ... is the only man to receive *le grand diplôme* from Le Cordon Bleu School of Culinary Arts in Paris by testing out. The French master chef faculty told him that his culinary creations and interpretation of American soul food was pure genius. All of this talent is packaged into a five-foot-eleven-inch-tall, 260-pound black man. Cee always said the agency was his side job and cooking was his real one.

Cee bought the restaurant 10 years ago. Since then, it has become a landmark in the area and Wilhelm eats their every time he stays in town.

He stopped in front of *Cee's* and looked at his pocket watch. It was 5:30 p.m. on the nose. Looking across the street, he saw his shadow standing there. Wilhelm turned, opened the restaurant door, and walked in. He strolled across the black and white checkered floor weaving between the few tables that were strategically placed and settled into his usual booth. He loved this place; the smells of home cooking and the atmosphere were like sitting in your own kitchen talking and gossiping with family and friends. The restaurant was small and quaint. It sat a total of 25 people. The décor consisted of wood and leather furnishings. Along the walls, booths were lined on both sides of the open center area. The walls were covered in African American artwork including bronzes and posters, some signed by famous artist. But the best feature was the menu, meaning he didn't use one. Cee cooked whatever you wanted, and the menu changed as his mind changed. So the regulars just asked for what they wanted. If he had it, you had it.

The bar was constructed from a variety of woods, built by a friend of Cee. It only had six barstools, three at each end. The arrangement of the barstools was a clear sign that drinking at the bar was discouraged. Neither he nor Cee liked their backs to the door or window, and this layout insured that wouldn't happen.

"So, Cee, what's on the menu?" Wilhelm said knowing the response that it would bring.

"You motherfucker, you know damn well I don't do menus yet you ask me this every fucking time you come in here. One day, I'm going to ban your black ass. And then where you're gonna eat?" Cee said all of this without turning around to face him. He just continued doing his crossword puzzle. Then with a smile on his face, he turned to face him said, "Good to see you, Wilhelm. How are you doing?"

"Fine, Cee, just fine. You have anything worth drinking in this place?"

"Very funny, Wilhelm.   Your usual?"

"Why not?" Cee told the bartender to bring Wilhelm a double shot of Glenrothes scotch, John Ramsay edition neat.

"So are you here for pleasure or business?" Cee inquired?" Wilhelm's drink arrived; and after the bartender left, he answered,

"Business, I'm afraid, Cee."

"Oh, I see.   I'll make sure not to put anyone in the next booth."

"I appreciate that, Cee, if it's not an inconvenience to you."

"Don't mention it, Wilhelm. Glad to do it." The two men conversed while Cee faced the other way. (If you weren't paying close attention, you wouldn't have thought a conversation was taking place at all between the two.)

Wilhelm ordered another drink. But before the bartender brought it, Susan and Wendy entered the restaurant.   They sashayed over and slid into the booth where he was sitting.

"Can a girl get a drink?" Susan said flirtatiously.

"Of course you can, my pretty," Wilhelm replied with a smile. The bartender returned with his drink, and the ladies ordered theirs.

"So what will it be for dinner?" Cee said addressing the two women.

"Oh, I'm not sure. Cee; tell us what you recommend."

"Well, since you two are casual sexy tonight, I think I will surprise you and you with something special. And Wilhelm, what can I get you this evening?"

"I'll have the chicken Kiev with all the trimmings," he replied."

"Good choice, I'll make it extra spicy like you prefer." Cee turned on his heels and disappeared into the kitchen.

"What's this all about, Wilhelm? What is the Toad up to this time?" Susan began setting the tone for the conversation. "I don't like this setup; its bullshit," she continued.

"He's out of his fucking mind is what he is," Wendy added. Although they complained in a low tone, their frustration was clear to him.

"This is why I invited you two to dinner besides the pleasure of your company. So since I've been put in charge of this mission, I thought we should have this little talk. I agree with you. The Toad is up to something. I think this is a bait job and we're the bait." Wilhelm paused a moment reading their reactions and body language. "I have a plan that might give us a fighting chance. If you trust me, I think I can pull it off."

"I'm with you," said Wendy.

"How can you say that? You don't even know the plan yet," Susan chimed in.

"You haven't had much interaction with this motherfucker before, Susan. Wilhelm and I have," Wendy said facing Susan. "As for me, I'm going with Wilhelm. I know that the Toad would kill us all and not lose any sleep over it. So whatever you're planning, I'm in all the way."

"And you, Susan, how do you feel about it?" Wilhelm asked.

"You've always been straight with me, Wilhelm. Jayne and I would've had a hard time after Mike was killed if it hadn't been for you. So I'm in all the way also," she said and then stuck her tongue out at Wendy and smiled. Their meals were served; and for the next hour, he told them his plan. After they had desert and drinks, one at a time, they left the restaurant. Wilhelm was last to leave.

"Goodnight, Cee, your creations were indescribably delicious and the company superb!"

"Thank you, Wilhelm. It's always a pleasure to see you, and I see you haven't lost your touch or appetite for beautiful women." They both laughed, and then Wilhelm headed out the door.

Wilhelm repeated his leisurely stroll back to the townhouse. When he was a half a block away, one of his guards emerged to escort him.

At that moment, he heard a soft voice say, "Goodnight, Shifu." And he smiled to himself.

He entered the house, went upstairs, and checked his watch. It read 8:00 p.m. on the dot. Then he hung up his coat, laid his pistol on the coffee table, and lit the fireplace. Outside, a car drove up. A black Lincoln Towncar pulled up in front of the townhouse. The two guards posted out front locked and loaded their submachine guns and waited. The rear passenger door opened and out stepped an older gentleman wearing a Spanish cape and black fedora.

"Gentlemen," he said in a baritone voice, "I believe I am expected." One of the guards called to confirm, and then they showed the gentleman inside.

"Sir, a visitor to see you," the guard announced as he entered the living room.

"Thank you," Wilhelm said as he stood up to greet his visitor. "That will be all and see that I'm not disturbed."

"Yes, sir." Then he left the room.

"Let me take your cape."

"Thank you. I see you have a fire going. Good, you must have known these old bones needed warming."

"Nonsense, you're not that old, but I do know how you enjoy a fireside chat."

"So, this is why you asked me over to pick my brain."

"That and to enjoy the company of the wisest man I know."

"Flattery will get you a long way in life but not with me," the gentleman said as he sat down in the wingback chair in front of the fire.

"What will you have?" Wilhelm asked as he headed for the bar.

"*Scotch*, of course, single malt preferably Bowmore Black Ceramic 30 years if you have it." Wilhelm smiled to himself and said,

"If I didn't, I wouldn't admit it to you." They both laughed. Wilhelm returned with a bottle and two glasses and sat down in the matching chair then placed the bottle and glasses on the table between them.

"This must be serious?" the gentleman said while looking Wilhelm in the eyes.

"Yes, it is very serious; and I need your counsel on the matter."

Linda entered her apartment, closed the door, and scanned the room. When she was satisfied that nothing was out of place, she laid her coat on the chair and put her purse and pistol on the coffee table. On her way to the kitchen, she kicked off her shoes. Once there, she opened the refrigerator freezer and perused her selection of ice cream.

"Hmmm, what's good to go with this file?" she said out loud. "That one, I think," she continued as she pulled out the ice cream. "Mmmm, death by chocolate … fitting I think for this occasion," she thought letting out a small giggle as she reached for a spoon. She headed to her couch and the file. Curled up on the sofa, she opened the ice cream, picked up the file, and started to read.

Mission Planning

Chapter Four

The Farm

Wilhelm sat at his desk in his library looking over the seven pictures in front of him. Only three targets posed a threat. Each were professionals who knew the consequences of their chosen profession. But the three scientists and moneyman didn't seem to fit. Somehow, maybe after he had a little more information, it would come together. For now, he needed to concentrate on putting a team together and sending a message to his boss. First things first, he'd send the message and then work on the team. At that thought, he got up, walked over to the shelves directly in front of his desk, and turned the head of the bronze crane statue which triggered the floor to open up to his right.

He turned, walked down the steps, and disappeared into the ground. Half way down, he touched the control panel. The secret door closed, and the lights illuminated a room revealing a large communications console that showed just how large the room really was.

"Computer on!" he said prompting the console to spring to life.

"Good morning, Wilhelm!" Do you want the night's reports?"

"No, computer; I want you to send a message to the boss."

"Special encryption, sir?"

"Yes!"

"When you are ready, sir."

"Sir, everyone is on board. The inner circle is secured.

A team of 8—consisting of 4 males, 4 females, all unknown to region.

Will keep main subject in the dark.

Details of mission to follow."

"Send message, computer."

"Message sent."

"Now you may give me the report on last night's Intel, computer."

"Report beginning." Wilhelm sat down and listened to the report while stopping the computer periodically to get in-depth information on certain aspects of the report.

"Thank you, computer; that will be all. Commence daily protocol."

"Very well, Wilhelm. Good day."

Wilhelm headed back up the stairs and touched the panel once more thus reopening the passage way.

Returning to his desk, he started to map out the mission. He knew logistics was the biggest problem in any op, so he started there. When he came up for air, so to speak, he glanced at the clock on his desk; it was 1:15 p.m.; he had been working since 7:00 a.m. Soon Gladys would be here with the final pieces of information he needed to complete his field team. As this and other thoughts ran threw his mind, he headed for the kitchen.

Gladys Bradley was travelling down Route 64 towards her bosses' house. She was enjoying the day; it was lovely and warm with the sun shining so bright and not a cloud in the sky. Her head gently rocked from side to side as she listened to her favorite radio station, the one that played songs from the 70s and 80s. Her canary yellow VW Jetta was rolling along the highway at a pretty good speed; she was going at least 20 miles above the posted speed limit. The cars GPS reminded her that a turn was coming up and brought her attention back to the road. Realizing how fast she was going, she slowed down. She made a left turn and found herself on a quaint country lane. Along the way, she looked at the scenery of trees and pastures and acres upon acres of grass.

"Wow," she said out loud, "so this is where he lives; no wonder he's never in the office. I wouldn't be either if I lived like this."

Just then, she noticed a jeep coming towards her very fast. She looked to her left and another jeep was headed her way. When she looked forward with the thought of out running the approaching vehicles, a third jeep was headed right for her. She hit the brakes and her Jetta slid a good 20 feet stopping inches in front of the oncoming jeep. Gladys looked to her left and right and saw the other two jeeps sliding on the grass towards her. She just knew they were going to hit her, so she closed her eyes and squeezed the steering wheel.

"You! in the car, stay where you are!" a loud voice shouted. Gladys opened her eyes to see a man in the jeep in front of her roaring through a bullhorn. Then she noticed two men pointing really big guns at her from the side.

"Don't shoot!" she yelled. "I'm here to see my boss!"

"Who's your boss?" said the man with the bullhorn.

"Mr. Libertaire! I'm his assistant at the office—You know, Langley!"

"Stay where you are and don't move while I check this out, miss," he said firmly.

"Don't worry; I'm not going to move while they're pointing those guns at me," she yelled back nervously. She saw the guard speaking to someone, and then he got out of the jeep and moved towards her. "Oh, shit, he's going to kill me; he's got orders to kill me," she thought as she watched him approach.

"Miss, you've been cleared; sorry for the inconvenience. If you will, follow me and please stay on the road. Did you hear me, miss? he continued. As he leaned into the open window on the driver's side to check her, Gladys was sitting there not moving not even blinking. Then she turned her head towards him ever so slowly and nodded. "Good then, miss; let's go," the guard said. Then he raised his left arm into the air and made a circle in the air with his finger. The other two men got back into their jeeps and backed up.

Gladys followed the lead jeep up the long winding lane towards the house. And just when she thought they would never arrive, she saw it and it caused her to catch her breath. The house was beautiful; it looked like a palace. She had never seen a house like this except on television. The jeep led her to the front steps of the house and stopped where George was waiting for her. As he opened the car door for her, he said,

"Welcome, Ms. Bradley. Sorry if the guards scared you back there, but you failed to stop at the intercom. And well, this is just how they're trained. You understand, don't you?" and smiled.

"No! I do not understand. Your guards nearly gave me a heart attack. And as for the intercom, I didn't see any intercom. A sign might be helpful, you think." Her outburst caught George off guard but he quickly regained his composer.

"You have a point, Ms. Bradley. I will take it up with the boss. Now if you would, follow me. Mr. Libertaire is waiting for you." George led her up the marble steps into the house and through the foyer into the library with such speed she didn't have time to get a good look around. But what she did manage to see was amazing.

"Sir, Ms. Bradley," George announced.

"Come in, Gladys," Wilhelm said from behind his desk. "Did you enjoy the trip down?"

"Yes, sir, I did. Here is what you asked for, sir." When she went to hand the flash drive to him, she looked at George.

"It's okay; he's with us," Wilhelm said. Then she approached and handed it to him. "Thank you, Gladys; I owe you one. Have you had lunch yet?"

"No, sir."

"Good, George will show you to the kitchen. George, tell the chef to fix one of his specialties for Gladys."

"You don't have to do that, sir. It's quite all right for me to get a sandwich on the way home."

"Nonsense, Gladys. It's the least I can do; besides, I may have something for you to take back to the office."

"Thank you, sir; I am a little hungry."

"Then it's settled. Just follow George; he'll take care of you." Wilhelm waited until they left the room and George closed the door behind them. Then he took out a silver box, lifted the lid, and plugged in the flash drive. He waited a moment until a green light appeared. Then he removed the flash drive, put away the box, and open up his laptop. He plugged the flash drive into it and clicked *download*. A list of the whole class along with their bios popped up. He searched through each and every one. Then he stopped and sat back in his chair.

"You're the one," he said in a quiet voice as he studied the picture of the young woman before him. He hit the print button and watched as her whole life churned out in front of him. "One down, seven to go," he thought as he continued his search for field agents who fit his requirements for this mission.

Then the intercom button light up.

"Yes, what is it?"

"Is there anything else for Ms. Bradley, sir?" asked George. Wilhelm had forgotten all about Gladys. It had been several hours since she had arrived.

"Yes, George. Please have Mrs. Bradley come to the library."

"Yes, sir." Then the intercom went dead. A moment later, a soft knock was heard at the door.

"Come in, Gladys," Wilhelm commanded through the intercom as he watched her in the monitor. Gladys slowly slid one side of the double pocket doors open and entered turning to close the door behind her. "Did you have a nice lunch, Gladys?" he asked her as she approached his desk?

"Yes, sir. I did, and your chef is fabulous. But I think I ate too much, though."

"Good, I'm glad. Listen, you did real good today; and tell your friend I hope she enjoys her new position. Also, I'm sorry for the reception you received when you arrived today."

"That's okay, sir. I understand," Gladys said in a soft voice. "What is it that you want me to take back to the office, sir?"

"Just this envelope, and put it in the front safe for pick up tomorrow by courier," he said as he walked towards her. "Now let me see you out."

"Yes, sir. But I have to stop by the kitchen first. Your chef fixed me a road bag as he calls it."

"That's okay; he does that for people he likes. You must have made a good impression on him." Soon after, Gladys returned with what looked like a fancy shopping bag, but it wasn't. It was one of the chef's hot and cold food bags. Wilhelm walked her to the door and watched her get in her car and drive away before he headed back to the library.

Back behind his desk, Wilhelm resumed his study of the agents. Finally, he selected eight agents with the skills necessary to carry out the mission. Seven were experienced field agents but not to the point of wide recognition by enemy agencies especially in the operating area, and one agent had never been seen. Wilhelm was satisfied with his selection; all of these operatives would do nicely. Next he focused on the weapons and transportation aspects of his plan. When he finished, he had spent sixteen hours on his plan and felt confident about what he had put together. He got up, reentered his secret room, and sent the plan to Rodney.

Mission Training: November 1, 2010

October had been a busy month for Wilhelm as he put the final touches on his plan. He took his time maneuvering agents and making them available so as not to cause gossip or suspicion when they were reassigned. (You wouldn't think a spy agency's employees gossiped so much even if it was among themselves. But they did and gossip drew attention.) As for his special agent, he had seen to it that she was assigned a desk job that kept her buried in paperwork and utilizing one or more of the languages that she had mastered in college and out of the eyes of other agents, especially Frank.

He looked at the clock it was 8:00 a.m. The team should have finished breakfast by now and should be wondering what this assignment is all about. He had them flown in earlier this morning. All they were told was where they would be sleeping and breakfast was at 6:30 a.m. sharp.

"We're ready, sir," George said interrupting Wilhelm's thoughts as he entered the library. "The men and horses are in place, and I've been informed that the agents have finished breakfast."

"Very good, then let's get going," Wilhelm said as he walked past George and headed for the side door were a jeep was standing by. The jeep crossed the highway where four guards on horseback sat waiting; one of them was holding the reins to two horses. Wilhelm and George got out of the jeep and mounted the two awaiting horses. No roads were constructed on this side of the property, nothing to suggest that anything was there but fields. But over the hill about five miles from the road was the training facility.

Wilhelm's appaloosa stud was feeling a little spirited, so he gave him his head and let the horse run awhile. Looking back, he could see George and the guards galloping behind him intentionally hanging back a little. At the top of the next rise, Wilhelm reigned in his horse and looked at the house below. A moment later, George and the guards joined him. Slowly, they all walked their horses down to the house, tethered them to the porch rails, and entered.

Upon entering, Wilhelm went straight to the living room with George close behind. Once there, he told George to gather the agents into the living room. George turned on his heels and headed for the dining room; he returned a few moments later with the agents.

Wilhelm watched them as they filed in. He sat in a strategic place where he could study their faces and body language. He already knew them—their histories and capabilities—from reading their dossiers. What he didn't know was how they would work together and what their true temperaments would be under intense stress. This was very important information that he needed to know. Wilhelm waited until the chef and the three instructors joined them. Then he began his introduction.

"For those who have not worked for me before, my name is Mr. Libertaire. You have been chosen for a very special operation. All of you except for one have the required field experience but not so overly exposed so that you would be recognized. This will work to your advantage on this mission. Also it means you haven't developed too many bad habits. In addition to this, all of you have unique ethnic backgrounds and your physical features allow you to blend into other ethnic groups. We will exploit these assets to its fullest. The three men you see standing to my right are your instructors for the next four weeks. They will teach you a variety of new tricks and new ways on how to kill efficiently and evade capture. These lessons will serve you well where you are headed. The chef will make all of your meals and only the chef and instructors are allowed in the kitchen.

"As for the instructors, they are simply known as Instructors One, Two, and Three. They will train you in all of the required conditioning, weapons, and hand-to-hand techniques for this op. You will find everything you need here; and if you need something, tell the chef and he will see about getting it for you. Your electronics and cellphones will be returned to you after the op is completed. Now for the operational area briefing," Wilhelm paused a moment and looked at the agents seated in front of him. "They are so young," he thought but he had a job to do. Then he began, "Lights please." The lights dimmed and the screen behind him lit up. We will be operating in three areas. The first is located at 35 degrees north latitude, 38 degrees east longitude; the second location is 39 degrees north latitude, 35 degrees east longitude; the last location is 35 degrees north latitude, 33 degrees east longitude.

"Now on the screen are the seven targets we are after. The three on the left are to be captured, interrogated, and eliminated; they will be found in Operational Area One. The four on your right are to be captured, transported, and held for interrogation. If this cannot be accomplished, then they are to be eliminated; they are in Operational Area Two. You will be split up into two teams each responsible for an area and its targets.

After the team in Area One has completed its task, the survivors will link up with Team Two and assist them. The third coordinates you were given are you're jumping off and extraction points, more on that later. These instructors will teach you how to handle the newest firearms that we'll use as well as unique and specialized forms of hand-to-hand combat along with edged weapons.

"Now before you begin your training, I will close with this last word. Some of you probably will not survive this op. It's going to be an old fashion cat and mouse hunt. I know that you're accustomed to technology- assisted communications and killing at a distance. All of you are familiar with the phase 'wet work,'" he said using his fingers as quotation marks. "Well, I choose to call it what it is—killing up close and personal. Trust me when I tell you that you will be eliminating people and there will be plenty of well-trained people looking to eliminate you.

"That is all I have for right now; I will talk to each of you individually today throughout the day's training. Now if the instructors would take over." George and a guard with a briefcase followed Wilhelm as he headed for the office. As they were leaving, they heard one of the instructors yell,

"Get off your ass and out to the firing range!" followed by the sounds of feet scrambling out the door.

Wilhelm went straight to the desk in the center of the room and sat down; the guard put the briefcase on the desk and left the room; George stood there silently but was an imposing figure nonetheless.

"What do think of this group?" Wilhelm asked.

"You're right on one point; in Syria and Turkey, they should fit right in."

"I see you have kept up with your studies and can identify countries by their L &L's.   Now let's see who else has this ability," Wilhelm continued.

"Do I get to go on this one, boss?" George asked.

"Yes, you do, I'm afraid.   I'll need your services.   I think we'll have to cover our front as well as our ass."

"You think something isn't kosher with this op?"

"I do indeed, George," Wilhelm said as he sat back in the chair and smiled.

Wilhelm and George arrived at the range just in time to hear the firearms instructor explain and demonstrate the pistol and assault rifle which they will use on the mission.

"Listen up," he began, "this is the FNH Five-seven N in 5.7 x 28 mm with the C-More system. This pistol has a 20 round magazine with one in the chamber as I know we all like to carry. You have a formidable sidearm." Then he turned, aimed down range, and fired off three rounds very quickly at three 12 by 12 inch thick blocks of ice. The ice exploded demonstrating the power of the rounds that hit them dead center and leaving very little behind. "That was the duty round, one of three rounds we will be training with.   Next is the sub-sonic round," he said while screwing on a suppressor. He repeated his performance but with much less noise. "And now, the fragmentation round." This time he fired at a steel target to show how the rounds broke apart on impact.

"Next is the P90 USG infrared (IR) assault rifle also by FNH; it has a fifty round magazine and fires the same caliber ammunition as the pistol." Pointing to the rifle, he continued, "As you can see, the magazine is located on the top of the rifle thus keeping the rifle compact and easy to maneuver." Then the instructor took aim at a side of beef hanging 50 meters away and opened fire. In seconds, he emptied the magazine and the side of beef was shredded. "Next we have the SLP MK1 tactical shotgun with eight plus one capacity capable of handling three-inch and three-and-one-half-inch shells. He loaded the shotgun and proceeded to pulverize the side of beef. "That's all for this demonstration. Now come over to the table, and I will issue you your weapons." The agents who were talking amongst themselves followed the instructor to the table to receive their weapons.

Wilhelm and George stood on the platform that overlooked the training area watching the agents fire their weapons. He was looking for who would buddy up with whom; of course, Wilhelm was paying particular attention to one agent. He was sure she could complete the training, but he wasn't sure if she could handle her fellow agents. From what he had seen thus far, she was a little standoffish. He could only hope she would settle in quickly because he needed her for a very special side job. Wilhelm tapped George on the shoulder and they returned to the office.

"Let's start with Randy," Wilhelm said to George. "I'm curious to hear what really happened on his last mission."

"I don't know why you selected this guy in the first place; he's a loose cannon...makes it up as he goes along kind of guy. I just don't like him."

"You don't like anybody, anyway, George. But I have a special motivator for our guy, and I think he'll behave himself this time. Now go and let Mr. Whitney know I request his company," Wilhelm said with a devilish grin. George left shaking his head while Wilhelm opened the file on Randy L. Whitney and begun reading. He looked up as he heard the door open and in walked Randy with George wearing his mean face. Wilhelm wanted to chuckle but restrained himself.

"Have a seat, Mr. Whitney," Wilhelm said without looking up. Randy sat down in the chair directly in front of the desk, and George backed up a few steps and folded his arms across his chest. "Now tell me about your last mission."

"Why? You have it in front of you," Randy said. George took a step forward and placed his hand on his pistol.

"That won't be necessary, George. I think Mr. Whitney will be a willing participant and tell us all about it." Wilhelm said as he looked Randy in his eyes. Randy turned his head to look at George.

"So you'll kill me if I don't talk to you? Is that how you run missions around here?" he said with no fear in his eyes as he stared back at Wilhelm.

"No, not exactly, you've been selected for this mission, not recruited. You're not volunteering; you're here to do the job you've been trained to do, nothing more nothing less. And since you are here and have enjoyed our hospitality, the least you can do is tell me about your last mission and why you've been on training duty for the past year. If you don't, you may very well find yourself as fertilizer for the field of flowers. Do we have an understanding, Mr. Whitney?" Wilhelm said in such a cold tone that it brought fear to the eyes of Randy and caused him to avert his gaze. When he looked back at George, he noticed that his pistol was out of his holster and he was holding it down by his side.

"It all took place about 18 months ago in North Africa, Morocco to be precise," he began. "I was given a mission to eliminate an information and money handler. It was supposed to be a public job to send a message. I did the usual set up on the target and decided to hit him in front of his house since the guy had three locks on his door and it took him a moment or two to get them all unlocked. I sent the details and was given the go ahead.

"Anyway, right about the time I was going to shoot him, his front door opened and a tall white guy appeared and shot him. So me and this guy get into a brief but brutal gunfight. He gets me in the leg and hand, and I hit him in the face…I think the jaw. Then he jumps into a car and poof, he's gone. Well, I make my way to a safe house, and they extract me. When I get back, they told me that I shouldn't have killed the whole family. I tell them the same story I just told you. After I recovered, they put me in the training division, and that's where I've been 'till now." Wilhelm leaned forward and slid a picture towards him.

"Do you know this man? Randy picked up the picture, studied it a moment, and said,

"No, should I?"

"Yes, you should. He's the man that shot you and killed that family you were blamed for. Tell me, Randy, who gave you your orders for that mission?"

"A man named DePore, Frank DePore. I hadn't worked for him before but the orders checked out; and well, you know the rest," he said as he gazed off in thought.

"You have any questions, Randy?" Wilhelm asked.

"Just one, is this man involved in this mission?"

"Yes, he is."

"Then whatever it takes, I'm in all the way. Is there a chance, I might run into this motherfucker?"

"I think there is more than a chance you'll run into this fellow, Randy. So I take it, we won't have the usual problems out of you on this op, will we?"

"No, sir, no problems from me," he said while looking Wilhelm in his eyes.

"Good, that will be all for now; you can go back to training and send in Alex." George waited until he had left before voicing his objection. Wilhelm listened and then told him why he chose Randy.

"Listen, George. He's a qualified expert in small arms, explosives, and CQB (close quarter combat) plus he speaks French, Germen, and Colloquial Arabic, not to mention he has five years in the field in a very hard place that's difficult to remain anonymous in. That's why I picked him. Now shut up, and let me do my job."

"Well, pardon me for giving a shit about you and your safety," he replied. "I'll keep my opinions to myself from now on," George said trying hard to conceal his anger.

"I can only hope you mean that, George, but the odds are against me on that one. Now let's get ready for Mr. Freeman, shall we?" Wilhelm said with a smile suddenly realizing how harsh his words were towards George. Wilhelm picked up another folder and began to read. George sat down in a chair near the door, crossed his legs, and stared into space.

Alex T. Freeman: Age: 25, Expert: in small arms, knives, guerilla tactics, Specialty: counter intelligence, Height: 5' 10", Weight: 210 lbs., Complexion: light, Eyes: hazel, Hair: black, Languages: German, Italian, Last area of assignment: Baltic region, Kills: 7.

Wilhelm heard a light knock at the door. Alex stuck his head in.

"You wanted to see me, sir?"

"Yes, come in; have a seat. I need to fill in some blanks in your record, nothing to be concerned about."

"Yes, sir. I understand."

For the next fifteen minutes, Wilhelm asked Alex a variety of questions, some personal some professional. Alex answered them all while accepting the process and dismissing it at the same time. Wilhelm took notice.

"Do you have any questions?" Wilhelm asked.

"No sir; I don't."

"Then that will be all; you can return to training and ask Jesse to report."

The interviews went on for two more hours as Wilhelm subtly interrogated each agent until he found out what he needed to know for this phase of the operation. Now he had one more agent to talk to. George sat stoically in his chair the entire time, not moving not saying a word. Wilhelm knew he was pissed. He would deal with him later over whiskey and cigars. But for now, he would just let him stew a little longer; besides, it was fun watching him sulk.

Pamela L. Tilyou: Age: 23, Height: 5'6", Weight: 130 lbs., Complexion: fair, Hair: black, Eyes: black, Last assignment: training Langley academy, Qualifications: small arms, long range shooting (sniper training), hand-to-hand combat training, knife fighting, Specialties: code writing, decoding, Special training: White Crane kung fu (10 yrs.), Languages: Polish, German, French, Turkish, Education: M.A. in Linguistics, University of Chicago.

This was the interview that really interested Wilhelm. If she could be trained enough within the short amount of time he had, then her special assignment had a good chance of succeeding. He was taking a big risk using an untested agent but it was a necessary risk. He couldn't take the chance that another more seasoned agent would be recognized. Another problem that he faced was her sexual history or lack thereof. According to her file, she only had two serious boyfriends and no one night stands. She was almost a virgin yet she did fit the type of woman who can captivate the target. Oh well, he had pulled off missions in the past with less resources to work with. He only hoped he had a life or two left out of these original nine; he could use a little luck on this mission. Wilhelm heard a light tap on the door.

"Enter," he said. In walked Pam; she was more beautiful in person than in her picture. He saw how fit she was as she walked across the room; he also saw the innocence in her face. It was a kind, soft face with a gentleness more befitting an elementary school teacher, not a trained agent. He smiled more to himself than at her, but she took it that way and smiled back. "Sit down please, Ms. Tilyou; I only have a few questions."

"Yes, sir," she replied in a soft voice.

"Your mother's maiden name is Zebloski, isn't it?"

"Yes, sir."

"And she comes from Koszalin, doesn't she?"

"Yes, sir." Wilhelm could see she was getting a little uncomfortable so he changed his interviewing tactics.

"Pam, did your mother ever tell you about what it was like growing up in Poland?"

"Yes, sir, she did."

"Good, as part of your training here, I want you to remember every detail of what it looks like according to your mother."

"That's easy, sir."

"It is?"

"Yes, sir. I've always pictured what it's like to live there. My mother and I played a game when I would close my eyes and she would describe her town." Wilhelm watched her closely as she spoke. He could see the joy in her face as she talked about her mother. His tactic had worked in calming her down and opening her up.

"Good, that's very good, Pam. Now I know you're wondering why you were selected for this op as you're straight out of the academy. I have a special mission for you, and only *you* can pull it off. Can I count on you, Pam?" Wilhelm asked as he leaned forward looking at her intently.

"Yes, sir, you can. If you think I can do it, I think I can do it, sir."

"Very good, Pam, because I will be counting on you and a lot is riding on you to pull this off. So learn all you can while you're here. And Pam, get to know your fellow agents; they need to know that they can depend on you and you on them, okay."

"Yes, sir. I'll do just that."

"Do you have any questions?"

"No, sir. I don't."

"Then that will be all for now; you may go back to training."

When she turned to leave, she noticed George for the first time which startled her.

"Excuse me," she said in a shaky voice as she reached for the door handle.

George waited until he was sure she was out of earshot and then walked over to the desk placing both hands on it. He leaned forward and said in a slow deliberate manner,

"You're going to get that child killed; she's just a baby. You heard her and saw how she acted. Have you ever seen a female field agent act like that boss? I mean really, she should be behind a desk, not on this mission not with this team." Wilhelm sat back in his chair and listened to George. He knew he was right; and even worse, he was in agreement with him. He was right on all counts. She did belong in the office but he needed her for this mission. If he had any chance of getting the information he needed, she could get it. She had to work out and he would make sure that she did.

He sat there and thought about the team that he had selected; they represented the diversity of his ethnic group. Their unique looks and skin colors allowed them to be invisible in plain sight. Undoubtedly, his adversary whoever he or she is, would not be looking for these Americans, especially the Syrians and the Turks. This team and this mission would show the company that it is underutilizing a valuable resource. After the operation, he would explain to George that more was at stake here. The success of this team and mission was of vital importance for more than one reason.

Wilhelm didn't say a word. He just stood up, placed the files back into his briefcase, and headed out of the office. George gathered the guards and they headed outside. George waited as Wilhelm talked to the instructors and handed one of them an envelope. Then he mounted his horse and the group rode off in the direction in which they came with Wilhelm not saying another word during the whole ride.

The Council of Five

Chapter Five

The one they called Number 1 was sitting on his wraparound porch in the section nearest to the kitchen. He watched the light rain falling steadily as he sipped his special blend of breakfast tea from a large porcelain mug trimmed in gold. He loved this house; it was his first house in this country and it was filled with all of his important memories. Decorated in the traditional Peruvian style, it gave him great peace of mind during his stays here. The house was located on a beautiful piece of land in the low hills that grew into the Andes Mountains, 50 kilometers south from the city of Tumbes.

He decided to walk around the porch to where he could see the mountain range that concealed the research center. Nestled a few kilometers from that center is his headquarters. Although, it is not visible from his house, he knew its exact location.

"Number 4 and Number 5 should be at their destinations about now," he thought. He had no worries about Number 5's assignment to hire a killer. In this organization, that was routine. But Number 4's assignment did cause him concern. Getting a spy to work for you is never an easy task even if he or she is retired. He took another sip of his tea then headed into the house, sat down in the living room, and refreshed his mug from the matching porcelain teapot resting on the coffee table in front of him. He let out a low sigh as he sat back and began to think about the feud that was taking place between Number 2 and Number 5. This year has been the worst between them so much so that the tension was starting to cause problems with ongoing operations with each one encroaching on the other's areas of responsibility.

He stayed out of it as much as he could and only intervened when things really got out of hand. After all, it was in their charter that only those who can prove their worthiness will remain among them. (And if you were cast out that meant a sure death sentence would be administered at the time of verdict.) He would hate to lose any one of them. But if it had to be done, he had no problem carrying out the sentence. His first priority was the preservation of the organization; he had spent the last twenty years building it up slowly, ever so slowly. This operation was not about the technology that was to be gained; he already had their work which was a precondition by him before taking them in and making them wealthy. No, this was about the elimination of Mr. Libertaire.

"The others believe that I'm giving Libertaire too much credit, especially Number 5 and Number 2. They think Frank can keep us informed then we can disrupt Libertaire as he put it. The information coming in from Number 5's newest asset has been very helpful, of course, even though he hasn't shared who it is. But this is quite acceptable by our rules. He was running a little high lately with his latest string of successes; he should be. But the pressure that he's putting on Number 2 is extreme."

If it wasn't for their opposition to his first plan, Number 1 would have been spared the headache of putting together this elaborate rouse just to kill a man. No matter how he explained his reasons for wanting this man dead, the others didn't see why he was so adamant about the issues. This man, the head of the CIA's Special Section, in the last seven years has ruined five major projects and cost the organization tens of millions of dollars, not to mention the personnel he has killed and made inoperable. Ironically, he has done all of this without any knowledge of their organization's existence. Number 1 could only image what Libertaire would cost them if he knew about them and targeted their organization. So he came up with this plan; and this time, he will kill Mr. Libertaire in Turkey before he becomes a real problem. Number 1 was pleased with himself. His plan was a win-win for him. He was also glad that he had given the Central and South American projects to Number 3 and Number 4 and that he was keeping Number 2 and Number 5 busy with this project. He only hoped that Number 2 could hold himself together until its completion. He would hate to have him eliminated. After all, he was a dear friend.

Rising from his couch, he headed for the kitchen. He loved this house, especially the kitchen. Every time he came here, he was glad he had installed a modern kitchen. And now that he was about to make crepe suzettes, he was doubly happy. This was his last night at the house and he was preparing a special meal for his guest. He loved cooking and young women. Today, he would enjoy both.

Final Preparations

Chapter Six

Linda sat at her desk thinking; she couldn't get the information concerning Wilhelm out of her head. It had been two weeks since she read the report that Sally gave her. Although she tended to believe what she read, it still was too incredible. If this was accurate information, Wilhelm was more dangerous than she thought and he very well could have been behind the killing of Tony as Frank believes. She sat there wondering about what her boss was so pre-occupied with the last month or so. He hadn't invited her over or made any indication that her company was wanted much less desired. Whatever it was, it was all-consuming. Even when he was in the office, he didn't notice her. She never thought she would miss his touch as much as she did. If he doesn't make a move soon, she would just have to find a replacement to scratch her itch. Just then, Frank walked into the office.

"Good morning," he grumbled as he headed for his office. Linda got up, smoothed out her skirt and headed for the coffeemaker. She knew Frank would ask for a cup any minute now. When the coffee had brewed, she fixed him a cup, and took it into his office. She found him sitting with his feet up on the desk, ankles crossed, and a stupid grin on his face.

"What's up, Frank? Why the face?" she said as she placed his coffee on the desk.

"Oh, nothing. I was just thinking about a meeting later today; that's all."

"With whom? I don't see it on the calendar for today," she inquired.

"It's with Rodney; that's why. He has the sudden need for my company." Frank took a sip of his coffee and made a face.

"What's wrong with the coffee, Frank?" she asked as she folded her arms.

"Nothing, it's good for a change," he said with a big smile. "Now sit down a minute." Linda sat down and then remembered that she didn't have her office notepad, the one with all of the information she needed on it. She left it open on her desk for anyone to see.

"Wait a minute; I need to get my pad." She was up, out, and back in her seat before he finished his second sip.

"Have everything, now?"

"Yes."

"Good, let's get started. Were you able to get all of the equipment I wanted?" he asked as he readjusted in his chair taking his feet down and leaning forward slightly.

"Yes, everything except for that special scrambler you wanted; it will be here on Monday, 8:00 a.m."

"How about that special team I want on standby. Did you have any trouble getting them?"

"No, I called in a favor and got you four men you can use at any time. Also the communications gear came in yesterday and is ready."

"Good, and the paperwork? What did you do with it?"

"I haven't filed any, Frank; it's in this folder," she said as she leaned forward to hand it to him.

"Good, I only have a few more assignments for you today. Since it's Friday, you can take off as soon as you're done."

"Thanks, Frank, but what is all of this special stuff for? I mean, you've been working on something big and I've been left out of the loop on this one."

"Sorry, but you're not a part of this one, Lin. It happens sometimes in this business; you know that. So just keep your pretty little nose out of this one, and life will be back to normal soon enough. I know I haven't spent much time with you lately, but I'll make it up to you when this is all over," he said in a soft caring voice as he looked into her eyes. He missed her and it showed.

Frank left the office at noon. As he was leaving, he noticed that Linda was working and eating at her desk. He said goodbye and headed to Langley for his meeting with Rodney.

Frank arrived a few minutes early and sat waiting for Rodney to call for him. Rodney sat behind his desk thinking about Frank and what new bullshit he was going to tell him this time. Rodney wasn't Frank's biggest fan, as a matter of fact he didn't trust the man. He knew what Frank wanted, and he was well prepared for the onslaught he was about to receive. But he was well informed about the op, and Wilhelm was following his orders. He reached over to press a button on the phone and told his receptionist to send in Frank.

"Frank, nice to see you; have a seat." Frank sat down in the leather chair and crossed his legs. "What's on your mind, Frank?" Rodney continued after Frank had settled into his chair.

"Wilhelm, he's on my mind," Frank said in a serious tone. "He hasn't given me any information on the team, nothing; and he ignores my requests for that information."

"And you want me to do what?" Rodney said as he leaned back in his chair and stared at Frank.

115

"I want you to remind him who's in charge of this mission and to start cooperating."

"I think he knows who's in charge of the mission, Frank. Didn't you tell him to run this his way?" Rodney said has he leaned forward to accentuate his words. "If this is the case, then he is following orders. Isn't that correct, Frank?" Rodney leaned back in his chair and studied Frank's reaction. Frank was getting angry and fighting hard not to lose control; but as usual, he lost.

Frank's voice was low and purposeful when he began to speak.

"All I'm asking for is a little help with your golden boy; that's all, Rodney. You let him do anything he wants. He doesn't respect the chain of command and he couldn't give a damn about protocol. The agency lets him live on his little farm with three wives like some self-imposed king or something. And with ten days to go, I'm really not in the mood to put up with his bullshit ultra-secret methods." Frank took a deep breath and noticed that he was sitting on the edge of his seat; he slowly slid back and re-crossed his legs.

Rodney sat there with his fingers interlaced listening to Frank vent and watching his body language. Frank was so far gone that Rodney doubted he was aware of what he was saying or how he looked saying it. Rodney didn't comment right away; he let Frank cool down. After a few minutes of uneasy silence, he began.

"I understand your position, Frank; it puts you in a delicate situation. But you'll have to take this up with Wilhelm. You can find him in his office, I believe. As for following protocol, since when do you or him give a damn about such things? If I recall correctly, your famous saying is 'It's the results that count.'" Rodney gestured using his fingers as quotations. "So if you have a problem, I suggest you find a solution and fast. As for him living on a farm with three women, they are all adults. As far as the agency is concerned, he has one wife and the rest of it is his business. So I strongly suggest that the next time you come to me with such bullshit and waste my time think again because I'll have your ass. And I don't care how many people come to your rescue; you'll be finished at the agency. Do I make myself clear!" Frank acknowledged with a nod of his head. "Now get-the-fuck-out of my office," Rodney said in a very controlled voice.

Frank got up and headed for the door. "Next stop, Wilhelm office," he thought. He also wondered why Wilhelm was in his office at all.

Rodney sat there thinking if he should call Wilhelm and warn him of the shit-storm coming his way. After a few moments, he decided against it. With a smile, he thought of the fireworks that would be coming from Wilhelm's office in a few minutes.

As Frank waited for the elevator, he thought about the problem he faced. He had to get the identities of the agents that Wilhelm was using. The Council was pressuring him for this and other pertinent information that Wilhelm was withholding on purpose. If he knew Wilhelm and he knew him pretty well, no way was he going to give him that information until his team was already on the ground.

Frank walked into Wilhelm's office and stopped in front of Gladys' desk.

"May I help you?" she asked looking up at Frank.

"Is your boss in?"

"May I ask who you are?"

"His boss!" Before she could reply, she heard Wilhelm say,

"It's okay, Gladys. Come in, Frank." Frank walked into the inner office and sat down.

"What can I do for you, Frank," Wilhelm said as he watched Frank closely. Frank didn't make house calls. This was definitely out of character for him. Wilhelm wondered what he was up to so close to the start of the mission.

"Hello Wilhelm, I was just upstairs in a meeting with Rodney and thought I'd stop by and get an update," he said nonchalantly.

"Nothing has changed, Frank, since my last report; everything is on schedule; there're no problems." Then he leaned back in his chair and formed his fingers in a tepee.

"What you left out of the last report was the identities of your team and your planned jump off date. Since I'm in the area, how about giving me that info?"

"Not a chance, Frank. You know how I work. I won't give out that info until the very last moment. You told me I could run this my way; so let me run it and stay out of the way. Don't worry, Frank; you'll come out smelling like a rose as always. Why the sudden change, eh, Frank?"

"There's a lot of interest in this op by the guys upstairs, and they're breathing down my neck. Look, forget I asked. I trust you'll do a good job; just keep me up to date with the latest Intel. I have to have something to tell the boys upstairs when they ask, okay," he said as he was getting up to leave.

"Okay Frank, I will," Wilhelm replied not believing a word Frank just said. Something was up with Frank and it had nothing to do with Rodney. Wilhelm was in constant communication with Rodney who wanted Frank to know as little as possible about the planning of this mission.

Wilhelm wasn't being told everything, and the way Rodney has been acting since this mission called for concern. Rodney hadn't asked for certain details like the departure dates and times or the identities of agents involved in the op. Rodney didn't seem interested in the targets when he was briefed two weeks ago. All in all, he has made a conscience effort to stay out of Wilhelm's way and not ask for too much information.

Something bigger is definitely going on, and Wilhelm has a limited time frame to figure it out. As this is a life and death game, one mistake, one miss read will cost him his life. He will have to discuss this with Wendy and Susan at dinner tonight to see if they have noticed anything out of the norm.

Wilhelm gathered up his camel hair overcoat and fedora and headed out of the office. On his way out the door, he said good night and good weekend to Gladys and headed for the parking garage. He pressed the button on his car remote, and his custom Corvette ZR-3ZR in blade silver metallic lit up and chirped. The engine started with a low rumble, *wooburrbubububububu…!* He got in and headed out. As he drove into the sunlight, his windows tinted automatically. He turned on the CD player using voice control and headed for his townhouse.

Frank sat in a booth at his favorite watering hole. He liked this place; he's been coming here for twenty years, and it still had the same décor. That was its charm. He decided nothing in this place ever changed except for the bartenders who tended to change every two years or so.

The present one is a busty brunette with a really nice ass especially when she wears a skirt like tonight. He had considered bedding her once or twice and should at least give it a try. Since the place is mostly empty this time of day, she is personally serving the few customers sitting in the booths. Maybe he will give it a try tonight. It's been awhile since he had enjoyed the company of a woman. He would rather be with Linda, but it is wiser to keep her at arm's length for now. Besides, the bartender is looking pretty sexy right about now.

He raised a finger signaling to her to bring him another gin and tonic. She smiled, nodded her head, and began making his drink. He watched her as she walked towards him with his drink. He noticed the sway of her hips and the light bounce of her breasts as she approached.

"Hi, Frank!" she said with a big smile.

"Uh, hi!"

"Sara, silly. It's Sara; how many of these have you had without eating?" she continued.

"Two, maybe three. Why, you hungry?" he retorted.

"If you're buying, I am," she said as she gave him a look that indicated he might get lucky tonight.

"Why of course, I am. What kind of gentleman would I be to let such a sexy young lady starve," he said laying on his charm.

"I get off in an hour, and I'll even let you pick the restaurant," she said putting on a sexy smile as she reached out and lightly touched his shoulder. Then she turned and walked away to see about the other customers. As he took a sip of his drink, he watched her and wondered just how soft she will feel naked next to him.

Wilhelm sat at his desk going over the latest Intel on the operational area. He wondered what he was missing. Usually, half of these people would be left alone by his department. Hell, they wouldn't even know that they were alive any other time. Then He turned his attention to the latest information on the Stanleys. Shadow One had reported that they were getting ready to take a trip and they may be out of touch for a while.

"Now what could those pompous asses be up to," he thought. He had never known them to travel to far from home and not often, especially during the winter months. Likewise, Shadow Two had nothing new on Linda. So far, she was acting like the faithful assistant. She hasn't even been sleeping with Frank, lately which could be a reason for him seeming so uptight. Maybe there's a little problem with the sleeping arrangements which may be throwing him for a loop. He knew these were only possible scenarios that he was telling himself. Something was really wrong with this mission and time was running out on him. He checked the time, locked up the files, and got ready for dinner.

Wilhelm and Cee were laughing when Wendy and Susan walked in and headed for the table.

"What's so funny?" Susan asked as she sat down.

"Oh, nothing much; Cee was just telling me about his latest conquest," Wilhelm said between laughs.

"I bet she nearly killed you," Wendy added.

"Now there's no reason to assume that, missy," Cee said. "It so happens that it was the most beautiful death and resurrection I've ever had. And if I play my cards right, I might be able to do it again," he said with a big smile and laughing so hard that his chef hat fell off.

Wilhelm waited until the girls ordered their drinks and Cee went into the kitchen to prepare the dinner that Wilhelm had preordered.

"Have any of you noticed anything out of the ordinary concerning preparations for this op?" he asked them.

"Yes!" said Susan, "Frank is having me use a secondary code and he didn't tell me not to tell," she continued.

"Why do you think that's unusual?" Wilhelm asked.

"Because all of the training on this new communication system has been hush-hush. And then, he gives me this new code book and says nothing…just gives it to me and tells me to learn it."

"Now that *is* interesting," Wilhelm replied. "And you, Wendy, do you have anything?"

"No, I've gotten everything I wanted and then some for that rainy day. Frank's been more than generous."

"Good, this is what I want you, two, to do. Susan, remember that special code I taught your daughter?"

"Yes, what about it?"

"When Frank asks you to use that secondary code, send me what it says using this code."

"Okay, but what frequency do you want me to use?"

"I'll give that to you later. But be prepared. I may use it for another purpose."

"Fine, I hope you know what you're doing," she said has she downed her drink.

"Wendy, do you have your teams in place?" he said turning his attention to her.

"Yes, one in the support/evacuation area; they've been there for a week now. The second is with me, and I have enough fire power to hold out for three days."

"And the necessary paperwork and photos of the target area? Are they ready?"

"Yes, I have them. I'll keep you updated on any changes in real time from the site."

"Good, then for now, we're ready. Here are the passwords." He slid two small pieces of paper towards them. After they had removed them from site, he ordered another round.

They laughed and drank and ate a superbly prepared rack of lamb with their favorite sides; and for desert, they had cherries jubilee. For those few hours, they had no worries; they were just three old friends enjoying dinner. Then one by one they left the restaurant going their separate ways. It was getting late. Wilhelm wanted to get an early start in the morning so he'd better get going.

Linda

Linda entered her apartment and stopped; she stood there scanning the area looking for anything out of place. When she was satisfied that everything was in its place, she laid down her coat and handbag in the chair by the door then headed towards the bathroom. She didn't want to do anything tonight except take a bath and fall asleep with the TV. She started her bath adding her favorite bath beads. On the way to the kitchen, she looked at her special friend that was laying on the bed right where she had left it this morning. "If I don't get any soon, I might as well marry that thing," she thought. She opened her fridge, took out a beer, and headed into the living room where she turned on the television. She was watching the news when the phone rang.

"Shit! Who could this be? It better not be Frank. I'm not doing any more work tonight," she thought. She turned the television to mute and listened to the machine.

"Lin, it's Sal! Pick up! I know you're home. If you don't pick up, Lin, I'll just keep calling you!" she heard her say. Linda smiled and reached over to pick up the phone.

"Hi, Sal! What's up?" she said into the speaker.

"Hi, Lin, I need a big favor. And before you say no, remember you owe me one, big time. Lin, Lin, are you there?"

"Yes, Sal; I'm here and I know I owe you big. But I'm tired and all I want is a bath and sleep."

"Come on, Lin. I really need you tonight; it's an emergency, honest."

"It can't be that bad, Sal; you sound as if you had a few already."

"Yeah, one or two. But listen, I have two guys, two gorgeous guys who are dying to party; and I need you," she said with a hurried breath.

"No thanks, Sal. I'm just going to take a bath and go to bed."

"You mean you're going to take a bath, pull out your special friend, put it on high, and rock yourself to sleep. That's what you're really saying, Lin." Linda laughed.

"It may not go in that order but I'm still not going out tonight; I'm really bushed, Sal."

"He's well-hung, Lin," Sally said softly into the phone. "Honestly, he is. So don't tell me you're not interested. Come on; be a pal, and hang with me. We'll eat, dance, and ride around in a limo. And if you don't like him, what did you lose?"

"What time, Sal?"

"8:30, Lin; and Lin, thanks. You won't be disappointed."

"Okay, Sal, I'll meet you down stairs at 8:30 sharp; and Sal, he better be well-hung; I'm starving, girl." They both laughed; Linda hung up and went to the bathroom. She turned off the water, checked the temperature, stripped, and stepped in. She had three hours to get ready, but for now she was just going to soak.

Linda looked at herself in the full length mirror that was next to her vanity in her bedroom as she stood there in her matching panties and bra. This was the third set she had tried on. Finally, she settled on this set, black lace panties and a lacy bra that opened in the front and gave her just enough support so her tits wouldn't bounce out when she was dancing. Then she sat down at her vanity and began the next phase of preparation. When she finished, she took one last look in the mirror and was happy with her hair and makeup. She got up, got dressed, and looked back in the mirror. The look she was after had come together. She was dressed in a black leather miniskirt, a black silk-satin blouse, black seemed stockings, and black ankle high boots with gold eyelets. She reached under her skirt and placed the LCP (light compact pistol) into the black lambskin holster attached to a black garter located high on her inner right thigh.

She smoothed out her skirt and checked to make sure the pistol didn't make an imprint. Then she turned sideways and looked. "Perfect!" she thought, "… not to slutty but very sexy. I would want to have sex with me if I was a man." Then she put on a three-tiered platinum necklace and a pair of pendulum diamond earrings, walked into the living room, put on a black mink fur trimmed three quarter length leather coat, picked up her clutch purse, looked at the Cartier watch on her wrist, and headed out the door.

She waited in the lobby for only a moment when a black limousine pulled up. The back door opened and out stepped a very well-dressed, six-foot-three gorgeous man. He walked into the lobby, approached her, stopped, and said,

"You must be Linda. I'm Josh, your date for the evening," in the most perfect baritone voice she had ever heard.

"Yes, I am and yes, you are," she said while flashing her innocent girlish smile.

"Then shall we get started," he continued. He took her hand lightly and led her to the car. Once inside, she saw Sally who was smiling and sitting close to her date who was introduced as Martin.

It was 3:00 a.m. when Linda and Josh entered his hotel suite. The evening had been fantastic for Linda up to now. "Dinner was fabulous and Josh loved to dance," she thought. As they laid their coats on the sofa, he leaned down and kissed her. Linda accepted his tongue into her mouth and gently sucked on it enjoying the sensation that she was feeling clear down to her crotch, and she was getting wetter by the second. Just then, Josh broke their embrace and headed towards the bedroom. When he reached the doorway, he turned and said,

"I'm going to take a shower; all of that dancing has made me sweaty; you can join me if you like." Then he turned and continued into the bedroom.

Linda waited until he was out of sight then she sat down on the edge of the sofa and took off her garter holster and pistol. She placed them in her purse and started taking off her boots. Afterwards, she walked into the bedroom just in time to see Josh entering the bathroom. He stopped and turned around to face her.

"I'm glad you decided to join me," he said standing their naked.

Linda didn't speak at first; she just stared at his cock. Linda was three for three on this one; he was very well-hung and she wasn't having second thoughts.

"I could use a shower myself," she managed to say. "I'll be there in a moment; you can start without me; you don't have to wait."

"Okay, that means the water will be perfect for you when you get in," he said as he stepped into the shower.

Linda undressed and got into the shower. He was right. The water was perfect, and it felt so good on her body. She stood there letting the water run over her, and she didn't move until her hair was thoroughly soaked. Josh took the mandarin orange scented soap and began to lather up her shoulders then he moved to her breasts, down to her stomach, and finally to her inner thighs. Linda involuntarily spread her legs where Josh lingered for a few moments before moving on. He took the hand held showerhead and rinsed her off then turned her around and repeated the process. Again, he lingered and again he used the showerhead to rinse her off. He leaned over her kissing the back of her neck, and then he gently pushed her forward. Linda placed her hands against the wall in front of her and braced herself.

"Uh, Mmmm," she moaned as he entered her from the back.

Linda woke up and looked around the room getting her bearings. She looked over at Josh who was sound asleep. Reaching over, she picked up her cellphone and checked the time; it was 6:30 a.m. Shit, she had only been asleep for two hours, she thought as she lay back down. After their "sexapade" in the shower, he carried her to the bedroom. And for the next three hours, they tried any and all of the positions they could think of before passing out. Afterwards, she thought about leaving but then remembered it was Saturday. She had nothing better to do. With that thought, she closed her eyes and wondered what Josh would come up with when he woke up. Then she drifted back to sleep.

Frank got out of bed and headed towards the bathroom. Once there, he turned on the cold water at the sink and splashed it on his face letting it run over his head. While he stood there relieving himself, he thought of the risks he might have to take. He gave himself two shakes and headed back to the bedroom. As he started to get dressed, he looked over at Sara who was still sleeping. He had answered his third question about her and discovered a few more things. "She really is a nice woman," he thought. He wrote her a quick note and quietly left her apartment. Once in his car, he took out his cellphone and made a call. A voice on the other end responded. Frank said,

"It's a go." He hung up, and then he headed for home.

Hiring Spies & Killers

Chapter Seven

Number 4 arrived in Philadelphia on Friday afternoon and settled into the royal suite at the Four Seasons Hotel located on the Ben Franklin Parkway. He would have a fine dinner and listen to some wonderful chamber music at the concert hall on Broad Street, he thought as he looked out of his window at the tree lined view of the parkway and the Philadelphia Museum of Art. He liked Philly and always enjoyed his time in the city whenever he found himself here. He was pleased that the Stanleys suggested it for their meeting place. He wondered whether he would be successful in his recruiting efforts; they were no-run-of-the-mill spies. Even if they were retired, they still controlled a vast intelligentsia network who's ability to get information was remarkable. He noticed that his glass was empty so he headed for the room's bar. He had enough time for worry, he thought. But tonight, he would forget everything and enjoy himself.

Number 5 had been in Las Vegas since Thursday and was partying from the moment he checked into the Hugh Hefner Sky Villa suite. He checked his watch as he stood in the living room; it was 5:00 p.m. He looked over at the two naked women sitting on the couch watching television and eating. He tried to remember their names. Looking around, he spotted his two guards who were sitting at the bar. Then he turned around and headed back into the bedroom. He needed a shower. He smelled like pussy and booze, he thought as he sniffed himself. He had to take it easy tonight because he had important business tomorrow in Green Valley at a location known as the District. He had never known such a place existed in Vegas. He had to look it up, and if an international killer wanted to meet at such a location, he had to be on his toes. Besides, who would name a desert attraction Green Valley, he thought as he scratched himself.

The Stanleys arrived at the Four Seasons at 11:00 a.m. on Saturday. A tall muscular German man met them. He greeted them in German and then escorted them to the elevator while Wilhelm's shadow watched them as he sat and drank espresso.

After they left, Shadow One went to the front desk. And after flirting with the young lady on duty, he learned that a very rich European was staying on the eighth floor. He decided to take a room for the night and booked the Logan Suite also on the eighth floor. Once in his room, he began to take inventory of his equipment. He would only need a fraction of what he brought to find out the European's identity, he thought.

"Thank you, gentlemen, for accepting my invitation and coming to hear my proposal," Number 4 began after they had drinks in their hands and were seated. "My organization would like to hire you to work for us. Now this can be a short-term arrangement or long-term as we hope it will be. In addition, we are prepared to pay you 50 million dollars per year for a long-term agreement and a fair negotiated fee for short-term or selective work," he continued.

"That's very generous of you but we'd like to know who we are working for," said one of the Stanleys.

"I find it hard to believe that neither one of you has never heard of my organization. But if this is true, then I've wasted your time and mine with this meeting."

"You are quite right; we have heard whispers about your organization but only whispers, mind you. And if the rumors are half true, why do you need us?" Stanley replied.

"Quite frankly, you have contacts in places we wish to expand into. With access to those contacts through you, our jobs will be a lot easier. And for this, we are willing to offer you not only money but a place in our organization."

"Of course, you will deposit all monies and/or precious metals into any account we designate," the other Stanley confirmed.

"But of course, you will be paid in any manor you choose and in any currency you prefer," he answered with a smile. He knew that when spies started talking about money, he was on the right track. The two Stanleys looked at each other for a moment and without speaking came to an agreement. Then one Stanley spoke.

"We accept your offer on a long-term basis; we will take payment in gold; I will give you the accounts later. Also we will not provide information on certain subjects and that will be on a case by case decision. And finally, we need to know exactly who we will be working for," he said somberly.

"Very good, I am very pleased. Let us have some lunch and work out the details," he said genuinely happy that he had pulled it off. Then he raised his glass in salute and all three gentlemen took a sip of their bourbon for the first time.

Shadow One waited in the hotel bar until the Stanleys came down, and then he followed them to the Latham Hotel. He had to ascertain the identity of the man at their meeting, although he had taken pictures of him with the Stanleys in their car. Something wasn't right with him; he didn't act like a spy but more like a business man. "So what did he want with the Stanleys?" he wondered.

Number 5 reviewed the information he had on Talaus. He was still impressed at what this master killer had accomplished. The report from the reconnaissance of the meeting place was most favorable. From the hotel to the meeting place was a 30 minute drive. He looked at his watch; it read 10:15 a.m. He placed the envelope that contained the information about the assignment in his briefcase and told his guards he was ready to leave.

He enjoyed his ride through Green Valley. It really was green and the neighborhoods were cozy like many others he had seen. He never thought of Vegas as residential; he only knew the Strip and up to now that was enough. But now that he had seen the mixture of shops and homes, he had a new appreciation of the place. After all, if this area was good enough for a man like Talaus, who was he to judge.

Number 5 rode the escalator down past the movie theater and went out the double doors to the crosswalk. He paused for a moment and looked down the open air mall before him; he was looking for any sign of Talaus or his men. He saw young mothers and their children, some in strollers, others following behind as they half ran and walked. On his left was the Elephant Bar and a row of boutiques as far as he could see. He crossed the cobblestone walkway and headed towards their meeting place, a coffee and tea shop. He didn't like open air meetings; they made him nervous. But he was doing the hiring, so he had to play along with the clients' wishes.

He reached the cafe, stopped, and looked to his right. On a bench directly across from the shop, a casually but expensively dressed man waited. Standing a discreet distant away on his right was a tall fit gentleman who appeared to be German drinking a cup of something; probably tea was his guess. Number 5 sent one of the guards into the shop for a double espresso and headed towards the gentleman seated on the bench with the other guard.

"Good morning, Mr. Talaus."

"Bonjour, Monsieur Cinq, please join me."

"This is an interesting meeting place for our business, don't you think?" he said in a low voice almost whispering.

"Why Mr. Cinq, it's a beautiful day and we should enjoy it; besides, who would start trouble here with all of these nice people around," he said with a smile. Just then, the guard showed up with his double espresso, handed it to him, and took up his position ten meters away. Number 5 took a sip, smiled, and said,

"Shall we get down to business?   I need you to provide security for a very important meeting. Also, I need you to eliminate any and all opposition or anyone else who may not want this meeting to take place."

"You can find any number of people to do this a job, Mr. Cinq. Why did you come to me with this routine request?"

"It's simple; there's a gentleman by the name of Libertaire who is very interested in getting his hands on the people at this meeting; thus, I require a person of your talents and resources."

"I see, Mr. Cinq. I may be able to help you. When do you need these services?"

"In ten days' time."

"That's cutting it close, Mr. Cinq; and that will cost you extra."

"Name your price, Mr. Talaus. I'm sure it will be reasonable."

"I don't know if it will be reasonable but it will be expensive, Mr. Cinq. So what part of the world are we talking about?"

"Syria and Turkey."

"That's two parts of the world, Mr. Cinq."

"I'm aware of this fact but it covers one operation. So if you will kindly tell me your price, Mr. Talaus."

"Let's see, two locations simultaneously in ten days' time, provide protect and remove any and all threats.... Do I have that right, Mr. Cinq?"

"Yes, you do; now what is this going to cost me?"

"30 million in U.S. currency payable up front. Is this acceptable, Mr. Cinq?"

"Quite, Mr. Talaus. Here is all of the information you need," he said as he handed him the envelope.

"And this is where you can deposit the funds by end of business today," he replied as he handed Number 5 a folded piece of paper. Number 5 got up without saying another word and walked away with his two bodyguards following closely behind. Talaus sat there watching him leave. When he was out of sight, his bodyguard came over.

"Do you think he's part of the inner circle of the Council?" he asked quietly as he stood their surveying the area.

"I'm sure of it. But is he really Number 5 is the real question," he replied as he prepared to leave the area.

Talaus

Chapter Eight

Talaus sat in one of the overstuffed chairs in his suite; it was quite comfortable and made reading the material he had been given more enjoyable. As he looked over the pages, he couldn't help thinking about Nicaragua and the close encounter he had with Mr. Libertaire. Number 5 didn't know it, but he would have taken this job at cost if he had known Libertaire was involved.

"Seven years ago, conducting what should have been a routine snatch, Libertaire and his team appeared from nowhere. And not only did he end up with the package, he caused me fifteen good people. I should have been better prepared. But the Intel I had was reliable as it came from an inside source who recommended me for the job," he thought.

Anyway, Talaus didn't find out who had pulled off that job until a year later and he has been keeping track of him ever since. He was up against a very shrewd and ruthless man quite like himself, except Mr. Libertaire has the protection and permission of his government to do his killing and give the orders to have it done. He had tried that route and found it to be all a bunch of bullshit; they train you to go out and kill their enemies and pay you poorly for it plus they give you shit for risking your life. No, he liked it the way it is now. He made tons of money for killing people and having them killed on the behalf of well-paying private and government clients.

He reached over and picked up his vodka martini from the marble pedestal table next to his chair and drank it down. Then he turned the page to the Syrian section and looked at the pictures inside. He recognized the three people in the photograph; they were all very capable of taking care of their own security. He knew the two women by reputation except he had never worked for them nor them for him, but the man he knew well. Talaus had retained this man's services on several occasions. He is a talented and resourceful killer who definitely doesn't need help securing his persons. He truly was sadistic and enjoyed his work a little too much. This tall handsome Pol had no boundaries; he would kill and torture anyone including children. Talaus remembered one case in particular involving a government who wanted a lady scientist with a unique specialty to defect. So they hired him who, in turn, hired the Pol. Talaus told him the intended outcome, sat back, and watched him work.

First, he roused suspicion about her by planting little hints that she was talking to a western government. (This is something you do not want to do when you work for an eastern government or any government for that matter.) Her bosses decided to interrogate to her and her family just to put a scare into them, just in case some truth was in the rumors.

Then the Pol made contact with her and offered to take her and her family out of the country for a better life which would be true to a certain extent. Of course, she refused. She was genuinely loyal—a patriot to her country—; she really didn't want to leave. But he left his contact number, did nothing for two weeks, and then sent her bosses a picture of him talking to her. Naturally, he was in disguise but it was a brilliant move nonetheless. Her bosses called her in, read her the riot act, and threatened bodily harm. But she didn't tell them which government had approached her or what they were offering.

His next move was to wait for her and her family to come home. One by one, he knocked them out and tied them up. He interrogated them in their native language asking them senseless questions. His goal was to convince the scientist that her government was orchestrating this and to persuade her change her mind. To drive the point home, he killed her husband in front of her then raped her and her two daughters. One week after her husband's funeral, she and her daughters became residents of their new country. The Pol is a dangerous man who lives in a world where sex and violence are not separated.

Talaus stared at the eyes in the picture. "Yes, it is you; although you have changed your face, you can't hide those dead eyes. I can think of a dozen people and at least that many governments who would want you dead. But for the life of me, I can't think of one who would want to protect you," he thought. Talaus got up and went to the bar and poured himself another drink from the martini pitcher. He had made a batch of the cocktail before he started studying the file. He looked over at Gernot, his personal bodyguard, who was watching horse racing and cleaning one of the three guns he had disassembled in front of him.

He returned to his chair and opened the file on Turkey. Now this was more like it—four paper pushers: three scientists and one money man. He began to read about them trying to figure out why they are so important and why an organization like the Council of Five would spend 30 million dollars to protect them. Just then, his phone beeped; he picked it up and looked at the message. It was a bank alert informing him that the money had been transferred. "Hmmm, apparently they are serious. Finally, I get a shot at Libertaire," he thought.

He heard the door to the suite rattle and looked up; Gernot was already headed towards the door with pistol at the ready. In wiggled his twin companions back from a morning of shopping.

"Hi, Bruce! Did you miss us?" one of them said as they walked past Gernot who tucked his pistol into the small of his back as soon as he saw them.

"Of course, I did. What did you two buy?" he replied as he got up to greet them. The two women kissed him and started to tell him about their morning.

He didn't hear them as they chattered; he just stood there looking at them in their minidresses, one in blue, the other in red, both in four-inch heels. He watched as they walked around the room pulling out clothes and jewelry. He didn't bother to remember their names; he just called them by the cutesy names he made up on the fly. When he had arrived, he ordered twins who possessed certain talents and looks; he wasn't disappointed. The women were beautifully tanned, young with full hips and perky breasts, and possessed the talents he desired.

"Bruce, are you listening?" the one in red said.

"Yes, I am; I was just thinking."

"I bet; I can guess what it is," the other one chimed in. "But you'll have to be a little gentler; my ass and body are still bruised from last night's session."

"You don't have to worry about that, Bruce. You can do whatever you like with me, the rougher the better," the one in red said with a smile.

"You have read my mind ladies," he said as he started for the bedroom with twins in tow.

Infiltration

Chapter Nine

Wilhelm sat in a lotus position meditating in the middle of the training platform in the martial arts garden. The sun had been up for an hour now and lit his face in brilliant yet soft colors of winter. He heard two sets of footsteps walking very lightly down the path. The two people that these footsteps carried were silent. He knew who they were without opening his eyes and turning around to check. They were his two eldest children, Wilhelm II and Elaina. They had arrived for their weekly training session with him. When he was home, he trained his family in the three main arts that they practiced and which he learned from his master Wuù Aìping. Today, his son would practice Hsing Yi Quan and his daughter, Emei Bagua Quan. Afterwards, he and Afef would fence and practice Classic Northern Wu style Tai Chi Quan. He was looking forward to training; his wife is an excellent swordswoman.

Wilhelm was dressed in a heavy silk traditional kung fu uniform in white with black trim. Without using his hands, he stood up and faced them. The children were dressed like him except their uniforms were black with white trim.

"Good morning, Father," his daughter said in a cheery and excited voice. His son echoed the same greeting but not so cheerily.

"So who shall be first this morning?" he said with a smile as he looked down on them from the platform as he stood with his hands behind his back.

"I will, Father; and I'm going to win today," Elaina said as she looked at her brother.

"She's been saying that all week, Father. Can I go all out today?" he asked with a smirk.

"Please say, yes, Father. I owe him big time," she said with determination while giving Wilhelm II the evil eye.

"We'll see after your lesson; now warm up and let's get started," Wilhelm said laughing a little. He watched them perform their prospective qigong sets and then their warm-up routine. He monitored Elaina as she practiced the Dragon Shape form also known as the eight palms set with a critical eye. He stopped her a few times to adjust her position and correct her posture. He was impressed with the speed, balance, and power she displayed. Now he stepped forward and they set up to practice the Dragon Shape fighting set. Facing each other about three feet apart, they bowed and then crossed their right arms across their chest with their left arm and palms facing towards the center. Next, they turned their bodies to the left. Finally, they took a step to the left with their right foot and began to walk in a circle. When they had taken eight steps, Elaina attacked.

They twisted and turned together never leaving striking distance. Wilhelm waited until the eighth interchange before catching her arm, sweeping her legs, and flipping her off the platform.

"Ha, ha, ha!" her brother laughed. "You should've seen yourself fly, girl!" he continued.

"Very funny, junior, wait until Dad throws *you* off the platform; you won't think it's so funny then," she said as she rubbed her behind.

"Okay, it's your turn," he said pointing to his son. "And, you, young lady, practice your swimming body form," he continued while he watched her get up and brush herself off.

Wilhelm instructed his son to start with the Shyr Er Hsing (Twelve Shapes) form representing the Twelve Animals of Hsing Yi Quan. Wilhelm stopped him periodically to correct him and repeat the movements until he was satisfied with the results. Then they took their places to begin the Ann Shenn Pau two-man fighting set. Elaina made herself comfortable sitting on the edge of the platform and yelled with the biggest smile,

"You're gone a get it now, junior!" Wilhelm and his son took their positions, saluted, and began. His son opened the exchange with a powerful right-hand Beng followed by a lightning fast Pi. Wilhelm responded with a Pi and a Pau fist of his own. Then they move in the characteristic movements that is Hsing Yi, back and forth and using angles to attack and defend.

Wilhelm waited patiently for the right moment; he could feel and see his son's overconfidence which was growing by the minute. Then Wilhelm II attacked with the sparrow technique; Wilhelm countered and attacked using the monkey technique. When his son started to backup, he followed using the chicken technique. He caught his son with two palm strikes in the chest and followed it up with a right Heng fist as he kicked out with his right leg striking him in the mid-section. His son went flying off the platform past his sister who watched wide-eyed and mouth agape. *Thud!* was the sound he made when he hit the ground.

"Ugh!" he muttered as he landed.

"Boy! That had to hurt, junior," she said as she looked down at him.

As Wilhelm walked to the edge of the platform to check on his son, he noticed Afef standing there in an all-black heavy silk kung fu uniform looking concerned.

"Are you trying to kill the children, my husband," she said has she helped Wilhelm II get up.

"No, but I couldn't resist; he left himself open," he replied as he sat down. "Are you ready for your lesson? I see you brought a sword with you," he said in a funny voice that caused her and Elaina to giggle.

"Yes, I am; and if you think I'll be as easy as these two, you're in for a surprise," she said trying not to laugh but not succeeding.

"That's not fair, Mommy Afef. We gave it our best shot!" Elaina exclaimed.

"Yeah, we tried. I left myself open that time but I won't make that mistake again," Wilhelm II said as he rubbed his chest where his father had kicked him.

"I know, children; I was watching, and I think you did just fine," she said consoling them as she kissed each one on the forehead.

"So what style do you want to practice today? I see you've brought a very pretty sword with you," Wilhelm teased as he got up and headed towards his sword resting in the stand by the platform.

"Northern Wu style against your Yang style," she replied very confidently as she walked up the stairs to the platform.

Wilhelm had a great respect for this sword form; it was, perhaps, the most complex and complicated of all of the Tai Ji Quan sword forms. It was a particularly dangerous form because of its use of left hand and two-handed techniques combined with interweaving movements and sudden changes in direction. Add agility and lively footwork and it becomes a very beautiful, graceful, yet deadly sword form. And when Afef performs this set, it has all of these characteristics with the added intensity that she brings to it.

When he reached the edge of the platform, he told his son to hand him his sword. He took it and returned to the center of the platform in time to see which blade Afef had chosen for today's workout. The wen jian that she brought was in the Ming dynasty style. Its handle was made from brown buffalo horn. The scabbard was also covered in wafer thin slivers of the same brown horn. It was adorned with silver inlay of a crane design and had brass fittings. The blade was hand-forged Damascus steel, twenty-eight inches long and weighed one pound.

Wilhelm's sword was in the Qing dynasty style and sported a black buffalo horn handle. The rosewood scabbard was covered in the flying bat motif in brass which represented good luck. The guard and pommel were gilded in steel with the guard formed like bat wings. Hanging from the pommel was an intricately tied knot fourteen inches long. It also was a hand-forged Damascus steel blade that was twenty-eight and one-quarter inches long and weighed one pound ten ounces. They unsheathed their swords and handed the scabbards to Elaina; then they took their positions, saluted, and took the en garde stance.

Afef's lunge set the tone for the match; it was fast and aimed directly at Wilhelm's chest. Wilhelm responded with a beat lunge of his own, and then he moved to his right. The ting of the blades as they met was slightly higher than a ping, and the vibration was very light. As he moved, she followed. She launched her second attack. This time, it came in low and then in high combination first striking at his knee then flicking the blade upward when he blocked the first strike. She took a step forward ending the technique with her blade at eyebrow height. After blocking the first strike, he quickly took a step backward to evade the second; and just as quickly, he advanced moving his sword from right to left. Afef quickly brought her sword down and blocked his attack as she backed up. Then she executed the technique Fair Lady Throws the Needle. Using the top third of her blade, she sliced first to the right and then to the left as she took a step forward finishing the technique by stabbing at his knee. All the while she was doing this, she kept perfect form with her sword finger placed on the pommel.

Wilhelm countered with Push the Boat with the Current as he brought his sword down and to the right blocking her strike, while simultaneously crossing his right leg over his left. As he stepped into a left bow stance, he circled his blade back and up ending in a stab to her forehead. Afef responded with Turn Around and Chop Sword as she raised her sword and her right leg blocking his stabbing motion. Then she pivoted on her left foot 180 degrees stepping out into a right bow stance and chopping her sword at his left shoulder. Wilhelm shifted his weight so that it rested on his rear leg, turned his waist to the left, and brought his sword across to block her attack. Then he stabbed forward towards her head causing her to take two quick steps backward to evade his attack as she blocked his sword.

They circled each other; and after one full turn, Wilhelm initiated the attack. He took one and a half steps to close the distance between them. As he did so, his blade was vertical and it traveled in a straight path towards her chest. Afef countered the attack easily and responded in kind. This started the back and forth exchange that he loved so much, nothing fancy just basic fencing which allowed them to speed up the tempo. Then Afef adhered to his sword and sent it outward to the left. As he recovered and swung his sword rightward, he was met with her foot hitting his right wrist. Afef had started her execution of Sweeps a Thousand Soldiers and he knew what this meant. Soon she would be employing the two-handed and switching-hand techniques that make this style famous.

Wilhelm calmly countered her technique and patiently waited until she switched hands and lunged. Then he lightly adhered to her blade and started to wrap his around hers by moving his wrist up and down causing his blade to wrap in tiny circles around and up her blade. When he had reached her guard, he executed the tiniest flick by quickly setting his wrist downward, causing her sword to fly out of her hand and stick into the platform as it landed.

"Very balanced blade," he said mockingly.

"How did you do that? Next time, you won't be so lucky," she said as she walked over and retrieved her sword.

"I'll tell you all about it over breakfast," he said as he walked down the steps of the platform. They gathered up their swords and the four of them walked to the house.

Wilhelm sat in the steam room thinking about Frank and his behavior yesterday in his office. He wondered what he was doing this Saturday morning. What was he planning? And why was he keeping Linda at arm's length? Of course, two of his previous assistants had been killed; and he might be thinking about that. But Wilhelm didn't think this was the case. Frank's behavior, the missing pieces of Intel, and notably, the reason for the importance of the targets were causing him great concern. And Linda acting like the perfect assistant and carrying on like this was normal procedure wasn't setting well with him either. She wasn't the type to sit back and be content being out of the loop. Then he rinsed off, got dressed, and went down stairs to the kitchen.

Wilhelm walked into the kitchen through the door that led to the family quarters upstairs. When he entered, he saw Afef and Afra sitting at the large butcher block table in the center of the room. Colleen was talking to the chef or more like having one of their tit-for-tat conversations about something. Wilhelm sat down at the opposite end of the table and one of the chef assistants brought him a cup of tea. He listened to the sounds of the kitchen: Afef and Afra discussing what was needed for the

145

stores at the mini-mall that Afef ran, the chef assistants preparing food and preforming other kitchen duties, and Colleen telling the chef not to give the children so much ice cream and cake no matter how much they pleaded their case.

He rose from the table, walked over to the dessert refrigerator, and looked through the glass door at the various pies and cakes and cookies. Deciding on lemon merengue pie, he opened the door, took out the pie, walked over to the counter, got a fork, and sat down. He felt the silence. Looking around, he noticed everyone was looking at him.

"You're not going to eat out of the pie, are you?" Afra said with a serious face. But before he could answer, Colleen walked over and removed the pie. She cut him a slice, put it on a plate, and brought it back to him. After she set it down, she shot him a look as she walked away.

Just as he was about to start eating, the kitchen door swung open. He looked to see who was coming in. It was Bonnie, their female French mastiff. He took a closer look at the dog and noticed a head just above her shoulders. As the pair came into view, he saw Tianna, Afra's first born and the baby of the family, for now.

"Hello Tianna," he said with a big smile as he looked down at her.

"I'm not Tianna; I'm Bubble Bee!" she replied.

"You are? Then hello, Bubble Bee."

"Hi, Daddy!" she said as she looked up at him with her smiling eyes. Wilhelm reached down and picked her up and placed her on his knee.

"Now why are you called the bubble bee?"

"Because she's been running around the house pinching us on the legs and running away," Afra said answering the question for her daughter.

"Is that true Bubble Bee?" he asked.

"Yes!" she said excitedly.

"Sounds like fun," he said as he tickled her tummy. "Do you want some pie?" Tianna nodded her head indicating that she did.

"She cannot have pie this close to lunch, Wilhelm," Afra said from the other end of the table. Wilhelm looked at Afra; and as he smiled, he feed Tianna not one but two bites of the pie before putting her down. Then he got up, picked up his pie and tea, and left the kitchen smiling to himself as he listened to Afra express her opinion on what he had just done.

Infiltration Team

Twenty miles south of Wilhelm's training facility, four men stood around a table in a motel room looking at a map of their target. The leader of the group was taking his team through the plan one more time. They would leave their vehicle five miles from the training facility and proceed on foot. When they reached the jump off point, they would split into two teams: Team 1 would set up position on the west side of the house where the living room was located. Team 2 would scout the grounds mapping and photographing what they saw. They would then meet up and leave the area by the southwest. He reminded them that this was a photo-recon, and they were not to do any shooting unless absolutely necessary. Then he instructed them to check their equipment and get some rest. They would jump off at 1800 hours.

The team leader stood in the doorway of the motel room giving it one last look to see if they had missed anything. As usual, it was perfect; they had wiped it down and left no trace of themselves especially hairs or fibers. He threw the keys on the bed, closed the door, walked to the waiting vehicle, and got in. They drove out of the parking lot and headed north. He put on some vintage Rolling Stones and began to sing along to himself. The other men bopped their heads to the beat as they adjusted the equipment that was attached to the web harnesses they were wearing. Everyone in the vehicle was doing something, even the driver who was constantly scanning his mirrors, monitoring the police scanner, and watching his speed.

The vehicle pulled off the road and traveled 50 meters into the field, and then stopped. The team leader got out and checked his watch. It was 1817 hours. "Good," he thought; he was on schedule. Looking at the night sky, he saw it was cloudy and the winter air was crisp. He took a deep breath filling his lungs with the cool night air; and as he exhaled, he could see his breath. As he put on his equipment, he thought about whom he was going against; and the thought made him a little nervous. The fact that he had a professional and experienced team who had worked together before made him feel confident that he could pull it off.

He had them do one final equipment check, and then they jogged off into the darkness towards their target. Half an hour later, they reached the jump off/rally point, stopped, and knelt on one knee.

"Remember, guys, this is a photo-recon mission. No gun play! What we're after are pictures of the agents and the training grounds. Got it!" he said looking at each of the men as they acknowledged. Then Team 2 started off in one direction. The team leader and his teammate headed to the west end of the house. He knew this was the best place to set up if he wanted to get a look at the agents. A big picture window gave a great view of the living room were the television was located. He figured he could snap the pictures he need as they watched television and milled around the room.

Randy was sitting on the railing of the wraparound porch just out of sight of the big picture window, smoking a cigar. Rochelle was practicing her knife and dart throwing techniques at a three-inch-square target at 20 meters in the outdoor knife training area. Pam and Alex were swimming laps in the indoor Olympic-size pool. The remaining agents were inside watching television while eating popcorn. The team leader and his partner crawled into position 300 meters away from the house and started to set up his camera. After he had done this, he called Team 2.

"Team 2, this is Team 1, over."

"Team 2, over."

"Are you in position? Over."

"In position, over."

"Begin operation, over."

"Roger, over."

Team 2 began sweeping the area; their first stop was the pool house where one of them looked into a small window and was greeted by a lengthwise view of the pool. He noticed ripples in the water. As he watched, Pam and Alex came into view as they started their run to the other end of the pool apparently racing each other. He whispered to his partner about what he had seen and then traded places with him. His teammate peered into the window just in time to see the pair reach the other end and stop. He raised his digital camera with a zoom lens attached, checked the setting, and then snapped pictures of them as they talked in the pool.

"How come we never work with women that look like her?" he whispered to his partner who shrugged his shoulders in response. And then, they moved on.

The team leader looked through the lens of his camera as he lay on the cold frozen ground. He was not happy with what he was seeing; he wasn't close enough, and the camera lens was starting to fog up from the cold. He signaled his partner who came in close. He told him that they were moving forward 150 meters. The man gave him a strained look and then acknowledged by nodding his head. He too was aware of whom they were spying on. It made him nervous to be so close to the house, but he didn't protest. They packed up and slowly moved forward; they both thought it was strange that no guards or patrols were there, not even a fence. And this fact caused them to be extra careful not just on their approach but in their planning as well. After he reached his new position and began setting up his camera, he hoped that Team 2 was having better luck.

Team 2 had finished with the northwest corner where the pool house was located and posted themselves by the outdoor pistol/shotgun range. After taking pictures of the range, they headed towards the northeast section approaching the knife range where Rochelle was practicing. As they approached, they heard the faint grunts that she was making as she threw the heavy blades. They stealthily crawled towards the sound, hugging the frosty ground and snaking along until they were behind a low log fence. Then one of them slowly peeked over the fence and saw that they were behind her. So they decided to move to a point where they could get a good picture of her. Rochelle was concentrating so intensely on what she was doing that she didn't notice him when he took the chance and placed his camera over the fence and took her picture.

When he finished and they moved on, his partner tapped him on his shoulder and made the "crazy sign" by circling his finger round his ear. His partner smiled and mouthed,

"No guts, no glory," and continued to crawl towards the next building.

The next building was the motor pool. It was full of tools, a tracker, and a few vehicles. As they took pictures and looked around, Rochelle finished her practice and was headed back to the house.

Team 1 had settled into their new position and the team leader was happy with the location. As he lay looking through his replacement lens at the four agents watching television with each and every photograph, he felt more confident that they would pull it off. He was also wondering if this was all of the agents and if Team 2 had captured any on their chip. If not, he still had hit the mother lode by photographing the mysterious secret agents they said were so important. As he laid there photographing the house and the surrounding area, his partner kept a keen look out.

On her way into the house, Rochelle bumped into Randy on the porch, so she stopped to chat with him. Meanwhile, Team 2 came out of the building and headed south which would put them right in front of Randy and Rochelle. The team had no idea that they were on the porch. The team kept well into the deep shadows away from the reach of the house lights, but they failed to notice the red glow of Randy's cigar as they passed.

"Team1, this is Team 2, over."

"Team 2, go ahead, over."

"We're on our way in, over."

"Roger, have changed location, will meet you at rally point, over."

"Roger, over and out." Team 2 headed towards the rally point and Team 1 started to pack up.

The chef and Instructor One were in the kitchen; the instructor was watching the chef preparing for tomorrow's meals and watching the basketball game. While dividing his time between prep work and monitoring the ground sensors, the chef noticed the sensor indicated movement at the southwest perimeter. He stopped what he was doing and watched the board. When he was certain that the intruder wasn't an animal, he told the instructor to investigate the area. The instructor immediately headed towards the kitchen door.

"Don't forget your comm piece," the chef called out after him. He backed up a few steps, grabbed two ear pieces, and headed out the door.

He tapped Instructor Three on the shoulder as he passed through the living room and motioned towards the door with his head.

"We have movement in the southwest sector," he said to him once they were outside. They pulled out their pistols and trotted towards the area. Randy and Rochelle noticed their urgency and decided to follow. After catching up with the instructors, they trotted alongside not knowing why or where they were going. As they were approaching the target area, Instructor One heard the chef in his ear piece,

"You're 75 meters from target. Be advised, there are four targets. I say again—four targets—, over." Upon receiving the information, he slowed down to a walk and gave the signal to come close. Once they were together, he stopped and told his team what they were up against.

Meanwhile, the chef was keeping an eye on the four intruders with infrared heat reading security cameras that were posted on retractable posts throughout the grounds. The four of them started off again, this time in pairs and 20 meters apart. They would approach the four intruders from two sides. Since they didn't know how heavily armed the intruders might be, they were being extra careful as they closed the distance. The defenders' greatest advantage was knowing the terrain which they intended to exploit to its fullest. Instructor One knew that a slight drop in the grounds was coming up so the intruders would have to step down a few feet. If he could get his team in place before the intruders arrived, he could launch his attack as they navigated the descent and catch them off balance.

Randy wondered what plan the instructor had in mind since he didn't have time to fully explain his intentions. But Randy was also familiar with the terrain, and he suddenly realized where they were headed. If his guess was right, a two to three foot drop off was coming up. He remembered because it caused him to drop suddenly on their first day cross country run. "That would be a perfect place for an ambush. This instructor knows more than he lets on; apparently, tactics is one of them," he thought as he jogged along.

The infiltration team leader thought he saw something on his left and halted the team. His men knelt down on their right knees and started to scan the area to their immediate front and rear. He had caught a glimpse of Rochelle as she disappeared into the darkness of the lower level of ground that was less than a foot away and directly in front of him. He focused trying to see into the dark; his ears were straining to pick up any sound of movement. Just as he was about to give the signal to move out, the night erupted into loud sounds of fighting to his right.

Randy and Instructor Three had come up on the two men from their right while they were still on one knee. When the two men heard them coming, they tried to pivot to face them; but it was too late. Randy and the instructor were on them. Randy kicked the side of the rifle as the man closest to him swung it towards him. Randy's kick stopped his motion causing him to lose his balance and roll off to his left. Then Randy quickly followed not wanting to lose sight of him in the dark. As the man jumped to his feet, Randy launched his attack first kicking him in his groin and then bringing up his knee to his face as he bent over from the pain.

"Ugh!" the man groaned. Then Randy hit him in his throat using a leopard fist. The man made a guttural sound and stepped backed disappearing into the darkness. As he fell off the edge, he hit the ground with a *thud!*

Randy jumped down landing beside the man's head and then kicked him in his temple. He quickly got behind him and snapped his neck hearing the cracking, crunching sound it made as he completed the technique. His assault took less than one minute. He remained crouched listening, wondering where was his partner. He had focused so intently on dispatching the intruder that he didn't hear the popping sound that the silenced pistol made when Instructor Three shot his target several times in the face.

"Where are you?" a voice whispered.

"Here," he replied after recognizing the voice. The instructor joined him and the two of them listened to the fight raging somewhere in the dark directly in front of them.

They listened to the hurried breathing and the dull sounds the blows made as they hit their intended targets. They couldn't tell who was fighting. They couldn't see them and they dare not move. So they crouched there listening, feeling helpless.

Rochelle had sunk one of her throwing knives into the neck of one of the intruders. The man dropped his rifle and grabbed his throat. As he tried to speak, he made guttural sounds instead. Then he fell over and died. His warm blood pumped out on the cold ground producing steam as it hit the cold air. While this was happening, Instructor One had closed the distance between him and the intruders' leader and engaged him in hand to hand combat. After the instructor disarmed him of his rifle and pistol, the man pulled his knife. He was better skilled with the blade than the instructor expected. His unorthodox techniques kept the instructor at bay causing him to dodge in and out to get in his strikes. Instructor One was trying to capture him and not kill him; he needed him alive if possible.

Just then, the clouds cleared for a moment. Suddenly, they were bathed in moonlight and his three companions could see the fight clearly. At only ten feet away, they watched in astonishment as the pair moved— dodging, blocking, and striking as the instructor slipped the stabbing and slashing techniques coming at him. Rochelle stood at the ready with her last throwing knife in her fingertips ready to throw. She saw her opportunity and launched her knife hitting her target on the side of his neck sinking it halfway into his throat. The instructor rushed forward catching the man before he fell and cradling his head as he laid him down on the ground. He tried to stop the bleeding, but it was no use. Her aim was perfect, and her knife had sliced his carotid artery and larynx.

The three gathered around the pair staring at the man on the ground.

"Where are the other two?" he asked as he looked up at them.

"Over there," Randy said as he pointed in the direction where the two men lay dead.

"Who's he?" Rochelle asked.

"We won't know the answer to that question thanks to your expert knife throwing skills," he said sarcastically. "Now I want you two to stay here while miss knife thrower and I go and report this." He and Rochelle ran back to the house. When they arrived he instructed her to say nothing to the others.

George walked into the room that housed Wilhelm's art collection and found him examining a new sculpture.

"There's been an incident at the training facility, sir," he said once he was standing beside him.

"What type of incident?"

"Four men infiltrated the grounds."

"Have we captured them?"

"Yes."

"Are they alive?"

"No, sir."

"Meet me out front in five minutes."

"Yes, sir," George replied as he turned and headed for the door. Wilhelm had held this conversation all the while he was examining the sculpture, never taking his eyes from it nor showing any emotion. In his mind, his thoughts were racing a mile a minute trying to figure out who could be behind this.

He placed the sculpture back on top of the pedestal and headed for the front door where he found George waiting. As he walked down the steps to the awaiting jeep, he saw three jeeps with five men in two of them and three in the lead jeep. He got in the lead jeep and George sat behind the wheel. As they were leaving, Wilhelm heard a helicopter take off flying above them towards the facility. When they arrived, George deployed the men after giving them their instructions. Then he drove Wilhelm to the motor pool building where the four men and their equipment were laid out.

"What do we know, so far?" he said to Instructor One as he looked at the bodies.

"Not much. They seem to have been conducting a photo-reconnaissance mission. We recovered these cameras, sir," he said as he showed Wilhelm one of the digital cameras.

"Did they have an uplink of any kind for these cameras?"

"No, sir. Whoever wanted these pictures didn't want to share."

"Identify these men as soon as possible, get me whatever is on those memory cards, and give what you find to George." Then he turned to George and said, "Take me to the house. I want to talk to our two heroes." The two of them left the building and headed for the training house. Wilhelm talked to Randy and Rochelle separately then he had George take him back to the manor. He told George to personally supervise the Intel gathering on their visitors and try not to take all night during so. Then he walked into the house, returned to his personal museum, and resumed examining the statute.

It was 2:00 a.m. Sunday morning when George entered the library and handed Wilhelm the folder. Six hours had passed since the incident and Wilhelm was becoming impatient. He needed to know who these guys were and whom did they work for.

"Well, what have you found out?" he said without looking at the folder in front of him. George sat down, crossed his legs, and began.

"The four men are professionals, of course. They have no unusual identifying marks on their bodies. Two are South African; one is British; the other is American."

"Any information about a possible upload of the pictures to an outside source?"

"No, sir, there was no evidence of that. The cameras they used are digital, and we have the memory chips. Also we found their vehicle about five miles south of the house; it was wiped clean, nothing inside. The details are in the report along with all of the pictures and chips; there are no duplicates," George stated in a businesslike tone.

"Thank you, George; that will be all for now. Get some sleep." As George got up to leave, Wilhelm stopped him. "George, were the bodies taken care of?"

"Yes, in the usual manner."

"Goodnight then," Wilhelm said as he opened the file and begun to read.

Rodney was sitting at the table drinking coffee at his suburban D.C. home and going through the morning briefings, when he came upon Wilhelm's report. As he started to read, he put down his coffee and concentrated on the report. When he was done, he picked up the phone and ordered a helicopter. He was going to hear what happened from Wilhelm in person.

Linda sat on her couch watching the Sunday morning news show when she heard the news that the guy she just had sex with only sixteen hours ago was dead. The reporter said he died from an allergic reaction, and the doctors aren't sure what caused it. She sat there in shock, not believing what she had just heard; this had CIA written all over it.

"That bitch!" she said out loud. "She *used me* to kill him; I'll kill *her*," she thought. Then she picked up the phone and called her.

"Hello."

"Sally, how could you use me to conduct business?" she yelled into the receiver.

"I don't know what you mean, Lin, but we shouldn't be talking about it over the phone."

"Save the bullshit, Sal; I know you had something to do with this."

"I really don't know what you're talking about, Lin. Calm down and tell me."

"On the morning news, Sal, they just reported that Josh was dead." The phone went silent for a moment as Sally was thinking; she had no idea that the poison would work so fast on him. It was supposed to take thirty-six to forty-eight hours to work giving her plenty of alibi time not to mention a continent away.

Just then her other cellphone rang.

"Hold on, Lin; I have another call, okay."

"Yeah, sure." Sally laid down the phone and answered the other one.

"Yes."

"If you haven't heard yet, you will in due time; the photo mission is cancelled."

"Why? This is our last chance before the mission starts. Are you sure?"

"Yes, when you're fully informed of the events that have transpired, you will understand. I will contact you later." Then the phone went dead. Sally picked up the phone that Linda was waiting on.

"I'm sorry, Lin, but I really didn't have anything to do with it. I had no idea you would fall for the guy; it was just dinner and sex."

"You're right, Sal. I sort of lost myself there for a moment; the sex must have been better than I thought. I'm sorry, Sal. Will you forgive me?"

"Sure, girl. But remember not everyone is pulling a fast one, you know. Listen, I gotta go but I'll see you soon, okay." The phone went dead before Linda could answer. She hung up the phone and thought, "You won't get away with this, Sal old girl." Then she headed into the kitchen.

Frank sat in his sunroom drinking coffee and enjoying the fragrance emanating from his orchards. He wondered who had ordered that failed mission, and he wasn't upset at all that his own mission was cancelled. He wouldn't have listened to Sally's plan if he hadn't been in a jam. Really, he didn't believe it would work. But she was sure; she had worked out the kinks and figured out what had gone wrong the first time it was tried. In a way, he was relieved now. He could do it his way and Wilhelm wouldn't escape his trap alive. Smiling, he took a sip of coffee and made a phone call.

Loose Ends

Chapter Ten

Monday Morning

As Wilhelm flew to D.C. in his helicopter, he looked over the photos of the four men who were killed. He was glad that he had withheld the information and photos of the agents which his men had collected. He was sure they weren't CIA which left about two dozen intelligence agencies that would pay a pretty sum for the information they had gathered. He had four days until the start of Operation Ophiuchus. With the added precautions, he wasn't too concerned that there would be another attempt on the training house.

He decided to work from the townhouse today. Going into the office wasn't such a good idea. Besides, he wanted to talk to his shadows; he was eager to hear their reports. He had a feeling they might provide a clue about who ordered the failed mission on the training house. This and many more thoughts went through his head as he flew along. He knew what he must do, what must be done to assure the success of this mission. He pulled out a legal pad and began to write. He was so wrapped up into what he was writing that the landing of the helicopter caught him off guard.

Wilhelm sat in the lower level open room of the townhouse drinking coffee from a porcelain coffee cup and listening to R&B, when Shadow One was announced by his guard. Wilhelm knew he hated coming in through the front door in the middle of the day. He smiled to himself at the thought, picked up the remote control, and turned down the music.

"You always play good music, Shifu," he said as he entered the room and bowed slightly.

"Thank you. Have a seat. Can I offer you some coffee?"

"No thank you, Shifu."

"So what have our friends been up to?" Wilhelm said as he poured himself another cup.

"The Stanleys travelled to Philadelphia this weekend and had a meeting with a man who appeared to be European. They met for four hours and then went to the Latham Hotel where they were registered. Later that evening, they dined out, went to a classical music concert, and then returned to their perspective hotels. The next day, they drove home and haven't left since."

Wilhelm sat quietly listening. When he heard that they had gone to dinner with this European, he knew they were up to something.

He knew the Stanleys had made a deal for their services; otherwise, they wouldn't have had dinner with him. The Stanleys are very cautious and prefer to eat at home. Like him, they found this to be a very sound policy. Also they like their entertainment young—very young. For them to leave their latest playmates at home meant this was an important and lucrative meeting.

"All of the details and photos are in here," he said as he placed the file and flash drive on the table interrupting Wilhelm's thoughts.

"You've done a good job; now this is what I want you to do. Bring me all of the files and microfilm and anything else that might contain information. Question them and find out who they are working for. Then eliminate them; leave no witnesses. I need you to have this completed by Thursday at the latest."

"What about their young companions?"

"What about them?"

"I was just checking."

"If they're in the house when it happens, then they go also. Understand?"

"Yes, Shifu." He got up, bowed, and quietly left. Wilhelm picked up the file and flash drive from the table and walked upstairs. After he locked the information away in the office safe, he checked the time and headed for the kitchen. He had a few hours before Shadow Two was due to report. He wondered what Linda was up to and if there had been any change in her behavior.

Wilhelm sat at the kitchen table playing dominos with two of the guards. They were laughing and slamming down dominos, when she walked in.

"Who's winning?" she said as she entered. The two guards got up and left the room. "Did I scare them away?"

"No, not at all, but that scarf might have blinded them though," he remarked as he pointed to it.

"What's wrong with my scarf? I happen to think it's very pretty," she replied as she looked at it. "I'm not listening to you on matters of fashion; you obviously don't know what you're talking about," she continued while pouting her lips. Then she bent over and kissed him on the cheek.

"Are you hungry? Do you want something to eat?" he asked.

"No, I'm okay; but I'll have some tea," she replied as she took off her coat and hat and sat down. Wilhelm poured her a cup of tea and sat down beside her at the table.

"What do you have for me?"

"Linda has had a little mental breakdown; it seems that the guy she had a weekend fling with got himself killed. They don't have a clue about what did him in. Linda thinks Sally had something to do with it."

"Who's Sally?"

"She's an old friend of Linda; they went through training together. She also works in Department 2."

"Oh, I see.   And how does she figure into this?"

"She's the one who arranged for them to be together. They stayed together until he left early Saturday evening as a happy man."

"What do you think happened?"

"I think Sally used Linda to kill Josh."

"Josh?"

"That's his name; anyway, that's what I think. And another thing, I haven't seen a chick go so ape-shit over a weekend fuck before; I think there's something more going on. Why else would she care so much? I don't get it."

"Anything else?"

"No, that pretty much covers it; photos and details are in the report." Then she handed him a flash drive.

The two of them sat in silence for a moment with Wilhelm thinking and watching her drink tea. What could cause Linda to cling so hard and so fast to a stranger? She should know better than to become emotionally involved. This definitely has something to do with Frank. Maybe she's trying to break from him. If so, Wilhelm wanted to be there when and if she does.

"I want you to stay close to Linda as usual, and I want you to get me all the information you can on this Sally gal also."

"Okay, I'll get on it right away. This Sally chick loves to party and she has good taste in men," she said with a smile.

"Well, you be extra careful; this sounds like there is more than meets the eye with this one.   I want a preliminary report on Thursday."

"Okay, anything else?"

"No, when you're ready, see yourself out. I have something to take care of; I'll see you Thursday." He got up, kissed her on her forehead, and went upstairs.

Thursday

Wilhelm was standing in the garage when he saw Shadow One standing in the doorway with two guards casually pointing their shotguns at him. Wilhelm smiled to himself; he knew this was annoying Shadow One immensely. He waited until George informed him about the contents in the van. Then he waved him in.

"You know all of the security wasn't necessary; I'm on your side," he said.

"Nice disguise, office supply delivery man, very old school," Wilhelm said ignoring his comment. "Come, let me show you some of the cars I've been collecting," Wilhelm said as he started to walk down his 100 yards long by 30 yards wide garage. They walked past his collection of American muscle cars starting with the 1966-1977 era classics. As they approached his collection of Corvettes, he began to speak.

"Did you get everything?"

"Yes."

"How many casualties?"

"Seven in all: three guards, two playmates, and the Stanleys. Did you know that they had a walk-in underground safe under their garden shed?" Wilhelm looked at him but didn't answer.

"Are you sure you got everything?"

"Yes, I am; besides, when I questioned them, they were very forthcoming with a little encouragement, of course," he said with a serious face.

"Did they tell you who they were working for?"

"Yes, something about a council or council members."

"Be more specific. What did they tell you exactly?"

"They weren't too clear at the time; by the time they decided to talk, the fuckers were pretty bad off. It took all of my medical skills to keep them alive, tough old birds. But that is what they said,—'council.' They work for a council."

"What was the job?"

"That's when it gets strange. They didn't know; they said all they were being paid for was to provide information on demand about any subject. They weren't told in advance."

"Did you believe them?"

"Yes, but by that stage, they just wanted it to be over and they were telling me everything." They started walking again in silence. As they got closer to the mechanic working at the other end of the bay, Wilhelm stopped and facing his shadow asked,

"Did they beg for their life?"

"No."

"Good, they were the last of an era; I'm glad they went out without begging," he said with a thoughtful look. "Now I want you to follow Frank. No matter where he goes, I want you there. Also, I want you to bed a young lady named Sally; she works in Department 2. I'm told she is quite beautiful and likes to party; you should enjoy this assignment. She's quite deadly too. I have reason to believe she has just completed an assignment. I'll forward you all of the information through the usual channels."

"Yes, Shifu, I'll do my best," he said with a big shit-eating grin.

"You don't have to be that excited. Remember, you may have to kill this woman so don't get cocky. Now come with me; I want to show you something special," Wilhelm said as the pair walked towards the mechanic. "This is the new Ferrari F12; it's a prototype; it won't be released until 2012. What do you think?"

"Now I know why you have all of this security; it's beautiful," he said as he ran his hands along the car's sleek lines and peered into its interior. "Boy, what I wouldn't do for a car like this!" he exclaimed as he sat behind the wheel.

"I know; I feel the same way when I look at it. Now be on your way; I have work to do and so do you," Wilhelm said has he walked him back to the empty van. They said,

"Goodbye," and he drove off.

Wilhelm headed for his private study located adjacent to the museum. He entered his study through a panel on the left wall. Turning on the light, he headed for the lounge chair in his favorite corner of the room. He sat down, kicked off his shoes, picked up the remote to the stereo, and pressed the *on* button. Then jazz filled the room with its soothing sounds. He sat back, reached over to the table next to the chair, opened a small wooden box, took out a joint, picked up his gold lighter, and lit it. He took a deep pull and let the smoke out slowly. As he started to feel the effects, he laid back and listened to the music. It had been an interesting five days. "If this was any indication, this mission was going to be a great big pain in the ass," he thought as he drifted off into bliss.

Operation Ophiuchus

Chapter Eleven

The Mission Begins

At 2300 hours Friday night, Wilhelm and George were running a check on the seaplanes they were going to fly and were supervising the loading of some last minute equipment. While they were looking over the second seaplane, a lanky figure stepped out of the darkness. George stared at the approaching figure trying to identify the person; then the figure came into view.

"Oh no, not this piece of shit, I thought they had locked you away in some dark hole," George said as the man got within earshot.

"They did. You ever work for the NSA? It's like being in a fucking hole," the man replied. "But it sure is nice to see you, George, and you, Wilhelm. And Wilhelm, thanks for getting me away from those assholes."

"It was my pleasure, Tommy, and hold the thanks. You may feel differently later," Wilhelm said as he shook the man's hand and slapped him on his shoulder. "You'll be flying with George in this waterbird; you can stow your gear in there," he said as he walked him around the plane to the entrance and showed him.

"This might not be too bad; after all with him along, at least it won't be dull," George said to Wilhelm as they continued their inspection of the plane.

Wilhelm walked down the concrete ramp to where it entered the ocean. Looking into the darkness, he drew in deep breaths of the ocean air filling his lungs with the cold salty stuff and watched his breath as he exhaled. The sting on his face from the sea water felt good, and this was a beautiful night for flying. It was clear and cold and moonless. This close to the water, the temperature had dropped a few degrees, and he could feel the chill through his leather bomber jacket. He rechecked the area on his way back to the parked planes. When he arrived, he saw Tommy, aka Captain America, smoking and talking to George.

He looked at his watch; it read 2320 hours. In a few minutes, the team and interrogators would arrive. Soon, everyone would be airborne and headed for the ship. Wilhelm lit a cigar and waited alone giving Tommy and George their space so they could catch up with one another. At that moment, he heard the helicopter. He looked up, spotted the running lights, dropped his cigar, and stepped on it. When the copter landed, he walked out and greeted three people who disembarked. He escorted two men and one woman to where George and Tommy were standing.

"George, show them where to stow their gear and prepare to leave." George nodded in response and started up the stairs with the three interrogators. Then Wilhelm heard the second helicopter coming in and turned to watch it land. His eight-member team debarked, grabbed their backpacks, and headed to where he was standing.

"Get in; stow your gear; and Rochelle, you'll be my co-pilot," he said as they gathered around him. He alerted the ground crew and blew a kiss to the image painted on the plane—a black female warrior holding an M-16 and riding a black eagle with the words *Black Betty* written above her. He got into the G-21G Super Goose and George got in the GL-130.

Wilhelm secured the door and checked on the seven agents; they had stowed their gear, selected a seat, and settled in. Settling into the pilot's seat, he put on his headset and started the pre-flight check with Rochelle. He started the four engines one by one; then he stuck his head out the window, pulled back the headset, and listened to the engines. Satisfied tha the engines were running smoothly, he sat back, readjusted his headset, and closed the window.

"This is 21G to GL taking off, over."

"Roger, 21G," George replied. Wilhelm eased the throttle forward and the plane began to move. He guided the plane down the ramp and into the ocean.

"Landing gear up." Rochelle reached over, flipped a switch, and waited for the green light.

"Landing gear up," she said after seeing the green light come on.

"Here we go!" he said as he turned the plane into the wind and increased the power to take-off speed. "Could you push that CD in for me," he said. When Rochelle did, she heard a loud "Wind me up!" in her ear as Bootsy Collins yelled through her headset and into the cabin. The plane skipped along the water, gaining speed, and then lifted off. Immediately, Wilhelm started to climb to cruising altitude. Behind him, George was doing the same. Soon the pair had linked up and started to cruise.

Wilhelm looked out the right window and saw George just off his right wing. He would stay there the whole flight. Wilhelm reached up and turned off the music giving Rochelle her first clue that something was happening. She looked at the clock; they had been flying for six hours. She felt the plane bank left and start to descend as they cleared the clouds. She could see the ocean for the first time. She didn't know where they were going; she guessed they were either going up or down the coast. But this looked like open ocean and no land was in sight.

"G-21G to C.A.A, over," he said into the mic breaking her out of her thoughts.

"This is the C.A.A., over."

"How do you read? Over."

171

"We have you on radar. Winds are out of the south by southeast. Swells are one to three feet, over."

"Roger, C.A.A., over and out." Wilhelm banked the plane right and descended to 100 feet above the water with George matching his every maneuver. They flew at that altitude for fifteen minutes. Then he suddenly climbed and banked right. That's when Rochelle and the others got their first glimpse of the C.A.A.

It was an old gray tub of a cargo ship flying a Liberian flag and sitting dead in the water. After flying for six hours to reach this tub, she thought, "God, this is going to be one fucked up mission." The plane made its approach and landed smoothly on the ocean and taxied up to the starboard side of the ship. There, two men waited on a platform connected to the ladder way leading up to the deck. Wilhelm and Rochelle shut down the plane and headed to the cabin where he opened the door and took a rope from one of the men and tied it to a hook.

"When you get off, go straight topside; don't talk to anyone; they won't talk to you. Now get your gear and file out. I'll meet you topside."

The agents gathered their backpacks and left the plane heading straight for topside in silence. Wilhelm was the last to leave. He said something to the men on the platform and then headed up the metal stairs. A side loading porthole opened up, and one of the men threw a rope to a man standing in the opening. Then he and another man started to pull the plane towards them. When the plane was clear of the platform, George guided his plane up, cut the engine, and opened the door. Tommy was the first one out, then the three mysterious passengers with their equipment, and last George. As George climbed the stairs, he could see the crew refueling Black Betty. When he reached the deck, he saw Wilhelm talking to the team. While he attempted to move closer to hear, he was intercepted by Tommy.

"Did you notice our three guests?"

"Yeah," he said half listening. "What about them?"

"They're torturers, man. The last time he worked with those types, it wasn't pretty, man." George looked at Tommy but didn't say anything. Instead, he headed towards the group.

As George approached, the agents were leaving with one of the crewman.

"What do you want me to do now," he said to Wilhelm.

"Come, let's have a drink; it's been a long flight," he replied. The two of them headed into the passageway which took them to his stateroom. Thirty minutes later, they heard a knock at the door.

"Come," Wilhelm said, and a middle aged man walked in.

"Sir, the team has been assembled in the briefing room."

"Thank you." Then the man left the room.

"Well, back to work," George said as he set down his glass and stood up. Wilhelm leaned back in his chair, swirled his scotch in his glass, and said,

"It seems like all we do is work lately, doesn't it? But, we *must* find out who sent those men. Then we get a vacation, George, only then."

"We'll find out who was behind that one, sir. I'm sure of it," George said. Then he left the stateroom.

The Briefing

The briefing room was large for being on a cargo ship and was finely decorated with artwork, carpets, and intricate wood molding. To the right of a small podium was a fully stocked bar. Next to it was a long table filled with finger foods, pastries, vegetables, and dips. On the left side of the podium were five posh leather chairs. In the center of the room were18 theater style chairs arranged in a semi-circle facing the podium.

When Wilhelm entered the room, he saw the eight agents and three interrogators silent at the table with goodies plates in hand. At the bar, George and Tommy were sipping on their drinks, watching the table, not saying a word. He thought, "This is strange. But again, no one trusts anyone. And when you are told not to talk to outsiders, you do just that."

Wilhelm headed for the control panel in the front of the room, approaching it from the left side so as not to disturb them. He inserted a special key, turned it counter clockwise, and watched the panel light up. Then he punched in an alpha-numeric code, and the large transparent computer touchscreen came to life behind the podium. He turned around and noticed that everyone was seated, the agents in theatre seats and the interrogators along with George and Tommy in leather chairs. He walked over to the bar, poured himself a double shot of Glenrothes John Ramsay Edition scotch, walked back to the control panel, and inserted a memory chip.

"Let's get started, shall we?" he said after he took a sip of his drink. "For the benefit of our guests, I will start with the four people of interest," he said as he looked over at the chairs. He touched the screen and four photos appeared.

"These four people are wanted for questioning. They will be brought to the ship for that purpose. Our guests will take care of that end. Some of you will be slated for deliver duty to assure that our end his held up." He paused to take another sip from his drink and continued. "That will be all. I will inform you of their arrival. You're free to enjoy the ship and go anywhere you like in the designated areas." The three interrogators got up, said,

"Good luck," and left the room. Wilhelm waited until they had closed the door before continuing.

"Now let's get down to business, shall we? If anyone needs a refill, too bad," he said as he took another sip and smiled at the agents.

"I see he still likes to fuck with people," Tommy whispered to George who nodded his head in reply.

"Now this is Dr. Agnes Slater," he said as he touched the screen and enlarged her picture. She has a PhD from Texas A & M, is 36 years old, five feet five inches tall, and weighs 135 lbs. She has brown hair and brown eyes. Her specialty is agricultural genetics. It seems that Monsanto, her former employer, thought her invention of a seed that would grow anywhere in the world was too profitable to share. So they discredited her work publicly and made billions from it privately. Dr. Slater dropped out of sight for a few years and reappeared about 18 months ago in Spain. At which time, she announced that she had improved on her original seeds and that her new seed would grow even in sub-Saharan regions of Africa, given enough water. Then she disappeared again and has resurfaced in Turkey at one of its resorts along the Mediterranean coast." He touched the screen again arranging several images of the woman with other people before continuing.

"Before she disappeared for a second time, agents in Spain managed to get some Intel on her and her habits. It seems Dr. Slater has a drinking and sex habit. She likes vodka straight and cold, and she enjoys the company of couples for sex. Role play and light bondage are her turn-ons. She likes to pick up her playmates at restaurants or cafés never at bars or clubs. These pictures taken in Spain show what her tastes in sex partners are like. The pictures are one and a half years old. But she does have a tattoo on her right inner thigh that looks like this." He showed them a close up of a lamb with a saddle on its back.

"Next, we have Peter Brumbaugh, a PhD from the University of Berlin, 34 years old, five feet nine inches tall, weighs 175 lbs., brown hair, hazel eyes, and a military engineer/weapons designer. He's a freelancer selling his designs to the highest bidder. He is now believed to be headed to a Turkish resort for a meeting with as of yet an unknown employer. He likes listening to classic rock, isn't a bad dancer, and drinks rum—Brazilian rum especially. He likes to be tied up and beaten; he's heavy into the B&D culture. He is an unassuming man who looks more like a company executive than an engineer," he said as he pointed to a large picture of him on the screen. He touched the screen, placed his picture alongside Slater's then pulled down the next image and enlarged it.

"Here, we have Charles Pimms, 35 years old, five feet eight inches tall, weighs 183 lbs., salt and pepper hair. He has a PhD in water purification/management and chemistry from Oxford University. This guy's claim to fame is that he invented a purification pill that will clean any type of dirty water. Since this is such an important invention, the British government stepped in to safe guard it. So this fucker decides to sell it anyway and gets caught then manages to escape and disappears. Thanks to our friends at Interpol, he was tracked from Lisbon to his present location at a Turkish resort. He drinks gin martins, plays the fiddle, and has a foot fetish. He likes to be jerked off using a woman's feet.

"Last, but not least by any means, is Derek Minh, 28 years old, six-foot-three, weighs 225 lbs., black hair, grey eyes, has an MBA from Yale. His specialty, of course, is moving and hiding money. Look at that face," he said pointing at the screen. "It's a face a lot of people love, and he uses it to great effect when talking clients into trusting him. He's not an angel, people! He's a dangerous man although he looks like a model and dresses like one. His mother is fifth generation Vietnamese organized crime. His father was a married African-American businessman from the upper eastside of Manhattan. His mother was tried and acquitted for his murder after shooting him in front of his apartment because she found out he was married with children and he wasn't going to marry her." Wilhelm brought up the pictures of the pair.

"It seems the witnesses, a doorman and one of the tenants, went missing. And this, of course, helped her case; so she walked. Her little boy witnessed the whole thing. He's been a cruel person ever sense, but he does it with a smile and a wink. But the end results are always the same: people are hurt or disappear. He is a person of interest, and our latest Intel tells us he's been in Istanbul for the last two weeks. Now he has moved down to a resort, which one we don't know yet. But what we do know is that he's traveling with his 15-year-old companion. He likes to party, drinks a lot, and has a penchant for young girls between the ages of 14 and 17 years old. We know he is a member of his mother's triad. In addition to his money laundering, he's a sex trafficker and white slaver.

"He can be identified by a dragon and European lion intertwined by their claws located on the right side of his chest. He is a world class trafficker moving girls and children from Vietnam through China and into Cambodia, Europe, Macau, and Taiwan for the purpose of prostitution and arranged marriages although most of the girls end up working in karaoke bars, restaurants, hotels, massage parlors and clubs. That's all for the first part of this operation." he said as he headed to the bar for a refill.

"Now for this next section, I want you to pay particular attention to every word I say. The personnel in this section are professionals. They know what they're doing every moment they're in the field. Don't make the mistake of underestimating any of them. Even if you do everything right, you still may end up dead at the hands of one of the next three people." Then he pulled up the picture of the Pol; he looked at Randy and watched him tense up for a moment and then relax.

"We'll start with this man known as the Pol to his friends. His real name is Andrzes Zielinski who was privately trained as an assassin. He has worked for and is wanted by twelve governments including ours. This is his new face; he is six-foot-one, 230 lbs. His hair and appearance will change frequently but his eyes never do. So pay attention to them and remember. He's staying in Syria at a resort on the Mediterranean coast to keep an eye on our next two guests."

Wilhelm posted a series of pictures of two women in various stages of nudity and dress. They were obviously Spanish and very pretty.

"This woman," he said as he pointed to the one in a bathing suit with a young girl at her side, "is Amaranta, flower that never fades, Adoración. She is a retired Argentinean major whose specialty is military organization. She is 30 years old, five feet eight inches tall and weighs150 lbs.; she is an expert with the pistol, rifle, knife, and hand-to-hand combat. The girl with her is her daughter who is eight years old. It is rumored that the father of this child is a well-known South American rebel leader.

"It seems that while Ms. Adoración was on temporary duty in another country, she was kidnapped and then released three months later pregnant. When she refused to have an abortion, she and the Argentinean army parted their ways. She's been offering her services in the private sector ever since. She drinks red wine, is a lesbian—a femme—, and is known for her orgies of beautiful women which she uses as business entertainment for potential clients. She has a tiny tattoo of a woman with a cock located just below her naval." Then he zoomed in on her tattoo from a nude photo of her. "This soft looking woman is credited with prolonging at least six conflicts with her organizational skills." He changed the screen and the second woman appeared. "Now this woman," he said as he put up her picture, "is a very special case, indeed. I want you to watch this short video of her at work. Then I'll fill in the particulars." He touched the play icon on the screen and stood to the side as it started. He watched the agents' faces as they watched intensely. When it ended, the agents looked at each other. Wilhelm could sense what they were thinking. How could a woman be so brutal, so cold, and do those things with a smile and a laugh? The video had the desired effect he wanted. Now they were worried; and from this moment on, they would be wired tight. And that is just where he needed them to be. He wanted them so wired that they would need a vacation from themselves when this op ended.

"The woman you've just seen is Bellona, goddess of war, Amaranta, a Chilean Colonel, Army Ret. Her specialties are small unit tactics, guerrilla warfare, and unconventional warfare. She's 33 years old, five feet seven inches tall, and 150 lbs. She is expert with the pistol, rifle, edged weapons, explosives, and booby-traps and is very adept at torture as you just observed. She has a tattoo of the infinity symbol around her navel and one of a tiny man with a hanging cock on her inner left thigh. She is a nymphomaniac and is known to pick up three to five men in an evening; she loves to dance and is a classical pianist. We know she just finished and assignment in Lebanon. Our guess is that she is on her way to Syria to meet up with our other two friends. Separately, they are a threat;

together, they are extremely dangerous. So whoever is assembling these three together has something big and long-term planned."

Wilhelm touched the control panel. The screen changed to a map complete with longitude and latitude lines of the operational area. He spent some time pointing out areas that they may find themselves working in and then went over the coast complete with tide information. Then he brought up the latest satellite information available on three of the possible resorts that they would choose. He had made his decisions purely by tactical deduction mostly from experience which he liked to call "what-would-I–do" logic.

"Okay, now we have covered everything. This is what you'll do with these people once you find them." He pulled up the first four profiles. "These four people are to be captured and delivered to the ship for questioning. They are not to be eliminated unless there is absolutely no other way. That means, ladies and gentlemen, that if you are not able to inject the tracking chip into them and you have to kill them instead and if it is reported that you had a chance to do that but took the easy way out by killing them, let's say having your retirement taken away will be the least of your worries.

"Now these three," he said with a little excitement. "The Pol is to be killed and his body disposed of; it can never be found," he said with a smile. "As for the ladies, they are to be interrogated in the field and then terminated. It will be up to the team leader to make the decision on how this should be carried out." He paused for a few moments letting it all sink in and watching their faces particularly their eyes. What he saw pleased him; they had steeled themselves to what was coming. Their expressions especially Pam's were serene.

"I am sure by now you realize this is no ordinary cargo ship although it does carry cargo in its forward holes. The stern is dedicated to our craft and is outfitted as such. You will find that traveling on board the C.A.A. is akin to traveling by private yacht; you have ample training areas and a fitness area. I wouldn't want you to get sloppy on this cruise. And as you already know, while on board, you have your own cabins; I hope you enjoy them. Now are there any questions?" He waited a moment. When no one said anything, he continued. "That will be all for this briefing. Go and enjoy the ship; get some rest; just generally enjoy yourself. Tomorrow it starts again. Pam, could you come to my stateroom at 1600 hours, please," he said as they started to file out talking to each other and shaking their heads.

"Yes, sir," she said in a low voice nodding her head at the same time. Then she turned and hurried to catch up with the others.

Pamela

Pam opened the heavy door that led to the hallway where Wilhelm's stateroom was located; she had come up from two decks below. She and Vanessa had been exploring the ship, and she had to hurry or be late and that wasn't an option. As she walked down the hall, she heard Prince's *Nicky* playing and passed a crewman who was lip syncing and strumming his air guitar. When she reached Wilhelm's stateroom, the door was open. So she knocked and walked in. Wilhelm was practicing with his putter when she entered. He looked up at her, looked back down, and putted. Then he said,

"Come in, Pam; you're right on time; have a seat, please," as he walked over and closed the door. He put the putter away and sat down at the small round table across from where she chose to sit. Wilhelm took her choice as a sign that she wanted this meeting to be all business because she could have chosen the more comfortable couch and chair situated just a few feet away. He smiled to himself and began. "It's time to fill you in on that special assignment I mentioned earlier." Her eyes widened a little. They did that when she was paying close attention. "I'm pleased with your progress and with the practice safe. They tell me you have it down to a minute."

"Yes, sir, I can shave a few seconds off if you need me to," she replied.

"No, a minute will do. But, keep practicing. I called you here to tell you about your target and what I need you to get from her." He paused while he typed on his laptop, and then he turned the screen to face her.

"This is Bryda Zielinski, aka the White Witch. She inherited the nickname from her predecessor whom she killed. She is 32 years old, five feet five inches tall, 120 lbs., black hair, brown eyes; she has a scar on her right side from a stabbing during her rise to power. She has a tattoo of a hummingbird on her left calf and another of her riding Pegasus on her back. She likes piercings and has several: two small loops on the corner of her left eye, one loop through each nipple, and one clitoris hood piercing. She's from the city of Wroclaw in Poland near the Sudetic Mountains. Her headquarters is an old mansion that she bought and restored in Verna, Bulgaria, on the Black Sea."

Wilhelm pressed the remote; the picture changed. He didn't bother turning the computer around; he knew what was in the file.

"This is the safe you'll crack. Pay particular attention to the way it is situated. It was placed that way for a purpose. Your target likes surprises; and she doesn't trust her own inner staff, hence the booby-traps." He showed her the next picture. "This is what happened to one of her assistants," he said as she viewed the photograph of a young blond woman lying dead on the floor with her face swollen and dark red. Blood was seeping from her nose, mouth, and ears. Pam cringed a little; she hoped he didn't see the shock on her face but the picture was gruesome. Her twisted swollen body on the floor suggested she experienced a painful death. "If this looks like a bad way to die, you are correct. What caused her death was a poison the White Witch put on the safe dials." Wilhelm pressed the button again; a picture of a young white woman who looked to be in her early twenties appeared. She was dressed in a yellow leather miniskirt and matching halter. "See anything familiar," he said. She looked harder, and then it hit her.

"Yeah, she looks a little like me," she said and then suddenly looked up at him. "She could be my sister except she's white," she continued. Wilhelm didn't say anything. He just went to the next frame showing three pictures of the woman, each highlighting a different body part. The picture on the far right focused on her legs; the picture in the middle focused on her breasts; and the last picture gave a close up of her face.

"Now look at the pictures carefully. You'll notice that *you* have a very similar body shape," he said in a low voice almost a whisper. Now this young lady was the love of Bryda's life. She was killed three years ago in Spain by one of her many enemies. Bryda never found out who did it and went into a deep depression for a while. When she emerged, she was twice as cruel and determined. Ever since her death, Bryda has been looking for a new soul mate; and *you* are *it*." Pam sat there staring at him. She didn't mean too, but thoughts were running through her head. She wasn't sure that she looked at all like the women on the screen, and she didn't have any tattoos. This woman had a pair of red lips on her right ass cheek. "Do you have a question, Pam?"

"Yes, I do, sir. I get that you want me to act like this girl so I can get to the safe. But honestly, I don't look that much like her, sir. Plus, I don't have a tattoo and I really don't want one, sir."

Wilhelm smiled at her and thought, "Why do I have to deal with this shit? Do they suddenly forget what they do for a living?" Then he leaned forward and turned the computer around. He looked at the tattoo and smiled. He got it: she must have been one hot number and not just in bed to make this evil bitch fall in love with her.

"Look, Pam, I know this is your first mission and it's an important one. But this is the deal, sweetie: You will play your part to perfection. You will not only get a tattoo but you will sleep with her if necessary. You will do whatever is required to complete your assignment, and then you will terminate her with extreme prejudice. If you fail in any way or let your guard down for a second, you will be the person in the picture that is dead on the floor. She will kill you in the most horrible manner imagined without hesitation, and I'll show the next agent your picture while giving her the speech. Do we understand each other?" He turned the computer back around. The picture of the dead woman stared at her. Pam looked up at him and saw how deadly his eyes looked. She was sure they hadn't looked that way a minute ago. The manner in which he looked at her was different now, and she realized for the first time that she was expendable. And he probably wouldn't even remember her name if she was killed.

"Do you have any more questions?" he said as he shut the computer down.

"Yes, sir. How will I make contact and what method will I use to insert and escape?" Wilhelm let a slight smile form on his lips. This was more like it; this is what he expected from his agents.

"When you return to your cabin, you'll find a laptop waiting for you; on it will be all of the information you'll need about the mission. You are not to talk about it nor let any of your teammates know anything concerning your mission. Do you understand, Pam?"

"Yes, sir, I do," she replied.

"Good, then that will be all for now. You can go." Pam got up, said,

"Good evening," and left. As she walked down the hall, she passed Vanessa.

"Where're you coming from, girl?" she said with a smile and a wink.

"From the boss's cabin, meeting."

"Oh, that's where I'm headed. Is he in a good mood?" she whispered.

"Yeah, I guess, hard to tell."

"Oh well, at least, he likes good music," she said and continued down the hall.

Pam listened a moment. Tupac's *Gangster Party* was streaming out of the hallway speakers. "How appropriate, he just acted like a gangster, and I guess we're his personal hit squad," she thought. She went straight to her cabin. Upon entering, she saw a pink laptop with a smiley face on the cover lying on her bed.

Cabin Party

Rochelle was the last to arrive at Teri's room; her room was picked because it was the farthest from the intersecting hallway where their cabins began.   She came in carrying a hookah in one hand and a bottle of red wine in the other.

"I see the gangs all here. So what's the subject of tonight's gossip fest?" she asked as she tiptoed her way past some of them sitting on the floor and made her way to the bed. Pam and Teri made room for her so she could sit down between them.

"I, for one, want to know how he got the CIA to let him have such a ship; I mean have you seen this ship; it has everything on it," Pam said while her hands expressed her words.

"You mean how the company let a black man have a ship like this, don't you?" Jamal said smiling and then took a long swig from the bourbon bottle he was holding.

"It's his ship," Alex said as he exhaled from a pull of the hookah, and a cloud of smoke accented his words.

"What did you just say, Alex?" Vanessa questioned. "Did I just hear you say this is *his* ship? What are you smoking in that hookah?"

"I'm serious, this *is* his ship. Doesn't anybody here know who our boss is? You can't be serious.   You mean you don't know who he is!"

"Okay, smartass, suppose you tell us who this black man really is," Teri said and then took a sip of the gin and juice in her glass. Alex took a deep breath as if preparing to speak and passed the bottle to Jesse who was sitting in one of the arm chairs; Randy occupied the other. He and Jamal along with Vanessa were sitting on the floor on pillows. He cocked his head towards Teri and smiled.

"Okay, miss thang, I'll tell you what I know about him. Some of you may remember an operation about seven years ago in Nicaragua. Others of you are too young in the game to have known about it."

"Fuck you," Vanessa and Pam said in unison. The room broke into laughter, and he waited for them to quiet down before continuing.

"Now that we have had our laugh, can I finish?"

"There's no reason to go into that Alex; tell them about the party," Randy said as he sat there puffing on his hookah enjoying the peach flavor and aroma.

"It was about five years ago in Lisbon," he began. "I was assigned to the embassy and during one of our V.I.P. dinners, in walks our boss. He's dressed much like the other men in the room—black tie and all except he's with two women. Well, my boss at the time is standing next to me checking out this blond when he sees him. Suddenly, he straightens up and makes a beeline straight towards him. I watched as he goes through his ass-kissing routine that he usually reserves for dignitaries, and then I turn my attention back to the blond."

He paused to take a pull of the hookah and a gulp of bourbon. "Anyway, another guy on staff comes up to me and says, 'You know who that is, don't you?' Well, of course, I didn't and told him so. Then he says, 'You should go over and introduce yourself; they say he is a real legend in agency.' I keep it in mind and start to make my rounds; so like two hours later, I run into him in the garden with his two lady friends. So I say hello and ask if he is enjoying himself. That's when I get the shock of my life. The guy says, 'Hello, Alex, and yes, my wives and I are enjoying ourselves; thanks for asking.' Well, I stood there looking stupid trying to decide if he was one of us or a counter agent and if I should shoot him or something."

"Aren't you glad you didn't shot him, Alex," Pam slurred.

"Uh-oh, sounds like somebody is a little drunk," Teri said with a giggle.

"She's not the only one from the sound of it; now if you don't mind, I'll continue."

"For Christ sake, go on already," Vanessa said and then took a drink from the bottle and fell over because she leaned back to far.

"Now I know you've had *too* much," Alex said.

"So instead of shooting him, I asked him who he was. After he told me, I was glad that I didn't try to shoot him. He introduced his two wives, and we talked for a few minutes; then he left."

"That's all! That was boring; I was expecting something else," Rochelle said with attitude.

"I have to agree with you; the only interesting thing about that story is the two wives and the fact I was drinking when you told it." Teri said laughing.

"Three wives."

"What did you just say?" Pam said a little louder than she was aware of.

"I said *three* wives," Randy repeated holding up three fingers. "And they are all fine looking women and none of them were poor when he married them, either."

"Now that's a man I can be proud of; he not only has three wives, they came bearing gifts and they're beautiful. Shit! Where do I sign up?" Jesse said.

"Fucking men, half of you can't satisfy one woman. What makes you think you could satisfy three?" Vanessa said with contempt.

"I think it's sexist and barbaric for a man to ruin the lives of three women just for his personal sexual perversions," Teri chimed in.

"To worship one god is civilized, to have just one woman is barbaric," Jesse said in a smooth, cool voice. Then he took a drink and said, "You want to tell me, Teri, you haven't fucked some other woman's man and called it good?"

"You sound like you know something, sitting on the floor talking in your cool sexy voice like you some authority on her sex life," Vanessa said coming to Teri's defense.

"You gotta be kidding me, right! You of all people, Vanessa, the girl who fucks both sexes and has had her share of married men. If you want to defend somebody, you better start with yourself," Jesse said as a matter of fact with no anger or animosity in his voice. After all, it was true. Pam looked at Vanessa and thought, "How could I have missed those signals? She was my roommate for a month, and I had no clue she was bi-sexual."

"You have a point, Jesse. I can remember a well-hung gentleman," Vanessa reminisced.

"How well?" Rochelle interrupted.

"Ten by three inches that is. Anyway, he had a wife, three kids, and a girlfriend. Come to think of it, I don't know how he had time for me but he did; and frankly; I didn't care. What's that old saying? 'Who's fucking who?' Anyway, we were fucking a lot," Vanessa boasted.

"I rest my case. If they're fucking around and it's okay with society, then why can't he have three wives?" Randy held up three fingers again. "I mean, what's the difference? If she's good enough to sleep with, then she might be good enough to keep. So why not is all that I'm saying."

Pam sat quietly on the bed, legs folded Indian style listening. These women seem to have slept with more than one married man, and now they were openly bragging about it. Jesse made a good point. If she was good for the short haul, why not the long haul? Hell, her mother even told her every man you sleep with is a potential husband, so spread your legs sparingly. But after listening to this conversation, she wasn't sure anymore whether mother was quite right on the subject. Then she took a long drink from the bottle of wine she was holding and kept listening.

"Actually, there are many academics and scientists that think monogamy is against the natural genetics of men," Pam said more to herself than to the others but louder than she had realized.

"Why are you on their side? You're supposed to support your fellow sistahs in this matter, Pam," Teri said laughing the whole time.

"On a different subject, has anyone noticed the crazy schedule? I mean this guy has us or at least me down for a full-body scrub and bleaching. What does our boss have in mind? If I get any lighter, no one will ever believe I'm black," Rochelle stated causing everyone to stop drinking and talking and to look at her.

"Yeah, I checked the schedule; and I'm down for a complete hair and face make over. I think Mr. Libertaire has something special planned for us on this trip to paradise," Randy said and then took another long drink from the bourbon bottle in his hand. "I mean, look at us, seriously. Take a good *close* look at us in this room. We can pass for anything; we have what they call the exotic look. Mr. Libertaire has something very special planned, indeed, for this ban of Americans of African descent."

"On that note, I think I'll call it a night; and I'm taking Pam with me," Vanessa said as she got up from the floor and grabbed Pam by the hand and pulled her to her feet. "Come on, little one, time to go to bed," she said as Pam stood up. Pam got up and realized just how drunk she really was and tried to say something but decided against it; instead, she waved goodbye.

George and Tommy were playing chess and watching a movie in Wilhelm's stateroom as he looked over the team's files. Wilhelm was putting the two teams together and was checking their psychological profiles to ensure a perfect fit.

"You know the children are having a gathering in Teri's room tonight; right about now they should be good and drunk. You want to listen in and hear what's up," Tommy said turning to address Wilhelm.

"No, you might hear something that might hurt your feelings; let them have their night," he replied looking at Tommy with a sly smile.

Counter Stroke

Chapter Twelve

Sunday, November 30, 2010

Number 5 wasn't surprised at the news of the failure and killing of the team he sent to Wilhelm's training facility. His spy had warned him and he should have listened. Now he would have to explain his actions to the Council, and he was sure that Number 2 would cherish that moment. But he still had twelve hours left in Vegas, and he intended to enjoy them. He would worry about the fallout later. He finished his drink, picked up the phone, and ordered two fresh whores; this time he wanted celebrity look-a-likes. They would help him relax and think about what to do next. With the failed attempt, Wilhelm would be on high alert; and the mission was due to begin in five days. He didn't have the time to waste wondering what went wrong. He had to figure out how to find Wilhelm and his team of hand-picked agents despite their anonymity.

Tuesday, December 2, 2010

Rodney sat at his desk reading the report on the Stanleys' death. He was deeply concerned, and his face showed it.

"Get Frank on the phone and tell him I want to see him ASAP!" he told his assistant then hung up the phone. He looked at the two gentlemen sitting in front of him; one was from the NSA, the other was from the FBI; both held the rank of deputy director.

"I don't mind telling you, gentlemen, that I don't give a damn that those two bastards are dead; the world's a better place for it. What is going to give me sleepless nights for the rest of my days is who has those files. And if you are wise, you will adopt this worry also," he said sitting there, staring at them but not seeing them.

The two men sat there in silence looking back at him. They knew firsthand that Rodney had sudden fits of rage and they didn't want him to go into one. So they sat there quietly until he spoke.

"So, do any of you have any idea who could've pulled this off right under our noses?" he said in a very controlled voice.

"Not just yet, there was no unusual chatter coming from their house before their deaths," the NSA deputy director said.

The FBI deputy director stated,

"We know that they went to Philadelphia the weekend before and met with as of yet an unidentified man from Europe. Then they went back to their house, they stayed close to home, and there were no visitors except the usual playmates."

"Is that all the FBI knows about this execution style murder? Can we account for everyone who has this special skill set?" Rodney inquired as he rocked back and forth in his chair visibly agitated.

"Yes, we can; everyone and anyone who could have pulled this off are accounted for, Rodney. This shit is in your lap. You and your special operations division guys kept those bastards around and protected allowing them to do pretty much as they wanted to. Hell, Rodney! You should've locked them up just for fucking minors. For Christ sake! You let them parade those little girls around like they were some type of benevolent uncles or something. You got the mess you deserve, and it has finally blown up in your face. Now you want to pass this off to our departments. Fuck you, Rodney!" the FBI director ranted flipping him the bird to accentuate the point.

"Neither of you ever complained when the information they provided was coming in regularly and accurately. How many cases did *these* perverts help the FBI and the NSA with, gentlemen? Now that they're dead, we look like asses because we didn't know they were dead for four fucking days. But that's nothing, gentlemen, compared to the information they had in that fucking vault of theirs. If it has fallen into the wrong hands, we are all truly fucked. The bigger issues here are who has that information and what will they do with it. So I suggest we stop pissing on each other and start working together."

The NSA deputy director sat quietly through the whole exchange; he really didn't care if they were dead; this wasn't his fight. He was here to get the new frequencies being used in the Libertaire operation. He knew sooner or later the culprits would use that information and *that* would be their downfall. So he sat back listening to them bitch and moan and laughed to himself as they did so.

"I've got real business to take care of, Rodney," said the FBI deputy-director. "I've wasted enough time here dealing with this *bullshit*. I really don't care who has the files that those traitorous assholes kept on all of you spies. Maybe, somebody somewhere will take care of the matter for you. Let's not hope it involves *you* Rodney; I would hate to receive a report on your death." Then he stood up, buttoned his suit jacket, and left the office without another word.

"Did he just threaten you?" asked the NSA deputy director.

"No, it was his way of saying I was on my own on this one. Now to our business," Rodney said as he opened his desk drawer and took out an envelope. "These are the trace and piggyback codes that Libertaire will be using; look for them to originate from Germany and somewhere in the area of the Stans. He has Susan and Wendy working with him on this one, so look out for his little oddities; you know how he is." Then he slid a sealed envelope across his desk into the waiting hands of the deputy director. He opened it, took a look at the three codes, and then placed it in the inside breast pocket of his suit jacket.

"What's really going on here, Rodney? This is looking more and more like a man hunt. Do we have a traitor in our midst?" he said looking at Rodney in the eyes as he waited for an answer.

"No, we don't, but I have my reservations about the targets we're after. It smells like a trap. I can ill afford to lose any more agents to traps I should see coming, and where Libertaire is headed looks like one."

"Well, you sent the right person; if it's a trap of some kind, he'll certainly spring it. Are you ready for the fallout when he gets started?" Rodney sat there thinking about just that and decided that he was, whether he really was or not.

"Good question, Troy, but it doesn't matter; the game has started, and I won't know what happens until it happens. So keep this close to the vest and only trust your top people. If I'm right, there's a whole new set of players ; and we know nothing about them." Before he could reply, the phone beeped. "Yes," Rodney said into the speaker.

"Mr. DePore is here, sir."

"Send him in. We'll finish this later, Troy; I'll keep you in the loop." The deputy director got up to leave and on his way out, he passed Frank; neither man spoke as they passed. Frank walked in, sat down, and crossed his legs.

"What's this about, Rodney; I'm in the middle of an operation," he said sarcastically.

"I'm well aware of that fact, Frank, so don't get your blood up. Have you seen the Stanleys' photos yet?"

"No, I haven't. Are they bad?"

"Yeah, whoever did this piece of work really enjoyed it; the torture methods used are a mix of old and new techniques. I haven't seen a body cut up like this in twenty years; here, take a look." Rodney pointed to a folder on his desk and Frank got up to retrieve it. He sat down before opening it. As he looked through the photos, Rodney watched him very closely; he knew Frank was examining each picture carefully. He was hoping Frank would spot something that the others had missed; it was a long shot but he needed something to go on.

Rodney sat patiently watching and thinking; he had his own idea about what kind of man had done this; he knew that man was trained in the old ways of torture. On one hand, he could count how many men had that knowledge. But they were retired and hadn't trained anyone or been active in years.

"Can I get a look at the bodies?" Frank asked snapping Rodney out of his thoughts.

"What?"

"I said, can I get a look at the bodies?"

"Yes, I suppose so. Why do you want to see them?" he questioned.

"Here, look at the base of the skull on the guard and notice how he was placed," Frank said as he stood up to hand Rodney the picture. "See, there's a small puncture; that means he used a steel dart to sever the brain stem; then he dragged him into the bushes and cut his throat. The man bleed out into the mulch; it's the same with the other guard; here, take a look." Frank handed him the photo, and then he placed the photos of the two dead girls in front of him. "Look at how he killed the girls; he shot them between the eyes; that's being kind in our business. I bet there are needle marks in key places on the Stanleys that correspond to nerve endings or acupuncture points that would cause great pain. But why would he need to torture them both in the exact same way?" he wondered out loud.

"I'll tell you why he did that," Rodney said causing Frank to look up from the photos. "The Stanleys' safe was in two stages, and he needed both of their keys and combinations to get in. The Stanleys shared everything; and for security reasons, they kept separate keys and changed the combinations often without telling each other what they were."

"Isn't that clever? What if something happened to one of them, then what?" Frank asked.

"That's simple; they would mail the new combinations to themselves using a code only they knew. So if something should befall one of them, the survivor would have the other's combination."

"That's ingenious; I wouldn't have thought of that one. How many people knew about this precaution, Rodney?"

"I'm the only one or so I thought. But it's obvious that someone else knew about it. So you really want to look at the bodies?"

"Yeah, I think I can help with this one."

"Okay, I'll make it happen."

Council Meeting

Number 1 paced back and forth in front of the large one-piece, curved, floor-to-ceiling window that provided a spectacular view of the valley below. The conference room was located on an upper floor of their headquarters imbedded in the side of the mountain. All of the council members were present and no one felt comfortable. They knew all too well of the violence Number 1 was capable of especially when he was angry, and he was very angry at the moment.

"How could you pull such a stunt so close to the start of this operation?" he said addressing Number 5. "To have it fail plus get the men you hired killed…I gave specific orders that no activity or operations were to be launch until this operation was finished. What part of that did you not understand, Number 5?" He had stopped in front of him as he finished his speech giving him a cold stare that started to unnerve him. "What do you have to say in your defense?" he reprimanded clasping his hands behind his back as he rocked back and forth.

"We needed to know who his agents are; without this key bit of information, we are at a distinct disadvantage. I thought if I could obtain this information, it would make life a lot easier on all of us," Number 5 said in a trembling voice as he looked up at Number 1 staring down at him. He listened to what he said, and then he returned to the head of the table and sat down in his chair.

"Does anyone have an opinion on the subject?" he said addressing all of the council members.

"Yes, what is our next move now that Mr. Libertaire has been alerted? And should we bring in additional resources to the operation?" asked Number 3.

"I think that would be a mistake; let's just wait and let Talaus do the job he's being well paid for," Number 2 said with a wave of his hand.

"With Number 5's failed mission and with the elimination of the Stanleys in addition to the loss of their files, shouldn't we abort this operation and attempt it at a later time?" asked Number 4.

Number 1 sat there silently for a minute, but it felt like an hour to the rest of them. He took a sip of his scotch and then began to speak in a monotone voice.

"Gentlemen, I will attempt to explain once again why this operation is so important to our organization. Like ourselves in this room, all gathered in support of a common goal here in this place, we can be who we really are. We sit here with no disguises and very few secrets." The other members laughed at his joke and began to relax. Number 5 took a big gulp of his drink and got up to get another from the bar across the room. Number 1 waited until he returned to the table bringing the bottle with him.

"Now in case you have forgotten, we are in the control and distribution of power business. In the past, we've achieved this though arms and force; those days are ending fast. The future is in resources, and I'm not talking about oil or any of those other minerals. What I am referring to is food, water, and renewable energy sources. The four people who are the bait are experts in these areas. Well, that's not entirely true. There's one gentleman whose business is personnel and his resources will be needed also.

"Number 2 has taken great care to get his agent to set up this operation. He's all of this so that we can eliminate Libertaire. If we do not get rid of him, we run the risk that he will disrupt our operations in Africa at the behest of his government. This, we cannot allow at any cost; he must be killed. Only when this has been achieved, can we continue with our plans."

"What if Libertaire gets to the scientists before we kill him?" asked Number 3.

"That will not be a problem, Number 3. We already have their research, and they each have demonstrated that their products and services perform outstandingly. So it doesn't matter if Mr. Libertaire captures or kills them. What's *important* is that we *kill Mr. Libertaire*. So we will increase our operatives in the areas of operation. Have our people focus on him and let Mr. Talaus do the rest. That way, we're assured that one of us will get him.

"As for the Stanleys, I don't think anyone in this room will miss them. As for the missing files, my advice is to wait and see who uses it. I'm sure we're not the only people asking that question. So if there are no more questions, I will say good day to you gentlemen. And if you don't mind, I suggest that no one leaves headquarters until after the operation ends." As the council members were leaving, they all were thinking the same thing. This must be bigger than they thought; he hadn't locked them down in years; this Libertaire must be getting *too* close.

"Number 5, got a minute?" Number 1 said as they were leaving.

"Sure, what's up?" he replied as he turned around to face him with his hands in his pants pockets.

"The next time you want to help, don't. Because if you pull another stunt like that one, I'll kill you personally. Do we understand each other?"

"We do, perfectly," he said as he turned and left the room leaving Number 1 looking out the window and swirling his scotch in his glass.

Linda Banally

Chapter Thirteen

Linda lay quietly on her back looking at the ceiling in the darkness and listening to Frank's steady breathing. "I knew that wasn't going to work," she thought. "Trying to infiltrate Libertaire's training facility was just plain dumb." She wasn't sure if Frank and Sally were behind the whole thing; she didn't put it pass them. But she did believe him when he told her about the failed attempt. Ironically, he was suspicious of her after closely watching her reaction when he told her about it and showed her the pictures of the four dead men.

"At least, I'm going to Paris in a few days," she thought. After the death of Josh, she could use a vacation even if it is a working one. Frank seemed to be back to his old self; she really did miss him and the last few days had confirmed it. He was back to giving her shit over every little thing but that was normal. The killing of the Stanleys has given him new vigor, and he has been working on that case more than the current operation. The photos of their bodies flashed through her mind. The sight made her cringe even though she'd seen dead bodies before some burned, dismembered, and even tortured. Their bodies were systematically torn apart; it was clear that the assassin was very skilled at his or her craft.

Frank stirred, mumbled, and then stuck his right hand under his pillow settling back into his slumber. She knew that he had his 380 caliber pistol under the pillow, the one that Wilhelm had given him. He always slept with it or at least since she's been sleeping with him. She had asked him about it once, and he said that someone he used to be close to gave it to him and it made him feel safe. She thought that was an odd explanation, but when she found out who that long lost friend was it made perfect sense.

Linda got out of bed and made her way to the bathroom and closed the door so that the light wouldn't wake up Frank. A few more years and she could retire from the agency. It wasn't that she didn't enjoy being a spy; it was the pay—it really sucked. She couldn't maintain her lifestyle on agency pay; she had to find another like Josh who was gorgeous, wealthy, and well-hung. She turned away from the dressing mirror and looked at her ass as she walked to the shower. She turned on the shower and sat down on the toilet to pee with her head in her hands. She got up, stepped into the shower, and as the hot water ran over her head and body she thought about the day ahead. She had a few hours before the house woke up officially, and she intended to enjoy the moment alone.

Shadow Times Two

Chapter Fourteen

Shadow One

Shadow One woke up at precisely 4:00 a.m. without the aid of an alarm clock; he didn't need one; he had been getting up at this time for 15 years now. He got out of bed, walked over to the window, and looked out into the darkness feeling it more than seeing it. He felt something behind him and smiled; he knew it was Freddie and Fanny, his two canine companions. The two superior red Doberman pinschers stood there happily wagging their short tails. He turned around and patted them on their heads.

"Want to go out? I bet you do," he said in his high pitched happy voice. He walked down stairs, across the large open space he used as his training area/garage, to the back door with the dogs leading the way. They sat patiently while he disarmed the alarm system and unlocked the heavy steel door that was built into the concrete wall. He turned on the flood lights briefly and scanned the area before opening the door and letting the dogs out.

He was glad this assignment allowed him to stay at home. He loved his carriage house, and he knew every inch of it because he had rebuilt it. Personally, he was pleased with the security system and precautions that he added which was a blend of electronics and natural deterrents. The carriage house was decorated with furnishings from his travels and artwork hung in his private gallery, some of which the world would not see for a while. From his security room using infra-green light, he watched the dogs run their patrol pattern around the perimeter. When they were finished, he called them home by blowing a silent whistle through speakers he had hidden in various trees throughout the property. He went to the door and let the pair in.

"Are we ready for breakfast?" he said to them as he headed back up the stairs to the kitchen. He turned on the TV and listened to the business news as he prepared the dogs' and his breakfast. He pulled out a two-pound bag of sirloin that was cubed and seasoned with garlic. He took down a skillet from the pot rack overhead, poured a little extra virgin olive oil into the pan, swirled it around, set it down on his professional grade gas range, and turned the burner on. Leaning against the cooking island, he looked at the TV as the pan heated up. When it was ready he dumped the sirloin in and listened to it sizzle.

The Dobermans watched this routine from their kitchen beds moving their heads in unison as he walked back and forth across the kitchen floor. He was naked as he prepared the dogs breakfast; he loved to be naked; it kept his body temperature regulated, and the cool Spanish tiles felt great on his bare feet. He walked to the counter that held all of his kitchen gadgets and plugged in the blender. He loved cooking as a proud foodie. And if he wasn't so good at killing and spying, he would have become a chef. He guessed he had Wilhelm to blame for that but not really. He went to the refrigerator and took out the juice of the day then returned to the skillet to stir the meat. It shouldn't cook too long; it was more of a warming of the meat; Freddy and Fannie preferred it bloody on the inside.

He turned it off and placed the meat on a platter to cool, and then he went back to the blender with juice in hand. He poured a measured amount into the blender, added various powders, dropped in a few ice cubes, put the lid on, and pressed the button. As the blender hummed away, he turned his attention back to the news. He turned off the blender and picked up two stone dog bowls with the dogs' names on them. He filled each bowl with a pound of meat then added yogurt and three different grains and mixed it all together. He placed the bowls on the floor and walked away; the dogs stood up, walked over, and sat down in front of their bowls. As they were waiting for his command to eat, he poured himself a large glass of his concoction, turned, and said,

"Bottoms up!" The dogs began to eat.

Then he went to his bedroom and got into the shower. Although he had showered last night before going to bed, he felt the need to be clean. He stepped out, dried off, selected a pair of sweats, went to his dresser, pulled open the second drawer, and opened up a fresh pack of undershirts. He never wore the same undershirt twice; and when he bought fresh ones, he didn't open them until he was ready to wear them. This was the same with his boxers. He dressed, picked up his cross trainers, and headed downstairs to work out.

Sitting on the polished wood floor, he put on his sneakers and crossed his legs. He began to breathe, first with light and shallow then with deep and slow breaths until he entered his place of emptiness. When he was finished, he stood up and started his temple exercises. After completing the eight specific exercises, he stretched doing full front and side splits. Next, he did two hundred push- ups, the last hundred as fast as he could. Then he went to his sit-up bench and started his five hundred count set.

Afterwards, he stretched again paying close attention to his upper body especially his wrists and shoulders. He stood quietly for a moment before suddenly exploding into movement. The movements belong to Bajiquan (Eight extreme fist), a Chinese martial art perfectly suited for close in-fighting. He liked this style because it was fast moving and deadly; also it was rare; few people practiced it, let alone knew of its existence. Next, he went to the wall that held his swords and knives and selected a Spanish epee. *Whoosh!* was the sound the sword made as it cut through the air. He gave it a few more warm up swings and then took the ready stance. He practiced his lunges, one hundred on each leg by repeating the exercise using his opposite hand to lead his lunge leg. When he was finished, he shadow fenced for twenty minutes ending the first part of his morning workout. As he wiped the sweat from his face and neck, he looked over at the dogs; they were fast asleep.

"Was I that bad?" he said to them. The dogs looked up at him and cocked their heads to the side as if they understood him. "Come on. It's time for a run!" he continued as he walked towards the backdoor with Freddie and Fanny close on his heels.

He set the alarm, put on a wool skull cap, and closed the door behind him before the security system armed. He started to run; and as he rounded the corner of the house, he looked at the sky. The sun was just rising, and the sky was full of color and darkness; the mixture painted a beautiful picture on the clouds. He took a few deep breaths feeling; the cold morning air filled his lungs. As he headed down the long driveway, he looked at his dogs; they were trotting alongside, one on each side of him. As he approached the end of the private lane that connected four houses, he heard,

"Good morning, Jonathan!" He looked to his left and saw Tara in her thin robe and short nighty that showed more than it hid. She managed to be out most mornings when he ran even on cold ones like this morning.

"Hi, Tara!" he yelled as he ran by. As he turned the corner heading for the park running trail, he looked at his dogs and said, "I'm going to have to fuck that woman." Then he sped up causing the dogs to break into a run.

Jonathan Merger, as he was known when he was in the States, is a well-respected businessman who sells expensive, custom toys to men and women who have nothing better to do with their money. His *Big Boy Toys Company* was a profitable and legitimate enterprise which he enjoyed running immensely.

He knew Sally had run his background at least twice since their last meeting at the night club. Her seemingly innocent questions and phony drunk routine must have worked on others. But he saw right through it and passed on her invitation to take her home; instead, he put her in a cab.

Today, he has a lunch date with her so he has to be careful. Libertaire was right; he might have to kill this woman. He turned onto the private lane having completed his morning run and sprinted to the house. He walked around the perimeter of the house pretending to stretch his legs. What he really was doing was checking to see if he had any visitors while he was gone. Satisfied, he went to the backdoor, opened it, and went in letting the dogs go first. He went upstairs to his bedroom, turned on the shower, and undressed. After showering, he dressed choosing gray gabardine pants, a matching sports jacket, and a cashmere black turtleneck. He selected a silver chain with a medallion and matching ring. Then he admired himself standing in front of his full length mirror. His six-foot, 220 lbs., athletic frame made his outfit look perfect.

"It should be summer so I can show off this beautiful body," he said out loud as he turned side to side looking in the mirror.

He went downstairs and opened his armory located behind the weight machines across from his collection of ancient armor. He entered the code and waited for the hidden door to open and then stepped into an arsenal of all types of weapons: pistols, rifles, darts, knives, and explosives, all organized by use. He selected a 25 caliber pistol and loaded it with hollow point bullets filled with a poison from Central America. He placed the pistol in a specially designed pocket holster in his jacket and left the room looking behind to watch the door close, and then he reset the alarm. He got into his Range Rover with keys already in the ignition. He always left the keys in his cars; he never knew when he needed to leave in a hurry. He pulled out of the garage and watched the door close in his rearview mirror while observing the dogs sitting there sending him off.

Shadow Two

From her window seat, she watched the human traffic scurrying to and from work. Her sublet apartment was located 200 yards away from Linda's place at the end of the bend on the same street giving her a clear view of the building's front door and the two windows to Linda's third floor apartment. Her vantage point was perfect for observation and had already helped her spot the two women who were following Linda.

She checked her email. She should know if they were family or not; and if not, she had to devise a way to dispose of them. She waited while the message was being decoded and then read it.

"Not family—find out all you can—then terminate."

"That's the boss, short and to the point," she thought as she erased and cleaned the hard drive removing the message forever.

Now it was time for her morning workout. Afterwards, she would decide how to solve her two problems. She settled on Bafaquan (Eight methods fist); this form would give her a good workout and ideas on how to deal with her guests. She began as always with temple exercises then a half hour of stretching before starting her forms. Her five-foot-six-inch, 125 lbs. body moved powerfully and swiftly with every muscle flexing especially her leg muscles. She moved gracefully but quietly around the empty living room floor. When she had finished her hand forms, she took her sword from its scabbard and began practicing a special form that Wilhelm had taught her. It had no name, at least he never told her; but it was special. It has techniques that can be found in European sword forms but with a Chinese twist. She really loved this form because it allowed her to strike from the most unlikely angles and pushed her athletic body to and beyond its maximum requiring 150 percent. After she had finished, she was drenched in sweat. She wiped down the sword and put it away. Then she took a much needed shower.

When she got out, she looked at herself in the full length mirror hanging on the bathroom door. She decided she needed a morning at the spa that included a bikini wax. But first, she needed to re-scout the area; she had two pests to remove. Turning around, she looked at the society's mark on her back. "This seems to be the right situation to use some of the society's special techniques concerning such matters," she thought.

It was 7:00 p.m. when she settled into the place she had selected for her ambush; she had made a clean entry or so she thought. On the way, she passed by an old homeless Black man who was sitting in front of his cardboard box home. She was sure he hadn't seen her. And if he did, she would have appeared to be one of the many shadows that were cast by the streetlights and headlights of cars passing by the park. She was betting that Linda would be home around 9:00 p.m. right after the reception that she and Frank were attending tonight. That would mean the women conducting the surveillance would be in place at least a half hour earlier once they were sure Linda was coming home.

Shadow Two settled in for the ninety minute or so wait time. She wrapped her cape around her and observed her surroundings. Then she noticed her targets moving into position; they came through the park approaching from her rear and passed by her ten meters to her right. She took out her injection pin and turned the dial to number 4; this would inject four times the poison needed to kill her opponents. She wouldn't take any chances with these two; she had to hit them hard and quietly. She waited and watched; and when she was sure they had settled down, she started her stalk. They were 15 meters in front of her. She crept forward slowly while crouching low and keeping her feet close to the ground so as not to step on any dried sticks that would give her advantage away.

When she was close enough, she charged breaking into a full sprint; she was upon them before they could react. She jammed the needle into the right choroidal artery of the woman to her left.

"Ugh!" was all she said as she grabbed her neck while searching for her gun. Then she hit the ground with a *thud!* Her partner turned to face Shadow Two and took a step backward; as she did so, she started to pull her pistol. The shadow stepped in close and stabbed the woman in the heart killing her instantly causing her pistol to slide out of her hand and back into its holster. She let the body fall to the ground following it down while looking around checking the area.

A couple walked by—a mother and child—; they hadn't heard the commotion. She grabbed the two bodies by their collars and dragged them further into the darkness of the park. Then she searched the bodies; she went through their clothing, every pocket, even checking their shoes. Once she had collected all of their personal things: money, jewelry, and identification, she placed the items in her bag. Next, she partially undressed them one at a time looking for body markings. She found a unique tattoo on the left hip of both women; the symbol was a world atlas with the Roman numeral five in the center. She took a picture of it along with their faces and then rolled their fingertips on her cellphone screen.

She double-checked that the information was stored and encrypted before putting the phone away and redressing the bodies. Then she took out the money that the women were carrying and made a quick count.

"Hmmm, not bad," she thought. Between them, they had ten thousand dollars. She gathered her bag and started to leave the area. But she deviated from her planned exit route and went back towards the homeless man. As she passed him, she tossed the money into his cardboard house and then disappeared into the darkness.

She returned to her apartment without anyone seeing her. She undressed and took a shower. Then she wrapped herself in an oversized cotton bathrobe, wrapped her hair in a bath towel, and booted up her laptop. After she sent the information and went through the clean-up procedures, she shutdown. She looked out the window towards the park then at Linda's apartment and said,

"You're welcome." She turned out her lights and went to bed; it was 9:30 p.m.

Shadow Two rose early as usual and went through her workout routine. After cleaning up, she prepared a bowl of granola cereal. She walked over to the window seat and sat down watching Linda's apartment and the park as she ate. Just as she finished breakfast, Linda's living room light came on. Then she noticed that the homeless man whom she had given the money was leaving the park. He seemed to have a pep in his step this morning or that could be wishful think on her part. She went to the kitchen, put the bowl in the sink, poured herself a glass of orange juice, and went back to the window. As she leisurely drank her juice, she heard sirens first off in the distance then coming closer. Finally, police cars and ambulances converged on the park half way between her and Linda's apartment. She looked through her spotting scope and saw Linda standing in the window watching the events unfolding on the street below.

The C. A. A.

Chapter Fifteen

Wilhelm stood outside on the external deck of the ship's wheel house looking skyward through his binoculars. Soon after, a crew member informed him that Randy was there to see him. He lowered his binoculars and told the man to send him out. When Randy reached Wilhelm, he was back to watching the sky, so Randy stood there for a moment looking out at the ocean. As far as he could see nothing was there but ocean; there wasn't a bird in the sky that he could see. He wondered what the old man, as he referred to him in his private conversations, was looking at.

"What can I do for you Randy?" Wilhelm said still looking at the sky.

"It's about the equipment list."

"Something wrong with the equipment?"

"Yes, sir, some of the stuff we need is not included, and I was wondering if I could make a request for the needed items."

"That equipment was selected because it will serve you the best on this mission. It will help you evade the Syrians' detection. Do you think you are better qualified to second guess it?" Wilhelm let the binoculars hang free around his neck, picked up a heavy leather gauntlet, and put it on his left hand.

Then he took the whistle that was hanging from a platinum rope chain around his neck and blew it. He tilted his head skyward and waited. Randy stood there wondering what the glove was for and if Wilhelm had finally cracked. Wilhelm blew the whistle again then raised his left hand. Randy first saw the shadow of the bird; it was huge. And when he looked up, he didn't believe his eyes. A large black eagle landed on Wilhelm's left hand.

"Ugh, RB! You're getting heavy; time for a diet, old boy," Wilhelm said looking like a big kid with his favorite toy. Randy took several steps backward when he saw the eagle land on his boss's hand.

"Holy shit, sir! Where did that eagle come from?" Randy said excitedly not knowing how to act around the bird.

"Relax, Randy; he won't hurt you; RB was just out for a little exercise." Randy started to relax as he watched his boss interact with the biggest-fucking-eagle he had ever seen. This black eagle was much bigger and heavier than the bald eagles which he was accustomed to seeing even in a zoo aviary.

"I didn't know you had a bird, sir, let alone an eagle. How long have you had him?"

"Since he was a fledgling; but you're not here to talk about birds of prey. I suggest you talk to Captain America about the equipment; I think he has the answers to your questions."

Wilhelm put a leather hood over the eagle's head and handed the bird to a crewman who was wearing a leather gauntlet. Wilhelm gave the man instructions, and then he left with the eagle.

"Now take a look at this ship; I bet you think this is just another company transport, don't you?" Wilhelm said as he faced Randy. "But you're wrong; this is a working cargo ship; come with me; I want to show you something." Wilhelm took Randy on a personal tour that ended at the lab where Captain America was working. As they entered, they saw George sitting on a bench playing with a pair of glasses.

"Randy has a few questions about the equipment, and I thought you're the best person to answer them," Wilhelm said. Then he left the room leaving Randy standing there and being stared at by a muscle-bound, Black man with dreadlocks.

"Don't just stand there; what-the-fuck do you want to say," snapped Captain America as he looked at Randy while leaning on his knuckles on the table. Randy looked over at George playing with the glasses as he chuckled then he looked back at the Captain.

"It's about the equipment. I want to ask you if I could get the items on this list." He walked over to the table and laid down the list.

Captain America picked it up, read it slowly, and then handed it back to him.

"Some items on this list are some of the same things I wanted, but the boss said, no. So it's no; got it. You'll just have to make do with what I'm issuing to you and your team. Now, is there anything else I can do for you? And don't ask me why they call me Captain America, either."

"No, that's it. You gentlemen have a nice day," he said as he turned to leave.

"There are no fucking gentlemen in this room, just killers. Which one are you?" George said.

"Both," Randy replied with a smile then step out of the room and went down the hall.

"I like him," said the Captain.

"He does grows on you, doesn't he?" added George.

As Randy headed for his cabin, he bumped into Teri returning from her workout with Pam.

"Hey, Randy! Why the long face?" she said poking him in the stomach and making him laugh.

"I just finished a tour of the ship with the old man then had a brief but interesting talk with Captain American and George. Now I'm headed to the bar to try to forget the last half hour with the help of my old buddy Jack."

"Sounds like a plan; I'll take a shower and join you later, okay," she said and then jogged down the hall.

Wilhelm sat in his stateroom enjoying a glass of hard lemonade when his computer buzzed indicating an incoming coded message. He wondered who it could be this time. Was it Frank wanting another update? or Rodney informing him of more bad news? He decided to ignore it for the moment; whatever it is, it could wait a few more minutes. So he turned his attention back to the notepad he was writing on and continued to draw lines to names. When he had finished with his list and three lemonades later, he opened his laptop.

Shadow Two's report appeared on the screen. He read it then looked at the pictures of the dead women. The first photos were of their faces, next were full body shots confirming their deaths, and finally, photos of the tattoo. He didn't recognize it but he would run it, and maybe someone else in the community will have information about its origins. He sat back on the sofa and wondered who-the-fuck did these chicks work for? And why did they choose an atlas with the Roman numeral five inside it? He looked at the photos one more time, and then he sent a description out general notice as not to raise questions among his colleagues.

He had two days left before they docked in Cyprus, and he didn't have the time to track this down; it would have to wait for now. The bigger problem was his team leaders who were having problems with some of the equipment. He decided to have Tommy hold a special training session. He understood their concerns. Some of the equipment was low-tech by today's standards but that's why he decided to use them. Staying off the Syrian grid was paramount; and if he used state of the art equipment, they would surely pick it up. The Syrians are no slouches when it came to counter-intelligence, and this young team didn't seem to grasp this very well. They were cocky because they knew how good they were. But none of them had faced anything close to this operation before or dealt with an enemy this skilled in a country that took great pride and put a lot of effort and money into their intelligence agencies.

Satisfied with his selection of code names, he entered them into the computer, shut it down, and sipped on his lemonade. He thought tonight he would finalize Pam's mission briefing by having Tommy instruct her on the use of the poison she would use. He should be hearing from Wendy soon. Although she had been silent, he knew she would be ready on her end. His real worry was Susan; she hadn't been under this kind of pressure before. In addition to that, she had the weakness of a child coupled with her misguided sense of patriotism which could become a problem. Especially if Frank gets wind of what he's up to, he would have no trouble exploiting her weaknesses to the fullest.

Wilhelm opened his humidor, took out a cigar, lit it, sat back, and began blowing smoke rings. His thoughts were interrupted by a knock on the door, and Tommy walked in carrying a covered tray.

"What do you have there?" Wilhelm said knowing full well what it was. What he was really interest in was how it was going to be administered. Getting close to the White Witch was going to be a big enough problem and poisoning her may prove to be impossible. Tommy set the tray down wearing the biggest smile that Wilhelm had ever seen on him. He lifted the tray's lid with a resounding,

"Ta da!" and sat down in the chair across from him and said, "Well, what do you think?"

"About what? All I see is a breath freshener spray bottle," he said as he eyed Tommy's new invention of death.

"Go on; you can touch it; you won't die; it's not filled yet." Wilhelm leaned forward and picked up the three-inch-tall bottle and looked at him. He even tested the spray top but pointed it at Tommy and pressed the button. "Hey, you really don't trust me, do you?" he said as the mist hit his face. "See, I told you it wasn't filled yet."

"Fine, now tell me what's your plan. And will Pam administer the poison using this sprayer?"

"That's easy, boss. You say the target is a lesbian, right? Plus, she's some kind of underworld super bitch? Well, this is how we get her." He leaned forward and told him his plan. When he was finished, he sat back with a shit-eating grin and said, "Well, what do you think?" Wilhelm sat there smiling slyly; he took a pull of his cigar, blew a smoke ring, and said, "You're an evil genius and ruthless son-of-a-bitch; I'm glad you're on my side. Hmmm, that's something I never considered."

They sat there for the next two hours working through any problems that could possibly arise. Tommy answered question after question, not just about his newest invention but about every piece of equipment that the agents would use. Satisfied, he told Tommy to get everything together and ready for disbursement to the agents. Then he picked up the phone, ordered dinner, and then called George telling him he needed to see him ASAP. Meanwhile, Tommy was leaving, but before he opened the door, he turned and said,

"You gotta admit that's a pretty cool plan; I think she'll appreciate the irony." Then he opened the door and left laughing.

Wilhelm and George leisurely walked down to the briefing room located two decks below his stateroom. Along the way, they talked about Tommy's plan.

"You know, that brother is a little touched in the head; only Tommy could come up with some wild shit like that," George said using his hands to accentuate his point.

"He's no crazier than you, George, and I keep you around," Wilhelm replied smiling at him and patting him on the back. "I think it will work if that prima donna of an agent you're so fond of doesn't fuck it up," he continued looking him in the eyes, no longer smiling.

"How did I become so fond of her all of a sudden? I stick up for her one time and now I'm her protector."

"Yes," Wilhelm said then broke out into laughter, "Don't sweat it; if she fucks up, she'll be dead and neither of us will be responsible." Then they realized that they were close to the briefing room, so they put on their game faces and walked into the room. The agents were gathered around the table on the left side of the room where Tommy was supervising the issuance of equipment.

Wilhelm stood quietly across the room listening to Tommy answer questions about the use of certain items and lit a fresh cigar. When Tommy had finished, the agents filtered back to their seats and looked over their action packs.

"Okay everybody, happy with your new toys, now listen up," Wilhelm said as he walked to the front of the room. "First, your code names for this mission," he said as the screen behind him came to life. "The names on the left side of the screen are Team One's; the names on the right are Team Two's. Take a moment to memorize the one next to your name; if you're curious about what they mean, look it up."

The names on the left read: Randy *Enki* team leader, Jesse *Pazuzu*, Vanessa *Tiamat*, and Rochelle *Ishtar*. On the right side, names read: Alex *Ninurta* team leader, Jamal *Nirgal*, Teri *Kubaba*, and Pamela *Oannes*. The agents looked at their names and each other's; they weren't accustomed to such exotic handles. Only Pam chuckled; she got it. It was just another fuck-with-you-moment for Libertaire; but a clever one, she had to admit.

"Team One," he said bringing the agents back in focus and silencing the chatter. Then he changed the screen image. A map of the Syrian coast along the Mediterranean came up. "This is Team One's operating area," he said as a red arrow pointed at a resort town. The area lit up in red. "It's located 100 kilometers from the Turkish border; this is where Team One will find their targets." He put up photos of the two women from South America and the Pol. "The team leader will decide how best to carry out your mission." He paused a moment and looked at Randy then brought up the Turkish coast. A yellow arrow pointed to the resort on the Mediterranean coast, and the area turned yellow. "This is Team Two's operating area; the team leader will decide how best to accomplish your mission. That means you, Alex." Next, he displayed four faces of their targets. "Remember, I need these people alive. And if that's not possible, I need proof of death." Then he gave Alex the same look he gave Randy which meant "Don't fuck up" which came through loud and clear.

Wilhelm stood there silently for what seemed like an eternity to the agents as he puffed away on his cigar and blew smoke rings into the air. Then speaking in a calm, deliberate voice as he looked each agent in the eyes, he said,

"I expect all of you to complete your missions; you've been trained and given equipment that will help you do just that. In forty-eight hours, we will dock in Cyprus where you will disembark to begin your assignments. Each team's communication person will use the codes that Captain America will give you before you leave the ship. He has spent a lot of time developing the program that corresponds with these codes. It is preset into every communication device that you will carry; so when you report, your communications will be harder to trace and decipher.

"It has also come to my attention that some of you are wondering why I selected certain equipment. And you have requested that you are issued more modern equipment—stuff you are more familiar with, things with all of the bells and whistles. This isn't *that kind* of mission. On this mission, you'll act like spies which means you'll have to rely on GLS which stands for God, luck, and skill. Once again, you'll act like *real* spies and that means leg work. Now I know all of you have been trained in this area; now is the time to use it. You were selected because you have the skills to pull this off, so prove me right and come back alive with your tasks completed. Now, are there any questions?" He waited a moment and when no one said anything he continued. "Good, then that will be all. And Pam, meet me in the lab; I have one more item to give you." Wilhelm cleared the screen and left the room with George and Captain America; the trio headed for Tommy's lab.

When Pam arrived at the lab, she saw Wilhelm and Tommy at the far end standing at a steel table, talking. Wilhelm was holding what looked like a small plastic bottle. She stood in the doorway watching them. Tommy looked over at her and said,

"Come in; don't be shy; we were just discussing you." He turned back to face Wilhelm and took the bottle from him. Wilhelm sat down on a stool and watched Pam approach; he scrutinized her carefully. He was happy with the results of her transformation. By looking at her, you couldn't tell she wasn't an Eastern European and the resemblance to the old girlfriend was scary.

"Let me see your tattoo," Wilhelm said when she reached the table. Pam unzipped her jeans and pulled them down just enough to show him the tattoo on her right hip. Tommy was all eyes. When she was done, she said,

"Hope you enjoyed the view," in her best Mae West imitation as she winked at Tommy.

"I sure did even if he didn't," George said from behind her where he was sitting, drinking scotch. Pam turned to look at him; when she locked eyes with him she said,

"Nothing makes a girl happier than being appreciated. And why don't you come and see me some time, big boy?" again in her Mae West voice. George raised his glass in salute and nodded his head then took a sip of his scotch.

"Sit down," Wilhelm said as he pushed a stool towards her with his foot. Pam sat down and noticed the vial that she first saw from the door resting on a steel tray. She also saw two glass vials and a pack of three pills from the shape of the packaging. "How are your safecracking skills coming along?"

"Really good, I'm down to two minutes," she answered enthusiastically.

"Good, and this takes into account that there are three tumblers on her safe?"

"Yes, it seems I have a knack when it comes to guessing the order."

"Now, are you clear on what you need to do? how you're going to infiltrate her headquarters? as well as how you'll get your ass out of there?"

224

"Yes, sir, I have; getting in shouldn't be too hard since she has such a large sexual appetite. And I plan to use the sea for my escape. It's figuring out the best way to kill her without alerting her guards…that part I haven't quite figured out."

"I understand your problem. But the Captain here has something to add to your bag of tricks, so listen and tell us what you think. After all, it is your ass on the line and your input is important. So don't be shy with your thoughts."

"Yes, sir," was her response as she sat tall on the stool and looked at Tommy.

"Okay Pam, in this vial is a special poison that I and my secret partner have invented. It contains a chemical that will react to a mixture of saliva and oils that you…well you know … make," he said nervously as he pointed to her crotch.

"You mean my kitty cat, don't you, Captain?" she said with a grin and a wink adding a quick opening and closing of her legs.

"Yes, I mean just that. Now as I was saying, in this vial is the poison that will do just that." Tommy picked up the vial and handed it to her. She took it and looked it over carefully turning it upside down and looking at it through the light. She examined it so thoroughly and without fear that he had to ask,

"Are you familiar with poisons, Pam?"

"No, why?"

"It's the way you're handling it; that's all."

"So how do I use this special kitty cat poison? I mean how do I get it on to her kitty cat?" she said with a puzzled look as she looked at the vial and Tommy.

225

"Oh no, it doesn't go on her; it gets applied to your kitty cat," Tommy explained with a big smile. Suddenly, laughter bellowed from George sitting in the corner.

"Bet you didn't see that one coming, did you, Pam?" George managed to say between laughs. "You should've seen your face; it was priceless," he continued.

"If you don't mind, I'd like to continue; this is important, George." Tommy chided in a serious tone.

"Alright! I'm leaving. I just wanted to see the look on her face when you told her that. And now that I have, I can die a happy man." Then he got up and headed for the door. When he reached the door, he turned around and said with a laugh, "'Kitty cat,' she calls it. Can I stay until the Captain tells her what he named it?"

"No," said Wilhelm, "now go and check on what I asked you to."

"Okay, I'm gone." And with that, he opened the door and left.

"Sir, what did he mean exactly when he said I would be using the poison?" Pam asked worriedly.

"I'll let the Captain fill you in; he knows a lot more about it than I do, Pam. I trust him; he knows what he's doing; he's the best I know at the sneaky stuff." Pam seemed to relax a bit. She took a deep breath and said,

"First, tell me what you call it. Then tell me how to use it."

"I call it, pussy poison. You use it by spraying it on your ... well ... pussy," he said letting his voice trail off at the end. "You see, it won't hurt you when you take one of these pills one hour before you use it." He handed her one of the pills. "This antidote will protect you from the poison's effect even with alcohol in your system. I just haven't figured out what flavor to give it."

"Why give it a flavor? Isn't it tasteless?" Pam asked as she put the pill back on the tray.

"Yes, it is; but the issue here is what flavor do you want for the regular spray?" Tommy said as he walked around the table. He was obviously happy to explain it to Pam; his demeanor was that of a child with a new toy. When he reached her, he was on his toes and his body seemed electrified. Pam sat back, a little out of sorts, not sure what to expect. "Here, take a look at the vial housing," Tommy instructed as he shoved the plastic bottle at her. "When you turn this ring one quarter turn counterclockwise, it will release the flavored spray. But, when you turn the ring clockwise one quarter turn, it will release the poison. Now if you turn the ring a full half turn clockwise, it will mix the two liquids." Tommy explained this by show-and-tell pointing out the starting mark to begin the turns through how the two vials fit into the outer bottle. "So you see, I need a flavor for the safe spray. With that in mind, I went to the galley and selected these." Then Tommy took some fruit from a draw underneath the table and placed them in front of her. First was grapes, then an orange, a grapefruit, a pineapple, an apricot, a plum, some strawberries, a mango, and finally a peach. After he put the last piece of fruit on the table, he stood there looking at her, waiting for her selection. Pam looked at the fruit briefly then turned to Wilhelm and said,

"Really, sir, a peach?" Wilhelm smiled and said,

"Yes, it's a peach. Do you like peaches?"

"Not really, sir," she said twisting her face.

"Then pick one, Pam; I don't have all day to waste on this, you know." Wilhelm rose from his stool and walked around the table to where Tommy was standing. He picked up the vial, looked at it, and then he shook it.

"You say this will activate when her saliva and Pam's oils mix?" he asked Tommy while he inspected the vial.

"Yes, sir, and not just with *her* saliva, sir, any will do since it's a sure bet that the White Witch will want to have sex with Pam. Well, sir, it's a sure fire way to kill her without making any unnecessary noise or getting into a fight."

"What makes you so sure she'll want to have sex with me?" Pam said looking at the two men and addressing them as she stood up and walked around the room stopping to look at the equipment.

"Have you looked at yourself lately? Why wouldn't she want to bed you? I've spent a lot of time and government money on you just to assure that she will. You're her wet dream, the love she lost oh so many years ago," Wilhelm said as he accentuated the point with his hands while he talked. "Trust me, when I say she'll want to fuck your brains out or whatever lesbians do in the privacy of their bedrooms. Now pick a flavor, Pam; I have a lot to go over with you after the Captain is through with you."

"Yes, sir, I guess it will be peach, sir," she said as she sat back on the stool.

"I thought you didn't like peach?" Tommy said genuinely confused looking at Pam.

"Somehow the irony is fitting; and to tell you the truth, I kinda like the idea that I'm sexy to my own sex. If you know what I mean?" she said the last part with her Mae West imitation and putting her hand on her hip wiggling a little.

"Then it's settled. Captain, finish training her on how to use this poison and walk her to my stateroom when you're done." Wilhelm was headed for the door as he gave him these instructions. Before the Captain could answer him, he was out the door closing it behind him.

"What did you do to piss of the boss?" Tommy asked Pam.

"Nothing, maybe he didn't like my Mae West," she answered with a thoughtful look on her face.

"Now that he's gone, let me give you some particulars about this poison," Tommy said causing Pam to turn and face him at the table. "This can be applied in several ways thus giving you many options on how to deploy this chemical weapon," he said as he held up the vial and spray bottle. "Sit down and let's go through them and their variables." Pam noticed his demeanor changed; he became authoritarian and was no longer shy. She took a closer look at him and for the first time noticed how handsome he actually was. He had to be at least six-foot-two. She guessed he was around 220 lbs.; his loose fitting shirt did a poor job of hiding his chest and arm muscles. She found his dreadlocks sexy and liked the way they framed his caramel face which had a soft look to it. To top it off or bottom it out, his small waist led to the cutest, tightest ass she had seen in a long time. And the jeans he wore did nothing, and she meant absolutely nothing, to hide what he was packing between those long muscular legs of his.

"Pam, did you hear what I just said?" he questioned.

"Yes, something about variables and uses ... ."

"Good, now this poison is unique in this way: it will irritate the skin on the face when it comes into contact with pubic hair, and it will wash off with the use of soap. But it won't activate when mixed with saliva, so you can use the spray with the poison and kiss all you want to," he said with a smile and a wink.

"What's the problem with pubic hair? I don't quite get that."

"Well, as you know, it's not popular to look like a little girl down there in Verna. So the women tend to let their pubic hairs grow a little bushy. If you get too much spray on the hairs and not directly on the vulva, your partner will get a severe case of the itchiest followed by an ugly rash."

"Oh, I see. But I don't have to worry about kissing if I spray it in my mouth to sell it. You're absolutely sure about that?" she said visibly concerned.

"Correct, it won't activate with saliva to saliva, only with the unique oils produced by excitement and saliva," he said as he leaned closer to her over the table. "Now if you don't have any more questions, I think the boss is waiting for me to escort you to his stateroom," he said as he locked up the poison and put the fruit in the refrigerator.

"You mean you're actually going to walk me to his stateroom; I thought he was joking. I mean really, where could I possibly go is beyond me? I'm on a ship for Christ sake!"

"The boss rarely jokes when he's working. If he says to escort you to his stateroom, you better believe that's what he meant. Now are you ready?" he said earnestly as he opened the door and waved his hand indicating she should go first.

Paris / Peru

Chapter Sixteen

Paris

Frank looked at Linda who was fast asleep in her fully reclined seat; her face was so peaceful with her lips smiling happily. He could imagine what she was dreaming about; she'd been jumping out of her skin with excitement ever since he told her that he was taking her with him. She had immediately requested ten days of vacation, so she could go skiing in the Bavarian Alps after their business in Paris.

"Get up, sleepy head," he said as he kicked her seat lightly with his foot. Linda stirred sitting up with the chair's help.

"Are we there yet or did you wake me for fun?"

"No, we're on final approach. So buckle up!"

A few minutes later, the private jet touched down and taxied to a special hanger reserved for the CIA. As they exited the jet, Frank paused and looked around the hanger; he noticed two other planes were parked. He watched the men who were dressed like mechanics milling around; he knew they were the security element assigned here. He looked out of the hanger towards the runway and saw that it was drizzling. He hated the rain especially in Paris; he never understood the romantic notions people had about Paris in the rain.

Linda headed straight for the waiting car, not bothering to look around or to notice the weather. When she got close, she recognized the driver; it was Kevin.

"Hi, Kevin!" she said genuinely glad to see him.

"I didn't know you were going to be here," she said with a big smile as she paused at the car door to talk to him.

"It was a last minute thing; you know how it is."

"Cheer up, Kevin; we're in Paris. I love this city, don't you?"

"Not in the rain, I hate Paris in the rain," he replied adding a shiver for effect. Frank reached the car by this time and the pair stopped talking. Linda slid into the backseat and moved over to the other side as Frank got in and Kevin closed the door.

Kevin got in the driver's seat, started the car, put on some jazz, headed out of the hanger, and turned on the windshield wipers as the car reached the hanger's opening. Frank had no reason to tell him where to go; Kevin already knew; the only person in the dark was Linda. For now, she was content looking out of the window at all of the familiar places she knew as they drove by.

Afef arrived in Paris the day before for her annual visit and shopping spree with her old university friend, Veronica who was married to the leading cardiologist in Europe. Afef was staying in their apartment overlooking the Seine River for the winter festivals and holiday. As she walked to her destination, the light rain stopped; and she was glad that she had decided to wear her cape instead of the rain coat. She planned to meet Veronica and her husband at a little café that sat across the street from the river. The establishment made the best coffee and orange-filled pastry to die for. She looked at her watch and saw she would be early which was just fine with her; this gave her a chance to relax and enjoy the sights and sounds of the streets and the people in the City of Lights.

Kevin drove the car skillfully through the streets of Paris only making one stop in the 7th district. There, Frank and Linda got out and entered the apartment where the station chief's office was located while Kevin stayed with the car. They stayed exactly forty minutes, and then they were back in the car headed for their hotel where they would be staying.

Linda thought that it was the strangest inspection she had ever witnessed. Frank barely looked at the action reports, and the station chief was trying very hard to please him. Frank seemed to be going through the motions and his actions caused her and the station chief to be confused.

Kevin pulled up to the Citadines Prestige Saint-Germain-des-Prés Paris, which is an apartment/hotel. The building sits opposite to Notre Dame, Pont-Neuf, and the café Les Deux Magat. They got out, gathered their few carry-on bags, and headed into the lobby. Kevin parked the car in the VIP section in front of the hotel for the night. Then he joined them in the lobby, and the three of them went up to the room. The apartment was spacious and decorated in the modern style but defiantly in a French manner. It had two bedrooms opposite each other with a living room in between. The kitchen was fully stocked with pots and pans along with silverware and matching plates. Intricately, hand-woven wool rugs adorned the wood floors. Of three windows, two overlooked the Seine River and the third towards the café where Afef was sitting.

Kevin walked to the kitchen, opened the refrigerator, and looked in.

"Hey, you guys! They even put fresh fruit, chocolate, and two bottles of wine in here. I think I like this place," he said as he took out one of the bottles.

"Which room is mine? I want to clean up before dinner; I'm famished," Linda said standing in the middle of the living room still holding her bag.

"It doesn't matter; choose one," Frank said.

"I'll take this one," she replied and headed off to the room that was located on the far side of the apartment.

"Set up the perimeter security in this room and hers. I'll take care of my room," Frank said to Kevin. Then he picked up his bag and headed to the other room.

Kevin picked up his field bag and the travel security bag, placed them on the kitchen table, and opened them. He took out a dozen monitors, checked and tested them; and when he was satisfied that they were in good working order, he began his work. He went to each of the windows and placed a monitor on it; he did the same with the door. Then he went back; and with a hand held device, he began testing each one by opening each window and door while looking at his device. The unit made a low beeping sound indicating that the monitors were working properly in that room. Next, Kevin knocked on Linda's door. Before she could answer, he had the door open and was walking in. When he entered the room, he caught Linda topless.

"Don't you knock before entering a lady's room?" she said without covering her breasts.

"I did knock, and those tits of yours could use some color," he said as he nodded his head at them. "They're the whitest set of breasts I've ever seen. Maybe you should be going somewhere warm with lots of sun where you could get a tan instead of the mountains."

"There's nothing wrong with my tits, Kevin; they're fine the way they are. Just put up those damn things and *get out* so I can take a shower, please."

"I certainly will; because if the rest of your body is that color, I'll end up swearing you are one of the walking dead. Does Frank know you're that pale?" he said as he began laughing and putting up a sensor on the only window in her room.

"Never mind what Frank knows; just hurry up," she said joining him in laughter as she turned her back to him and continued unpacking.

Kevin finished his security set up and system testing. Then he sat down at the kitchen table, took out his Sig Sauer 45 caliber pistol, and laid it on the table. He took the laptop out of its case, plugged it in, and booted it up. After logging in, he began to type; he was sending in his day's activity report and situation assessment to Rodney back at Langley. As he was finishing, Frank came out and told him that the shower was all his. Kevin signed out, closed the computer, put it back into its case, picked up his pistol, and headed for the bedroom.

When he reemerged, he was dressed in brown wool gabardine pleated trousers and a brown and white pinstriped shirt and was carrying a light brown sports coat. Linda and Frank were sitting at the kitchen table drinking a glass of wine.

"Well, did you save any for me?" he said as he walked towards them.

"Of course, we did. Frank even acted as the official taster. Here, sit down; have a glass." As he sat down, Linda started to pour him a glass of the red wine they were drinking. He picked up the glass, gave it a swirl, and then took a good sniff before taking a sip.

"Now tell me that's not good wine; go on; tell me; I dare you," Linda said leaning forward on her elbows waiting for his answer.

"Yes, that actually is a good tasting wine. Now where are we going for dinner?" Kevin said as he looked a Linda.

After two bottles of wine and a not-so-serious conversation on the matter, they ended up at a little restaurant not far from the hotel. For the next two and a half hours, they were not intelligence agents; they were three friends having dinner and drinks in Paris. They laughed and talked about things that were otherwise trivial but tonight they seemed important. After dinner, Linda wanted to walk along the river. Frank conceded after a feeble attempt to get out of it, so she didn't bother to nag Kevin.

When they were half an hour away from the hotel, Kevin let them out of the car and followed them driving slowly a few feet behind. He kept a constant eye on his surroundings checking his mirrors often as he listened to jazz and hummed along. He thought as he watched them, "This was a very dumb idea to be walking out in the open this way when god and who-knows-else know you are in town. But Paris…and a girlfriend who's also an agent whose boss is her boyfriend…throw in the rain and what you got is one fucked-up mess." His attention was diverted when he saw a police car slow down behind him then drive past him and the officers gave a nod as they did so. He knew it was the diplomatic plates that kept them from stopping him; this was the third police cruiser in twenty minutes.

Frank and Linda walked along the river mostly in silence, and Linda was just fine with that. She was enjoying herself more than she had hoped to. The rain had given the air that fresh perfume smell that only nature could provide. The lights along the river were spectacular in the way they cast shadows that seemed to move with her every step. She walked along lost in her own thoughts sometimes singing a French song she remembered softly to herself. When she looked back at Frank, he was walking slowly with his black full length wool overcoat around his shoulders and his hat tilted just at the right angle. Coupled with the street lights, this made him look like a spy from the old movies she watched as a kid. "That was part of his charm; he liked being a spy. This game turned him on and maybe me a little as well," she thought as she slowed her pace letting Frank catch up to her.

"Let's get back in the car, Lin. We've been out here too long as it is, and you know Kevin is having a security crisis about now."

"Okay, we're almost at the hotel anyway. And Frank, thanks for the walk," she said as she stopped and turned to face him. Frank smiled and signaled to Kevin. When he brought the car up, they got into the back seat; and Kevin headed for the hotel. Unbeknownst to them, they had company waiting for them back at the hotel. Kevin pulled the car in front of the hotel and stopped. Linda and Frank got out on the passenger side and stood on the steps talking.

To Frank's left about 100 meters away was a South African mercenary looking through his scoped 308 caliber suppressed sniper rifle at the pair who were talking and laughing. He thought about taking the shot if his target gave him even the briefest opportunity. At this range, he couldn't miss. But he decided to wait; he was in no hurry.

On Linda's right at 150 meters away, Taylor looked through her scope on top of her 7.62 x 39 caliber sniper rifle. She had no need for a suppressor. She sat far back into the room, so the report from the shot would be muffled. If her target cooperated, she could complete her task and go dancing and drinking with friends. But her intended target was obscured at the moment, and she may miss out on what promised to be one hell of a night on the town.

Linda and Frank watched Kevin park the car and walk towards them. The three entered the hotel totally unaware of how close two of them came to dying. They went straight to their rooms. Once there, Linda stood watch keeping an eye on the exit door, elevator, and stairs as Kevin checked the security system. Satisfied that there had been no intruders, he gave the okay and they entered the room. Next, Kevin did a quick check of the interior; when he was finished, they all started to relax and talk again. Linda excused herself and went to her room to change leaving the two men in the living room talking. When she returned, only Frank was in the room.

"Where's Kevin?" she asked.

"Outside, smoking one of his skinny cigars," he answered. Linda walked to the window and looked out. She located Kevin and watched him for a moment as he leaned against a chest high wall looking at the river and leisurely smoked his cigar.

"I think I'll join him," she said without turning around.

"What! Are you going to have a cigar with him and talk about the latest jazz sensation?" he said jokingly as he joined her at the window. "Look at him; you would never guess he was one hell of a field agent once."

"I never knew that about him. I always thought of him as the cool driver who made me feel safe," Linda said not turning from the window.

"Well, that's the reason why you feel safe around him; he has that effect on people."

"Why did he quit and join the executive security department?"

"I don't know; it was for personal reasons. So he called in a favor and here he is."

"Well, the things I learn hanging around you," she said as she turned to face him and gave him a light peck on the lips. "I'm still going out and not for a cigar either but for a breath of fresh air."

"How much air do you need in one night? You just walked for a half hour getting air."

"Be nice. This air makes me really horny you know," she said as she rubbed his crotch.

"In that case, please get all the air you need but be back in forty-five minutes," he said. Then he kissed her deeply and longingly with a kiss she felt way down in her loins.

"Well, that sure got the juices flowing," she said breathily. Then she headed for the door grabbing her coat on the way.

Afef and Veronica sat at the café across from the hotel where Linda and company were staying; they were waiting for Veronica's husband to join them. Afef had no idea that they were in Paris, and it was apparent that Frank didn't know she was there either. Otherwise, he would have made a point to find out why she was in town and to inform her that he was around.

They sat at a table where they both had a clear view of the river and the hotel that was illuminated with lights and made the river sparkle. They sat, ate, and drank wine with their pastries and talked about the clothes they had purchased. Afef was in the middle of describing a collection of dresses she had ordered when Veronica's husband arrived.

"Sorry, I'm late, dear," he said to his wife as he leaned over and kissed her lightly on the lips. Then he ordered a cognac as he sat down and said, "What have you ladies been up to all day? No doubt, you're trying your best to break your husbands' piggy banks."

"Oh my love, you of all men shouldn't complain about money; it's just not like you," Veronica said in French as she winked at Afef and touched his leg near his crotch under the table. "Besides, Afef is being good this year; she hasn't spent nearly as much as on last year's visit." Both ladies smiled and took a sip of wine.

"That's good to know; few men have the resources that Mr. Libertaire has," he said and then took a sip of his cognac. "So Afef, I hope Paris hasn't disappointed you this season. My wife tells me that the weather has been awful."

"No, not at all, I find the rain refreshing and it has kept the crowds down in the stores," she replied as she bit into another pastry.

Linda walked over to Kevin.

"Hi, I thought I'd give you some company if you don't mind," she said as she pulled the collar of her coat tightly around her neck.

"Now what brings you out in the night air?" he replied taking another drag of his cigar.

"Paris, what else?"

"Do you love this city that much?"

"Yes, yes, I do; I really do. This city makes me feel special. It's a place where I can get lost in and nobody cares who I am when I'm here."

"Interesting, I've heard a few reasons for loving this city but you said it the best," he said jokingly.

"Why, have you heard it before?" she asked seriously.

"Yes, I have but not as beautifully put as you said it." Then he turned away and looked at the river.

The two snipers were intensely watching the pair. The South African had taken his weapon off safe and started to control his breathing in preparation for the shot. Taylor sat calmly looking at them with curiosity rather than focusing on a target; she wondered what they were talking about.

"Kevin," Linda said getting ready to ask him another question. As he turned to face her, his head snapped violently forward causing his body to do the same. She instinctively reached out and tried to catch him. Then her head snapped back and to the side causing her body to spin before it hit the ground with a *thud*. "Ugh!" was the only sound she made. She lay motionless, unconscious bleeding from the bullet wound to her head.

Taylor couldn't believe her eyes. She pressed a button on her trigger housing and switched her scope to camera. Now when she pulled the trigger, she would take pictures instead of shooting bullets. She watched, took photos, and panned the area looking at every place she would have used due to the angle. Nothing…she saw no shooter or anybody leaving a building with anything in their hands that could possibly hide a rifle. She refocused on the two bodies lying on ground. A crowd was starting to form, and a few people were trying to help them. Taylor knew there was no need for that; they were dead. Whoever the shooter was, he or she had put two bullets into two people in the span of seconds. Not many shooters out there could do that with a semi-automatic rifle. "He or she wouldn't be too hard to track," she thought as she continued watching and taking pictures. She scanned the window of the room that they had been in, looking for Frank. But she saw no sign of him; perhaps, he couldn't hear the commotion going on below him.

A man ran across the street towards the café where Afef was sitting. He stopped to tell the waiter to call an ambulance.

"What's happened?" asked Veronica's husband.

"A man and woman have been shot…over there by the river," the man answered in hurried French.

"I am a doctor; take me to where they are," he told the man, and the pair headed off with Afef and Veronica close behind.

The South African mercenary calmly disassembled his rifle and put it in a hard case. Then he placed the case in the back of an armoire and left the apartment. He knew someone else would remove the case which left him free to make his escape unhampered and unnoticed.

Veronica's husband arrived at the scene and pushed his way through the crowd. What he saw when he reached the area was horrific. A large pool of blood formed around the heads of both of them; he had no idea that the blood was mostly Kevin's. Carefully, he stepped around the pool of steaming blood and squatted down next to Kevin's body. He noticed the small hole in the back of his head; he took him by the shoulders and slowly rolled him over just enough to see the front.

He was greeted by half of a face; the top portion including the forehead had been blown away. He gently laid Kevin back down and made the sign of the cross over him. Next he examined Linda who was lying on her back with her head not far from Kevin's. Her face and chest where covered with Kevin's blood and brains, so he had to wipe some of it away from her neck to feel for a pulse. Astonished, he yelled,

"She's alive! For Christ sake, where the hell is that ambulance?" He wasn't talking to anyone in particular; he just had to say it.

Afef recognized Linda right away. But it took the doctor rolling Kevin over for her to recognize him; and it took all of the control she could muster not to cry out. Her mind was racing. She had to let Colleen know right away because where Linda is chances are Frank is not far behind.

Taylor was breaking down her weapon and was preparing to leave; the night hadn't been a total waste; she still had time to meet her friends. Soon, she heard sirens in the distant. She stopped packing to look out the window. Frank heard those same sirens and walked to the hotel window.

When he saw the crowd below and the police cars pulling up, he got his cellphone, pressed the speed dial letter that corresponded to Linda's phone, and waited. When she didn't answer, he hung up and did the same to reach Kevin. He let it ring four times then hung up and walked back to the window. He was just in time to see the ambulance arrive. He picked up his binoculars and zoomed in on the center of the crowd. When he saw the blood and the large area it covered, he put the glasses down and headed for the door holstering his pistol and grabbing his coat and hat. Taylor had missed him in the window because she was busy scanning the crowd for him.

"Surely, he would be in the crowd with two of his people down," she thought. But when she didn't see him, she went back to breaking her rifle down and missed him as he left the hotel wading through the crowd to get a closer look.

The ambulances arrived and the medics went to work. With the help of the doctor, they laid Linda on a stretcher and wheeled her to an ambulance. After putting her in the ambulance, the medic pulled a sheet over her head signaling that she was dead. The driver closed the doors, got in, and sped away with sirens blaring. The second ambulance crew did the same with Kevin, but it took them longer because they had to place him in a body bag and get more information from the doctor.

Frank took this opportunity to talk to one of the medics from the second ambulance.

"Where are you taking the bodies?" he asked the man in a calm voice as not to alarm him.

"To 1 place du Parvis Notre-Dame," he answered. Frank was familiar with this hospital; he thanked the man and walked away. As he left, he pulled out his cellphone and placed a call to the station chief who he had visited earlier in the day.

"Yes," the voice said.

"I need you to get over to 1 place du Parvis Notre-Dame hôpital and shut down any information about my two companions. I need a total information blackout; also send a team; I'm leaving this location."

"Understood," was all the voice said, and then the phone went dead. Frank headed back to the hotel. He had a million things to take care of, not to mention how to explain this mess.

Afef slipped away from Veronica in the middle of her talking about the horrible scene they had witnessed. She was talking more to herself than to Afef anyway; thus she didn't notice when Afef stepped away to use her phone.

"Hello! Colleen! There's been an incident here in Paris and it involves Kevin and Linda!" she said breathily.

"Slow down, Afef! I can't understand what you're saying. Take a breath and start over!" Colleen said as she sat back in her chair at her private desk. She removed her glasses and glanced at the crystal encased clock resting on the right side of the desk; it read 4:00 a.m. "You said something has happened to Kevin and Linda?"

"Yes, something bad. They've been shot, Colleen," Afef said in a clear and calmer tone.

"Where are they taking the bodies?"

"Hold on a moment, I'll find out." Colleen waited. In no time, Afef had returned to tell her the name of the hospital and what she had witnessed.

"Don't do anything until I get back to you, Afef," Colleen instructed. When Colleen had finished, she told Afef she'd call her back. Then she hung up. Afef went back to where Veronica was standing and talking to someone in the crowd. She hadn't noticed Afef's absence.

"Fuck! Fuck! Fuck!" Frank said as he paced back and forth in the living room of the hotel apartment. "This is all I need right now—another assistant killed. Rodney will never believe *this* story. Fuck, I have more important things to deal with at the moment like who'd want her and Kevin dead. Are they waiting for the chance to kill me, also? Fuck! I really don't need this right now." A knock on the door stopped his stride. He pulled his pistol and looked at the monitor. It was the team whom he had ordered. He went to door; they exchanged the day's password, and he let them in.

The Farm

"Samuel, are you awake?" said the voice on the phone.

"I am now! Colleen is that you?"

"Why yes, Samuel. What other woman calls you at four in the morning?"

"What do you want?"

"I need a favor, Samuel, and only *you* can help me."

"No! Colleen."

"You haven't heard what it is yet, Samuel. How can you say no so quickly?"

"Easily! Whenever you call me *Samuel*, I know it's bad. And what I mean by bad is that it will probably get me in trouble so the answer is *no.*"

"I didn't want to remind you that you *owe* me a favor or two," Colleen said as she took her glasses off and walked crossed her bedroom while enjoying twisting his arm.

Samuel had gotten out of bed when his phone rang to answer it in the other room. His wife was sleeping peacefully. He was sure she had heard the phone but the years had taught her to ignore such calls; they came with the job.

"Samuel, do I need to remind you who helped you get your current posting?"

"No, you don't. What do you want me to do?" he said as he sat down on the couch.

"I need you to go over to the hospital. A friend of mine has been injured and I need you to arrange for her privacy while I arrange for transportation back to the States."

"What happened to your friend?"

"She was shot in the head earlier this evening."

"Oh! Well, give me the information and give me an hour; I'll be in touch." He hung up and dialed another number. Colleen called Afef and filled her in letting her know there was no need to cut her trip short.

Back on the C.A.A.

Randy, Teri, and Vanessa were the first agents to enter the lounge. They were greeted with music and the sight of their boss doing a two-step with the chef.

"Come in or get out but close the door; you're ruining the vibe," Tommy called from the couch where he was sitting. The eight agents filed in and headed for the bar where George was sitting, smoking a cigar, and drinking a Kentucky mule.

The agents ordered their drinks and spread out through the lounge sitting on couches and overstuffed chairs that framed the dance floor. Randy sat on a barstool next to George and watched his boss dancing to an R. Kelly song.

"What are you drinking?" Randy asked.

"Kentucky mule," George replied without looking at him.

"And what's the name of that dance the boss is doing?"

"It's the Philly bop." Randy told the bartender he would have what George was drinking. After the bartender gave him his drink, he took a sip and said,

"This is really good!"

"Be careful with that, junior; it has a hell of a kick," George said as he finished his drink and ordered another.

Vanessa sat down next to Tommy, crossed her legs, took a sip of her drink, and said in her best sexy voice,

"Why are you sitting here all alone?"

"Waiting for you, of course," Tommy said as he turned his head to look at her and smiled. "Like to dance?"

"Yes, but I don't know how to two-step."

"No problem, I'll show you as we go; it's easy. Why do you think the boss likes it?" He got up, extended his hand; and the pair headed for the dance floor. The song changed to a Marvin Gaye tune, and Wilhelm and the chef changed steps.

"Now what dance are they doing?" Randy asked.

"That, my man, is the West Philly version," George said.

"How many versions are there?"

"I really don't know but the boss knows them all." They sat there watching Tommy trying to teach Vanessa how to two-step and chuckling at the sight. By the fourth song, the dance floor had four couples dancing with drinks in hand and smiles all around.

"What's the reason for the party tonight?" Vanessa asked Tommy as they sat on the couch playing touchy feely with each other.

"Tomorrow you start your mission, right?"

"Yeah, so?"

"So tonight, we dance and drink because it may be the last time for some of us to do so. Understand?"

"I get it; so enough talking and more drinking and who knows what the night will bring," she said in an upbeat tone. The night went on. Everyone was having a good time, seemingly with the same sentiment as Tommy's.

Peru

Number 1 rode down the length of his headquarters building in an electric golf cart to his office that was at the other end. The headquarters section is 125 meters long, 125 meters wide, and 50 meters high, all carved out of the side of a mountain. This was just one section of three that made up the above ground portion of the complex. The section he had just come from is situated to the right of the main building and serves as the council members' personal living quarters. It is equipped with a gym, sauna, and gourmet kitchen complete with staff and every professional and convenient appliance you could imagine.

Each member's apartment is two stories high and has 2,000 square feet of luxury living space. Each is equipped with individual security systems, state-of-the-art communications, and counter electronic measures. The building to the left of the headquarters building is the command and control center where the master controls for the compound's defensive armaments are housed. The Council employed a private army of 150 men who are experts in mountain warfare and other military special skills.

Underneath the headquarters building are additional living and working spaces in an underground structure that extends one mile deep and a half mile wide with connecting tunnels to the other buildings. This structure contains living quarters for the army, scientists, and other personnel including its armory. The entire complex is located on the west side of a mountain that overlooks a Y-shaped canyon. On the far side of the canyon sits S.A.M. (surface-to-air) missiles and four electric powered, radar guided, 20-millimeter Gatling machine guns supported by three twin 40 millimeter anti-aircraft guns. In the center of the Y are stationed the same weaponry minus the anti-aircraft guns. The area around the building complex is similarly armed with the added protection of mine fields. The whole outer structure is camouflaged to blend with the surrounding mountains making it nearly impossible to spot from the air. It also is protected by an electronic screen that jams all unauthorized signals.

As he rides down the long corridor, he notices all of the activity around him; every department is busy. A department exists for every country that the Council operates in. They are organized by continent along with a special department for spies and dignitaries who work for them. But his favorite department is planning or as he likes to call it, "the devious group." Here, he assembled people who do nothing but think of ways to turn spies, plan attacks, and identify the best places for the Council to position itself. When it's three new members arrive—the ones from South America and the extraordinary assassin known as the Pol—, this special group would be complete. Then he could turn his attention to Africa full time.

As he passed the communication center, he collected his thoughts because the next stop was his office. His driver stopped in front of the glass elevator. Number 1 got out, thanked him, and entered the lift. He rode up two floors and exited into his large office. He didn't have a secretary; instead, he had a female companion who saw to his office needs.

"Good morning, sir!" she greeted him.

"Good morning!"

"You have three new artifacts this morning; they're from the underwater city in Lake Titicaca."

"Great! I've been waiting for these," he said excitedly. He went over to the large wood table where three stone statues were displayed. The statues were 18 inches in height, 5 inches in width, and a good representation of the ancient culture that lived in that region. His office was filled with artifacts from around the world; collecting such objects was a perk that he fully enjoyed.

He walked across the open space between the table and his desk to look out of the window. He saw a puma sunning itself on a mountain ledge. He stopped and looked at the animal as it lay there without a care in the world. After all and why not, it was the top predator in these mountains. He continued to his desk, sat down, and started looking over the morning reports. He stopped at a message simply marked important and opened it. After reading it, he sat back and thought about what he had just read. Who would want to kill Frank's assistant and driver? Does someone else want him dead? It was obvious that it wasn't Talaus' man. The message is from him, and he's not prone to making mistakes.

Number 1 read the rest of the reports before contacting Talaus; their brief fifteen minute conversation gave him the facts he was missing. Then he called his second in command on the view screen.

"I have a bit of news for you," he said as soon as Number 2 answered. Number 2 was in the middle of his morning workout; he was squatting 300 lbs. at that moment.

"Oh, what is it?" he said after placing the weights back on the rack. "And who would want them dead?"

"I don't think they were after them; I think the assassin was after Frank." Then Number 1 paused watching his reaction. Number 2 took his time wiping the sweat from his upper body; he already knew about their deaths; his assassin had already informed him.

"I'll look into it, Number 1, although I can't imagine that his cover is blown. I'll contact Frank and get the details."

"Fine, let me know what Frank says by end of business."

"Will do." Then he pressed a button on the remote and turn off the monitor.

Number 5 sat in his living room drinking vodka. He was angry and somewhat sad over the news of Linda's death; his pipeline into the CIA had been severed. His first thought went to Wilhelm. Perhaps, he discovered who she was; he had a knack for sniffing out spies and double agents. Maybe, just maybe, Number 1 was right about his ability to cause turmoil for us.

Number 1 sat in his office watching his companion going about her routine and thought about the news. On the very day Wilhelm is due to land in Cyprus, his boss' lover and driver are killed. He didn't know why, yet. But he had a feeling someone was jockeying for position or getting rid of loose ends.

Cyprus

Chapter Seventeen

Wilhelm sat in his state room eating breakfast and reading the morning intelligence reports when he came across the notice of Kevin's death. He sat back in his chair and swallowed hard then started to read the details. When he had finished, he contacted Rodney; he wanted to know the particulars. As he waited for a reply, George walked in.

"Good morning, sir, the captain says we will be off shore of Cyprus in two hours."

"Thank you, George; and see that the teams are ready."

"Yes, sir and sir, I'm sorry about Kevin." Wilhelm looked at George and said,

"He knew what could happen; he took his chances like the rest of us." Then he went back to eating his breakfast.

The agents gathered in the number 3 cargo holding area conducting an equipment check. They had broken up into their separate groups and each had picked a corner in the huge hold. (If you were a stranger looking at their behavior, you would think they didn't know each other.) Wilhelm knew that each team leader was going over the insertion plan and checking the equipment for what seemed like the hundredth time. He watched the preparations from the bridge monitors and observed the captain as he maneuvered the ship towards Xylofagou.

Once there, the ship would sit idly for an hour to allow the teams to disembark and head for the landing point and their transportation. There, they would be picked up and taken to their final staging area to wait for darkness before making the water crossings to Turkey and Syria. Then the C.A.A. would head down the coast to the port of Larnaca where it would unload its cargo, and Wilhelm and his team would disembark.

Randy and his team landed. When he looked down the beach, he could see that Alex's team had done the same. Randy looked around and saw a man 50 meters away so he took out his pistol and waited. Then the man gave the correct hand signal and Randy approached him cautiously with pistol at the ready.

"Long trip, short night," the man said in a distinctive British accent.

"It depends on the season," Randy replied as he started to holster his pistol. Then he turned and waved, and the rest of the team grabbed their gear and headed towards him at a run. Down the beach, Alex and his team were doing the same.

They loaded up in the waiting van and took off. From landing to transport took less than ninety seconds. The ride was brief. Only ten minutes had passed when the van pulled into the garage, and then a second van parked alongside it. Randy got out, saw Alex, and breathed a sigh of relief to himself.

"Enki, Ninurta," a man addressed them as he came out of a door to their right; he was British. "Will you and your team follow me, please?" They followed the man through a hallway, down a flight of stairs, and into what appeared to be a living room. "I assume you'll want to send a message. The communication room is down that hall on the right. You and your team can relax in here. There's food in the kitchen and rooms for sleeping, so relax. If you need anything, just ask."

Alex waited until the man left. Then he called over Kubaba and told her to send the message informing their boss that they had arrived and are holding. She headed down the hall to the communications room, sent the message, waited a moment, and received the confirmation. Then she returned to the living room and gave him a nod.

Wilhelm was sitting in the communications center when the signal came in. Tommy was in front of the communications console. He wrote down the message and handed it to Wilhelm. He read it, put it in the shredder, picked up the phone, and told the captain to head for Larnaca. In a moment, the ship was underway. Wilhelm sat there and thought, "First phase is completed; now if they make the crossing, game on." He got up and left the room without saying a word.

The captain had set the ship's speed at six knots. At that rate, he would reach port just before sunset. By the time he docked, it would be dark and the off-loading of cargo would have to wait until tomorrow.

Wilhelm went to his state room and checked on the information that he requested. It arrived and read:

"Security Agent shot in the back of the head—Paris 2230 hrs.

Unknown assailant.

Assistant skiing running—check.

Lead in zone five."

"That's strange," he thought. "Who would put a hit on Kevin while Linda is off skiing and Frank takes off to Germany? While Frank's in town, he would have one of his assets keep an eye on him. If I'm right, Frank will be the poster boy for the agency while there. But if he had nothing to do with it, he will be calling in a favor or two to find out who's the shooter." All Wilhelm could do was wait and see which way it would play out.

Langley

Rodney wondered if Frank had killed another assistant. The one in Nicaragua was understandable; she had been turned. But if he had this one killed along with the driver, for Christ sake, he would have Frank's head. And Wilhelm ... with the history he and Kevin shared, he could be a problem if he suspected Frank had anything to do with it. Rodney seriously doubted that Linda was skiing, but he had sent an agent to check on it. And according to Susan, he had shown up at her station in Germany in the middle of the night and stayed in a safe house. If he didn't kill them that meant someone had them on their to-do-list. At least, Wilhelm was on schedule. This trap was delicate enough without these outside complications and unexpected developments.

The Farm

Colleen sat in the jeep alongside the private airstrip at the east end of the property. With her was Anthony, the security chief when George was away. She looked into the sky and spotted the plane. She watched the Medijet land, turn around, and taxi back towards her and the waiting ambulance. She looked at her watch; it was 7:12 a.m. EST. She supervised the transfer of Linda, and the small caravan headed back to the house. When the ambulance arrived at the house, a group of four security personnel took over, not allowing the EMTs to go any further. They took her through a back hallway to an elevator then down one floor. The doors opened revealing a room equipped will all of the medical equipment and supplies needed for her care and recovery.

Dr. Bell and a nurse stood by; the pair took charge of Linda and hooked her up to the medical equipment that would save her life.

"What are you going to tell your husband when he finds out? And he will find out, you know." Dr. Bell asked Colleen.

"I'll cross that bridge when I get to it, but I need her to be able to talk. Will she make a full recovery?" she asked as she turned to look at Linda and watched the nurse connecting the IV to a pump.

"Yes, I think she'll recover just fine. I'll do a complete physical and let you know for sure. Now you must have some business to attend to this morning, children and the like." Colleen smiled and nodded. She knew a gentle shove when she got one so she turned to leave. "Colleen, she'll be alright; and by the way, that's a very pretty dress," he said with a smile.

"Thank you, Doctor; you're not only a credit to your profession but a flatterer as well.

She left the room closing the door softly behind her. As she stepped into the elevator, she thought, "The doctor doesn't know how right he is. Wilhelm would find out. My job is to delay that until I have all of my ducks in a row so to speak." The elevator door opened and her youngest son was standing there.

"Mom, I don't want to wear a tie today. Do I have to?" he asked. She smiled, touched his check lightly, and said,

"Maybe. Let's talk about it over breakfast, shall we?" as they walked to the kitchen.

Port Larnaca

Wilhelm read the message that Captain America had delivered. Team One had departed for Xeros and Team Two would be departing for Varosha in two hours. In a few hours, both teams will be in place. Now he could get ready to receive his guests. He was looking forward to seeing his two fathers-in-law and Afef's younger brother now a major. This business/family gathering afforded him the opportunity to make sure that everything on their end was in place.

His calculations were right. When the ship finally docked, it was too dark to unload; so the ship was given the last berth, the one nearest the cruise liners. He liked the port's configuration; it was horseshoe shaped. "It accommodates both cargo and cruise liners," he thought as he stood on deck watching various passengers from the *Queen of the Sea* returning to their ship. He leaned on the railing smoking a cigar and watched the people, wondering just how many of them were spies. Then he turned his attention to the crew and watched as they checked the ropes that tied the ship to the dock and checked the hull for damage.

Checking his watch, he headed for his stateroom; it was time to prepare for dinner. When he reemerged, he was dressed in tan summer wool trousers and tunic with Italian loafers, no socks. He was joined by George, and the pair headed for the gang plank to greet the men who would be arriving soon. Wilhelm and George arrived and conducted a final check with the security personnel going over their duties. Satisfied, Wilhelm turned his attention to the docks; he carefully and methodically scanned every inch of the dock with infrared/heat sensitive binoculars. He found nothing of concern; the wharf was clear of humans; all that remained was a cat or two and quite a few rats.

A call came over the radio announcing that three black sedans were headed his way. Wilhelm knew it was his fathers-in-law plus their security. Within moments, he saw the cars' headlights. He watched until the cars stopped at the gang plank and the men got out. He stood at the top of the gang plank where they could see him clearly, and he waited. The first to reach him was Afra's father and her older brother Abdullah.

Her father was a slender man, five feet eleven inches tall, 190 lbs., fair complexion with jet black wavy hair, and well-dressed in a dark blue Italian-cut suit.

"Son, I am very pleased to see you! And how is my daughter? Does the pregnancy go well?" he said in Arabic as he shook his hand.

"I am pleased to see you also, Anwar, and your daughter is doing fine. I have a letter for you from her. "Welcome Abdullah," he said turning his attention to him.   "How have you been? I hope business is good."

"All is fine, Wilhelm. It's good to see you; but does it always have to be business," he said as he shook his hand and smiled. Her brother was an inch or two shorter than his father but he was his spitting image and dressed in the same manner.

"Please, come aboard and enjoy my hospitality," Wilhelm replied in Arabic waving his hand in jester.

Right behind them approached Afef's father and older brother, the major. Her father was five feet eight inches tall and 210 lbs. of muscle. His tanned skin was a testament to the amount of time he spent in the field. With the rank of major general, one would think he would stay indoors more often but not him. His son was at least four inches taller than he and just as fit. Wilhelm liked him; he had a keen wit and the same passion as his sister when it came to living life. Being in military intelligence suited him; he took to it naturally, and having a general for a father was certainly a career booster.

"Wilhelm, my son! It's good to see you! And it is also nice to see that my daughter hasn't run you through yet," he said in Turkish as he laughed and patted him on the shoulder.

"It's good to see you, Mustafa, and congratulations, Omar, on your promotion to major. Now if you will follow me, we can catch up on a few things before dinner," he replied in perfect Turkish.

The group headed towards the dining room in silence with Wilhelm and George leading the way and the remaining bodyguards following. When they entered, they were greeted by a beautifully decorated round table in the center of the room surrounded by five plush leather chairs. The Crusaders singing "Street Life" was playing softly in the background. On the right side of the room, couches and lounge chairs were arranged in such a manner that the openings faced the table. Standing to the left of the table was Marsha, the ship's head chef dressed in kitchen whites wearing a white chef beret with the ship's patch. She is five feet five inches tall, slim 120 lbs., brown-skinned woman from West Philadelphia sporting the perfect afro under her cap. She had worked for Wilhelm for five years, and he had promoted her to head chef of this ship. She stood there flashing a brilliant smile as they took their seats and the guards settled on the couches.

"I hope you've prepared one of your superb dinners of American soul food, Marsha; I've thought of nothing else all day," Mustafa said to her with obvious affection. He really enjoyed her cooking and had offered her a lucrative contract to cook for him and his family more than once.

"Of course, General, the moment I was informed of your arrival, I started preparations," she replied in her usually soft but purposeful voice. "Now if you, gentlemen, will excuse me," she added and left the room.

They sat around the table talking about family and laughing at bad jokes while they ate dinner and drank wine. When it was time for cigars and cognac, the bodyguards thanked Wilhelm for the meal and they filed out of the room. The general's aide placed a packet on the table in front of the general as he passed by. The guards would take up positions outside the room along with George as the men conducted their business.

Wilhelm started to ask each man pointed questions. It was clear that business was being conducted and that he was in charge. Mustafa slid the packet to him as he puffed on the hand-rolled custom tobacco blend that Wilhelm grew and rolled on the farm. These were the only cigars he smoked since the first time Wilhelm gave him a box many years ago.

Anwar did the same after reaching into his thin leather briefcase producing a similar packet. Wilhelm turned his attention to Mustafa as he went through the pictures and information contained in the packet. He questioned him thoroughly on every aspect. When he was sure no more questions were needed on the subject, he turned his attention to Anwar. He followed the same procedure with him but his inquiry took a little longer. Syria was a more delicate operation than Turkey, plus Anwar was a hot head and was leading the support team. So Wilhelm was extra diligent in his questions to him.

After Wilhelm finished informing them of what he intended to do and reassured them that no bombs would go off nor would he leave a trail of bodies behind, he reminded them of the importance of this mission and raised his glass in salute. Then he looked at his watch. He pressed a button on the floor with his left foot, and George came in.

"Would you bring in my special guests?" George nodded and stepped back into the hall. A minute later, he knocked and opened the door. Four young women entered the room, and then George closed the door.

"Gentlemen, since it is too late to travel, I have arranged for you to get a little help in making you comfortable aboard the C.A.A." He introduced each woman. Each woman stood five feet ten inches tall weighing 130 lbs., and none wore a bra size under a D cup. They were dressed in black

261

form-fitting cocktail dresses, designer fishnet or seamed stockings, and heels. Around each woman's neck rested a string of pearls complemented by diamond ear rings and a matching tennis bracelet. They stood there shapely and fit oozing sex appeal. Each dark haired beauty smiled and waited for Wilhelm's signal. "Ladies, I have wined and dined them. I leave the rest in your capable hands," he said with a smile and a raise of his glass. The women started to move, each going to her prearranged gentleman. They were paired according to each man's sexual taste, so Wilhelm was assured that each man would be fully engaged for the rest of the night.

He didn't want any of them wandering around the ship tonight, and this would guarantee that he would know exactly where they are and what they are doing. He was glad he added these four specialists; they would not only keep them busy, they would give a full report on everything they said and did in the morning. Wilhelm relaxed at the table taking his time drinking his cognac, smoking, and enjoying the scene unfolding in front of him.

As Wilhelm slipped quietly out of the room, Abdullah had his hand under the dress of his partner. Judging by the motion, he was finger fucking her with enthusiasm. The others were snuggled up and oblivious to anything around them.

Wilhelm went to the communication room. Tommy handed him a message; Wilhelm read it, checked the time, and handed it back to him.

File it!" he said, and then he left the room.

Ophiuchus: Day One

Chapter Eighteen

Wilhelm watched the four-car caravan drive away on the surveillance monitor as he ate his unusually large breakfast. In an hour, he and George would leave the ship and head for the temporary headquarters located close to the Turkish controlled region of Cyprus in the north. They would leave amongst the congestion and activity of unloading the ship's cargo. Captain America had gone ahead to make final preparations and set up his personal security precautions.

The morning report was what Wilhelm expected; the major players knew he was in town. The only surprise was from Susan. It seems that Frank showed up in the middle of the night and stayed in a safe house but left early the next morning for parts unknown. Also, there was no sign of Linda. It was starting to look like Frank was trying to stay one step ahead of somebody. The satellite photos showed no signs of activity near his first base of operations in the north. The NSA reported no unusual chatter coming from either sector where the teams were operating. He wouldn't get too happy yet; the day was early and he hadn't left the ship. But when he did, he expected a little trouble from his peers on the other side.

South Africa

Talaus sat crossed-legged on the natural rock outcrop just off his living room. The panoramic view of the valley and mountains made this his favorite place in the 12,000 square foot house that sat on a one hundred acre spread which he called home. Taylor dressed only in shorts sat a few feet away brushing one of the five boerboel dogs that he kept around the house. They were enjoying the warm winter sun as he bounced ideas off of her about the best way to eliminate Wilhelm and his agents. The morning report from his agent in Cyprus had confirmed Wilhelm's presence there with a photo of him standing on the deck of his ship. Now he wondered if Wilhelm would be running the operation from there or if this was just a jumping off point.

He might take Taylor's advice and kill him the first opportunity he gets and not fuck around with this guy. But he had other plans for him. Besides, he wanted to wait for Theresa to return and hear her opinion on the matter. He still had to find and remove Wilhelm's team of agents, so killing him too soon would not be wise. Maybe a snatch and torture move might be more appropriate in this situation. That way, he could have a little fun getting the information and then let Taylor kill him. But if he did that, how could he trust the information? And how many men would he lose in the process of the capture? This and many more questions and scenarios had to be examined. He had time for reflection for now. At this point, all he could do was to sit and wait and see where he goes when he leaves the ship.

Syria

Randy stood looking out the front window of the beach cottage and watching people walking back and forth to the beach and to points unknown. Behind him, Vanessa was busy checking the equipment for the tenth time since they arrived early this morning. The drop and pickup went without a hitch, and he liked the civilian he would be working with. The guy seemed to know what he was doing and could be very helpful to him with the terrain and places that a person could use to hide in the area.

Jamal and Rochelle were at the other end of the row of beach cottages. There, they could keep an eye on as much beach as possible. When they went to town or to a local night spot, the route back could be covered easily since each cottage was within eyesight of the other.

This was day one of the mission. Randy had to find his targets and fulfill his mission in ten short days. After breakfast, the team would start their search in earnest. He walked over to the communication gear and started to send his report. He knew his boss was expecting it; he reminded himself to use their code names and began.

Turkey

Alex and his team had settled into the safe house. He liked it; the mixture of modern and traditional features made them feel at home. The safe house had enough room for the equipment and a space for holding the targets before transport. But what he really liked was the location of the house; it gave him clear views of every approach to the house, and it was halfway between the beach and the hotel. His counterpart, a Turkish military intelligence officer, seemed amicable enough although he wondered why Turkish intelligence was involved in this op. Anyway, Pam had caught her ride on time and he was on schedule, so far so good.

Pam

She had gotten into a different car than her team when they landed in Turkey. The two men in the front seat wore Turkish military air force uniforms. They didn't speak, and the two-hour drive passed silently. They entered a side gate at the airbase and went straight to a parked cargo plane. She got out, stretched, straightened her black skirt, smoothed her black tights, put on her waist jacket, picked up the backpack that held her equipment, and walked towards the plane. A man standing at the loading ramp greeted her and showed her where to sit. Then an alarm sounded and the ramp started to close. The plane taxied and took off. When the plane leveled out, she unbuckled her seat harness, took out a pen light, and started looking through her backpack. Next she took out a file and with the pen light in her mouth began to read.

Ophiuchus: Day Two

Chapter Nineteen

Langley

The CIA deputy director sat silently across from Rodney and waited for him to continue. Rodney had paused when they reached the subject of Frank. The deputy knew of the trouble Rodney was having with him, and he also knew the decision he had to make. So he sat there quietly drinking his tea and waiting for him to begin again.

"We haven't found Linda. She sure isn't skiing or laid up fucking some stud somewhere. And knowing Frank, she's probably in a dozen pieces never to be found. He hasn't checked in, and there's only been one confirmed sighting from the station chief in Hamburg. It's time we put an end to this cat and mouse game and either bring him in or remove him from the equation."

The deputy knew that the last part was a question directed at him; he knew Rodney wanted to kill Frank as much as he did. He had been waiting for Frank to fuck up and he finally did so. Now he could kill the cocksucker, and the best part was—it would be legal.

"Frank has a few well-placed friends in Europe, and they would be more than happy to help him out. Not to mention, there is a possibility that he could go private, or rouge, or traitor. We should take that into consideration," the deputy stated.

"Frank's an asshole; I'll give you that. He has fucked up in the past but I've never thought of him as a traitor."

"Fine, he's not a traitor then. So how do you want to handle this? If you put this through normal channels, he is bound to find out and really go to ground."

"I think you already know how this should be handled, but make sure he can have a funeral. You understand me?"

"I understand. I'll activate three contractors in the region and issue a shoot-on-sight order. Are there any other special orders for them?"

"No, but I want you to oversee this personally, and no mistakes. We need to eliminate him as soon as possible *and quietly.*" With that, the deputy rose from his seat and left the office with a smile. Finally, he could get rid of the man he hated the most.

Peru

Number 1 listened intently to what Number 5 was saying about the sudden turn of events concerning Frank. He theorized about why Frank wasn't shot and no attempt was made on his life. But why those in his team were targeted didn't make sense. What Number 5 didn't know was that Talaus had been given the green light to remove him but failed. Number 1 sat their wondering why Number 2 was acting so smug lately, and why he lied about the incoming call that he received on his cellphone, a couple days ago. Then Number 5 said something that made him sit up straight and lean towards him.

"What did you just say?"

"Linda was my agent; I was running her. That's where the inside information was coming from. Do you think Frank found out and had her killed?"

"That's a possibility, and that bit of information adds another dynamic to the equation. I'll have some of our people look for him. In the meantime, where are we on the Wilhelm project?"

Number 1 listened to the update but didn't really pay attention; the news he just received really didn't change things. If Frank had his team killed, he had jumped the timeline. That means he was going with his own plan. He had to contact Talaus; he had new instructions for him concerning Frank.

The Farm

Afra was reclining on the chaise lounge and was reading, when Linda woke up and asked if she could have some water. The physician's assistant handed her a cup with a straw and she began to drink. When she finished, her caretaker changed her head bandage. Afra closed her book and observed. She was really big now; her belly was swollen, and the baby was riding low. It was becoming more and more difficult to move around. She was glad to sit and read with her feet elevated, refreshments close by, and the company of the medical staff who all were good at board and card games, not to mention the gossip and stories they told to pass the time.

Linda had been there for five days now, and the doctor informed them she was recovering fast. The bullet hadn't penetrated her skull; it just dug a shallow furrow about one and a half inches long and one-quarter inch wide on the left side of her head. It looked worse than it actual was; and the doctor told them that when her hair grew back, it would hide the scar. He suggested that in a day or two, she could get some air and walk around a bit. Colleen was particularly eager to hear that news. She had a few questions for her, and she was anxious to find out how Kevin was killed.

But for now, Linda rested comfortably waking periodically and talking little which was just fine with Afra. She would continue to relax and hope her husband would be home for the baby's birth.

Verna, Bulgaria

Pam checked into the hotel using the name and ID that would let her contact know she was here. Since her arrival, she had changed her attire. Now she looked like a college student complete with mannerisms, and the little bag she was carrying didn't look out of place. She spoke to the desk clerk in fluent Polish as she received attention of a sexual nature from men and a few women in the lobby. Next she took the elevator up to the sixth floor. As she walked down the hallway, she took mental notes of the exits and stairway. Then she entered her suite, put down her bag, took out her gun, and proceeded to clear the room. She repeated the procedure with the debugging device that was concealed as an mp3 player and also doubled as one.

Satisfied, Pam called room service and ordered a cheeseburger and fries. A few minutes later, there was a knock on the door; Pam picked up her gun. "It's too soon for room service," she thought. She went to the door, stood to the side, and asked who was there.

"Room service!" a female voice answered. Pam cocked the hammer, unlocked the door, and then took a few steps back. Holding her gun down by her right thigh, she turned sideways pointing her left shoulder at the door and said,

"Come in; it's open." A sandy blond haired woman about five feet eight inches tall, slender with an athletic build, and dressed in a hotel uniform walked in.

"Your order, miss.   Where would you like it?"

"Over there will be fine."   After the woman finished setting out her meal, she turned to face her.

"That's really fast considering I just ordered it five minutes ago," Pam said as she leveled her gun on her.

"I didn't want the mysterious Oannes to wait for her cheeseburger and thick-sliced fries."

"Identify yourself!"   After the woman went through the proper protocol and gave the correct counter-sign, Pam lowered her weapon.

"So it's true; those who are trained by him are the best. For a moment there, I thought you were going to shot me."

"I thought about it even after you gave the counter-sign."

"Why didn't you?"

"You seemed sincere."   Then she smiled and the woman breathed a sigh of relief.

"I have some news for you, and it's going to fuck up your timeline," her contact said as she began to eat the French fries from the plate. "Your target, the White Witch, is out of town and won't return until the day after tomorrow."

"Do you know why?"

"No, we don't; all we know is that she took off for Germany yesterday and is not due back until the day after tomorrow," she said as she moved from the fries to the burger taking a big bite then sat down on the sofa.

"Yes, that does present a problem but it could work for me as well. While you're enjoying my burger, you can answer a few questions for me starting with where can I get a good fish dinner?" Pam said smiling slyly at her contact.

Vietnamese / Chines e Border

Wendy sat a few yards away from the group of men whom she was leading on this field operation and stripped her Smith and Wesson M&P in 40 caliber. She was going through the plan and still couldn't figure out why Wilhelm wanted a remote border post shot up and a few girls rescued. It just didn't make sense to her. The girls would just be rounded up again and resold. He knew this and never gave a fuck before. So what's the interest in this slaver and this group of girls? With instructions to kill a particular man and the Chinese soldiers at the crossing, she wondered, "What does Wilhelm have in mind?" She should be back in Bulgaria supporting *that* operation. "That crazy bitch doesn't mess around; she will blow up a building to get one person. Not to mention, the agent he sent has no field or any other experience, to speak of, to kill the bitch. He must be out of his fucking mind," she thought. She put the reassembled pistol in her shoulder holster, stood up, picked up her scoped semi-automatic sniper rifle chambered in 300 short magnum, and walked towards the men.

"You don't fire until I do. Then make sure all of the border guards are killed. And for Christ sake, don't shoot any of the girls! Understood!" The five men nodded signaling that they did. She turned and walked into the darkness of the jungle with the men close behind. Wendy and five mercenaries crawled out to the edge of the jungle to where they could see the border guard shack. She looked through her binoculars, pressed the button for heat sensing, and scanned the area.

Immediately, she picked up two men standing outside of the shack. She did a grid-search until she located the last four—two were in bed with women, she assumed; the other two were asleep in their bunks. She retreated back into the jungle about 20 meters before stopping. Then she whispered to them their final instructions, and the men moved out to their assigned places. Wendy setup where she had a clear shot at the guardhouse. If the Intel was reliable, there would be four men escorting the girls. That totaled ten armed men all together. Her mission was to take out the leader of the group, escort the girls, and allow the girls to escape.

It would be light soon and the traffickers should be arriving. The exchange is to take place at day break. Wendy scanned the area checking to make sure her men were in place. Each man lay quietly waiting; they were professionals. She liked working with professionals. They didn't mind the killing: the money was more important. As long as they were paid, they were reliable. And not only were they being paid *well*, they could keep any money that was found; but the girls were off limits. This was Wendy's add-on to the orders; these filthy killers wouldn't enjoy these children whose average age was 13 years old. How and why a person sold people was beyond her, but she sure didn't mind killing them when she had the chance.

Wendy heard faint voices and knew it was them. She took her rifle off of safe as she shouldered the weapon. She watched the line of girls and four guards walk by and head for the border. The girls were quiet with their heads down as they passed by. She waited until four of the Chinese guards were in view before she squeezed the trigger. The head of the lead trafficker exploded sending brains and bits of skull onto the two guards standing in front of him. Then her team opened up. Despite the noise and confusion, the shots were well aimed and not one girl was hit even though they were scrambling around holding their heads and screaming.

Wendy stood up, put her rifle across her back, drew her pistol, and walked over to the men gathered in front of the guard shack. As she passed each bandit, she put a bullet into his head even though they were already dead.

"Did you get the money?" she asked casually.

"Yes," one of the men answered and held up the canvas bag containing $150,000.

"Good, then our business is concluded here." At that moment, one of the men walked up with one of the girls who had been hiding in the guards' sleeping quarters.

"Look what I found; I think I'll keep her," he said with a smile. Wendy raised her pistol and pulled the trigger three times. The man's body jerked violently backwards as the hollow point bullets tore into his body.

"What part of no girls was unclear," she said to the remaining four men. "Anybody have a problem with *this*?" The men shook their heads no and took a step back. "Good, now take him *or not*. But I suggest we get out of here." One of the men picked up the dead man's rifle, pistol, and ammo, went through his pockets, and then dragged him into the jungle. When he returned a moment later, the four men said their goodbyes and disappeared into the jungle.

Wendy told the girls that they were free and to return home. She stood a moment watching them huddled together slowly meandering up the road. Then she too headed into the jungle. She had two hours to reach her extraction point. After the helicopter picked her up, the crew chief handed her a sealed envelope. She opened it, read the message, and then said under her breath, "*Fucking* Frank."

South Africa

Talaus sat at the workbench in his armory carefully measuring out grams of gun powder onto a digital scale. After taking the powder and pouring it into the rifle casing, he began to set a 338 caliber bullet, when Theresa interrupted.

"You have a half dozen presses in this room to do that for you yet you insist on doing it by hand. Your *goon* told me you were down here. You know I don't think he likes me very much," she said in a low sexy voice he could barely hear. He continued pulling the lever on the old press setting the bullet. Then he placed it into a wooden box with the others before looking up.

His eyes were greeted by the most beautiful woman he had ever known and one of the best killers in the business. Her five-foot-ten-inch,160-pound frame glided towards him as her three-inch heels echoed softly on the tile floor with every step her long legs took. Her coco-complexion was glowing. As he gazed at her face, he saw that pleasant but faraway look complete with a smile and framed with shoulder length brown hair. Her tan leather pants tapered at the ankle showed off the curves of her thighs and ass. Her yellow blouse hung loose and low allowing those magnificent breasts to sway and bounce with each step. When she reached him, she leaned over and kissed him lightly on the cheek. Then she picked up one of the finished cartridges and examined it. He watched her, looking into her eyes—those pretty hazel eyes, those dead eyes. He searched for some sign that she had a soul; he was hoping maybe this time he would see it. He knew it was a silly pursuit—a stupid dream. But of all that he had taught her, he couldn't teach her compassion and without that she could never have a soul.

"What's so special about this round?" she said breaking his thought.

"It's my new explosive round; it's still experimental, but I think it will work." He peered through the opening in her blouse as she leaned on the bench studying the bullets. Catching a glimpse of her areola made him aware of the stirrings going on in his loins. "Did you have any trouble removing your targets?"

"No, not at all, the first one was easy, a simple car accident. The second one, well, let me tell you. He liked kinky sex. Well, his version of kinky sex was pretty tame so I decided to introduce him to the wild side. Anyway, long story short, after I made him come twice, I cut his throat. So there, both targets down and a little fun in the process. Where's Taylor? I looked for her in the house and hoped she'd be down here with you."

"She's out riding. It's good your back. We have an important job, and I need your talents on this one."

"Oh, what's the job?"

"Libertaire." Theresa straightened up, and a serious look came over her face. Then she smiled.

"So we're finally getting a crack at him, are we?"

"Yes, and this won't be a walk in the park. Remember Oscar."

"You mean this guy took out Oscar?"

"Yes, the same, and we don't want to end up like him, do we?" She shook her head in response; then she walked around the bench and sat on his lap.

"I want to fuck; I want your cock in every hole I have. So enough talk, let's fuck," she whispered in his ear.

"I'll meet you in the bedroom as soon I finish this."

"Okay, but if Taylor gets there before you do, I'm going to start without you," she said then kissed him deeply with their tongues intertwining.

She stood up and walked towards the door with him watching her ass sway causing him to get hard. He reached down and rubbed his cock a few times then went back to filling his cartridges.

Talaus reached the master bedroom after checking Taylor's and Theresa's bedrooms. He found them fondling in his custom king size bed. He undressed and sat in a chair at the foot of the bed and began to watch. He knew what he was about to witness was pure lust between two women. He watched as they kissed, licked, and sucked their way across each other's body. Taylor stopped suddenly, got out of bed, and returned with two dildos. She crawled back into bed and handed one to Theresa.

He sat there with his manhood at full attention and watched as they worked the wet dildos in and out of every orifice. After they made each other orgasm multiple times, they separated. And as Theresa lay there lightly rubbing her clit, Taylor beckoned him to bed. He crawled between them lying on his back, taking turns kissing each woman, and tasting their private juices. The two women started kissing down his body; and when they reached his cock, Taylor started to lick its length while Theresa did the same to his balls.

He arranged the women into the sixty-nine position with Theresa on top. He entered her and steadily stroked her as Taylor's tongue flickered back and forth over her clit. He held onto her hips pumping hard and deep until she stiffened and shook letting out a scream between Taylor's spread legs. She rolled off breathing hard with hair matted from the sweat and a smile on her face as she watched Talaus position himself to enter Taylor. She spread her knees and rolled them towards her chest, reached between them, and guided him into her ass. He slowly pushed until he had sunk his full length into her. She hooked her legs around his thighs urging him on, and he began to pump her in earnest. He kept this pace up until his body started to spasm; his face contorted, and then he stiffened emptying into her.

He lay there on top of her lightly kissing her until he regained his breath. Then he got up and took a shower. When he finished, he put on a robe and walked barefoot towards the communication room.

Ophiuchus: Day Three

Chapter Twenty

Verna, Bulgaria

Pam was sure her plan would work, but she knew her new partners weren't at all crazy about it. As they drove to the club, Pam looked at the street hustlers; both sexes were selling themselves or being sold. Her two companions pointed out places of interests such as the headquarters of the major gangs. They also pointed out the major buy/sell houses of women and children for the international sex slave trade and the number two gun runner who was the White Witch's main competition.

Pam sat in the backseat taking it all in as she smoothed out her stockings. She was thinking about how she could lure then trap the White Witch's head of security. If the Intel was good, she had dressed the part. Dressed in a minidress, seamed stockings, garter belt and four-inch fuck-me heels as she liked to call them with blond hair, black eyes, and makeup, she would catch her eye. She felt around in her black velvet purse and touched the vial. If she could entice her to bed, maybe just maybe she could get a look inside that fortress. The BMW pulled up and parked a half block away from the club; the agent on the front passenger side handed her a pair of binoculars.

"The woman dressed in the white pants suit, red hair, black pumps talking to the woman in the red miniskirt, that's your mark. She doesn't look the part, does she?"

"I didn't know what to look for but I was expecting a more butch-looking chick, I'll admit," Pam said.

"Yes, she looks quite feminine. But that, my dear, is one of the most feared women in Europe; and she protects her boss like a rabid bulldog.

Lucky for you, her appetite for pretty young things like you is the chink in her armor; and with that lavender minidress, you can't lose."

"She's going to want to eat you up, girl," the driver said laughing as she looked at her in the rearview mirror.

"Shall we get this show on the road?" Pam countered. The three female agents got out of the car, gave each other one last look over, and walked towards the club. They pushed through the crowd and made their way to the red velvet rope that was restraining the crowd. One of the agents spoke to the guard, and he waved them through giving them a big smile as they passed.

"What did you say to him?" Pam asked.

"Simple, I told him I would suck his cock after work. Don't worry; I promise him that every time I come here," she said and winked. As they approached the main room, Pam could feel the music; and when they entered, a resonating wall of thumping music greeted her.

The club was spectacular. The decor, the seating, the people, all looked like they belonged together. She noticed a dozen go-go dancers, some wearing only a G-string. As she looked closer at the men sitting at the tables, she realized they were really women in drag. In fact, the only true men were the bouncers outside and the ones standing at the end of the bar which spanned the length of the room and accommodated eight bartenders working feverishly behind it. They found a table and ordered a drink. Pam scanned the room for the security chief.

"If you want to get noticed, we should dance and the sexier the better," her escort said then grabbed her hand.

Cyprus

Wilhelm sat in the rear room of the safe house going over the latest reports from his teams. Team Two was on schedule but Team One was behind. He expected that since they are down one. He picked up the message that he had received from Rodney who informed Frank was to be apprehended or terminated. He couldn't believe it. What could Frank have done to warrant such an order? He also wondered if he was able to give the order to kill Frank. Of all of his faults, none rose to the level that would cause for this action to be sanctioned.

He sat there and stared at the message for a moment. Then he checked his watch and headed for the living room. Captain America was sitting at his consul comprised of four flat computer screens that monitored the security cameras. George was cleaning his rifle with his pistol disassembled on the table in front of him.

"George! Get weapons for the Captain and me … and hurry up … and put that back together!" he said as he pointed to the table.

"Captain, I want you to download everything. But leave the computers on and deploy the inflatables." Then he left the room. When he returned, he had a briefcase.

"Ready?"

"Yes!" they responded.

"Let's go!" He led them across the street from the house.

"What's going on, boss?" George asked in a hushed voice as he looked around checking the area.

"We're going to have company in a few minutes, and this is the best place to watch the festivities," he replied as he placed an earphone in his left ear. George turned to Captain America and told him to prepare for action and to find a good place to provide cover fire. Wilhelm looked at his watch again; fifteen minutes had passed. "They should be here anytime now," he thought. A minute later, a dark-colored van drove slowly down the street and stopped just shy of the front of the safe house.

"Nobody fire until I say so," Wilhelm ordered. The men stood silently with weapons at the ready except for Wilhelm who turned on his mp3 player, and *Street Life* by the *Crusaders* started to play softly in his ear. Six men poured out of the van and headed for the front door at full speed. They breached the door and entered. They were in and out in sixty seconds and back in the van. At that precise moment, four men stepped out of the darkness—two from either side of the house—and opened fire. Their suppressed submachine guns aimed at the van. In less than fifteen seconds, they had sprayed the van completely even flatting the tires. Then one of the masked men opened the side door, stepped in, and shot all seven men in the head.

A flatbed tow truck pulled up, and the driver jumped out and hooked up the van. The gun men pulled a dark colored tarp over the van and tied it down. The wench began to whine, and the van was loaded unto the flatbed. The driver got in and drove away slowly while the shooting team poured an absorbent on the blood that had dripped out of the van. They swept up the glass and debris, bagged it, got into a waiting car, and drove away slowly as if nothing had ever happened all in less than twenty minutes.

"Alright, let's go! I think we've worn out our welcome here," Wilhelm said as they started across the street.

"Where to, boss?" George asked.

"Istanbul! To the office," Wilhelm replied.

"How did you know we'd have company tonight?" Captain America asked as they entered the house.

"I'll tell you on the flight. Make sure you render everything we leave behind unusable. Be ready to move in three minutes."

Hamburg, Germany

Susan sat at her desk in the office above the childcare center which was the front for the CIA signaling station that she is in charge of. In front of her, sitting nonchalantly with legs crossed and drinking coffee was Frank. "He sure isn't acting like a hunted man; maybe he doesn't know yet," she thought.

"You've heard about the killing of Kevin in Paris by now." Susan nodded her head and leaned back in her chair. Frank took another sip and watched her over the rim of the cup then continued, "Have you any news? ...anything to report concerning the operation?"

"No, everything is on schedule as far as I can tell. I sent you this morning's report an hour ago, did you receive it?"

"Yes, it was just a question, nothing to worry about. I only stopped by to say hi and have a cup of coffee," he said as he placed the cup on the desk and got up. "I have a few more stops to make, so I'll be on my way." He picked up his coat, laid it across his left arm, put on his hat, and left the office. He got into a waiting car, and it drove away. Susan opened her laptop and began to type.

"Frank just in office at 10:23 a.m. this time.

Left 11:13 a. m. to destination unknown at this time.

Waiting for instructions."

She encoded it and sent it to Langley. Then she repeated the message minus the last sentence and sent it to Wilhelm. Frank's visit troubled her the rest of the day, so she took off early and picked up her daughter. She went straight to her apartment making none of the usual stops for gas or groceries. Once home, she quietly checked the security measures she had in place, all the while careful not to alarm her daughter.

Her neighbor Nancy and daughter stopped by. The women had some wine and cheese and talked while their daughters did their homework and gossiped about school. When they left, the two had dinner and watched a movie. She tucked her daughter in bed, kissed her goodnight, turned out the light, and went back to the living room. She turned on the late news, filled a glass pipe, lit it, took a deep pull, held it; and when she exhaled, she could feel the effects of the marijuana and started to relax.

She was in the middle of paper work when she looked up to check the monitor that focused on the little enclave directly under her side window. It was a blind spot from the street by the way it was situated, and the trees hid it from view. She methodically checked each camera. The next one monitored the view directly in front of her door. Then she checked the ones for the apartment entrance way and finally the street views. Something caught her eye. A young man standing in front of the building was talking to a young woman and smoking a cigarette. She watched the pair for a moment. "Something was out of place," she thought. She zoomed in on the two and noticed they were lightly clothed for Hamburg in the winter at night, and they didn't act or look cold. The young woman walked away in the direction of the blind spot when two men joined him.

The three men headed towards her building; Susan watched until they approached the elevator. At that point, they would be out of camera view until they reached her hallway. Even if they proceeded down the hallway, she might be overreacting, she thought. Nevertheless, she locked her daughter's bedroom door, readied her 9 mm pistol, placed it on the coffee table in front of her, and stared at the monitor. When the three men came back into view, she knew her hunch was right.

Susan slid the coffee table into position and turned off all of the lights except the lamp by the side window. She hid behind the right side of the couch and pressed the alert button on her cellphone to call in the reaction team. She knew it would take the team three minutes to get to her, so she had to keep her daughter and herself alive until then. She breathed deeply to calm herself and control the adrenaline rush that was suppressing her fear. "*If you are afraid to die, you will die,*" she heard her husband's voice say to her. She smiled and a calmness came over her; she was ready.

The three men stopped two doors down the hall from hers. She hoped Nancy won't open her door. They took out their pistols, screwed on silencers, and approached the door in a triangular formation—one man on either side of the hallway, the third a few steps behind in the middle. The men positioned themselves at her door; and the middle man readied his pistol, looked at his companions, and fired at the door locks. In an instant, they rushed into the apartment, one behind the other firing their pistols. The first intruder burst through the door and tripped over the coffee table. Susan fired and hit the second intruder in the chest and stomach. She crawled quickly to the other side of the couch avoiding the return fire that ripped through the couch like a paper target. She popped up and fired six more shots hitting the man who had tripped over the coffee table; he cried out then fell silent.

Susan and the third intruder exchanged fire as they jockeyed about the room until they heard the heart sinking sound of their pistols locking back signaling no more ammunition. Her opponent immediately dropped his gun and drew his knife and headed straight for her with his eight-inch gleaming blade leading the way. Susan lowered her stance into a crouch spreading her legs and shifting her weight onto her rear foot with hands at the ready. He attacked with a slashing movement completing a figure eight before stabbing forward. Susan waited for it then parried the thrust and countered with a back fist to his face smashing his nose.

"Ugh!" the man gasped as his head snapped back from the blow. He reversed his swing coming back across her stomach.

Susan jumped back tripping over a chair and getting cut in the process. Her attacker pounced; she met his attack with a knee to his chest causing him to spinoff to her left. Instantly, she was on her feet moving towards him no longer on the defensive and attacked. He scrambled to his feet in time to block her first punch but the second one found its mark; his newly broken nose caused his eyes to water. She pressed her attack connecting with a front kick to his chin sending him reeling backwards until hitting the wall which stopped him from falling. She continued forward blocking his two punches and striking him in the throat with a leopard's fist. When he grabbed his throat, she attacked his head with her elbows. He countered with an uppercut and right hook. She blocked his attack grabbed him and kneed him in the groin. At that moment, she heard footsteps approaching fast down the hall; she hoped it was the reaction team. He heard it also and took the opportunity to break free from her grasp and jumped through the window.

The five-man team entered the room.

"He jumped!" she yelled looking out the window and pointing. By the time two of the men reached the window and looked out, he was gone. But Susan had kept her eye on him and noticed that same woman appeared and helped him.

"We have to move. Where's your daughter?" one of the men asked.

"In her room; it's locked," she said as she pointed to the room.

"Are you hurt?"

"No, just a scratch." At that moment, she heard her daughter's room door being kicked in.

"Where is your laptop?" he asked.

"Somewhere over there, I think.   Are they dead?"

"Yes."

"Good!" Then they heard the police sirens.

"We have to go!" The team hurried Susan and her daughter out of the apartment and past all of her neighbors who were standing and watching. As she passed Nancy, she smiled and said,

"I'll be in touch."   Then they were gone.

As they rode towards the village of Bitburg, Susan held her daughter tightly stroking her hair and thinking. "That bastard tried to kill me and my baby. Wilhelm and Wendy were right about the Toad. Well, he won't get away with this, I promise you."

Ophiuchus: Day Four

Chapter Twenty-One

The Farm

Linda and Afra were sitting in the sunroom talking when Colleen walked in with one of the security personnel.

"Glad to see you're up, Linda; the doctor tells me your recovery is coming along just fine. He suggested to me that you get some air, and walk around a bit; this, young lady, will be your escort." Colleen left the room without saying another word leaving the guard behind and Afra looking a little bewildered.

"If I thought she didn't like me before, it's settled now, don't you think?" Linda said.

"I'm afraid you might be right. If you'll excuse me for a moment ... ." Afra left the room leaving Linda alone with her guard. "Why the guard, Colleen?" she asked when she caught up with her in the kitchen.

"Have you forgotten who she works for? Aren't you the least bit curious as to why somebody wants her dead? Now I want you to keep doing exactly what you've been doing and leave everything to me; besides, you're close to term and we don't want any complications, do we?" Afra nodded in agreement and went back to the sunroom; she knew Colleen was right. When she returned, Linda and the guard were in their same places, the guard staring at her.

"Let's go for a walk, shall we?" she said with a smile.

"Yes, let's," Linda replied and stood up.

Syria

Randy paced across the room thinking. He had found the two women,

289

but the Pol was nowhere to be found. He was worried that his nemesis had left the area. And maybe, he wouldn't get his chance to even the score.

He had a lot of payback, and he wanted the chance to repay it.

Vanessa sat on the beach under the cabana eyeing the little girl playing in the surf with her mother. They looked happy, not a care in the world. "Why do all the really bad ones look so innocent," she thought. "Too bad though, in a few days, the kid will be an orphan and she'll be dead; and it wouldn't be a quick death." She pressed a button on her sunglasses and began recording then she spoke quietly.

"Are you receiving this transmission? Because this is such a touching scene, I just have to share it."

"Yes, we are receiving you, Tiamat; but that gorgeous man to her right has my attention," Ishtar replied.

"Have you tagged the girl?" Enki said interrupting the conversation.

"No."

"I need her tagged. Ishtar is ready and waiting for your signal, so get on with it."

She acknowledged, reached into her bag, and removed the small syringe that contained the nano-tracking device.

Tiamat walked towards the water where the girl was playing. She looked to her left and saw the asset who was assigned to help them. She reached up and took off her sunglasses giving him the signal. He and another man started to jog towards the target laughing and playing along the way. When the child was in place about knee deep in the water, both men began running at full speed. They timed their collision precisely as both men hit the girl causing her to spin and fall face down into the water.

Tiamat rushed to the girl's aid reaching her moments before her mother did which gave her just enough time to inject the child and hide the syringe.

"Are you alright?" Amaranta said with the excited voice of a mother. "Those bastards, didn't they see my baby playing there?" Then she turned her attention towards Tiamat. "Thank you so much. I don't know how to repay you for your help."

"It's okay; I would do that for any girl as pretty as her," she replied as she bent over and smoothed the hair from the child's face. "At least, come back to my cabana and have a drink."

"Alright, that sounds refreshing." The trio walked back to the cabana, grabbed towels, and began drying off.

Amaranta ordered a pitcher of L'orange. While they waited, the two talked about nothing special; and her daughter went back to playing with some children. The waiter brought the iced pitcher of this potent elixir and placed it on a small wooded table between them while smiling and eyeing them both hungrily as he poured the drinks.

"Abelie, your name means honeysuckle, doesn't it?" she said in Italian testing Tiamat.

"Yes, your Italian is very good. Where did you learn it?" she responded nonchalantly then took a sip of her drink. "This is really good; it's called L'orange. I love it!" she continued staying in character. They talked and drank going in and out of Italian as they downed two pitchers.

When Tiamat returned to the bungalow, Enki was waiting for her with Pazuzu; they both sported shit-eating grins.

"If you're not too drunk, tell me it all went according to plan," Enki inquired.

"Not only did it go according to plan, but I've been invited to lunch tomorrow; thank you very much. And she has at least two shadows watching her. How's that for a drunk girl?" she touted slurring some of the words.

"Good work, now take a cold shower and go to bed." He waited until she left the room before talking again. "I'm going to find out who is watching our gal. You stay close to the bungalow. I'll be back in a couple of hours and inform Ishtar." Then he went out the door.

Turkey

Ninurta walked down the street heading for the coffee shop situated across from the beach where Kubaba was lounging. As he enjoyed the sun and perfect December weather, he couldn't believe that he hadn't taken a vacation here; this place was beautiful. He sat down at a table and ordered some tea, and then he touched his sunglasses and scanned the beach in front of him looking for Kubaba. His glasses zoomed in and out focusing on the different faces then he spotted her; she was talking to the target.

He watched her and was careful to keep his sunglasses on her. He wished he had audio; but then again, he really didn't want to hear the sex talk.

"You'll have company in a few minutes," Nirgal said in his ear.

"Which direction?" he replied softly.

"Your four o'clock." Ninurta turned his head and looked around. "There, in the yellow bikini!" Ninurta focused on her.

"Oh my!" he said.

"My words exactly," Nirgal said in his ear. "Here are her stats:" he continued, "five years in the field, the usual qualifications, five feet six inches tall, and 120 lbs. soaking wet. Her specialty is counter-intelligence. So this is what your target likes."

"Yeah."

"She sure has good taste in women." Ninurta ignored his last statement; he was watching this strange women approach him. He didn't care how beautiful she was. If she gave the wrong countersign, he would killer her where she stood. He watched her as she paused at the road's edge and tied her sarong. He saw her looking for him and then spotting him. She sat at the table to his left and ordered an espresso. While she waited, she took out a notepad, then her cellphone, and placed them on the table. After the waiter brought the coffee and left, she asked Ninurta for some sugar.

He answered in German and stared at her waiting for a response. She smiled and answered in kind giving him the first part of the code. He finished the code, got up, and sat down at her table with the sugar in hand. The waiter returned to check on them and smiled at him. He asked if he needed anything, winked in approval, and left. A few minutes later, they left the café; and the pair walked nonchalantly down the street blending in with the other couples and disappearing from sight.

Ophiuchus: Day Five

Chapter Twenty-Two

Verna, Bulgaria

Pam sat across from Wendy and stared at her in disbelief. She didn't know this woman and that meant she didn't trust her. Wendy sat with her legs crossed hoping Wilhelm would reply to her message before she had to kick this young bitch's ass and fuck up his operation. She had to give it to her; for a newbie, she was sharp and stuck to protocol. It was obvious that she didn't believe nor trust her. "Good, girl," Wendy thought.

A woman walked in; Pam watched her as she handed Wendy a message.

"Thank you," Wendy said. Then she read it, handed it back to her, and said, "Show her." The woman walked over and handed it to Pam then left the room. Pam read it twice, looked at Wendy, and then re-read the message again.

"Now, Oannes, did I pronounce that right? Your boss does have a knack for creative code names," Wendy said. "What you have just read should relieve some of your mistrust, do you agree?" Pam nodded in agreement. "Good, you're still in charge of this op, understood? This is your mission. I'm here to kill the White Bitch only if you fail to do so or you're killed in the process. Personally, I think you can handle it. If you can't, you should be killed and I should be with my own people, not hanging out with lesbians. But orders are orders. So forget I'm here and do what you do. I'll step in," she paused. "Well, you won't know when because you'll be dead," she said sarcastically.

Before Pam could respond, her counterpart walked in.

295

"The witch is back," the woman said. "Get dressed; it's time she sees you in the flesh." Pam stood up, looked at Wendy who was still sitting, and said,

"You should be with your people; you're wasting your time hanging around here; I'm sure your services won't be needed," she said with equal sarcasm. Then she left the room.

Wendy watched her closely as she said this saying nothing but thinking. "This is one tough bitch to be so young; he sure knows how to pick'em," she thought as she watched her leave.

Pam selected a pair of skinny jeans, a light pink blouse, black four-inch heels, and a denim waistcoat. She put on her makeup, fixed her hair, took one final look in the full length mirror, and said softly,

"Alright, Oannes, let's go to work." She checked her twenty-five caliber pistol and headed for the car. As they rode along, Oannes sat in the backseat and silently steamed. "How could he send that woman? Didn't he think I could pull this off? And to tell me that she is just a backup...Fuck him," she thought.

The driver looked in the rearview mirror and saw the intense expression on Oannes' face. Whatever was in that message sure got under her skin. She hoped it wouldn't throw Pam off her game.

"We'll be in the area soon, you alright?" she asked.

"Yes, just a change in orders; I'm fine," Oannes lied. The car pulled up to a café and stopped.

"This is where you get out," the driver said without turning around. "Your target has coffee here every day about this time."

"Isn't that a little dangerous for her?" Oannes asked.

"Not at all, she owns the place and there will be guards all around. She'll be here in fifteen minutes. So out you go and good luck."

Oannes got out, watched the car pull away, and felt the feeling of loneliness although she knew they would be close by. She took a seat outside in the back away from the street, ordered a cappuccino, and waited. She spurned several advances from both men and women and was in the middle of getting rid of the latest would-be-suitor when a Rolls Royce pulled up and out stepped the White Witch. She looked better than her photo. Pam focused on her security chief who was talking to her as they walked by.

Neither one of them looked at her as they passed and entered the café. She sat and waited sipping her cappuccino. That was all she could do until one of them made contact. She hoped she wouldn't have long to wait. A waiter approached her and told her that Ms. Zielinski would like a moment of her time. She got up and followed him to the back to the private table where the White Witch and her security chief were seated.

Bitburg, Germany

Susan stood up when Dieter came into the room. She was glad to see him; her big smile and out-stretched arms indicated that sentiment.

"Dieter, it's good to see you," she said when they hugged.

"I came as soon as I heard," he replied when they separated. "Can we talk here?" he asked as he looked around the room.

"Yes, the guards are only a pre-caution," she said as they sat down on the couch. "Did you find out anything?" she asked as her eyes relayed a message of urgency. He nodded in answer. "Well, do tell," she said as she reached out and touched his knee. "Who are they and why target me?"

297

"They are members of an organization simply known as Talaus; the word is he is a killer who turned his business into a global enterprise. Nobody knows how he got his start or where he hangs his hat. What they do know is that he hires and recruits the best killers he can find."

"Did you find the man and the woman who helped him get away?"

"Yes, they are holed up in an apartment in Hamburg; the doctor who patched him is a friend of mine. He told me you did a real number on him, lots of broken shit. The leg, of course, was broken by the landing but everything else is all yours." He flashed a big gin and settled back into the couch. "So what's our next move?" Susan looked past him in thought. Then she re-focused, took a deep breath, let it out, and cocked her head a little to the left.

"I want to do this personally, Dieter. Will you help me?"

"That will be a pleasure, fräulein," he replied as he reached out and held her hand.

Istanbul

Wilhelm sat behind the handmade Cyprus wood desk that dominated the office at his import/export company. He was looking over some papers and listening to a new R&B/Soul songstress. The window was open, and the sounds of the traffic going by—horns honking—and the aroma of street food wafting through the window went well with the music. He was considering hiring her for the holiday party when George stuck his head in and broke the mood.

"What is it?"

"You have a visitor; he's Chinese," he said with a serious face.

"Send him in, George," Wilhelm told him as he adjusted himself and checked the pistol he kept under his desk.

The man entered the room and gave him a quick bow before he began to speak.

"I am here to deliver a message to you of a personal matter, Mr. Libertaire." Wilhelm waved George off and gestured to the man to sit down. He eyed him cautiously. He knew he was with Chinese Intelligence and wondered what they wanted from him.

"What can I do for you?" he said in Mandarin. The man reached into his inside suit coat pocket and produced an envelope. He stood up and handed it to him and sat down again.

"This is a request from my superior; he wishes to meet with you on a matter which he feels will be of great interest to you and your agency. The details are in the envelope. If you find that this information is of value, please follow the instructions." Then he stood up, bowed, and left the office having to walk around George who was standing just outside the office door.

"Have the Captain check this," he said as he washed his hands. George put on a rubber glove and picked up the envelope. In a few minutes, George returned.

"It checked out, boss," he said as he placed the envelope on the desk. Wilhelm opened the envelope and read the content then looked at George and said,

"Looks like we're going to Egypt, Alexandra to be exact."

"When?"

"Tomorrow."

"I'll make the arrangements," George answered and left the office. Wilhelm turned the CD back on and thought about what was in the message. He trusted its source, and he knew the mark that was affixed to it. The person that sent it was an old enemy/friend. They had risen through the ranks of their perspective agencies together and had opposed each other many times. Some would say he was a worthy opponent but Wilhelm referred to him as a man he would love to kill. But he was an honorable man, and he wouldn't have sent a message requesting a meeting in territory that favored Wilhelm.

George knocked once and entered.

"You have another visitor, sir," he said standing their looking puzzled.

"Are you going to tell me who it is or do I have to guess?" Wilhelm said as he put the message in his desk drawer.

"It's Viviana, sir."

"What the hell does she want?"

"'A moment of your time,' she says."

"Oh, *does* she. Well, let's not keep the lady waiting then. Send her in, George." Viviana sashayed into the office and stopped in front of his desk with hand on hip.

"Nice music," she said flashing a sexy smile. Wilhelm leaned back in his chair and took in the sight standing in front of him. He looked her up and down knowing that this made her uneasy. He admired her choker—a tear drop pearl with a diamond inserted into its center. She wore a light wool dress made of crepe in taupe that ended four inches above her knees; and her perfume, he knew it well; it was Somali Rose. All of this beauty was carried on a five-foot-ten-inch, one-hundred-forty-pound frame sporting perfect thirty-six D-cup tits leading the way.

He looked at her legs and the way the material wrapped itself around her thighs; he wondered if her stockings were held up by garters or if they clung lovingly to those thighs without any help. Next he looked at her eyes; her makeup was perfect as he expected. Her jet black hair framing her face made her brown complexion all the more stunning.

"Are you going to ask me to sit down or shall I just stand here and look beautiful?" she said.

"Please, by all means, sit your pretty ass down," he said with a grin. "What can I do for you, Viv?" Viviana waited until she had settled into one of the overstuffed chairs to the left of his desk before answering.

"I was told of a mysterious killing of some Chinese border guards and several traffickers at a remote crossing in Vietnam a few days ago."

"And that means what to me?"

"The way it was carried out reminded me of Wendy." Just then, George knocked and entered carrying a drink for her and tea for him. Wilhelm waited until he had left before talking.

"Why do you think Wendy or I had anything to do with it?"

"For one reason, there were no girls found at the scene; and a few days later it was rumored that several nearby villages came into some money. Second, Derek Minh is in town with his latest plaything; and boy, is he mad."

"Oh, what has made him that way?" Wilhelm said now interested in what she was saying. It seems this was not an information-seeking visit but the opposite.

"It seems," she started. Then she stopped and took a sip of her drink. "Mmmm Hendricks, you remembered. Anyway, as I was saying, it seems that a shipment of girls was destined for the Witch of Bulgaria." She paused and eyed Wilhelm curiously looking for the slightest reaction. She was indeed fishing for information and hoped he would add to what she knew.

"Again, what does this have to do with me, Viviana? I don't deal in flesh. Now if you have any information I might be interested in, please continue." Wilhelm rose from his chair and walked around his desk stopping at the small table near the window and picked up a cedar box. He continued across the room and picked up a decorated tin box then headed towards her. He sat down in the chair next to hers and placed the boxes on the low wooden table in front of them.

"Let's enjoy a smoke, shall we? It has been awhile since we last did so," he said as he opened the two boxes. "What's your pleasure hashish or Pakistani Ryder?"

"A little of both, I think, and a refill if you please," she replied as she crossed her legs exposing the top of her stockings, raised her glass, and swirled the ice. Wilhelm called George and told him to bring her a refill and him a pot of tea. Then he filled a tall hand-blown water pipe with a mixture from both boxes; after her drink had arrived, he lit it for her. He waited for her to exhale before asking her to continue. "As I was saying, he's in town; and someone, if not you, has a bone to pick with him. This is not the first shipment of girls he's lost this year, and the Witch's people are thinking about another supplier. And you know what that means; he'll be dead very soon."

Wilhelm drank his tea as he watched her slowly pull on the water pipe filling her lungs with vapors from the sweet sticky mixture. He watched as she relaxed and waited until that familiar look came over her face.

"Why would his people kill him over a lost shipment of girls? That makes no sense. He's much more valuable to them than just running girls."

"You would be correct if that was all he did for them; it seems he's been making financial deals of his own and not cutting them in on it. This latest blunder is the last straw, and they want him dead." Then she took another pull and sat back.

"Where did you say he was staying?"

"I didn't."

"What do you want, Viv?" he asked her as he got up to get a cigar; it was deal time and Viviana could be demanding even when she was high. "What do you need from me, Viv?" he repeated.

"There's a businessman in New York that I need some information on. I was hoping that you could help in this department. In return, I'll provide you with all the information I have on Derek."

"What's the name of your target?" He had her write it down and sent it to Captain America. While they waited, he caught up on what she had been doing since going private. When the information she wanted arrived, he looked it over then said, "Your turn." For the next hour, Viviana laid it all out. He handed her the packet and walked her to the door. "We have to do this again sometime, Viv, but not too soon," he said as she left the office. She smiled over her shoulder and walked down the stairs to the street. (Watching her walk in those high heels, you would never have guessed that she had drunk three gin and tonics and smoked a good amount of hash and bud in the last hour and a half.) She never wobbled.

"George, we have some planning to do," he said to him after she had left.

"What are we planning, sir?"

"We're going to snatch Derek Minh and cause a lot of people heartburn and quite a few sleepless nights," he said. He and George worked on the plan for an hour before he had to stop and head for the club. He called Tommy to his office and quickly explained what was worked out already and what needed to be done. Then he and George checked their weapons, knives and pistols and George's brass knuckles; he liked using them in close battle. Wilhelm preferred his Sykes blade; the eight-inch double-edged knife was his favorite close battle weapon. Satisfied, the pair walked down the steps and out the front door, turned left, and started the short three-block walk to the club. Wilhelm loved to walk; he didn't have that luxury all the time but here he often walked despite the crowds. People were hurrying to and from whatever business they were conducting. The mixture of men and women who were dressed in suits, miniskirts, traditional dress, and something in between represented modern Turkey. He listened to the street sounds—a blend of voices, cars, and trucks each singing a tune distinctive to the attentive ear.

Walking drove George crazy although he had learned to hide it better, but Wilhelm knew it still did. He never learned to feel his way through the city; but out in the bush and desert, he had no problem. This environment made him very uneasy.

"Too many variables," he would say. So as usual, he was stiff trying to look relaxed yet eyeing everyone as if they were a threat. They went inside the building passing under a sign that read *International Chess Club* written in English and Turkish.

Inside were tables for drinking coffee and tea and tables inlaid with chessboards for various games to be played. Of the sixteen dedicated game tables, twelve were for six kinds of chess and two each for dominos and backgammon.

On the other side of the large open first floor was a tea and coffee bar where a jukebox was located and the young men and women hung out. As they passed them, Wilhelm stopped at the bar and told the woman behind it to bring him a pot of his special tea blend. He lingered for a moment watching several couples do a two-step that he taught them to the sounds of Marvin Gaye. Then he and George disappeared into the private area in the back separated by long beads with a motif depicting a black eagle.

The private room is large, 20 by 30 feet in size. To the left as you enter is a rug covered area—a space he uses for those guests who prefer the traditional way to talk business. In front of that space is a set of four conference chairs made from hand-tooled tanned leather arranged around a round sandalwood table. On the right side center is an eighteenth-century antique desk. Couches and chairs line the wall in front of it. On the walls hang tapestries depicting ancient battles and the hunt which always includes horses, dogs, and falcons. The center area is left open, free from obstruction leaving a clear field of fire to the entranceway.

The young woman brought in the tea, poured him a glass, and asked if they had eaten lunch yet. He told her,

"No," and she left the room without another word.

"That woman gives me the creeps. Why do you keep her around?" George said as he watched her leave.

"Ever since she threw that knife at you, you haven't liked her much," Wilhelm chuckled. "Maybe if you stop looking at her as if she's crazy, she would warm up to you."

"No thanks, boss; I just wondered why you pay her so much to do so little and she never talks except to you. I tell you she gives me the creeps, and it doesn't have anything to do with the knife; I've had knives thrown at me before."

Wilhelm sat back in his hand-studded leather desk chair and smirked, crossed his legs, and said,

"I need you to cover the snatch tonight and have them take him to the northern safe house and keep him under wraps for a few days. After we get back from Egypt, I'll have a talk with him and find out what our friend

305

has done to warrant a hit that even mommy can't stop." Before he could answer, the woman returned with a tray of lamb kabobs, fruit, and yogurt; she set it on the table and left.

Wilhelm strolled over to the table and inspected the food; he called the woman back and asked for his custom brand of hot sauce. Then he sat down to eat while George changed his sitting position so that he could cover his boss better. Halfway through his lunch, his private telephone line began to ring. He looked at the number and saw it was Susan's daughter. He touched his earpiece and said,

"Hello," in their special language. Wilhelm and she had created a special pig Latin that was comprised of words and sounds that he and she only understood. They tried to teach it to Susan once but to no avail; she just couldn't speak it without laughing thus never learning it.

"How are you, sweetie? Done much skiing yet?" he asked her in their language.

"No, but Mommy wants me to tell you something."

"Okay, go ahead," he said. He sat with legs crossed listening to what she was telling him; he knew her mother was sitting their monitoring. When she finished, he told her to get some slope time and her mother good hunting. Then hung up. He sat back in his chair and thought, "So I may get the chance after all to kill a toad. The way that hit went down sure smells of Frank." It's been seven years since Nicaragua, and now it seems he would finally get his chance to repay Frank.

The young lady returned, stood in front of the table with her hands clasped in front of her, and waited. She cut her eyes at George, and he taped the grip of his pistol that he wore in a cross draw configuration. It took a moment for Wilhelm to notice her; he was deep in thought.

"Yes."

"There is a man here who wishes to speak to you about some brass."

"Okay, you may send him in," he said to her as he rose from the table and headed back to his desk. The woman gathered the dishes on a tray and headed out of the room with George a few steps behind.

George patted down the man and escorted him to Wilhelm's desk. Then he stood behind the man off to the man's left. The man was in his mid-forties, five feet five inches tall, thinning gray hair, and dressed in a not-so-new gray suit. He nervously looked over his shoulder at George, took out a handkerchief, and wiped his upper lip.

"That will be all, George," Wilhelm said. George backed off a little but just a little. The man was one of Wilhelm's assets, one of his better informants. "So what do you have for me?"

"There is a new player in town, and word on the street says they are gunning for you," the man half whispered then looked back at George before continuing. "They are also in the south near the sea looking for some of your people; I mean American agents," he stammered.

"Do you know who they work for?"

"No, they appear to be private contractors." Wilhelm pulled open the top draw of his desk, took out an envelope of money, and handed it to the man. The asset took it and counted it fast then looked back at Wilhelm wide-eyed. "This is more than usual," he said surprised and worried.

"You have done a good job; this is your reward."

"Thank you," the man replied. "What do you want me to do about the strangers?"

"Get some pictures of them for me and keep a close eye on them and, of course, keep me informed of their every movement."

"Yes, sir. I will do whatever you say," the man said as he stood up and placed the envelope in his coat pocket. Wilhelm stood, shook his hand; and George walked him out. Wilhelm thought about the information he just received. His first thoughts were that Frank was behind this. If he was, what group did he hire to kill him?

Wilhelm waited for George to return then told him of his change of plans concerning Derek. He decided to head back to the office. It would be dusk in a half hour. It wouldn't be wise to be caught out after dark especially when a new enemy was around—one he didn't know anything about, mainly their numbers and capabilities. George sent two of the young men who hung out at the jukebox to check the street. They returned and reported that no new or unfamiliar faces were seen; then George rechecked. When he was satisfied, he informed Wilhelm; and they set off for the office.

The first two blocks were intense. Both of them were on high alert; their eyes darted through the crowd as they passed the same people they had seen coming in. The faces were comforting; many of them greeted them as they passed. Then George looked behind him and caught sight of a pair of young men trying hard not to overtake them. He scanned the area in front of him until he settled on two young men coming towards them from across the street.

"We have company, sir," George said in a low voice.

"Are you referring to the two young men headed our way?"

"Yes, and the two behind us, as well."

"I see; they wasted no time."

"No, sir. But I wish we had a little more privacy and space, sir."

"Maybe I can help with that, George. At the next corner, we'll turn left; it's a false street and goes back about sixty meters then dead ends. Let's see what our friends are made of, shall we?"

"Do you want to question any of them?"

"No, I have a feeling that won't be necessary, George."

They held this conversation while they walked increasing their speed gradually so as not to be noticed by their pursuers. George checked on the two men behind them; they were almost at a trot in their haste to keep up. Wilhelm and George turned left and then made a slight right up the false street into the darkness. The four men were not far behind. Wilhelm stopped once they were cloaked in the shadows. Then he and George spread out and waited. The four men paused at the entrance, pulled their knives, and slowly began to walk towards them. Wilhelm and George backed up slowly drawing them deeper into the darkness of the dead end street.

The four men separated; two went towards George and two for him. Wilhelm watched them approach. They stayed up right until they felt in range; then they assumed a fighter's crouch with knives out front but not too far. Wilhelm slid his right foot back a half step and prepared for the attack. He had taken off his suit coat and rolled up his sleeves earlier, and now he was ready for battle.

The two men advanced; the one to Wilhelm's left a few steps in front of his partner came in fast and low. But Wilhelm didn't lower his stance instead he remained upright forcing the man to stab upward then slash to his left. Wilhelm stepped back evading the stab and slash. His opponent stepped forward and stabbed again. This time, Wilhelm responded. He grabbed his attacker's right wrist with his right hand and gave it a twist inward. Next, he attached his left hand to his assailant's right elbow and pushed up and down simultaneously breaking the man's arm at the elbow. Wilhelm slid his hand across the man's palm and removed the knife; he kept moving until he was behind the man before plunging the knife between the opponent's shoulder blades killing him.

Then he pushed the slumping body into his other assailant who was coming in fast and swinging wildly. The man stumbled trying to avoid his dead partner which gave Wilhelm an opening, and he attacked. He sliced the man's forearm, but his opponent changed knife hands and countered with a slash. Wilhelm parried the next attack, circled to his right, and attacked with a stab to the man's ribs; but this was a faint. When the man went to block it, Wilhelm changed direction and came straight at him stabbing the man in his throat killing him. He left the blade in his assailant's throat and turned looking for George. He was just in time to see George finishing off his last opponent with a few well-placed strikes and sinking a knife into the man's neck in the soft spot between the collar bone killing him. The fight took a little over three minutes.

"You alright!" Wilhelm asked him.

"I'm okay, sir. Are you okay?"

"Fine, let's check them and see what we can find." They went through the dead men's clothing and took everything they found. Then George took a picture of each of their faces with his cellphone. They gathered their belongings and headed out. By the time they reached the busy street, Wilhelm had on his suit coat and George had tucked in his shirt. To look at them, no one would have guessed that they had just killed four men. They arrived back at the office without further incident and headed into the living quarters to clean up and give Captain America the pictures of the dead men.

"Now that we have had a little exercise, you should be warmed up for tonight," Wilhelm said to George as they stood in the communication room. "And take the Captain with you when you go; he needs the practice," he continued. Then he left the room and headed upstairs.

Ophiuchus: Day Six

Chapter Twenty-Three

Hamburg, Germany

Susan and Dieter sat in the car up the street from where her target was hiding. She was looking through the night goggles watching the building's entrance and the shadows going by the window of the apartment where her target was staying.

"It's not too late to call in some help," he said to her without moving his head to look at her.

"Why Dieter, don't you think we can kill them all by ourselves?" she replied as she put the goggles down on the seat beside her. "I count six milling around outside; and judging by the shape of the shadows that have passed that window, there are three to four people inside and one of them is a woman. I think we can manage to kill them all without any outside assistance."

"Okay, what's the plan?" he said.

"I thought we would walk right up and kill the ones out front then go upstairs and kill the ones in the apartment."

"Sounds like you gave this a lot of thought. But what-the-fuck, killing people is what I do so let's get to it." The two of them rechecked their pistols. Susan checked the small explosive she would use to blow the door to the apartment.

They got out of the car and started down the sidewalk. Susan hooked her arm through Dieter's right arm and laid her head on his shoulder. The six men standing out front looked at them as they approached but dismissed them as just a couple. When they were in range about ten meters away, Dieter started shooting. Two men fell where they stood taking the other four by surprise. Before they could react, Susan pulled out her silenced pistol and fired killing the remaining four. Dieter was already at the entrance; he looked inside quickly then signaled her to follow him. He raced down the hallway to the backstairs, opened the door slowly, and peered in.

"Come on! These stairs will put us closer to their apartment without going down that long hallway," Dieter said in a hushed voiced.

"Sounds like you've been here before," Susan said with a smile and an equally hushed voice. They started up the stairs to the second floor. They checked the hallway and it was clear. So they darted down the carpeted hall and stopped at the apartment door. Dieter stood watching as Susan attached a small explosive to the door lock and set the timer for ten seconds.

"Let's go!" she said. They backed off about five meters and waited. *Boom!* And the door blew open. They were in the apartment in seconds with silenced pistols firing. They both held pistols in each hand as they sprayed the room with bullets.

When it was over, three bodies lay lifeless—two on the floor and the third one on the couch clutching his pistol.

"I thought you said four," Dieter said.

"I said three to four. Stop being a pain and help me clear the place," she said as they reloaded and started their search. Susan found the woman in the bedroom cowering in the corner. She looked at her then shot her in the face three times and walked away. Then she met up with Dieter in the living room.

They left the same way that they came in except for the building entrance. They left by the service door in the rear and walked down the back street towards the second car that they would use to go home. As they walked, Susan hooked her arm through his, laid her head on his shoulder, and smiled as she listened to the approaching police sirens.

Langley

Rodney sat at the head of the conference table and looked at the three people also seated there. He knew two of them who were station chiefs; the third person was from the NSA and new to him.

"So what do we know so far? Let's start with you," he said as he looked at Karen, a tall fit black woman who was in charge of North Africa. She had risen from the field to this position and knew her way around when it came to the players in her area of responsibility.

"Well sir, we've lost five agents—two in Algiers, one in Egypt, and two in Tunisia. All were deep cover and had been imbedded with their target organizations for two to three years. There are three people other than myself who knew their identities. You, of course, Mr. Libertaire, and Mr. DePore," she said as her voice trailed off a little.

"And you, Steve, what do you have for me on the subject?" Steve started as an analyst and now is the station chief in charge of Central Africa.

"Sir, I've lost seven agents in the last two weeks from Mali, the Congo, and both Northern and Southern Sudan. Again, sir, the same people knew about their existence including the person you issued the recent order to apprehend or kill—Mr. DePore. The analyst in me says he's behind it." Rodney didn't respond to his statement; he already knew it was Frank. What he was thinking was how much damage would Frank inflict before he stopped him.

"Now what news does the man from NSA have to contribute?" he said

313

with a smile which caused the desired effect that he wanted as he watched the man relax his shoulders.

"Good morning, sir. My name is Gary, sir. What I have for you is a replay taken by one of our satellites as it captured an assault on Camp K5. The camp was attacked at 2200 hours; the casualties are high; there are nineteen dead and six seriously wounded. The head of this group, a Ms. Liang, was not present at the time of the attack; her whereabouts are unknown at this time. What we are about to see is the assault from start to finish and a person who we believe to be Mr. DePore according to survivor reports."

Then Gary started the replay and what they saw was alarming. Three helicopters landed one hundred meters away from the site. Thirty men jumped out and started a picture perfect assault on the building, hitting it from two sides in an L-formation, firing on full auto as they approached, and killing or wounding everyone in their path. Next, a lone figure proceeded from body to body as if looking for someone then knelt beside one of the bodies for a moment and left. The three helicopters loaded up and took off.

"That's all we have, sir. We believe that the lone figure is Mr. DePore. As for the team that conducted the raid, we have no information on that at this time. We're lucky that a satellite was passing overhead; otherwise, we wouldn't have as much information as we do." Gary sat back in his chair with a slight smile; he was happy with his presentation, his first in front of the director of the CIA.

Before Rodney could comment on what he just saw, an aid came in and handed him a folded piece of paper. He opened it and read it.

"Need you to come out to the farm right away—most urgent. C. Libertaire."

Rodney refolded the note and placed it into his inside suit coat pocket. "Karen, Steve, write me a report on just what kind of damage we have sustained and what we can do to recover from it if we can. And Gary, thank all the people over at the NSA for this footage. I have another appointment so that will be all for now. And I want those reports on my desk in the morning." The two station chiefs said,

"Yes, sir," and started to pack up their papers as Rodney left the room. He went back to his office and put on his grey wool three-quarter length overcoat, picked up his hat and gloves, and walked out the office. He stopped at his assistant's desk, told the man to have his helicopter ready and that he would tell the pilot where they were going en route, and continued out the door.

As he flew towards the farm, he thought of the worst scenario. Then he emptied his head of all thoughts and looked out the window. When he landed, he was met by Anthony who is in charge of all security matters at the farm when George is away.

He got into the waiting jeep and they headed for the house in silence. Anthony escorted him inside and a woman took his hat and coat. Then he was directed towards the kitchen where he found Colleen waiting. She stood near the stove with a teapot in her hand. As he came in, she turned to face him.

"Thanks for coming on such short notice, Rodney. I was just having some Imperial Black Oolong tea; join me?" she said as she glided across the kitchen towards the table; on it were three tea cups and saucers. Rodney noticed and silently wondered who was going to join them; he wouldn't be surprised a bit if it was Wilhelm.

"Yes, I believe I will join you for a cup," Rodney said.

"Good, pull up a chair. I'll pour you a cup; I'm sure you'll agree it's perfect for this occasion."

"What is the reason for this occasion, Colleen? It isn't often I receive an invitation like the one you sent. I hope you're not wasting my time." Colleen smiled as she listened and poured tea into all three cups.

"You wouldn't have come if you thought for one minute that my note was bullshit. So let's be civil about this, Rodney. I'm sure you'll want to know about this before anyone else does. And by the way, you owe me one; and this is a fucking big one, understand," Colleen said in a normal tone, never raising or lowering her voice as she finished pouring the tea and sat down at the head of the table. Rodney sipped his tea.

"You're right, this is good tea," he said.

"What I have to tell you is better told by the person that it happened to; my information will fill in the gaps." Then she dismissed Anthony, picked up the phone that sat on the table by her left hand, and said,

"Bring her in," and hung up.

Rodney sat back in his chair and watched the door open. In walked Linda, head bandaged, with the help of one of the guards. The guard walked her to the table and helped her sit down then left.

"What happened, Linda? How did you get wounded? And how did you end up here at Libertaire Manor?" Rodney asked in a nonchalant voice.

"Well, sir, I can fill you in up to being shot; after that, I'm afraid Colleen will have to take over," Linda said in a steady, strong voice. Then she took a sip of her tea and flashed a nervous smile at him and began.

Ophiuchus: Day Seven

Chapter Twenty-Four

Verna, Bulgaria

Pam rolled over onto her back as she listened to her target talk. "God, this woman sure could talk, and her weird pitched voice was truly annoying," she thought. Pam got out of bed and felt the coolness of the marble under her feet as she walked towards the bathroom which was an apartment in itself.

"What was the flavor you used last night?" the White Witch yelled after her.

"Grape!" she replied turning her head to speak over her shoulder. "It was grape. Did you like it?" Who knew that they really had pussy flavoring in Bulgaria of all places. Her boss, that's who. She was receiving a hell of a lesson in spying. Pam turned on the shower and looked in the mirror; she looked tired. The heavy partying and fucking the last couple of days was starting to show. She had decided to make her move at tonight's special orgy/business party here at the mansion. She didn't know why the White Witch was throwing it, but it was going to be huge if the preparations were any indication.

She would pass this information on to her helpers and see what surprises they could devise. She would do this today when she left to go shopping, and her tail wouldn't return with a report of her movements this time. Just as she was getting into the shower, the Witch walked in.

"What are your plans for today?" she asked as she kissed the back of Pam's neck.

"I'm going shopping then hang out for a while," she replied smiling at her in the mirror.

"Why don't you let me take you shopping and buy you anything you want?"

"No Bryda, for the last time, I don't want anything from you. I like hanging out with you but I buy my own things. You know how I feel about this," Pam said putting on a convincing face to go along with her speech. Then she got into the shower and began to wash while the White Witch sat on the edge of the large tub and watched.

Pam finished and stepped out.

"Hand me a towel," she said. Bryda brought her a towel and began to dry her off. As she squatted down to dry off her legs, she stopped and traced her finger across the tattoo on her hip. It was an African rose with a naked woman intertwined with its stem; her arms were outstretched and over her head with her palms facing up holding the rose. The vibrant purple color of the rose, the green of its stem, and the shapely, light brown body of the woman drew her attention every time she saw it. Pam knew what she was doing and stood patiently while she looked. She didn't like the tattoo but it had grown on her; and maybe she'd keep it when the mission was over. But she couldn't think of that now.

"Stop it, Bryda! I have to go," she snapped when she felt her hand snake between her legs to her clit.

"Alright!" she said with a sigh and continued to dry her off. Pam fixed her hair, put on makeup, found her panties and bra, put on her jeans and a sweater top, picked up her coat and purse, and slipped her feet into three-inch heels.

"Walk me out. I still get lost in this big place, you call home," she said as she kissed her lightly on the lips. Bryda put on a robe and in her bare feet walked with her towards the front door.

Pam stepped onto the sidewalk and looked up the street. There, in a yellow *VW Rabbit* was her backup. She started walking towards them then passed them going to the next intersection where she made a left. She picked up her pace; she wanted her shadow to be a little nervous worrying that she may lose her. Pam watched the windows across the street for her reflection, but it was in the side mirror of a parked car that she spotted her. "Good, it was the same woman," she thought. This made it an even fight. Her shadow was roughly the same weight and height, and she felt confident she could take her. Pam went into a shoe store and bought a pair of flat shoes. When she emerged, her shadow was waiting across the street; her backup kept close watch on both of them.

Pam headed east away from the store; she crossed the street and walked the short distant to an ally that she would use to keep the pressure on her shadow. Now that she had on flats, she could walk faster taking long strides to cover the distance without looking suspicious to her tail. By the time her shadow reached the ally, she had been swallowed up in its darkness. Her tail hurried down the semi-dark corridor and into the light at the other end just in time to see Pam enter the adult bookstore in the middle of the block. She walked into the store. A clerk was sitting behind the counter eating a breakfast sandwich of sausage and egg. A large cup of coffee sat steaming while he was reading the paper as the morning news stories on the TV played in the corner.

The clerk looked up from his paper when he heard her come in. He took a bite of his sandwich and went back to reading his paper. Pam didn't bother to look at him; instead, she headed straight to the video booths located in the back of the store. She was halfway down the narrow hall that was lit with red light bulbs when she heard the doorbell ring. That would be her tail. The woman came in breathing heavily after

319

fast walking the half block to catch up to her. As she looked around the room, she took the time to catch her breath. Not seeing her target, she too headed towards the video booths and into the red hallway.

As she looked down its length, she saw a figure at the far end; it was squatting down with its back towards her. She couldn't tell if the figure was Pam or if anyone was in front of her because the back wall was completely dark. The woman started down the hall slowly pushing each door, checking as she went, and taking care not to make any more noise other than the sticky, squeaky sound her rubber shoes made on the dirty floor. When she was almost to the squatting figure, she heard the faint sound of sucking; so she stopped.

At that moment, Pam stood up, turned around, and walked slowly towards her opponent as her face was illuminated by one of the red lights. Her shadow recognized her and took a half step back involuntarily. Pam pounced launching her attack with a front kick to her solar plexus knocking her back and through the door of a video booth. Pam followed her in and pinned her body down in the tight space within the booth. She grabbed her hair with her left hand and slammed her fist into her opponent's temple three times in quick succession. Then she cupped her right hand under her chin, slid her left hand into position at the back of her head, and with a quick snapping motion broke her neck.

Pam quickly checked the hallway; it was empty. She could hear the clerk's TV but she was listening for his footsteps. Not hearing anything, she sat the woman up on the bench, put five dollars in the machine, and pressed the button to start the movie. In a moment, she heard the moaning of the porn movie beginning. She leaned the broken door back against the opening, walked back down the hall, and retrieved her bag. Then she left the store with the clerk still sitting there reading his paper and drinking his

320

coffee. Once outside, she looked for and found the car, signaled; and they picked her up.

"What happened in there?" the driver asked her.

"A little workout is all. I'm going to need a cleaning team to remove the body," she answered nonchalantly. As they drove to the op house, the woman in the passenger seat got on the phone and ordered a body disposal.

"What's your plan, Oannes? Why kill your tail?"

"When we get to the house, I'll fill you in, okay."

"Okay," she replied, and they rode silently the rest of the way.

Once back at the apartment, Pam went to her room then into the bathroom and stood in front of the mirror. She took a deep breath and let the trembling in her stomach which she had kept control of until now take over. It exploded and caused her to shake; she let it happen then stopped it cold regaining her composer. She looked at herself in the mirror; she stood there and stared awhile. She was feeling a combination of elation and humility. She had her first kill and that felt good. But at the same time, she felt humbled and she didn't know why. She shook it off and turned on the cold water then washed her face and checked her hands for bruising.

"Okay!" she said as she entered the living room where her two partners were sitting. "This is the plan, ladies, and it's a crazy one. So gather around and let's get started. Tonight is the first sex slave selling event of the season, and the Witch has pulled out all of the stops. She's been busy with phone calls from all over Europe. Everyone at the top of the game in sex trafficking will be there. The party will be packed and the security will be a nightmare. Her security chief has added extra electronic security, not to mention extra guns. The auction will take place at 1900 hours in the great room and afterwards is the orgy."

"Orgy! Is there really going to be an orgy? Do we get to go?" the black haired agent asked.

"Yes, actually I'll need both of your help. One to be my guest and the other to cover our escape."

"I volunteer for the cover duty," the sandy blonde said. "I don't mind killing them but I'm not going to fuck the bastards," she continued as she twisted her face to accentuate her point.

"Okay, I got it; so enough with the face already," Pam said half laughing. "First me and miss hot ass over here are going shopping; we need something new for the party. While we're out, I want you to notify Interpol and that do-good captain you know. We'll need their help getting out, I think. So make sure they're on time and not early; you know how cops are."

"How do you plan to kill her?" the sandy blonde asked.

"Very quietly after sex."

"Why after sex and not after the auction?"

"If my guess is right, Bryda will be very horny after making all of that money; and one thing Bryda loves more than killing people is money. It makes her so horny she literally wets her pants and not with pee either; then she just has to fuck. Trust me on this, ladies; men are easier, one nut and out; this chick needs three, at least." They sat back in their chairs and had a good laugh at what Pam had just told them. Then they went to work on the preparations for tonight.

Pam walked into the living room barefooted and sat down on the couch. She held her stockings in her left hand, her shoes in her right and looked at her partner. She was standing by the dining room table smoking a joint and grooving to a song on the radio.

"Do you need that?" Pam said.

"Need what?" she answered with a puzzled look on her face.

"That joint!"

"Oh no, baby, I don't need it but it's sure good to have," she said then took a big pull on the joint and blew out a big cloud of smoke. "You don't smoke?"

"No."

"Why not?"

"I don't need it."

"Who needs it; most of the agents I know smoke. It beats drinking and you can still function on it. Not like the old time agents, they drank; and drinking makes you sloppy and sloppy gets you killed."

"I get your point; I just never smoked is all," Pam said then put down her shoes, crossed her legs, and began to put on a stocking. Her partner went back to dancing to the music. The dark haired woman came into the room.

"Don't be a hog," she said as she reached for the joint.

"She doesn't smoke so don't ask," she half whispered to her friend. "Really," she said then took a pull.

"Too bad, this is some damn good bud she's missing." Then she let out the smoke and coughed. Pam ignored them and continued putting on her stockings. In an hour, they would be in the lion's den. And who knows, maybe she wished she had taken a hit of that joint.

The car pulled up to the curb on the opposite side of the street, a block away from the in-town mansion that the White Witch called home. Pam sat in the backseat going through her handbag making sure she had nothing to cause suspicion, nothing out of place. Her counterpart was doing the same beside her. Pam looked at the driver; and when she caught her eye in the rearview mirror, she spoke.

"Are Interpol and the cops clear about the signal to move in?"

"Yeah, simple, wait 'till you come out shooting. I gotta tell you for a chick who can kill before breakfast, doesn't smoke bud, and comes up with plans like this ... well sistah ... I got to hand it to you. You're a credit to the service and your ethnic group even though you pass well."

"Thanks, you guys have been great; I'm glad we got to work together. Are you ready?" she said to the woman beside her.

"Let's do this, Oannes; fucking and killing happens to be a hobby of mine. Didn't you know?" she said with a big smile. The pair exited the car, walked across the street, and paused.

"How do I look?" Pam watched her partner do a slow turn around then stopped to face her. She was dressed in a rose colored microminiskirt, matching waist jacket, sequined sheer blouse, three-inch heels, and fishnet stockings. The color of her outfit complimented her skin tone perfectly. She was hot, and Pam knew she would have no problem finding partners for the night. Pam had selected yellow leather for tonight and her miniskirt seemed long compared to her partner's. Her sheer black blouse was covered by a matching waistcoat. She wore seamed stockings and open-toed three-inch heels. Both ladies were braless and sported color coordinated thongs. With a final check, they began to walk towards the mansion.

As they approached, it was hard to tell that a major event with really bad people in attendance was going on inside. The outside of the mansion was softly lit, and the guards were cleverly hidden. Only two women standing outside of the entrance gates were in clear sight. They took turns greeting the guests as their cars pulled up, never more than two at a time, and ushered the occupants through the gate. Pam walked up to one of the women and stared at her not saying a word. The woman stared back then placed her right hand next to her ear and listened. Next she walked to the gate and opened it stepping aside as Pam passed but gave her partner the once over.

They walked up what felt like a hundred steps, through the twelve foot high wooden and iron doors displaying a hand craved motif, and into the foyer where they found a small crowd waiting to go through the metal detector.

"Come with me," Pam said and headed around the crowd by-passing the machine. One of the guards started towards them with his hand on his hip where his pistol rested. Pam turned to face him; he stopped, turned around, and headed back to his post.

"Wow, you got some clout around here."

"Yeah, the boss loves this pussy; and for that, they dare not fuck with me."

"Hurray for the power of the pussy!" she replied and they laughed. They stood at the top of the entry way and looked at the party going on in the living room if it could be called that. The huge room was twenty by fifty feet, and it was filled with guests. Women and men were dressed in sexy customs mingling among the guests. Hanging from the ceiling cages were naked go-go dancers; every other cage had a well hung semi-hard man in it. In the center of the room was a round platform set low to the floor and covered with pillows, white satin sheets, and about seven people laying on it. Four men and three women were having sex in an intricate daisy chain. People sat around the platform on chaise lounges and couches and watched while drinking, snorting coke, or smoking bud from tall hand-blown glass bongs. The women servers wore G-strings and silver bow ties, nothing else as they went about; the men wore cock socks and gold bow ties; both wore black dancing shoes. Spaced around the room were booths with neon signs above them which contained men in some and women in others.

"This is my dream party!" her partner said. "It's a shame we have to kill people. It seems kinda rude, don't you think?" she said to Pam with a devilish smile. Pam looked at her and nodded her head.

"I'm going to the auction room; you get to know the place. Look for the excitement to start around 2 a.m. and try not to enjoy yourself too much. Remember, we're here for work," Pam said. Then she placed her hand lightly on her shoulder and they started down the stairs into the party. When they hit the crowd, they separated; her partner disappeared quickly into the mix of people. Pam maneuvered her way through the crowd smiling at faces that looked familiar and swiping away the random hands that tried to cop a feel under her skirt.

She reached the auction room on the other side of the house; auction was being held in the music room. Pam was sure it was some kind of sick joke that only the Witch knew the punch line. The guard at the door stopped her and called the security chief who came out and gave her a hard look.

"What-the-fuck, I can't go in?" Pam said with attitude.

"You can go in; she's been asking for you. But first, I would like to ask you something," she replied. "Where have you been all day? You knew what was to take place tonight yet you disappear 'till now." The security chief stood there waiting for an answer. Pam crossed her arms and stared back. After a minute of this, she stepped aside; Pam entered the room just in time to see Bryda walk up to the podium. She was dressed in black leather with her hair pulled up into a bun. Her milky white skin was more apparent especially her stomach since she was wearing a midriff.

Pam selected a seat in the back and took a good look at each of the men and women who sat there waiting.

As Bryda began her speech, Pam zoned out for a moment; she was calculating her odds on her escape. There had to be three hundred guests and sixty or more guards.   Bryda had doubled her security force for tonight added to the fact that everyone was locked in until dawn as is the custom at one of these gatherings.   So her chances of survival weren't looking too good.   Then she heard Bryda start to call people by name so she re-focused on her.

"It's good to see some old friends and some new ones. I trust my good friends from Israel, Germany, and of course, Vietnam will enjoy the selection I have for you tonight. Due to the economic misfortune of the United States which is my good fortune, we have a special diversity package up for auction thanks to our new friend from America."   She pointed to the newcomer, a white woman who looked to be in her mid-thirties with brown hair stood up. Then she continued, "As usual, payments are made electronically and all sales are final. Also, there will be two virgin sales and all the girls have been certified. The girls are all between twelve and eighteen. So let's get started so we can enjoy the party that's raging just down the hall."

Pam sat there amazed at how professionally the White Witch ran the auction as she brought out each group of girls. They were well-groomed and didn't appear drugged. They stood on the stage with wide-eyed fear as strangers bid on them. A few of the girls cried and Bryda comforted them and gave them tissues. When the last group from the States—indeed a diverse bunch—was showcased, the Witch demanded and received a higher price for them.

Afterwards, Bryda and the buyers congregated at the side of the stage and talked. Then she nudged them towards the door, went over to Pam, grabbed her by the hand and said,

"Baby, are we going to have fun tonight!" Then she kissed her, took her by the arm, and began to walk. "I love your outfit; the color is perfect on you," she said.

"Thanks, I hoped you'd like it and I couldn't resist when I saw it," Pam replied in the little girl voice Bryda liked.

"Yes, I like it very much. You know how I feel; you make me very happy. I wish you would reconsider ..." Bryda said giving her hand a little squeeze.

"Not tonight, Bryda. Can't we just have fun?" Pam said has she removed her hand from hers.

"You're right. I just made a shitload of money, and not all from the girls either. Now it's time to party. I have something special for you, and I guarantee that you will not only love it but it's going to make you in creditably horny."

She led her into the party. As they entered the main room, the volume of the music caught Pam off guard. After the quietness of the auction, this was quite loud but the people dancing were enjoying the beat. Whoever was the DJ knew her or his business; the crowd was jumping just like at the club. She stood there watching the crowd and feeling the beat while Bryda was talking to somebody.

"What are the booths about?" Pam asked her.

"Let's go see," she replied with a sly grin. They made their way through the sea of people while Pam searched for her partner as she went. "This is the cum dumpster. As you can guess, it is for my guests who prefer an oral release." They headed for the second booth located across

328

the room. Pam steeled herself against the crowd and followed her. She looked around and saw her partner who was standing near the booth watching the goings-on with a crowd of people.

"This is the ATM booth," Pam heard her say. When she looked into the booth, she was just in time to see a man cum all over a young woman's face. The crowd cheered her on as she began to lick the milky white substance from her lips using a finger to gather up the rest. Pam looked over at her partner who was smoking a joint and talking. When she caught her eye, she smiled, winked, and then turned her attention back the man who had his hand under her skirt.

"Where's this surprise?" she yelled over the music.

"Right this way, my lady," Bryda said with a sweep of her hand. Bryda guided her back to the bed stage that she had passed on her way. Now the chaise lounges and loveseats were arranged differently, and the sheets had been changed to gold. "Sit here, baby," Bryda said pointing to a loveseat. They sat down, and a waitress placed a silver ice bucket with champagne next to them, handed them glasses, poured the champagne, and left. Pam took advantage of the moment to look at the other people sitting around the bed. She recognized three from the auction. But of the remaining, she had no idea; fifteen people in all were seated. They reclined in various positions of relaxation depending on what they were lounging on. All had companions of their choosing, and some had started to enjoy them.

Pam focused on the American woman sitting on the couch directly across from her on the other side of the bed. She had two handsome young men on either side of her who were taking turns kissing her and rubbing her pussy; she looked blissful. Just then, Bryda tapped her on the thigh.

"Wait 'till you see these studs. Since you like the occasional cock and god only knows why, I did this for you." Pam watched Bryda's face and her mouth twist when she said this; this intrigued Pam. For the first time, she was interested in Bryda's show. Two young men showed up; they looked to be in their early twenties. They had thick curly black hair and golden brown skin that looked like a tan. Their eyes were dark and alluring black pools. Their bodies were perfect at least what she could see of them above the black towels they were wearing. Both men were well-muscled but not overly so. Their chests and arms were cut with definition but not bulky, and their eight packs brought attention to their narrow waists. She wondered what was swinging under their towels; if it was half as good as she hoped, she would be a very happy woman indeed. The two men dropped their black towels and stood there for a moment before turning around in a full circle giving everyone a good look at their naked bodies. "Wow!" was all she thought as she gazed at their cocks that were huge at least six inches long and still soft. Pam wondered how big they would grow when fully aroused and which lucky girl or girls would get to sample them.

The two men crawled on their knees across the bed to its center. Pam watched their brown manhood swing powerfully from side to side as they moved. The men were joined by a petite woman with long blond hair who looked like see couldn't handle the two of them. They began kissing very tenderly and rubbing their hands over each other's bodies until she settled on the men's now hardened cocks. She began to slowly jerk them off as they continued kissing. "Bryda sure knows how to conjure up a fucking-wet-dream; this certainly is what I like," she thought. Just when she was deeply interested, the two men changed into the sixty-nine position with the woman in the middle. She had to watch this as curiosity got the best of her. She refilled her champagne glass and crossed her legs.

When the two men were completely hard and enormous from the attention that their mouths had given each other and when she saw the signs of the impending explosion, they stopped.

"What-the-fuck!" Pam said out loud. "Why did they stop?" she said looking at Bryda. Bryda just looked at her and then gestured with her head back towards the bed. Pam looked back just in time to see an exotic looking woman, average height with thick black hair that hung to the center of her back. Her flawless light brown skin glistened with oil as she stood there naked, her body devoid of all hair. Her large breasts with dark brown areolas and large nipples rose and fell rhythmically with her breathing.

She maneuvered herself between the two studs, and they pounced on her licking her pussy and sucking her breasts simultaneous. Pam watched thinking this was more of what she had in mind; and looking at the American seller, she could tell she felt the same way.

The American woman now had her companions' dicks firmly in hand. They had her squirming and moaning with the attention they were giving her twat and tits. She changed position and now was giving head to one and receiving it from the other. Then Pam turned her attention back to the show. The entertainers were changing into many different positions with each stud taking his turn riding her. The exotic woman caused the studs to explode in unison spewing their spunk high into the air for the grand finale.

"Whew! Now that's what I call a sex show; thanks, baby," Pam said as she leaned over and kissed Bryda.

"I hope it made you horny as hell."

"Oh, it did just that and more."

"Good, now let's dance," Bryda said and got up from the sofa. The music was thumping. Pam could feel the bass vibrating through her body. By the time they reached the dance floor, she was already moving to the beat. She danced for two hours straight sometimes with Bryda but mostly with any stranger who wanted to dance. She just wanted to forget for a while. Soon, she would kill Bryda or be killed by her. But for now, all she wanted to do was dance. Then Bryda approached her with a redhead in tow.

"Let's go upstairs; I'm horny," she yelled over the music. Pam could see how drunk and high Bryda was. The young woman hanging onto her was in the same shape. Pam shook her head in acknowledgment, and the trio headed for Bryda's bedroom which was two floors up. The young redhead hung all over Bryda as they rode her private elevator to the top floor. Bryda kissed and felt all over the woman as they walked down the hallway and passed the guard who was stationed outside her bedroom door. Pam hadn't figured on a guard but it made sense for a night like tonight. This just meant killing one more person during her escape.

They walked into Bryda's bedroom which was decorated very femininely in pink, lavender, and pastels. Bryda and her new plaything wasted no time undressing and jumping onto the huge four-poster bed that dominated the center of the room, laughing and giggling. Pam took her time undressing and using the distraction to pull out her poison spry. She got into bed and slid the vial under a pillow then joined them in the middle of the bed.

Pam lay there looking at Bryda who was across the room rummaging through her sex toy collection. The redhead who turned out to be a natural redhead was lying on her back with her feet towards Pam looking up at the hand-painted motif on the ceiling. Pam slid her hand under the pillow where she placed the poison. She felt for it then brought it out. She checked to make sure Bryda was still occupied then she removed the top and turned the spray nozzle one turn to the right. Then she reached over and started to rub the redhead's leg getting her attention.

"Want to taste something peachy," she said to the woman when she sat up to see what Pam wanted.

"Yah, sure, I like peaches," she said smiling broadly. Pam raised her knees and spread her legs pausing for a moment as the young woman positioned herself between her opened legs.

Then Pam depressed the spray nozzle a few times lightly coating her crotch.

"Taste this and tell me how you like it." The young woman started out cautiously not sure if she would like it.

"Mmmm, this tastes good," she said raising her head a little. Pam started making moaning noises and gradually raised the volume to attract Bryda's attention.

"What's going on over there?" she said turning around to look.

"You two starting without me?" she continued. Then she headed towards the bed with sex toy in hand and walked across the bed on her knees to where they were.

"Peach!" the young woman said to Bryda stopping only long enough to say this. Pam kept up the moaning and now added a little squirming to the act.

"Get out of there, you little slut; I want to taste it too," Bryda said pulling the redhead out of the way. "Here play with me with this," she continued as she handed her the apparatus. "And you, my tasty whore, spray some of that peach shit on your cunt and let momma have a taste."

Pam turned the nozzle one more time and mixed the poison with the flavoring and pumped the nozzle. She closed her eyes and waited until she felt Bryda's tongue. Her eyes opened, and she focused on the redhead kneeling behind her.

"How long does this shit take to work?" she was thinking when she heard Bryda cough. Suddenly, Bryda started to convulse and grabbed her throat. Pam quickly rolled over and sat up on her knees. She watched Bryda's violently convulsing body and her eyes darting back and forth looking for help. Then she went limp and her body gave one last shudder before going completely still. The redhead had been silent through all of this staring wide-eyed in disbelief to what was happening in front of her.

"Shhh," Pam said as she put her index finger to her lips. She moved closer to Bryda's lifeless body and checked for a pulse. Finding none, she moved closer to the redhead who was visibly shaking. "It's all right," she said in a half-whisper as she reached out and softly touched her. The young woman didn't move when she did this so Pam positioned herself beside her then quickly snapped her neck. She laid the young woman down on the bed gently and covered her up with a bedsheet. She jumped out of bed and got dressed. Then she went to where the safe was kept and examined it.

She returned to the bedroom and started looking around until she found a pencil. Then she went over to Bryda's body and proceeded to remove her right eye being careful not to damage it. When she was done, she grabbed Bryda and dragged her to the safe room. Pam studied the three dials for a moment and selected the bottom one first. She took out her hearing aid that was disguised as her earphones for her mp3 player and began. When she had all three tumblers aligned, she held up Bryda's eye for the scanner and then placed Bryda's left hand on the hand scanner.

Pam heard the safe unlock. She swung the heavy door open and started going through the shelves. She knew exactly what to look for and went about her work. She gathered up all the flash drives as well as the paperwork along with three hard drives that she found. But what she didn't take were the many velvet bags of precious stones and bars of platinum. She checked the safe once more then closed it knowing that if anyone tried to open it, they would be in for one hell of a surprise. Bryda had rigged it to blow. If tampered with, the charge would go off seven seconds after opening it.

Pam took the custom forty-five that she found in the safe; it had great balance and a magazine that held ten rounds of the deadly caliber. She took all four magazines and loaded them as she readied the pistol. She decided she would hold on to it as sort of a souvenir.

Ready now, she opened the door. When the guard turned around, she shot him in the face blowing the back of his head out. She stepped over his body and headed for the elevator and the first floor. The elevator opened and the party was still in full swing. Only now, she didn't hear the music nor feel its beat.

Pam slung her oversized pocketbook across her body, headed for the door, and looked for her partner. She had decided to make her exit from the eastside of the house avoiding the heavily guarded front entrance. As she crossed the dance floor and started down the east hallway, Pam ran into Bryda's security chief.

"Where are you going?" she said blocking Pam's path.

"I'm leaving," she replied with attitude.

"No, you're not. Nobody leaves before dawn; you know that. This goes for you also so take your pretty little ass back to the party." She took a step towards Pam reinforcing the point. Pam removed her hand from behind her bag. Upon seeing the forty-five, the security chief started to reach for the gun in her shoulder holster.

Pam leveled her pistol and fired twice hitting her in the chest which slammed her body against the wall behind her. Then the wall above Pam's head exploded with chunks of marble falling everywhere. She ducked down looking around and spotted a guard firing an assault rifle and running towards her. Pam fired two quick shots hitting him in the stomach and leg; the last bullet caused the guard to flip over. When he tried to sit up, she shot him in the face taking half of his head off. Pam changed magazines and just as she was getting ready to move, she heard screaming coming from the front room. The music was still playing loudly but she could hear gunfire and cries of panic. She moved in that direction. As she turned the corner, a woman was firing an assault weapon at a half dozen guards on the stairs leading to the front door. Pam looked at her; it was her partner and she started towards her. When she reached her, she yelled,

"Let's get-the-fuck out of here! Follow me!" and headed back across the room. Her partner close on her heels was changing magazines as she ran. The pair headed back down the east hallway past the two dead bodies being careful not to slip on the blood and brains. They stopped in a blind spot to check if anyone was following.

"What do you see?" Pam asked her.

"All clear, nobody trailing us. Now how do we get the-hell-out of this maze?" she said without turning her head.

"Down this hall about fifty meters there should be a door that leads to the street."

"We have company, Oannes, a half dozen guards coming our way." Pam peered around the corner and saw the guards. They were approaching cautiously checking every room as they passed.

"We have to deal with them before we go. I don't want to get caught between them and the guards outside," Pam whispered to her. Her partner nodded and readied herself. Pam moved to the other side of the hallway where she could see the approaching guards. She held up three fingers and began to silently count down. When she made a fist, they both jumped out into the center of the hallway and opened fire. When they stopped, all of the guards were dead except for two. Pam walked over and shot them in the head. They changed to fresh magazines and headed down the hall leading to the street.

When Pam opened the heavy door, they stepped out into a firefight between the White Witch's forces against Interpol and the local cops. Pam put the pistol in her pocketbook, and her partner threw the assault rifle in the hedges. They crouched down and began running and screaming blending in with the guests who had managed to escape the carnage. Once clear of the mansion, they looked for the car, saw it, and ran full speed towards it losing their shoes in the process. They piled into the car, and it pulled off passing police cars headed to the fight.

"I guess things went as planned," the driver said.

"Hell, yeah! That was some dope shit; you should've been there. Oannes was shooting guards and taking names. Hey, did you kill the bitch?"

"Yes, she's dead," Pam said.

"Good, I can report mission success then," the driver replied. They rode the rest of the way recounting the night's events. The car pulled up to a secluded dock with a sailboat tied to it. Pam and her team got out.

"You have everything you need in that waterproof bag. It's been a pleasure working with you even if you don't smoke," the driver said and smiled.

"That goes double for me, Oannes. I'll work with you anytime. You sure know how to show a girl a good time," she said. Her face was bright with a smile.

"Ladies, I feel the same; and if I get the chance, I'll definitely ask for you two," she said pointing at them. They walked down the dock to the sailboat. Pam got in, and they helped her cast off. Then they watched until they couldn't see her anymore.

Pam used the small sailboat's motor until the docks and the Bulgarian coast were no longer in sight. A light rain started to fall and the wind picked up a couple of knots. So she decided to shut off the light engine and raise the sail. She had no reason to waste such a strong breeze. She sailed along for the next hour or so carefully avoiding any of the small and large sea crafts in the area.

She sailed along in the dark enjoying the ride as she skillfully tacked back and forth catching the wind. Then she noticed that the wind had picked up and the waves were getting choppy. Pam checked the compass and looked at her watch; she was on course and on time. But she still had about two hours before she landed on Turkish soil, and the water was getting rough. Pam checked her one and only sail and saw it was full of wind and stretched to its limit.

She adjusted her rudder a little to port to ease the strain on the canvas and settled back. The small craft was moving at a good speed now. She estimated around eight knots, and the swells had to be at least eight feet high now. She pulled her waterproof bag closer to her in case this little boat capsized and she had to swim for it. Then see remembered what her father taught her about maneuvering in rough water. So she started using the small craft to ride the waves like a surf-board with the sail acting as a balancing point.

She looked through the rain and saw the lights of the distant Turkish shore. She had made it. If she could just keep this up for another hour, she was home free. Pam tied the boat to a large rock that was half-buried in the ground. She was soaked down to her skin. She checked her surrounding, got her bearings, and headed off into the darkness.

Ophiuchus: Day Eight

Chapter Twenty-Five

Alexandria, Egypt

A black Mercedes pulled up in front of the library. Wilhelm saw it was his Chinese counterpart; the car had Chinese diplomatic plates. Wilhelm and George got out of their black sedan and headed for the entrance leaving the driver with the car. George bought two tickets, and they headed for the Sadat exhibit where he found Mr. Chìen waiting with his bodyguard.

George and Chìen's bodyguard walked to the giant ink press and stood by as their bosses greeted each other and headed into the exhibit.

"Thank you for accepting my invitation, Mr. Libertaire. I am confident that your time will be well spent. I hope you do not mind me speaking in this dialect. I know it was your masters," he said in Shanghainese. Wilhelm smiled and nodded his head, and Mr. Chìen continued speaking in a soft voice just loud enough for him to hear. "This man Talaus is sometimes a problem to my government, and I have heard he is looking for you and your team. We have no interest in whatever the United States is doing in Turkey but we do have an interest in Talaus." He handed Wilhelm a white 8 by 10 inch envelope as they stopped to look at Sadat's swords. "Inside, you will find all of the information we have on him. I would consider it a personal favor if you could help him on his way to the afterlife." The pair walked the last few feet to the exit then out to where their bodyguards were waiting.

Then they turned to face each other. Wilhelm stretched out his hand and Chìen did the same. As the two men shook hands, Chìen said,

"Remember the three." Wilhelm replied,

"Revere the five." Then the two men headed for the exit each taking a separate route to their cars with their bodyguards following nervously.

As his car headed for the private airfield, Wilhelm opened up the envelope, took out the picture and paperwork, and started to read. Then he put the papers in his briefcase. He rode along looking at the desert wondering just how much trouble this man really was to the Chinese government.

After the Lear jet had taken off and reached its cruising altitude, Wilhelm told the pilot to head for Nigeria.

"Why are we going there?" George asked curiously.

"I need to see an old friend," Wilhelm replied. "I think he has information on Talaus that the Chinese missed or neglected to tell me," he continued as he opened his briefcase and took out the picture of Talaus. "It seems our new found friends want me to eliminate this man for them, and I want to know why."

"I thought you wanted him dead, sir."

"Yes, George, I do. The question here is why do the Chinese and why are they trying to use me to get it done."

The Lear jet circled a few times above an air stripe cut out of the jungle that was part of a vast compound. The fasten seatbelt light lit up and the plane started its descent. It made a smooth landing and taxied to a hanger. Wilhelm and George stepped out of the plane and felt the intense heat even though it was early evening. They stood there for a moment and smelled the jungle. Both men were silent, but thinking the same thoughts. The jungle was a second home to both of them. They got into a waiting sedan. The air conditioner was on full blast. The cool air felt good, for the little time they had spent outside had caused them to sweat.

"Who are we going to see, boss?"

"A friend of mine, he worked for MI6 for a while and now he's in business for himself. The Nigerian government lets him live out here in the middle of the jungle with his own private airstrip." The car stopped, and the driver got out and opened the door for Wilhelm and George. They waited by the car while the driver talked to the guard standing in front of the house. Then the driver turned and waved them on, and Wilhelm and George started towards the house. The guard let them in and passed them on to another guard just inside the door, stationed in the foyer. He led them down a long hallway, turned left, and walked down another hallway to a set of double doors.

When the guard opened the doors, they were greeted by James dancing with a beautiful woman to an R. Kelly song. Wilhelm stood there for a moment taking in the sight in front of him. He glanced over at George and his expression said it all. Wilhelm placed his hand on his shoulder, and they entered the great room with the guard leading the way. Wilhelm looked around the room and noticed two more lovely young women lounging on chaises and sharing a joint the size of a small cigar. Just then, the song ended and James turned to greet them.

"Wilhelm! It's been a long time my friend!" he said with a big smile showing all of his brilliant white teeth. He stopped a few feet in front of him and George before continuing. "When my tower informed me that it was you who wanted to land in my little paradise, well, I just didn't believe him. So I had him double check, of course. I was certain no one would impersonate you but one can't be too careful in this business. You must be George. I have heard a lot about you, the retired captain from the Legion. You are well known in Africa, Captain, for your extraordinary jungle fighting skills. Welcome to my home!" George stared at him. His face was blank and expressionless but his mind was working overtime trying to put a name to his face.

"I see you've not suffered for lack of comforts, James," Wilhelm said as his hand did a sweeping motion. And the company seems to be getting younger every time I visit," he said looking over at the three women.

"Unlike you, my friend, I can't bring myself to marry every woman I fall in love with. I just don't have the fortitude. Of course, you married well but still it's marriage." Then James flashed his smile and they began to laugh in earnest. "Come, sit, and relax. Enjoy my hospitality while you tell me of the purpose for this most welcome visit."

"Thank you, James. Is there somewhere I can clean up a little before we talk?" Wilhelm asked.

"Yes, of course, we'll talk later. Right now, clean up; and after a little dinner, I shall help you all I can." Then James instructed one of the women to take care of their needs and show them to the guest suite.

Once there, Wilhelm and George gave the room a sweep for listening devices and found ten in all.

"He sure likes to hear people's conversations. Half of these would have covered the room," George said as he held the bugs.

"He should. His business is information, and he is good at gathering it as you can attest to," Wilhelm replied. "Now let's get ready for dinner; we're on a tight schedule." Then Wilhelm headed for the bathroom. After they both had showered and redressed in fresh clothes that were brought from the plane, they headed for the dining room with the same young lady leading the way.

The six of them sat down to a light meal due to the heat and travel; James thought it would be best. Of course, he would rather have had his usual feast that guests of Wilhelm stature warranted. But it was clear; he was here for business and on a time schedule. And James would give his left nut to find out what he was working on. After dinner, James and Wilhelm went out by the pool and sat at a table that allowed George to keep his eye on his boss from his seat in the living room.

Wilhelm opened the envelope, took out the picture, and slid it to James.

"Tell me all you know about this man, and I don't care who you made promises to." James glanced at the photo. He didn't have to look at it long to know that it was Talaus.

"My usual fee," he said looking at Wilhelm. Wilhelm nodded. "Talaus," he began, "this is a very dangerous and cunning man, and he isn't your run of the mill killer for hire. He is well-educated and started his career in his teens killing a man that cheated him out of some money. He now lives in South Africa somewhere in Zulu country in a mountain estate. He has two helpers both women. The most dangerous is Theresa; she is a psychopath and enjoys killing. The second one is called Taylor; she is in it strictly for the money and is one of the best snipers out there working.

"They both stay with him and are his personal killers and lovers. They carry out the special hits. Talaus is the head of an international organization that deals in espionage, murder, and mercenary work. Word has it, he is working for some secret organization providing security somewhere on the coast of Turkey on the Mediterranean side. He has sent Theresa to oversee the operation which makes it an important assignment. Listen closely, my friend. This man is smart and ruthless; he will do anything to fulfill a contract. In a lot of ways, he reminds me of you. If you come across him, kill him without hesitation and do the same to his women if you have the chance. Is there anything else I can do for you?" he asked.

"Yes, can you get me a picture of the women?"

"Yes, of course, I'll have a copy brought to you immediately. How long are you staying?"

"Long enough to re-fuel and conclude our business."

"I understand. I wish you could visit longer; we could have some fun. I tell you what, I'll throw in the jet fuel and none of that watered down shit I sell to the others." James sat back and laughed at what he just said. Then they got up and walked back into the house. James summoned a man and told him what he wanted, and then he looked over at George. "I have met that man before but I just can't put my finger on it," James said to Wilhelm. Wilhelm didn't answer him; he didn't even look at him. Instead, he walked over to the bar and poured himself a drink. The man came back and handed Wilhelm a manila envelope. He opened it and took out the photos of the two women.

"How long to fuel the plane?" he asked.

"It's already fueled," James said. "I thought you might be in a rush so I took the liberty."

"Thanks for the hospitality, James, and the help."

"My pleasure, Wilhelm."

"Let's go, George," Wilhelm said as he headed out of the room. Wilhelm waited until the plane had taken off to talk.

"Relieve the pilot, George, and set course for the southern office in Turkey." Then he laid out some papers on the table in front of him. He felt the plane bank starboard then level out. The door to the pilot's cabin opened, and the pilot stepped out and nodded as he passed. He sat down in the rear seat, reclined; and in a few minutes, Wilhelm could hear him softly snoring. He turned his attention back to the paperwork in front of him and began to read the information on Talaus and his killers.

They arrived at the office which was connected to a traditional Turkish house in the middle of the block. A stone craving of an eagle with the words *Black Eagle Exports* was its only identifying mark. Arriving in time for brunch, he and George ate as Captain America brought him up to speed.

"I have our friend in the safe house ready for transport," he began. "Did he give you any trouble?"

"No, sir, after the beating George gave him, he's been a good boy."

"What beating? I didn't authorize any beating did I, George?"

Wilhelm said as he looked at him. George saw his bosses eyes darken, and he knew he was in serious trouble.

"My apologies, sir, but when I saw him with that young girl I sort of punched him," he explained. Wilhelm's eyes softened until they were normal.

"Please continue, Captain," he said turning his attention back to Tommy.

"The information you relayed checks out about this Talaus guy and the two women. The reason we have so little information on him is he usually stays in the background. But for some reason, he has taken a personal interest in this particular case. Or the money is really good. It cost a lot to hire this guy; he is strictly big time, government-like big time."

"Thanks, Captain. Now I want you to send the photo of Theresa to the teams and instruct them to kill her on sight. Also I want you to help George prepare and deliver Derik to the pickup point; he's going out tonight."

The rest of the morning, Wilhelm did paperwork and the office buzzed with activity. After all, it was a working export office. Clients came in and out all morning only slowing down after three in the afternoon.

Wilhelm finally got around to what he called "the bad news reports." In fact, they are the reports of the major actions taken and incidents that may affect his area of operation. He came across the report concerning the attack and casualties on Wendy's group. As he read on, the report stated that Frank was behind the attack and his present location was unknown. Wilhelm pressed the intercom button on his desk phone.

"Captain, come in here," he said then he re-read the message. Pam may have completed her mission by now, and Wendy would be headed back to her now dead group. He had to stop her and re-route her. Just then, Tommy walked in.

"Yes, sir."

"I need you to get a message to this agent," he said as he started to write. He handed it to him. "And wait for a reply then bring it to me," Wilhelm said with an intense expression looking at Tommy in his eyes as he gave him his instructions. Tommy took the message, said,

"Yes, sir," and hurried out of the office and back to the comm center. Wilhelm picked up the next message which had a picture attached to it. From the look of it, it was taken at night and the street lights gave it an eerie glow. He read the message then looked at the photograph closely. "I'll be damn, that's Susan and Dieter. So she put in some wet work, good for her," he thought and continued through the messages. Tommy came back and told him that the agent was still in-house and will proceed to Washington right away.

"Thanks, Captain," he said and went back to his paperwork. One of the office workers knocked on his door.

"Yes."

"There is a woman here to see you, sir," she said.

"Does this woman have a name?"

"Yes, sir, it's Carla."

"Well, show her in."

In walked Carla big as life and wearing a hat just as big. When he saw her, he couldn't help hearing the song, *Don't Mess with Sexy Ida*. Not only did the song describe her ways, it described her. He thought of it every time he saw her.

"Have a seat, Carla," he said as he opened his humidor and took out a cigar. Carla sat down in a large leather wingchair and crossed her legs as she took off her sunglasses. Wilhelm looked at her exposed thigh; he could see a good part of it. The short dress she was wearing did little in the way of concealment. He lit his cigar turning it in a slow circle ensuring an even lighting of the tobacco. He blew out some smoke and stared at her for a moment focusing on her face. If he hadn't had intimate knowledge of her age as a young forty-six year old, he would believe her when she said she was an aging twenty-eight year old. She accomplished this with no plastic surgery; he had to hand it to the sistah; she handled her business well. "What brings you to sunny southern Turkey?"

"Why so blunt, Wilhelm? Can't an old friend drop in on another old friend?" she said adjusting herself in the chair. You could at least offer a girl some refreshments before you interrogate her, can't you?"

"I don't think you'll be here long enough to enjoy it, Carla. So whatever your reason for dropping in, let's get straight to it, shall we?" he said then drew on the cigar and blew a large cloud of smoke in her direction. Carla waved her hand that held her gloves a few times in front of her face fanning the smoke away.

"Okay, here it is. I hear the agency has a kill/capture order out for Frank, and I want to stay out of the line of fire," she said with all seriousness. Then she waited for his response.

"Alright, Carla, but what makes you think the agency has you in their sights?"

"I've had a tail on me for the last week for one thing and a break in at my Madrid apartment, and it wasn't the agency." Wilhelm put his cigar in the ash tray and picked up the phone. He told Tommy to come to the office. Then he called the house girl, and Carla told her what she wanted. Tommy arrived; they waited until the house girl brought Carla's drink and left before Wilhelm spoke.

"I need you to tell me everything, Carla; and I want you to give all of the technical information to this gentleman. I need to know everything, Carla; otherwise, I won't help you. Now do we have a deal?" Wilhelm said and then locked eyes with her.

Carla uncrossed her legs and tugged at her dress before crossing her legs again. Then she took a big gulp from her drink.

"Okay, we have a deal. But I do have your word I won't be targeted by the agency?" Wilhelm nodded. She took a deep breath and began talking and alternating her attention between him and Tommy. Wilhelm was surprised at the amount of information she had to offer. Some of it filled in the gaps to cases five years back. It was when she handed Tommy a pair of disks that it turned dangerous for Wilhelm, and he realized that she was clearing her conscious. Somebody wanted her dead and she had run to him. She wasn't part of the agency; she hadn't been for the last six years. He couldn't help her if he wanted to, but he kept pumping her for details and she kept delivering.

This went on for several hours; when she was done, she looked different somehow. She got up, smoothed out her dress, fixed her hat, put on her sunglasses and gloves, and walked to the office door. Without looking back, she opened it, walked out, went down the stairs out the front door into a waiting car, and drove away. Wilhelm watched her from his window as he puffed on his cigar. On the street, a young Turkish man on a motorcycle kept his eyes on him. Wilhelm looked at him and nodded. The young man put on his helmet, jumped on his bike, and followed her.

"Find out everything that's on those disks, Tommy, and keep this to yourself. This is strictly off the books."

"Yes, sir, and sir, who was that fine woman?"

"A dead woman, Tommy. She just wanted to make amends before she dies; that's all. Now get started, and Tommy, send an action message to Team Two. Have Nirgal and Kubaba report to me this evening after dark." Jamal and Teri arrived at the office via the roof. They had entered a house two doors up from the office, went up to the roof, and crossed over two houses until they reached his building. Then they had to go through two check points before seeing him.

"I want you two to check on this person and report on who she sees and where she goes. You are not to interfere in anyway even if it is life threatening. Do you understand your orders?" Then he handed them Carla's picture. "This is your subject." The two agents took their time committing the image to memory. Jamal placed the photo back on the desk.

"So we can't save this chick no matter what. Is that what you're telling us?" Jamal asked talking with hands and a puzzled look on his face. Teri stood there and watched him. She couldn't believe that he was questioning the boss. Wilhelm leaned back in his chair and smiled. He liked the young agent because he had a light-hearted approach to his work.

"How much Italian is in your blood?" he asked.

"None, sir. Why?" Jamal replied. Now his face became serious.

"The whole hand thing; it reminded me of an old friend. To answer your question in a word, yes. Now are there any more questions?" Wilhelm said looking at Jamal. Both of them shook their heads no. "Then Nirgal, Kubaba, I suggest you get going."

The two agents parked their car down the street from Carla's bungalow. They had circled the block once in the car and a second time on foot. When they were satisfied that the block was safe and no other watchful eyes were there, they took up a position where they could observe their subject. Kubaba looked through a mini-telescope at the bungalow. She could see three shadows that looked like they were dancing, but she couldn't be sure.

"I'm going to take a closer look; I can't see anything from here," Kubaba said.

"Remember, no interference," Nirgal said as she slipped out of the car closing the door quietly behind her. Kubaba made her way to the bungalow and slid down the side of it into the shadows. She heard music and laughter coming from inside. She went to the first window and peered in. She saw nothing; the window covering prevented her from seeing anything. She moved furtively around the structure until she was on the other side that was in view from the street.

Nirgal watched helplessly through the telescope. "What is that woman doing? If she gets caught, I'll kill her," he thought. Kubaba checked her surroundings then looked through the window. She stayed there for what seemed like an eternity. Then she retreated and returned to the car.

"What were you doing? You could've been seen," Nirgal said with concern.

"You should have seen what I just witnessed," she said ignoring him. "She was naked dancing around the living room with two fine, well-hung guys who looked to be in their early twenties, twenty-two if I had to guess. All three of them were dancing and drinking. She's my new hero, I tell ya."

"Good, that makes this assignment easy. As long as she is fucking and sucking, she's not going any place soon."

"You got that right. The way they are going—easy night, late morning," she said and slid down in the passenger's seat placing her feet on the dashboard. They sat watching and engaging in small talk and took turns checking the bungalow's blind side. Around 1:00 a.m., Carla's lights went out.

"I guess it's bed time," Nirgal said to Kubaba as he tapped her knee to wake her. "It's your turn, I believe, young lady."

"Alright, I'm going. All I'm going to find is three sleeping bodies. Why did the boss have us watch this woman anyway?" Kubaba got out of the car and headed for the bungalow as Nirgal watched her approach. He watched her disappear around the other side. Then suddenly, she headed back towards him trying hard not to run. He took out his pistol and checked the mirrors looking behind him. The car door opened and she got in. The look on her face was one of surprise.

"What happened?"

"They're all dead."

"Oh, fuck! Are you sure?"

"Yeah, pretty much, we have to make sure though; that's why I came back."

"How the-fuck could that happen? Shit, the boss is going to kill us. What-the-fuck are we going to tell him?" Nirgal said as he checked his weapon and grabbed a flashlight. "Let's go see what happened and take no unnecessary risks. Hear me?"

"Yeah, I hear you. Let's get going already," she said racking a round in the chamber of her pistol. They exited the car and made a tactical approach to the bungalow. Once there, they went to the back door to gain entry. Nirgal took the lead and the pair made their entry. Their training kicked in, and they started to clear the rooms, first the main room then the second bedroom. It was in the master bedroom where they found the three of them. One of the toy boys was slumped in the corner next to the bed. He had been stabbed in the heart with a throwing knife. The second one was across the room. He was cut up badly but from the angles of his wounds, he had put up a fight. His throat was cut and he was placed in a chair.

Carla was lying on the bed; she had been stabbed in the stomach. When Kubaba checked her, she moved.

"Shit, she's still alive. Nirgal, get over here!" she said as she leaned close to her body. "She's trying to say something." Then she leaned closer placing her ear near Carla's mouth and listened.

"What did she say?" Nirgal asked.

"She said she had nothing to do with Nicaragua."

"Let's search the place and get out of here."

They searched the bungalow, returned to the car, and headed back to the office and Wilhelm. A half hour later, they were standing in front of him giving their report. He sat there listening expressionless, watching his agents fidget as they told the story.

"Anything else? Is this all you found?" he asked pointing to the two suede pouches. They both nodded. "Open them." Jamal reached down and opened each pouch pouring out the contents. Wilhelm looked at the array of diamonds, rubies, and emeralds and thought, "This must have been her retirement fund." He looked back at the two agents standing in front of him. "As far as I'm concerned, I don't see any pouches full of stones; I want you two to play nice and fair when dividing them. Now get out of here and go back to work." Jamal scooped up the gems. He and Teri left a little bewildered. They expected him to say just kidding, but he didn't.

Theresa sat on the couch sipping a cup of tea and replaying the evening's events. She couldn't believe what that bitch told her and could it possibly be true. She smiled to herself and took another sip; she was reminiscing on her kill. The second guy did try to put up a fight. He gave her a chance to try out a few new moves with the blade, but he didn't last long. The woman was the most interesting. Carla lasted longer than she would have thought, and her pain threshold was amazing. "Killing her was the highlight of the evening. Besides, the information which I think I'll keep to myself for now... . There's no need for Talaus to know just yet," Theresa thought then took another sip of her tea.

South Africa

Talaus was sitting, drinking scotch, and thinking, as he scratched the head of one of his three dogs and watched Taylor watch TV. He was wondering if he had made a mistake by sending Theresa to oversee security on this project. Knowing how she felt, he hoped she wouldn't go off on one of her killing rampages trying to lure Wilhelm out. He was seriously thinking about retiring her; she was becoming increasingly harder to control. Maybe, Wilhelm will do him the favor and kill her for him; that would make life a lot easier. Talaus drank the last drop of scotch in one gulp. He got up and headed to the bar for a refill. As he poured, he smiled. Wilhelm killing her would solve the problems associated with having her removed. Then he went over to Taylor and sat down next to her. She laid her head on his lap, and he played in her hair as they watched TV.

Ophiuchus: Day Nine

Chapter Twenty-Six

Turkey

Alex sat at the head of the table drinking tea and looking at the photos spread out in front of him. Tonight, they would collect their targets and remove the guards around them. He didn't like to say or think the word *kill*. But he knew that's what they would do—kill them. He couldn't chance one of the guards getting away and sounding the alarm. He picked up the photo of his target. "She's pretty enough, alright," he thought. Sleeping with her should be the easy part. But he wondered about his partner. Would she, could she pull it off? He had little doubt she could kill. But could she have sex with a woman? He had no way of knowing until it happened. Now he really wished the bitch had liked Teri, but he would play the hand he was dealt.

He heard a sound and looked up towards the end of the table. In walked Kubaba, Nirgal, and the two Turkish agents. He had given the woman the name Sahara. The man, he called Big T because he was a large and powerful looking Turk. They both seemed to like their names. They said,

"Good morning," and he waited until they had filled their mugs with either coffee or tea and sat down.

"Our seed lady will be the first target tonight. Me and Sahara will handle this one. Big T, you will be security and transport. Kubaba, you will keep your target, the water guy, busy until you get the signal from me. Then prepare your target for transport. Now here is where we could run into trouble; it's the last target, the engineer. Unlike the seed lady and the water guy, he's not indulging in his kink; he just has been plain boring so we can't use it to exploit him.

357

"The only opening I've found is that he and one of his guards play cards and drink the night away; and for that reason, I have saved him for last. Plus, we'll have enough man power for the snatch if I use all of us except for you, Kubaba; I need you to guard the other two. So let's recheck the equipment we need for tonight and make sure you go over the latest Intel." Alex looked around the table at each agent then said, "Now go and have a good breakfast and see to your preparations." The four agents left the room as quietly as they had entered. Alex got up, refilled his cup with hot water, put in a fresh tea bag, sat down, and then picked up the photo and stared at it. He knew this would be a bloody night, and the engineer would be the most problematic as he looked at his picture.

Syria

Randy sat in the main room of the beach house watching the sunrise over the ocean and drinking espresso. He was contemplating the coming events of the day and wondered if he would survive. All of their targets were as dangerous as they come, and the odds were slim on their side of the fence. He sat quietly calming his mind and watching the sun slowly rise above the water. He rose from his chair and refilled his cup. As he did so, Ishtar walked into the room.

"Good morning," she said. He nodded and returned to his chair.

The rest of the team filtered in one by one, first Tiamat then Pazuzu; their Syrian assistant wasn't present. Enki waited until they had gotten their coffee and started to talk softly among themselves keeping their distance from him.

"Okay, pull up a chair and gather 'round," he said. The agents took seats around him and waited. "This is how we're going to work this.

Tiamat, we're going to take your target first. I need you to be ready to move on her at 2200 hours because I'll need you and Ishtar for a distraction mission before you pick up our Chilean firecracker. I want you two not to take any chances with this woman. She's a skilled killer so be on your toes. As for the Pol, Pazuzu and I will take care of him. Now let's go over the plan once more. I want to be sure everybody knows what to do before we jump off. Any questions?" No one had any, so he got up and headed for the communications room. It was time to send the morning report.

Argentina

Frank sat on the balcony sixteen stories above the city of Rawson and looked at the view as he enjoyed his cigar. In forty-eight hours, it would be all over. Either he would be sitting on the council or he would be dead. He had played his hand and did his part even going as far as removing that uppity bitch's team and eliminating a dozen agents. He hadn't counted on Wilhelm moving around as much as he did. He really put on the disappearing act this time. He smiled at that thought and pulled on his cigar.

Now it was up to Talaus. Frank hoped he could pull it off although he had his doubts. Wilhelm had survived better plots. He still had a few friends and enough money to disappear if it came to that, and he had no problem sending hitters after Wilhelm. But he'd rather avoid that scenario. A battle with Wilhelm would be costly in lives and money. Oh well, c'est la vie. If it came to that, he knew of a half dozen countries that would pay handsomely for the information he had on Wilhelm.

If he had any regrets—which he didn't—, it was the loss of Linda. He really did love her; he didn't trust her but he loved her. "And that cunt Susan, she thought she could send Wilhelm my messages and I wouldn't find out. If she hadn't started using that pig Latin that only the three of them knew, I wouldn't have sent that kill team after her. Too bad they missed. If I had known she was such a talented killer, I would have recruited her." Frank stood up and walked to the railing. He looked over and plucked his cigar into the wind and watched it fall out of sight. He wondered whom it would hit when it landed and smiled at the thought. Then he walked back into the apartment.

C. A. A.

Wilhelm was back on the ship where he could monitor the teams and help with their extraction if necessary. He had Tommy watching Derik as he decoded all of his records revealing not only his secrets but those of his mother's tong as well. It was a wealth of information; and if Pam was successful, he would have the other half of the arms and white slavery trade that they shared. The agency would love the arms smuggling section, and Interpol would be very appreciative for the slave routes.

For most people in this position, this would be a highly stressful time but not for Wilhelm. He used this time to gauge his agents. He was most interested in how creative they would be under the circumstances and if the stress of it all would make them falter. He expected them to be successful and not lose anyone; after all, he had trained them. But he knew they would take casualties. He could only hope they would be minimal although he knew he would lose at least two. He looked at the clock on his desk and noted the time. He had ten or more hours to go before either team made their move.

Turkey

Alex was sitting on the couch when he looked at his watch. It read 2100 hours. Kubaba had just left for her rendezvous with the water guy. She was wearing a light pink tube dress with two-inch open-toed heels and had her toenails painted pink to match her dress.

"He likes pink. I even put on pink panties, see." She pulled up the corner of her dress and showed him.

"Very nice, Kubaba, are you clear on the plan?" Alex said.

"Yes, he won't be a problem. While he's busy sucking my toes and looking up my dress, he'll never see it coming," she said as she demonstrated with her left hand how she would stick the needle with the sedative in him. She reached into her clutch bag and produced a needle that was half the length of a regular one, showed him, and then put it back. "Well, how do I look?"

"Good enough to eat," he replied then smiled. She smoothed out her dress, winked at him, and with a little extra wiggle of her hips walked out the door.

Alex went back to his thoughts. He was hoping that Oannes would make it and in one piece. He also hoped she would be on time; he would hate to leave her and have her make her own way out. Just then, Sahara walked in barefoot carrying her shoes in her hand. She was dressed in a sleeveless mustard colored dress that ended six inches above her knees. She had no makeup on, and her long black wavy hair hung freely except for a hair comb that held her hair away from the right side of her face.

The color of her dress brought out her complexion in a way he had not noticed before. She sat in the chair opposite from him, placed her shoes neatly beside her, and stared at him.

"What?" he asked.

"Nothing."

"Then why are you staring at me?"

"When do we leave?" she asked changing the tone of the conversation.

"As soon as I get the call. Big T has some of his people staking out the three clubs that the seed lady likes to frequent and when she shows up at one of them, I'll be notified." An uncomfortable silence fell over the room and both of them felt a little nervous in each other's company. Alex got up to leave.

"Please, do not leave. I have something I wish to talk to you about," she said in a soft voice. Alex sat down and crossed his legs.

"Well, what is it, Sahara?" he said flatly.

"I am aware that you are not confident in my skills as an intelligentsia officer but I am very good at my job. Even though I have never slept with a woman before I will not fail this mission. I promise you, she will never know that this is my first time. After all, I'm a woman; therefore, I will know how to please a woman. Do you not agree?"

"Listen, Sahara, you're going to be fine. It's only sex and I'll be there also. So if you run into any problems, concentrate on me, okay."

"Okay, Ninurta, I will do just that. You have much experience in this area, yes?"

"No, so if I get into any trouble, I'll concentrate on you; and in that dress, I'm sure that won't be hard to do," he said as he smiled at her. He watched her body relax which helped him to relax. He hated waiting on anything but waiting for the call to action was by far the worst. Just then, his phone vibrated. He was glad for the distraction and wished it was the call from Big T.

"Yeah," he said.

"Target at location three," the voice on the phone said and then hung up.

"We're on," he said to Sahara as he got up and left the room. Sahara put on her shoes and stood up. She smoothed her dress then opened her purse. After taking out the 25 caliber pistol, she removed the clip and visually checked the ammo. She reloaded it and chambered a round. Alex walked back into the room and asked her if she was ready. Sahara nodded and walked towards the door.

Syria

Tiamat sat observing the three other girls smoking hashish and talking. They seemed to be enjoying themselves. But her target, Amaranta, seemed to be nervous; she was walking around checking and double checking everything. The two guards protecting her were stationed outside. They looked capable and professional and both were armed with machine pistols. Tiamat wondered who the guests would be. She hoped they were men but she wasn't sure with this one. She hoped the party would start soon or she may run into a time problem. With Enki wound up as tight as he was, he might get impatient and jump the gun.

"What time is it?" she asked.

"Why, you have somewhere to go?" one of the girls replied as she blew out some hash smoke.

"I'm going to find something else to do if this do-nothing continues much longer."

"I hear you, girl. This hash is making me horny, and I'm going to fuck something soon or bust," she said then burst into laughter.

Enki sat in the backseat of the car listening to Ishtar and Pazuzu talk about what they had planned for their time off after the mission. He paid little attention to what they were saying; his mind was on the Pol. He looked at the beach house where the present target was located and wondered when the party would begin.

Amaranta came into the room and spoke to the women.

"Our guests will be here any moment and there is one change. You will be with me for a special guest," she said pointing to Tiamat. "I expect you, ladies, to be very accommodating to our guests. Remember, the word *no* does not exist when it comes to our guests," she continued. Then she walked around the room re-checking and re-stocking the drug bowels that held hash and marijuana and replaced what the girls had smoked while they waited. She didn't care how much they smoked as long as they could perform when the time came. And besides, she preferred them high, not drunk or stoned on heroin or coke.

The door swung open and in walked three men dressed in grey suits. Amaranta approached them. The short one in the front smiled and greeted her warmly. They talked quietly for a moment; then he left leaving the two men standing there eyeing the women. A short time later, he returned this time with a woman who looked to be in her late twenties. She was tall, busty, and shapely with long brown hair. She also was dressed in a grey suit, heels, and stockings. She looked all business as she greeted Amaranta.

"Ladies, these are our guests whom we have been waiting for. Please, make them comfortable," she announced. The men smiled and headed straight for them. Tiamat took a deep breath and smiled as the short man made a beeline straight for her. Tiamat watched as Amaranta and the woman went into another room. Meanwhile, Enki took note of the new players; he hadn't expected so many men at this party. In fact, he expected women since the target was a lesbian.

"The plan stays the same, just a few more people to kill is all," he said to Pazuzu and Ishtar as he screwed a silencer onto his pistol. Pazuzu screwed a silencer onto his carbine and now was doing the same to his pistol.

Tiamat rubbed the man's head and played in his hair as he smoked on his bong kissing and sucking on her nipples in between pulls. She talked softly to him and giggled at the appropriate times while keeping him from sticking his dirty fingers in her snatch. Just as she was tiring of this game of hide the fingers, Amaranta came into the room and summoned her with a wave of her hand and not a moment too soon for her taste. She stood up and smoothed out her outfit, what little there was of it, and pressed the center snap on her bra sending the signal.

"I've just received the go signal," Ishtar announced from the front seat.

"Okay, we go in twenty minutes," Enki said chambering a round. Tiamat followed Amaranta to the master bedroom. When they entered, she found the mystery woman naked on the bed.

"Now that business is out of the way, it's time for a little fun. I have told our guest all about you. And she can hardly wait to, shall we say, taste you," Amaranta said as she began to undress. Tiamat did the same and crawled across the bed towards the woman with a devilish smile.

Pazuzu stepped quietly out of the car and started up the street towards the beach house making sure he kept close to the shadows. He moved quickly and cautiously. His soft rubber shoes made no noise as he walked and his black uniform made him invisible in the dark. When he was in position, he radioed Enki. Then he and Ishtar started to slowly walk up the street. When they were close to the beach house, they started talking. When the two guards turned their attention towards them, Pazuzu fired his carbine that whispered its death. Not making any noise, the two guards fell dead. Enki and Ishtar rushed up to the front door, grabbed the dead men by the collar, and dragged them off hiding their bodies behind some bushes.

Pazuzu soon joined them. He and Enki went to the front door and waited while Ishtar went around back. Then Enki tried the door; he turned the handle slowly until he felt it open. He looked at Pazuzu then counted mouthing the words. When he reached ten, he opened the door and walked in with Pazuzu right behind him. The two of them spread out and started firing their FNH five-sevenN pistols loaded with subsonic ammo. They shot everybody in the room; the three men and women all died in their various sex positions; it was over in seconds. At the same time, Ishtar shot the backdoor lock and was making her entrance when she ran into her partners. They formed up and headed for the bedroom. When they entered the room with pistols at the ready, they found Tiamat sitting on the bed.

"What happened?" Enki asked.

"I broke this one's neck when she came up for air," she said pointing to the dead woman on the bed. "And when this one ran back into the room from the gunfire, I knocked her out. Did you find her daughter?"

"No, Ishtar, Pazuzu, search the place for her," Enki instructed.

"And if we find her?" Ishtar asked.

"Tie her up or something. Just keep her out of the way 'till dawn. Now go," he said. The pair came back and reported that the daughter was not in the house and that they had gathered up all of the information from the bodies and brought in the two guards' bodies as well. "Good, Pazuzu, go get the car. We'll take Ms. Amaranta to the holding house then go after the last two targets." They put Amaranta in the truck and headed off to the holding house.

Once there, they dressed her in a black jumpsuit, placed a hood over her head, and bound her hands and feet with flex cuffs making sure they were not too tight. Tiamat and Ishtar changed into very short tube dresses and thongs then headed out the door with a small vinyl drawstring bag that held a change of clothes. Enki gave Big T's men who were guarding the prisoner their instructions, and then he followed the women out to the car. As Pazuzu drove, Enki went over the plan with Tiamat and Ishtar. Then they rode the rest of the way in silence.

They parked the car half a block away from where the Pol was staying at the bend of the road near the corner. This position hid the car from view but allowed Enki a good line of sight to the Pol's house and to a car with four men in it. Tiamat and Ishtar got out and started up the street; there wasn't much traffic and the street was clear. When they got within ten meters of the men in the car, they started to put on their drunken act. Tiamat started talking loudly and stumbling while holding on to Ishtar. Both women were barefoot holding their shoes in their hands. The men in the car turned to look at them. They watched as the women stumbled up to and a little past the car where they paused. Ishtar watched as Enki slowly drove up the street in their car towards them. She squeezed Tiamat's shoulder giving her the signal.

At that moment, Tiamat dropped her shoes and bent over to pick them up without bending her knees giving the men in the car a good look at her thong and ass. She fumbled a few times trying to pick up her shoes as she wiggled a little for effect. When their car was in place, muffled shots rang out as Enki sprayed the car with bullets from his P90 assault rifle. The four men's bodies jerked as the armor piercing rounds slammed into them at point blank range. When he had finished firing, Ishtar stepped up to the car and checked; they were all dead. She gave the signal; Enki and Pazuzu jumped out of their car, and the two women got in and drove away. They had their own target to secure.

Enki and Pazuzu approached the house from the eastside, the side furthest from the street. They split up with Pazuzu taking the backdoor and Enki going around to the front. Enki paused and listened. He knew the Pol was in there. If he wasn't, his shadows wouldn't have been out front. He was glad he didn't tell the team that the Pol's babysitters were Mossad. He had informed Anu of this fact and had received the go ahead. In a few moments, he would have his revenge or be dead. He was sure it would be revenge.

"We enter on three," he said into his ear piece. "Roger, that," came the reply.

"Three, two, one, go," he said and shot the lock and kicked in the door. He entered hard and fast staying low with his pistol pointing everywhere his eyes were looking. He could hear the same thing going on in the back of the house as Pazuzu made his entrance.

The living room was dark except for a small lamp that illuminated the corner where a book sat on a chair. Enki cautiously and quietly crossed the room staying as far away from the light as possible. He made his way to the hallway and waited for Pazuzu who quickly joined him. Pazuzu told him that the kitchen and adjoining room were clear.

"Then he has to be upstairs," Enki whispered as they approached the stairs. Suddenly, muffled shots impacted the wall just above and to the right of their heads. Neither man said a word. They began returning fire shooting up the stairs into the darkness at a target they could not see. Then a burst of automatic fire came at them. This time the shots were more accurate causing them to retreat back into the living room.

They changed magazines and waited. Hearing no movement, they entered the hallway again with pistols firing. Pazuzu fired high as Enki walked his rounds up the stairs, both men methodically placing their shots. Enki felt a button on the wall against his shoulder; he pressed it then moved his shoulder in an up-and-down motion turning on the hallway light.

The Pol came into sight. He was halfway down the steps when he had jerked his night vision goggles off; his eyelids were blinking wildly. He was temporarily blinded by the sudden light. As Pazuzu was reloading, Enki rushed up the stairs and grabbed the Pol by the ankles pulling hard.

"Ugh!" was the only sound he made as he hit the stairs and started sliding down them. He made no attempt to resist. Instead, he relaxed and went with it. But when he reached the third step from the bottom, he sat up and punched Enki hard in the forehead. The punch sounded like a slap but the impact knocked Enki back causing him to let go.

The Pol was on his feet and attacking. He threw a side kick catching Pazuzu in the throat. The impact made him drop his weapon and threw him against the wall, hard. The Pol followed up with a punch to the temple dazing him causing him to go down on one knee. When the Pol turned around, Enki hit him in the face with a palm strike. Then he grabbed him and kneed him in the groin. Next he hit the Pol with an uppercut and two strikes to the ribs. The Pol pushed him back and delivered a front kick to Enki's mid-section knocking him into the living room. The Pol was in close pursuit when Enki recovered. He faced the

Pol who was now armed with a knife. Enki pulled his Sykes blade and took a combat stance. Just then, Pazuzu appeared in the doorway with his pistol aimed at the Pol's head.

"Don't shoot him! He's mine!" Enki yelled at Pazuzu. The Pol stood still taking it all in; his eyes darting back and forth between the two men.

"Who are you? independent? or agency?" he asked.

"Agency," Enki replied.

"Good, a professional should only kill professionals," he said in a thick eastern European accent. "So you want the pleasure and reputation of killing the Pol. Are you sure you are up to it?" Then he laughed a good hearty laugh. Enki and Pazuzu watched as he did so. They were thinking the same thing. "He really has lost it. He's a madman in the mad world of espionage."

"So you are the chosen one they sent," he said to Enki looking at him in the eyes. "Well, let's get to it. If I win, your partner will shot me."

"Fucking right, let's just shot him and get out of here," Pazuzu said in a hushed voice. Enki said nothing. He resumed his stance and started towards him.

"Well, we have our answer," the Pol said as he began to circle to his left.

Enki had his knife in a reverse grip with the blade lying against his forearm. The Pol had his out front pointed towards his opponent. They completed a half circle before the Pol attacked stabbing and punching at the same time. Enki blocked and parried the attack managing not to get cut in the exchange. He waited for the second attack. He didn't wait long. This time, the Pol mixed it up. He stabbed at Enki's face then kicked him in the stomach. Bringing the knife down across his chest, he cut him then he reversed his direction and came across his stomach. Enki jumped back avoiding the second cut then came forward quickly slashing low catching the Pol across his left thigh leaving a deep gash.

"Motherfucker!" he said as he started to favor his left leg. Enki came at him again slashing and stabbing. The Pol blocked and parried but got cut two more times in the process, once across the chest and another on his right arm near his wrist.

The blood was flowing freely and being splattered around the room from their rapid movements. The Pol fainted an attacked to Enki's right side and ended up stabbing him in the left shoulder sinking three inches of his blade into him. Then he hit him with a knife hand on his collar bone. Enki punched him in the throat. Staying close to him, he moved to the Pol's left side, pinned his left arm next to his body, and sank his knife into his side pushing the blade up to its hilt in between his ribs and puncturing his lung. He turned the Pol towards him as he withdrew the blade and replanted the knife this time in his sternum. The Pol stiffened. His eyes widened. Then his body went limp. Enki laid him down, removed his blade, and then sat on the floor beside the body.

"Come on, man. We have to go," Pazuzu said as he helped Enki get up. The pair headed for the backdoor. As Pazuzu helped him to the car that they had staged the day before, he realized just how hurt Enki really was. He placed him in the car, got in, and headed for the holding house. As he drove, he noticed the trickle of blood leaking from the corner of Enki mouth.

Ishtar and Tiamat sat in the car waiting for Bellona to arrive. They had received news that she had left the club with her newest playmates.

The women had changed into their all black work outfits, checked their equipment, and were now watching the lone guard. They didn't talk. They sat in silence each in her own thoughts, each in her own private world. This target was dangerous. The bitch was a true killer. Ishtar wondered if she could take her alive if things went south. Tiamat looked through her binoculars searching for any sign of Bellona. She wanted this to be over; she was tired of Syria. She had no doubt that she and Ishtar could take this bitch. The guards were just a formality. As for her fuck friends, oh well…wrong place, wrong time.

Then Bellona came into view. She was walking in between a couple with her second guard about ten meters behind her.

"Here she comes," Tiamat said. "She's the looker in the miniskirt and heels. The guard is ten meters behind. See them."

"Yeah, I got them; and, Tiamat, you got to give up eating pussy. She's not such a looker. Look at that nose and she's knocked-kneed," Ishtar replied.

"Fuck you, Ishtar, and don't knock it 'till you tried it. Now can we snatch this chick so I can go home already," Tiamat snapped back.

"Alright, you know the plan, stick to it and this should go smoothly, okay."

"Yeah." They watched Bellona approach, speak to the guard briefly, and go into her beach house. The second guard took his post next to the first, and the pair lit their cigarettes and settled in for the night.

Tiamat watched the house and waited. The living room light came on, and she could see the outline of the three people through the window. Shortly after, the bedroom light came on then went off.

"Let's give her a few minutes; after all, this is her last go round," Ishtar said matter-of-factly. They waited ten minutes. Then Ishtar started the car, and Tiamat got into the back seat and rolled down the window. She scooted down to where her head was just out of sight. With her black skull cap on, she blended in with the darkness with her silenced assault rifle at the ready. Ishtar pulled out and slowly drove up the street. She knew her motions would draw the guard's attention. While they were staring at her trying to ID her as friend or foe, Tiamat would strike.

As the car approached, the two guards took notice. They strained to see who was driving while Tiamat took aim. The short controlled burst hit the two men across the chest knocking them backwards against the steps. Ishtar made a U-turn and stopped in front of the house. Tiamat jumped out and shot the men again making sure they were dead. The two agents dragged the bodies around the side of the house and left them. They returned to the front door, and Ishtar began to quietly pick the lock. She looked up at Tiamat, took out her pistol, slowly opened the door, and stepped in. With the door closed behind them, they made their way to the bedroom. As they got closer, they could hear the sounds of lovemaking.

They paused and listened for a moment. When they heard the distinctive moans and grunts of heavy fucking, they burst through the door. They saw Bellona being taking from the rear as she buried her face in the young woman's snatch. Ishtar fired two shots into the man. The first one hit him in the neck; the second blew a large chunk of his skull away. Bellona scrambled towards the nightstand and in the process placed the young woman between her and her attackers. Tiamat fired two shots striking the woman in her chest. The bullets ripped open her left breast as they slammed into her body killing her. Bellona reached the nightstand. She grabbed one of the three knives she had there. Then she turned and threw it into Tiamat's throat. Tiamat grabbed at her throat and tried to yell out to Ishtar. Her eyes were wide with fear. Ishtar glanced at her then turned her attention back to Bellona who had gotten to her feet and was armed with knives in both hands. Ishtar took aim at her. Bellona raised her right arm in preparation to throw. Ishtar shot her in the shoulder then in the left hand disarming her.

"Don't you move, bitch! Stand right there and bleed!" Ishtar snarled at her then she made her way over to Tiamat and bent down to check her. Tiamat smiled up at her then closed her eyes.

Ishtar approached Bellona who tried to kick her when she was close enough. Ishtar blocked the kick and hit her on the head with her gun knocking her out. She secured her hands and feet with the flex cuffs and gagged her. Then she picked her up and carried her out to the car placing her naked body in the trunk. She went back in and brought out Tiamat and laid her on the backseat and covered her face. She got in and headed for the holding house allowing herself to cry a little as she drove.

Ishtar pulled into the garage and took Bellona out of the trunk and into the house where she found Enki receiving medical care from Pazuzu.

"Good, you made it!" Enki said to her. "Put her over there. Pazuzu, stop wrapping me up like a mummy and see to our guest."

"Hi, Ishtar, glad you're back. Where's Tiamat?" Pazuzu asked as he walked past her.

"She's dead," Ishtar said.

"How?" Enki asked.

"That bitch put a knife in her neck and she bled to death."

"Where's her body?" Enki continued.

"In the car," Ishtar said as she pointed over her shoulder with her thumb.

"Bring her in and place her here," he said pointing to the corner of the room. Ishtar left and returned with Tiamat's body and gently placed her on the cot in the corner and covered her body with a blanket. "How is Bellona, Pazuzu?" Enki asked.

"She'll live, she's a little weak from the loss of blood but a half hour of this stuff and she will be just fine," Pazuzu said as he prepared an IV drip.

"Ishtar, help Pazuzu strap her in the chair," Enki said. Then he went into the next room to check on Amaranta. When he returned, Pazuzu had the IV up and running; and now he was on the laptop making contact with Anu on the C.A.A.

Wilhelm sat in front of the large screen looking at Enki and his team.

"What's the situation, Enki?" he asked.

"I have one dead, one wounded but not seriously; and all the targets have been neutralized. One guest is injured but will be able to talk in thirty minutes," he replied.

"Proceed with the interrogation of our first guest and make sure you are recording," Anu instructed. Enki told Pazuzu to watch Bellona and took Ishtar with him to the room where Amaranta was being kept. Ishtar set up the camera and checked the image of Amaranta who was now dressed in her black negligée and matching panties with her breast hanging freely and uncovered.

"How are you receiving me?" Ishtar said into the headset.

"Connection is good, proceed," Captain America replied. Ishtar walked over to a table that had a syringe and a vial on it and began to fill the syringe. Amaranta watched in silence. When she approached her, Amaranta spoke for the first time.

"What have you done with my daughter?" she asked. Ishtar looked back at Enki who was sitting in a chair out of camera sight.

"She's fine. We didn't hurt her. She's being taken care of by some really nice people. If you tell me what I want to know, you can be back with your daughter in a matter of hours," he said in a soothing voice. Amaranta smiled then shook her head no. She knew they would kill her anyway. She just hoped they really did give her daughter to nice people. Enki nodded his head and Ishtar injected the solution. "You should have taken the deal Amaranta this stuff is going to turn you into a vegetable," he said. Ishtar was back at the laptop making sure everything was being transmitted and recorded. Enki waited a few minutes then he began to ask her questions. She tried to give wrong answers but it didn't work. She told him everything.

The interrogation lasted an hour. Afterwards, Ishtar cut Amaranta loose and left her in the chair. She sat there limp. Drool ran down her cheek. She was no longer a threat to anybody.

"Good job, I hope we get the same quality Intel from our next guest. Notify me when you're set up. Anu out."

"Break it down and take it next door," Enki said as he left the room. "How's the patient?" he asked.

"Fine, she's ready," Pazuzu answered.

"Good. As soon as Ishtar sets up, we'll begin." Ishtar came in and went through the same routine. After checking in, she went to the table and filled the syringe.

"I know you aren't going to talk, bitch, so I'm just going to shoot you up and skip the preliminaries." She injected Bellona and walked back to the laptop and checked the image.

Enki went through the list of questions and double checked that everything was being recorded and that Anu was receiving it clearly. The information that Bellona was giving was fantastic. It contained details of operations they had no clue ever existed, let alone the fact that she was on her way to train a special guerrilla force whose mission was to go out and train other groups. What was disturbing about all of this was the fact that there was no fanatical reason behind it, just money. And even more, the target area was Africa specifically the western and central regions.

"Pack it up and head to the extraction point. I'll notify them about the body. And, Enki, good job," Anu said before ending the transmission.

"Okay, pack it up! And, Ishtar, make sure there are no loose ends," Enki said as he picked up his cellphone and walked into the outer room. After they had put the equipment and Tiamat's body in the van, Ishtar went back into the house and shot both women in the head. She came out of the house and got into the van.

"It's done," was all she said. The driver started the van and they headed for the extraction point.

The van pulled up. The driver who's a family member of Afra and Pazuzu got out and walked down to the dock. Halfway down, they found a cigarette boat, painted black and silver, gently rising and falling in rhythm with the waves. Nearby, a young man was standing with a machine pistol pointed at them. They stopped; the driver spoke to him, and then they briefly hugged.

"This is my cousin; he and his brother will take you from here." Pazuzu greeted the man then headed back towards the van with the driver. Pazuzu told Enki what was going on. Then he and Ishtar began loading the equipment onto the speedboat, loading Tiamat's body last.

Enki went into the small cabin and lay down; the pain killers that Pazuzu had given him were starting to kick in. The boat cast off. As they started, the low rumble of each of the four engines caused the boat to vibrate. They headed for Cyprus at a steady speed; and for the next half hour, it was a pleasant ride. Pazuzu and Ishtar sat and enjoyed the salty air filling their lungs with each breath. Both were glad this mission was over and they were going home. Suddenly, a searchlight was spotted behind them. Then they heard the engine.

"Coastal patrol! Don't worry. We can out run them!" the man piloting the boat yelled.

He steadily increased the power to the four engines and the cigarette boat's nose rose out of the water in response. Ishtar and Pazuzu readied their P90 USG assault rifles that are equipped with infrared (IR) sights and loaded a fifty round magazine. They took aim at the searchlight and waited. The speedboat bounced violently as it skimmed across the water towards Cyprus.

"That patrol boat is gaining!" Pazuzu yelled. Just then 20 mm cannon shells hit the water alongside their boat creating water spouts as it did so. Pazuzu and Ishtar opened fire sending three-round controlled bursts at the patrol boat's searchlight. After a few attempts, they hit it and it went out only to be replaced by a second light.

"Can't this boat go any faster!" Pazuzu yelled.

"Not if I want to keep control of it, I can't," the pilot replied. Just then off to their left, Ishtar saw a light. She hit Pazuzu on the shoulder and pointed.

"Fuck, just what we need another patrol boat." The pilot of the speedboat was zigzagging now and doing his best not to get hit by one of the shells that the patrol boat was shooting at them. His motion was making it impossible for Pazuzu and Ishtar to return fire. The other craft was gaining steadily, and now their pilot seemed to be heading for it. "What are you doing!" Pazuzu yelled. The pilot ignored him and kept zigzagging towards the boat. Pazuzu and Ishtar watched as the boat got closer. He leaned over to Ishtar. "If he doesn't change course soon, I'm going to shot him and take control." Ishtar nodded and pointed her weapon at the second man standing next to him.

Just as Pazuzu was ready to fire, the second boat opened fire. It was shooting at the Syrian fast-attack patrol boat. The Syrian boat changed course and headed straight for the second boat. That's when Ishtar and Pazuzu resumed fire on the patrol boat as well. The two larger vessels continued to merge firing at each other with the speedboat in the middle and the two agents along for the ride.

Suddenly, the speedboat turned hard to the left laying the boat on its side and exposing two of its engines in the process. As they leveled out, a large explosion and a great ball of flames pierced the night sky. All on board the speedboat looked on in awe at the sight as the Syrian patrol boat went up in flames. As they looked for the second boat, they saw its silhouette as it disappeared into the darkness in the direction from which it came. The pilot of the speedboat cut the throttle back, and the boat settled down to a normal cruising speed. Then he turned and waved Pazuzu forward. When he was standing next to him he said,

"My father and your boss thought that there may be trouble. So they had my cousin meet us at that point. Now we head to Cyprus to refuel then out to the ship. My cousin will escort us to Cyprus." Then he flashed him a big smile and let out a hardy laugh.

Ophiuchus: Day Ten

Chapter Twenty-Seven

Ninurta looked at his watch; it was midnight. "Enki and his team should be on their way to the ship or at least headed to the extraction point by now," he thought as he watched the seed lady flirt with Sahara. So far, the plan was working. Sahara's looks and body sucked the seed lady right in. Sahara's flirting method was uniquely different since she was making it up as she went. Ninurta leaned over to her and said,

"Time to move on." Sahara knew what this meant and went into her act.

"I really liked spending time with you, but my man is bored and wants to leave," she said to the seed lady as she whispered in her ear.

"What is he looking for tonight?"

"Oh, he's horny and wants to fuck," Sahara answered then stuck her tongue in her ear. Sahara sat back on the barstool and pulled her dress up a little as she crossed her legs and smiled sexily.

"Do you think your man will go for a three-some?"

"Of course," Sahara said as she leaned forward and placing her hand on the seed ladies upper thigh close to her crotch then gave a little squeeze and blew her a kiss. "Let's take this party to a private place."

"Okay, let's go back to my place; it's quiet and we won't be disturbed," the seed lady offered. Sahara raised her index finger as to say wait a minute and turned to face Ninurta.

"She's primed and ready let's go," she said then bent over and kissed him deeply. Sahara turned back around and said, "It's just what he needs. But I warn you, he's well-hung and hungry." The seed lady squirmed slightly in her seat.

"That just made me wet," she said and slid off the barstool, smoothed out her dress, and walked to the door. Ninurta and Sahara followed her, arm in arm. Her guard whom she introduced as her driver drove them to her place on the beach. They entered the small beach house and the guard stayed outside. "Make yourself comfortable; there's liquor and something softer if you prefer at the bar. I'm going to change...be right back," she continued as she went into the bedroom and closed the door.

"When she comes out naked, no doubt, you give her the dose; I'll take care of the guard," Ninurta said. Sahara nodded her head in agreement. Sahara took out the syringe from her clutch bag, placed it behind her left ear, and fixed her hair to conceal it from sight.

Ninurta attached the silencer to his 380 caliber pistol and tucked it in the small of his back. Then he poured both of them a drink and waited. Agnes, aka the seed lady, came out wearing a bathrobe.

"Good, you have drinks; I think I'll join you," she said as she headed to the bar. Sahara followed her. When she reached the bar, she stuck her with the syringe and injected the sedative. Ninurta covered her mouth and helped restrain her while the drug to affect. They laid her body on the floor and arranged it so it looked like she had fainted. Then Sahara went to the door and summoned the guard. When he entered, he saw Agnes lying on the floor and rushed over to her. As he was bending over to check her, Ninurta shot him in the back of the head.

Ninurta went outside and checked the perimeter then signaled the waiting van to come up. When he reentered the house, Sahara had tied the seed lady's hands behind her back and bound her feet with flex cuffs. They picked her up and carried her to the waiting van, placed her in, and got in themselves. Ninurta dialed a number sending the signal to Kubaba to get ready.

"Okay, let's go and collect the foot fetish guy and I hope he is as easy," he said as the van pulled off.

Kubaba received the signal through her tiny earpiece; the sequence of the tones told her they would be there in thirty minutes. She looked across the table at Charles, aka the water guy. He was pouring her a glass of wine and looking at her with puppy dog eyes. He was a nice guy, polite and gentlemanly towards her. She enjoyed his company; and as far as she could tell, the guy just wanted to get paid for his invention. Kubaba smiled back at him and winked.

"Charles, you have been such the gentleman all evening. I think you deserve a treat," Kubaba said as she sipped her wine looking at him over the rim of her glass. She got up and walked to a wicker chair that sat low to the floor then kicked off her shoes. She called him over with the wiggle of her index finger. The water guy half ran to her, and she could see his full erection; it made a decent size tent in the front of his pants.

He sat down on the foot stool in front of the chair. His eyes went straight to her crotch where he could see her pink panties.

"Charles," she said softly causing his eyes to jump up to meet her, "would you like to worship my feet? These pretty pink toes need some attention." The water guy nodded his head vigorously up and down then swallowed hard. "Good! And for being such a nice guy, I'm going to give you a treat," Kubaba said as she raised her hips and hooked her thumbs under the waistband of her panties and pulled them off. "Now I want you to take off your pants and undershorts," she commanded. He stood up and removed them in one fell swoop stepping out of them and kicking his pants across the floor.

"Oh, I think somebody is glad to see me," Kubaba purred then reached up with her left foot to play with his balls. "Sit down, baby, and suck my toes while mommy plays with your balls," she said as she spread her legs giving him a better view. Charles sat down and started licking and sucking Kubaba's right foot. She played with him making sure not to make him cum which was the tricky part. If he came too soon, that is, before Ninurta got there, the snatch may get messy. But if she timed it right, he would shoot his load; and while he was recovering, she would administer the drug knocking him out in seconds. The two guards would be taken care of by the team.

Kubaba encouraged him with moans and giggles. To tell the truth, she was enjoying herself; in fact, she was more than a little wet.

"Baby, why don't you put that talented tongue to better use," she said breathily then she spread her legs and scooted to the edge of the chair. Charles wasted no time burying his head between her legs and snaking his tongue around her clit. Kubaba laid back and prayed Ninurta wouldn't show up until he finished. After three mind blowing orgasms, she stopped him. "When I tell you that was fantastic, I mean it, baby. Now why don't you finish yourself and let mommy watch," she said as she sat up and removed her hair from her face.

As she watched Charles jerk off, her earpiece sounded again. This time, the tones told her that the team was outside and ready. "Shit!" she thought then looked at the water guy. He was staring at her crotch and jerking away. "They can wait a minute or two. At the rate he's going, he won't last long; he does deserve to have one good memory considering what's ahead of him," she thought. Then she sat back spreading her legs wider and watched the show. Five minutes later, he grunted and shot his load all over her foot then collapsed with his head in her lap. Kubaba reached into her clutch bag, took out the syringe, and injected him in the neck. Then she sent the signal, wiped up his cum with his shirt, got up, put her panties on, and prepared for the team to enter.

"Okay, Sahara, you're on," Ninurta said. She smiled, got out of the van, and started walking towards the house. Nirgal kept an eye on her through his scope.

"She's almost there, and you're telling me you didn't tap that beautiful ass," he said to Ninurta.

"Keep your eyes and mind on the target and to answer your question, how do you know I didn't hit it before we left the safe house."

"She's in front of the house; now she's talking to the guards." Just then, the door to the house opened. The two guards turned their heads to look giving Sahara time to get her gun out. Kubaba shot the guard standing closest to the door and Sahara shot the other one. The van pulled up to the house. Ninurta and Nirgal jumped out and grabbed the bodies carrying them into the house.

"That could sure please a girl," Sahara said looking at Charles' naked body which still had a hard on.

"No, girl, it's his tongue and he knows how to use it," Kubaba said flashing a big smile.

"Get him dressed and ready for transport; you can tell lies later," Ninurta said breaking the giggle session that the ladies were enjoying. They dressed, cuffed, and hooded him. Then the two men took him and put him in the van next to Agnes.

"Get changed. Your clothes are in the bag," Ninurta said to Kubaba and Sahara. The van took off and the women started to change. Ninurta looked at his watch; it was 0230 hours. "Good time," he thought. "The engineer should be half drunk by now, and his guards may be a little buzzed which would help me and the team if they were." The van pulled over, and Big T turned off the headlights a block away from the target. Nirgal got out and took his assault rifle with him; Sahara was with him armed with the same. The pair slipped off into the darkness. Both were glad the Turks didn't spend much on street lighting. Ninurta watched them as they snaked their way from shadow to shadow staying out of sight with their black fatigues hiding their outlines.

He waited until they had reached a position to cover the teams' entrance and extraction. Then he told Big T to move. The van started to move. When it was almost in front of the house, Big T stuck his left arm out of the window and started firing his pistol. He hit the guard standing out front but not before he sounded the alarm. Ninurta was out of the van before it stopped and headed for the front door. He came face to face with the second guard as he was climbing the front stairs two at a time; he pumped five rounds into the guard's body knocking the guard back into the house. Ninurta kept going. Once inside, he started to look for Peter, aka the engineer.

Kubaba caught up with him. "Where is he?" she asked.

"He's hiding. Check all the rooms and be sure not to kill him," he replied. They split up and began to search.

"I found him!" Kubaba yelled out. Then she reached under the bed, grabbed him by the hair, and pulled him out. She rolled him onto his stomach, and placed her knee in his back. Just then, Ninurta arrived. He helped her cuff his hands and place the black hood over his head then stood him up and headed for the door. As they passed the living room window, it exploded with gunfire. Ninurta and Kubaba hit the floor reaching up to pull the engineer down. Then they heard the return fire.

Ninurta knew it was Nirgal and Sahara. Next he heard the sound of a semi-automatic shotgun being fired.

"Come on!" they heard Big T yell. Ninurta jumped up taking the engineer with him and headed out the door with Kubaba hot on his heels. They raced to the van and threw the engineer in as bullets hit the van's windshield and raked its side.

Kubaba turned and saw two men rushing towards them and fired. Her bullets caused them to be knocked backwards downing them. Then she ran forward and put a round in each of the men's faces before returning to the van. She jumped in, and Big T tore off heading down the street as fast as the van would go. Ninurta looked in the side mirror and saw seven bodies lying in the street and hoped Nirgal and Sahara had made it out. As the van turned the corner, its headlights illuminated a car with a woman sitting in it. Ninurta looked at her as he passed by then looked back at the car as the van maneuvered down the street.

They returned to the safe house driving the van into the garage. Their three guests were secured and the team started to stand down.

"I'm going to contact Anu and report our situation and tell him we have a problem," Ninurta said. Kubaba looked at him for a moment as if to ask what problem but decided against it. "Kubaba, I want you to keep a watch out for Nirgal and Sahara and let me know as soon as they get here," he instructed then left the room. Kubaba looked at Big T; they locked eyes. Both of them knew something had gone south; they just didn't know how far. Kubaba left the house going out the back and circled around to the front ending up fifty meters from the safe house where she took up her observation. Ninurta sat at a small wooden desk that was the only furniture in the room except for the chair he was sitting on and a cot in the corner. He opened a folder and took out a picture of a woman and looked at it. "It was you and you didn't even bother to hide," he said to himself. The picture was of Theresa, the one Anu had sent along with the kill order.

Ninurta started to type out his report. He didn't want a visual meeting not knowing the capabilities of his new enemy. He sent it and waited for a reply. Kubaba noticed a red sedan pull up and park at the end of the block. Two figures got out and headed her way. She watched them approach the safe house. She focused on how the man was walking and knew it was Nirgal and Sahara. She called Big T and let him know they were about to enter the safe house. Then she stayed in place to see if they had been followed. Nirgal and Sahara walked in and went straightway to talk to Ninurta.

"Good, you're back. How did you evade and get here?" he asked.

"We moved maybe 20 meters after you got clear and waited. And you'll never guess who showed up with the clean-up crew...our girl in the picture...the one with the kill on sight order. Well, she shows up with about fifteen men and women and started to clean up. I mean, they took all of the bodies even the guards and left. The whole thing took about five minutes," Nirgal told him.

"I think she was watching the entire time, Ninurta," Sahara added.

"What makes you think that, Sahara?" Ninurta asked.

"Because she entered the scene from the same direction you left from, so it's safe to assume she has had us under surveillance," she answered. Before he could reply, the laptop lit up and a message started to come through.

"Will you excuse me a moment," he said as he turned his attention to the screen.

"Proceed with plan. Target is highest priority.
Capture if possible. Will send pickup as requested."

Ninurta sent his acknowledgement and shut the laptop down. He sat there for minute and wondered if this was the right plan. He couldn't leave until Pam arrived if she arrived at all. Plus, he had to find a way to draw his target in. Now he had to tell his team his plan and sound convincing. When he decided to do so, he got up and walked into the room where they had gathered, all except Kubaba.

"Kubaba to base," the radio sounded. Ninurta picked up the mike and acknowledged. "We have two visitors." she said.

"If possible, return to base," Ninurta told her then ended the transmission. "Nirgal, go up to the roof and see if there are any more uninvited visitors. Sahara, go and meet Kubaba and make sure she's not followed," Ninurta instructed. The agents left the room. Big T went to check on the packages. Kubaba and Sahara came back first then Nirgal and Big T. Kubaba filled Ninurta in on the particulars that she did not tell him over the radio. He listened. Then it came to him as to how he would bait Theresa and eliminate her and her team of killers.

Theresa sat in a wingback chair drinking vodka, straight, no ice, and stared into space as she thought of the early morning activities. She ignored the noise coming from the men and women talking as they cleaned and organized their weapons and equipment. "Whoever is running that ground team is smart. I hadn't counted on a cover team. And how did they get in place without being spotted? Oh well, time for plan A. I will hit them with a full assault before they have time to move the targets," she thought to herself. Now all she needed was for them to sit right where they are until she comes a calling. Then she smiled to herself and took another sip of her drink.

Oannes sat in her private compartment on the Mediterranean Express and looked out the window at the darkness. The rocking and swaying of the train should have soothed her some but not tonight. It was 3:00 a.m. In a few hours, she would be back with her team then home. She needed to see them again. They never would believe the time she had and the shit she did. Oannes smiled to herself. Finally, she would be a full-fledged agent and no longer the baby. She had completed her first field assignment. All she had to do now was stay alive until she reached the ship and safety. The thought seemed to relax her; and as she thought of Alex, she dozed off.

Ninurta told his team that there was a change in plans. He informed them about the new plan to ship the targets out early and how they were to accomplish this. He answered their questions. Then they set about the task at hand and started packing up the equipment. They loaded the van. Nirgal and Kubaba started to take the captives one by one out the back escape route to another waiting van. Ninurta and Sahara rode with the captives to the pickup point where Captain America was waiting by the helicopter.

Captain America approached Ninurta as his team loaded their targets into the helicopter.

"Anu said to tell you if you're not at the pickup point on time, he will have to leave you and your team. If that should happen, you should look up a friend. Here's the address and good luck," he said then boarded the helicopter. It lifted off disappearing into the darkness.

Ninurta and Sahara headed back to the safe house in a car that was waiting for them as the van took off in another direction. He took the risk and drove past the front of the house. Two men in the surveillance car were still their watching. But now, they were joined by a second car at the other end of the street. This one had a man and woman in it. They were talking when he passed by them. When he was back in the house, he informed his team of the extra eyes. His decision to move his guests early was a good one. Now he knew how he could draw them in, but he had a feeling Theresa was coming straight at them.

It was 6:00 a.m. and the train pulled into the station. Oannes was packed and waiting. She stayed in her compartment until the train came to a complete stop. She left her compartment, walked to the exit, and left among the crowd of people departing.

Ninurta looked at his team. Half were armed with the FNH P90 assault rifles in 5.7 x 28 mm caliber. Each had two fifty round magazines. He and Big T were carrying SLP MK1 semi-automatic tactical shotguns. Around their waists were ammo belts holding twenty-four extra shells in double 00 buck including exploding slug rounds all in 12 gauge. He placed Nirgal and Kubaba on the second floor where they had a clear field of fire down at the oval shaped reflecting pool and the front door. He and Big T would be on the first floor on the other side of the room. There, they would engage whoever came in and could cover the open room with their shotguns. Sahara would circle around front and take out targets as they presented themselves. He gave her one of the FHN pistols with two extra twenty round magazines.

It was 6:00 a. m. and time to spring his trap. He gave Nirgal the signal. Then Nirgal cautiously walked out the front door. He walked a few meters up and down the street so that he could be seen then he went back in the house. Once inside, he sprinted up the stairs, took up his position with Kubaba, and waited.

"Five, no, I mean nine armed men moving towards the house," Sahara said into her throat mike.

"Stay put and no firing until they come out," Ninurta said to her. "Curtain call, people, pucker up," he said to the rest of the team as he took the safety off his shotgun.

Nine men approached the house. Two of them set small explosive charges to the front door's hinges and lock. The others stood guard and waited. They were getting a little nervous because the neighborhood was starting to stir. Three loud pops sounded and the door fell into the house. The men streamed in firing their assault rifles in three round bursts. Ninurta waited until they had reached the reflecting pool before he opened fire. The team rained bullets, buckshot, and exploding rounds down on the doomed men tearing their bodies apart. The engagement was over in ninety short seconds. Then Nirgal and Kubaba looked down at what was left of the dead men's bullet riddled, dismembered bodies.

Sahara walked in and looked around. She tried hard not to throw up.

"We have to go. There're people outside and more coming," she said anxiously.

"Go and get the car, Sahara. Everybody okay?" he asked Nirgal and Kubaba. They answered and came down the stairs being careful not to stand in the pooling blood gathering around the men's bodies. "Get out of that gear! And, Kubaba, go check outside on that crowd Sahara says is gathering and keep an eye out for Oannes." She handed Nirgal her weapon and magazines and took off her body armor and headscarf. Then she carefully stepped over the bodies and various body parts and intestines and went outside.

Kubaba saw Sahara sitting in the car just out front and nodded. A crowd was gathering but not a large one. Some neighbors were talking amongst themselves trying to figure out what all of the gunfire was about no doubt. She approached them and told the small crowd that everything was fine, and that it was a government operation capturing a cell of terrorists. Then she showed them her identification and continued to calm them down. As she did so, she kept an eye out for Oannes. She looked up the street, over the crowd. She knew she had to come that way.

Then she saw her and radioed Ninurta.

"It's about time. Take the gear to the car. I'll be right behind you now get going." Nirgal and Big T picked up the two black duffle bags and left. Ninurta pulled out a camera and began to take pictures of the scene. Then he left and headed for the car. When he reached the sidewalk, he looked up the street and saw Kubaba headed his way. He couldn't see Oannes.

Just as Kubaba reached him and Oannes broke through the crowd, Theresa pulled the trigger on her carbine. The 30.06 caliber round slammed into Ninurta's chest throwing him violently back against the side of the house and killing him instantly. Kubaba ran to him looking all around with her pistol drawn. Nirgal and Big T jumped out of the car to assist her.

Oannes saw the entire thing unfold but couldn't warn them. Instead, she drew her pistol and ran towards the car that Theresa was sitting in. Theresa didn't see her coming until it was too late when she looked up the street after placing the rifle on the seat beside her. Oannes raised her gun and fired as she ran up to the car. The 45 caliber bullets made Theresa's body jump around in her seat. When she stopped firing and looked into the car, half of Theresa's head was missing; and her left side looked like it had been put through a meat grinder. Oannes turned and headed towards the house and saw Nirgal and Big T loading Ninurta's body into the trunk of a car. Kubaba screamed to her and waved her towards them. She got in the backseat with the two men, and Sahara sped off.

"Who-the-fuck did I just kill?" Oannes asked.

"Theresa," Nirgal answered.

"Is she the one that killed Ninurta?"

"Yes," she answered flatly. Sahara maneuvered the car through the narrow city streets driving much slower now. No one was talking as they headed for the extraction point. When they arrived, Nirgal and Big T took Ninurta's body out of the trunk and laid it down on the ground covering him with a blanket.

"I'm sorry about your friend. I liked him. He was a true professional. He will be missed. But this is where I must leave you. I too have my orders. Good luck, and may Allah bless you," she said sincerely. Then she and Big T got into the car and drove off.

"Now that we have a minute, will one of you tell me what happened and who-the-hell this Theresa chick is or was in this case?" Oannes said as she kept a look out for the helicopter.

"Alright, I'll bring you up to speed then you can share," Kubaba said sarcastically, "because Nirgal is not the best storyteller." She gave Oannes the condensed version. By the time she finished, they heard the woompwoompwoompwoomp! sound of the helicopter. They loaded Ninurta's body and gear then themselves. Nobody looked back as the helicopter took off and headed for the C.A.A.

The Holiday Party

Chapter Twenty-Eight

Wilhelm stood in front of the window that looked out over the gardens, sipping a scotch. The snow was sparkling under the moonlight, undisturbed. No footprints were visible for as far as he could see. Just as his mind started to wander, he heard the right door panel slide open then closed. He listened to the footsteps approach then stop.

"Sir, they're ready," George said.

"Has Rodney arrived?"

"Yes, sir, and he has Ms. Banally with him."

Then Wilhelm turned around, put his glass on a coaster on his desk, and walked out the library. He headed for the east wing of the house where the family's annual holiday party was in full swing. In the hallway just before the grand ballroom, he saw his three wives standing and talking among themselves. He stopped to look at them. He watched them as they checked and re-checked their gowns and noticed the way they smiled at each other and laughed at whatever was being said. "Family," he thought. Maybe it was time for him to retire and spent more time with his family. Deep inside, he knew that wasn't possible. Even in retirement, he would always be involved with the community. Then he resumed walking down the hall.

"My, don't we all look beautiful. And, Afra, are you sure you just had a baby? Looking at you, one wouldn't know," he said making her smile. He was glad that he had made it home in time to see his daughter's birth; it did a lot in the peacekeeping department.

"We keep telling her that; maybe she'll believe you," Afef said.

"Enough with the chatter, already. Let's go in," Colleen said as she ran her hands over his lapels.

Colleen had decided to dress them in Halston retro, and the ladies had pulled out their best jewels and pearls. Wilhelm wore his silver inlaid hand scrolled 380 caliber pistol with bison horn grips that was engraved with the family crest. He wore no jewelry except for a two-carat diamond tiepin, Cartier watch, and wedding ring. George talked into his collar mike and waited.

"Any second, boss," George said to him. Wilhelm and his wives got ready. Colleen stood on his right and Afef and Afra on his left. They waited for the announcement.

"Ladies and gentlemen and distinguish guests, it is my pleasure and honor to present to you our host and hostesses," the announcer said. Wilhelm and his wives walked into the ballroom and stopped in the center of the floor. Next, a man came out and handed him a microphone.

"Thank you for coming to our annual holiday party. As some of you know, we have this celebration to enjoy the company of old and new friends out of sight of prying eyes and away from the world's problems which many of us are charged with solving. So please, enjoy the hospitality of Libertaire Manor and let the festivities begin," he said. Then he danced with each of his wives, first with Colleen doing the Philly two step and then changing partners throughout the song.

With his responsibility done, he headed for the bar and caught the eye of Rodney. Wilhelm stopped and spoke briefly with some of the diplomats, senators, congress members, and select businessman. As he made his way across the room, his wives had spread out and were now working the crowd. The ballroom held one hundred fifty people and was filled to capacity with guests and waitstaff. A beautiful tall dark-skinned woman was singing on the stage, and more than a few couples were dancing. Wilhelm took a lamb kebab off the tray of a passing waiter and made his way to the bar. Once there, the bartender handed him a scotch; as he waited for Rodney to work his way through the crowd, he ate.

"Can we go to your library and talk? I have some information I need to share with you," Rodney said when he finally reached him.

"Have a kebab, Rodney. They're really good," Wilhelm said ignoring him.

"I have a report that Frank is back in the country," Rodney said as he got the attention of the bartender. "And I need you to find and kill him, Wilhelm," he continued.

"I'm not killing anyone tonight, Rodney. Frank will keep for a while," he said and then took a sip of his scotch. Rodney took his double gin from the bartender and drank half of his drink in one gulp.

"It really is important that I talk to you, Wilhelm. So stop fucking with me and let's go talk in your office," he said through clinched teeth and then threw back the remaining gin.

"Okay, Rodney, let's go." Wilhelm notified George, and they were met in the hall by two guards dressed in black tuxes and the five of them walked to the library.

After they were alone, Wilhelm turned to him and said,

"Fix yourself a drink, Rodney, then tell me how the agency is in peril." Wilhelm knew Rodney had a way of making the smallest thing an emergency; it was his nature. He also knew Rodney was a good administrator and better than most when it came to hunches.

"Frank was spotted in Seattle five days ago around the docks then again in Long Beach two days later and again at the docks. Since then, there have been no further sightings. What do you think about that?" Rodney asked.

Wilhelm's mind went into overdrive. "Docks...Cali...disappeared," he thought. He walked over to his desk and pressed a button on his phone and walked away. Rodney turned around with a double gin in his hand.

"Where's the ice?"

"Behind you on the left." Rodney turned back around and opened the silver ice bucket and pulled out a frozen colored marble cube and dropped it in his glass.

"I love these; they keep my gin cold without the water," he said as he swirled the marble around in the glass.

"Why do you think he went to the docks?" Wilhelm asked.

"I think he's setting up something; and with the information he has in his head, he could do a lot of damage to us. I need you to find him and kill him before he can do that damage," Rodney said then sat down in a chair and sipped his drink.

"I don't know what to tell you, Rodney. With such little Intel, there's very little me or my people can do," he said then walked to the chair across from Rodney and sat down. Then Bonnie his French mastiff came over and lay down beside him.

"Does that dog ever leave this room?" Rodney said with a smile taking another sip of his drink.

"No, Rodney. She never does and neither do I." Then the two men burst out into laughter.

"Thanks, Wilhelm, I needed that. This shit with Linda whom I still don't trust. And Frank...well...I don't need to tell you how I feel about him. Now it wasn't enough for him to be a top operator and run his own department; he had to turn traitor. I never would have predicted that in a million years, not a million years. What-the-fuck made him turn? Before you kill him, Wilhelm, you ask that son-of-a-bitch why he turned."

Wilhelm sat there and listened and watched Rodney's face contort with rage and anger and hurt. He knew Rodney favored Frank over him. He had accepted that fact but he had to agree with Rodney on this one. And yes, he would ask Frank that question. He wanted to know for himself what made him turn. Why betray his country and friends?

"I will ask him for you, Rodney, before I kill him."

"Good. Now for some good news, you've been promoted. You now run the section. This means you will take over Frank's old office and all of his cases. You bring whatever personnel you want. I assume it will be Gladys and one other. I didn't see you at the ceremony," Rodney said changing gears in mid-stride. Wilhelm took notice Rodney was back. That moment of honesty was rare in this business especially at this level, and Wilhelm was honored by it.

"I haven't been to one of those in years; you know that. Why would I change, now?"

"Because of Kevin, that's why." Wilhelm didn't respond. He thought of the promise they had made never to attend each other's star ceremony, only the funeral. Wilhelm and Colleen went to his funeral; they both had lost a close friend.

"Because of a promise... ." Rodney nodded his head and finished his drink.

"Will that beast rip my leg off when I head to the bar for a refill?" Rodney joked as he stepped over the dog. Just then a short buzz sounded; it came from the phone on the desk. Wilhelm now knew that Shadow One was ready and awaiting orders.

"You're not going to get that?" Rodney asked from the bar.

"No, it's Colleen reminding me I'm being a bad host," he said as he got up.

"Is there anything else, Rodney? If not, let's go back to the party." Rodney shook his head no; they headed back to the party and Bonnie headed for the kitchen. When they reached the party, they split up. Wilhelm went to check on his guests at the indoor pool located down the hall from the ballroom. He had discovered over the years that some of his guests liked to swim and drink even before he opened the pool for his annual parties. In fact, they were the reason he started to include the pool in the festivities.

Next he returned to the ballroom and started to mingle with his guests. While he was dancing with his eldest daughter, he saw George approaching and so did she.

"Daddy, tell him to go away; we're dancing."

"Okay baby, I will," he said. Then he held up his hand stopping George. George waited until the song ended before approaching again.

"Sir, there's an urgent message for you; it was delivered at the gate," he said in his ear as he leaned close. Wilhelm looked at George and nodded. Then they headed for the library.

"Who delivered the message?" Wilhelm asked as they walked.

"A young man on a motorcycle; he was familiar with the protocol," George informed him. When they reached the library, Wilhelm turned on the TV, tuned into the gate footage, and watched.

"Where is the message?" George gave him the envelope.

"We did the usual checks, no finger prints or contagions," George said as he handed it to him. Wilhelm opened the letter and read it in silence.

"Meet me at the hill. I'll be waiting," it read. *He new it was Frank.*

"Go and ask Ms. Banally to join me and get the jeep ready," he told George. After George left the room, Wilhelm picked up his cellphone and pressed the pound button.

"Yes," a voice said on the other end.

"I'm sending you the coordinates. Be there in thirty minutes," he said then hung up. George walked in with Linda then left. "I think you should take a ride with me," he said staring directly into her eyes.

"Why?" she asked as she stiffened her body becoming tense.

"There is someone you should meet. It won't take long; it's a short distance from here." He took note of the change in her body posture. Bonnie did also by standing up and moving to his side. George came in with her coat.

"Everything is ready, sir," he said then headed out the door as Linda and Wilhelm followed. They left by a side door where a jeep was waiting. The three of them got in, and the driver pulled out of the garage and down the lane using no headlights. The driver turned left onto the highway then turned on the headlights. Linda sat quietly in the backseat with Wilhelm and looked straight ahead. They rode for twenty minutes then the driver made another left turn onto a snow covered road. (You would have to have known that it was there because it wasn't visible from the highway.)

The driver put the jeep into four-wheel drive, turned off the headlights, put on the fog lights, and continued up the side road for another ten minutes. Then he stopped, turned off the fog lights, and got out of the jeep taking an assault rifle with him. For the first time, Linda noticed that he was dressed in white. The man walked behind the jeep and into the darkness. Then George got out and took off his overcoat. He was in white also; he too walked off into the darkness. Linda didn't see if he had a weapon. But she was sure he wouldn't walk into the woods without one.

"Who are you meeting?" Linda asked.

"Frank," he said as he looked at her. "Wait here. Do not leave this vehicle and keep your eyes on that hill," he continued as he pointed.

Linda looked out into the darkness and up at a hill that was dotted by shadows and lit with what little moonlight there was. She watched Wilhelm carefully walk up the hill. When he was half way up, a man's silhouette appeared at the top. Her heart skipped a beat and her breath got caught in her throat at the sight of Frank. She knew his body shape and the way he stood when he was faced with danger, and meeting Wilhelm way out here was a dangerous move. She watched Wilhelm walk up the hill and stop a few feet from Frank causing him to turn sideways to face him.

"I knew you would come. So where's George? Does he have me in his scope?"

"Why the meeting in the cold, Frank? You could have thought of a warmer place?" Wilhelm replied ignoring Frank's inquiry about George.

"I thought a night talk might be beneficial to our health since I know how you enjoy fresh air. Besides, it harder for anyone to sneak up on us and interrupt. I would hate for that to happen," Frank said as he looked around.

"Rodney and a few others would like to know why you changed your allegiance."

"Does that mean you're not interested, Wilhelm. I called this meeting just to tell you why I did it. Now you tell me you're not interested."

"Alright, Frank, tell me why you did it," Wilhelm said as he took out a cigar.

"Is lighting that cigar the signal to kill me?"

"No, Frank. If it makes you feel better, I'll put it away."

"I would feel better if you did," Frank said then changed his position.

"Now can we get on with it? I have a party to host," Wilhelm said as he put the cigar back into the case then back into his coat pocket.

"It's simple. I did it for the power."

"And Nicaragua, Frank?"

"He was a psycho, Wilhelm.   He needed to be put down."

"He was with me, Frank, and he had information about an assassin named Talaus when you killed him," Wilhelm said taking a step closer to Frank. "What do you know about this assassin?"

"Nothing, Wilhelm. I killed him for the reason I gave you, nothing more. He was out of control and didn't care who he killed. That's why I blew his brains out and nothing more."

"Okay, Frank. If you say so. Why come back? With your resources, you could have dropped off the grid."

"I still may do that but I wanted to see you first, one last time. You know I still believe you killed or had Tony killed. Although you have always denied it, I know you did. He was getting too close to the great Wilhelm, so you killed him.   And the company let you get away with it but I guess I should have expected that. With the way they let you get away with, well, anything you want to."

"Is this about me, Frank? You telling me you turned traitor out of jealousy? That's bullshit, Frank. I worked for you. You had all of the power and position. What-the-fuck do you have to be jealous about?" Wilhelm said through clinched teeth.

"Oh that's rich, Wilhelm. Where do I start? Let's see," Frank said as he started pacing back and forth. "Oh yeah, you have three wives. What agent has three wives? Most of us can't hold on to one wife and yet you manage three. Let's see, one is from Syria whose father is a major smuggler. One is from Turkey whose father starts a miraculous climb up the military ladder soon after you married his daughter. You have two cargo ships. Tell me, Wilhelm, how many black men have two fucking cargo ships, not to mention your gentleman's farm? Shit, give me a break.

I knew you when, motherfucker! ...gentleman my ass! You're a cold blooded killer. I watched you shoot through a young girl to get your target, remember!" Frank said getting visibly angry and pacing in a circle in the snow. Wilhelm stood there and watched him closely keeping his hands in his coat pocket.

"Anything else on your mind, Frank. I mean, while we're having this heart to heart you should get it all out in the open," Wilhelm said coolly. Frank stopped, looked at him, and then smiled.

"You really are a bastard. You were always better at this spy game than I was. I just wanted to say I hope they don't send you after me. I would hate to have a fight with you. Let someone else do it. So I'm asking you to just walk away and let someone else hunt me. Can you? Will you do that for an old friend?" he said sincerely. Wilhelm looked at him for what seemed a long time then nodded yes.

"Yeah, Frank, I can do that I promise. I will not be the one to put that bullet in your head," he said as he looked Frank in his eyes.

"Thank you, Wilhelm. I have big enough problems ahead of me and knowing you're not behind me...well...need I say more."

"What kind of problems, Frank?"

"Nothing to concern yourself about, Wilhelm. Don't you have a party to attend? You'll be missed if you stay any longer."

"I take it our business is concluded then."

"Yes, it has. Take care, Wilhelm. I suspect I'll never see you again and congratulations; I hear you have a new baby girl." Wilhelm nodded his head and turned to walk away. Frank stood halfway in a shadow watching him go down the hill. Just then, Linda thought she saw a fleeting shadow go by Frank. Then his body collapsed. Wilhelm turned around and walked back. When he reached Frank, he looked down at his lifeless body. Frank's face had a look of surprise on it and there was a small hole in the side of his head. Other than that, he looked very peaceful. Wilhelm headed back down the hill to the car and got in. George and the driver appeared out of the darkness and joined them.

"Was that Frank?" she asked.

"Yes."

"Is he dead?"

"Yes." Linda turned her gaze forward and sat quietly as the jeep turned around and headed back to the house.

As she listened to the tires on the highway, she thought, "You were right, Frank. He's cold and deadly to kill you without a second thought—a man he knew for twenty years. I wouldn't have believed it was possible. This is a lesson I will never forget." Then she looked over at Wilhelm who was sitting next to her, emotionless. He had just killed a man in the snow. (To look at him, you wouldn't know he had done anything except go for a ride in the snow.)

The jeep pulled back into the garage. They got out and waited while Wilhelm took off his boots and put on his shoes. Then he, George, and Linda went to the library.

"What you witnessed tonight was the execution of a traitor, nothing more. You are to keep tonight's activities to yourself; it is now deemed classified. If you want to go home, that's understandable. You were once lovers and this can be a little upsetting. My advice is that you rejoin the party and get drunk. I can promise you Rodney will be evaluating your performance. Can I get you a drink or something? Do you need to sit down and collect yourself?" he asked.

"No, sir. I'll be fine and I understand. Thank you for letting me witness this," she said looking at him through glazed eyes.

"I thought you deserved to see that. After all, he did try to kill you; and you needed to see how we deal with such matters in Special Section. George will see you back to the party." George touched Linda on the shoulder and they headed for the door. Linda stopped and turned around.

"Sir, are you going to leave him in the snow?" she asked.

"For a little while, it was one of his favorite places," Wilhelm said then smiled.

Wilhelm saw the last of his guests out and stood on the front steps until the last car was out of sight before going in. He went upstairs and looked in on all of his children and lingered over the newest member of the family. Then he said,

"Good night," to each of his wives and went down to the library. He patted Bonnie on the head and poured himself a double scotch then stood in the window looking out at the snow. The snow started to fall lightly, gently and there was no wind to disturb the flakes. "Here's to you Frank," he said in a whisper. Then he took a large swallow from his glass and looked out at the snow.

Le Fin

Epilogue

Peru

Number 1 looked down the long conference table at the other four members seated along its length.

"Gentlemen, I have received confirmation that the operation to eliminate Mr. Libertaire and his team of special agents was a failure. And Number 2's agent Frank DePore is dead, no doubt at the hands of one Mr. Libertaire." He paused as two men walked up and stood behind Number 2's chair. "It has also been confirmed who the shooter was that killed the two CIA agents in France and who had hired that shooter. Do you have anything to say in your defense Number 2?" Number 1 said looking at him. The other members turned to face him.

"The target was Linda Banally, I suspected. *She* is Number 5's agent and the one feeding us all of that Intel. I didn't want you to start thinking about replacing Frank. After all, he was right about our plan. Now we don't have the scientists or Wilhelm," Number 2 said very calmly, very matter-of-fact.

"You know our rules and the punishment," Number 1 said. Number 2 nodded yes. The two men standing behind him seized him. One pinned his arms down; the other put a silk cord around his neck and began to strangle him. Number 2 bucked his hips and kicked his legs violently under the table as his life was drained out of him. When a slight cracking sound was heard, he went limp. The man kept the tension up for a minute longer then released it. The four members watched in silence as the body was carried away. "Now that we have closed that business, is there anyone present who still thinks Mr. Libertaire is not a threat to our organization?"

Number 5 had just returned to his private quarters when his cellphone rang; he looked at the number. "It can't be," he thought. Then he answered,

"Hello."

"I bet you're surprised to hear from me," a voice said.

"That's an understatement. You're the ghost who walks."

"I've been inside, and I have the information you want."

"Good! We'll meet and talk about it."

"Fine, just bring lots of money with you," the voice said then the line went dead. Number 5 smiled to himself. "Greedy bitch," he thought. Then he threw the phone on the sofa and headed for the pool.

South Africa

Talaus and Taylor stood by the grave of Theresa and watched the men throw dirt on her casket. He had buried her on the hill overlooking a stand of trees that a flock of colorful birds used as a place to roost. Theresa liked watching them return each evening. Wilhelm had saved him the trouble of killing her yet he still felt the loss. Taylor stood there patting the mastiff on his head lightly. She looked impatient and wondered how much longer and who would replace her in bed. When, the men finished, he paid them.

"You ready to go?" he asked Taylor.

"Yes. Who's going to replace her?" she asked as they started to walk.

"I have my eye on a lovely young lady, an American. I think you'll like her. And training her will not only be fun but pleasurable. What do think about that?"

"I love that idea. When do we start?" she replied as she looked up at him.

Epilogue

Libertaire Manor

"They're waiting for you, sir," George said as he entered the library.

"Help me with this parka." George walked over and picked up the black mink parka and helped his boss slide it over his head.

When he walked outside, he saw his entire family, all of his children and his wives. The younger ones were playing with two of the security guards who stopped when they realized their boss was watching. Wilhelm didn't mind; the closer the guards felt towards the family, the harder they would fight to protect them.

"Why are you always late?" Afra said to him.

"I had no idea I was late," he replied.

"Well, you are. We can't start our evening walk until you get here," she continued trying to keep a straight face.

"Very well then, since I'm here, let's get going," he said as he walked down the steps to join them. His children ran ahead of him and the security guards melted into the darkness on either side of them. Wilhelm took a deep breath and looked at the fog his breath made when he exhaled. "I have to give Shadow One a bonus; he did a good job on the hill," he thought. Then he smiled at Colleen as she took his arm. They walked behind the others with George and Bonnie pulling up the rear.

About the Author

P. W. Hand is a scholar, a former marine, an all-around adventurer, and outdoorsman. He is an avid golfer and sailing enthusiast and enjoys equestrian cross-country and trail riding, hunting, hiking, mountain-climbing, and the shooting sports. He earned three degrees from the University Nevada, Las Vegas, which are a master's degree in educational leadership, a B.A. in history, and a B.A. in Asian studies. As an expert in Asian history and culture, he is fluent in mandarin Chinese and is a skilled calligrapher and teacher of Chinese internal boxing arts and swordsmanship. He has studied and has practiced Chinese martial arts for forty-four years as well as French and Italian swordplay for fourteen years. He teaches the arts of Yang Style Tai Chi Quan, Hsing Yi Quan, Classical Northern Wu Style Tai Chi Quan, and European swordsmanship.

His travels have taken him to the four corners of the globe which has inspired his research on exotic peoples, cultures, and places. His most recent adventure took him to Egypt just before the fall of the Mubarak regime. There, he conducted research for his upcoming fiction book series, *Wilhelm Libertaire*.

He has chaired creative writing sessions at the Far West Popular Culture and American Culture Associations' 2012 and 2013 conventions held in Las Vegas, Nevada. He is a member of the Golden Key International Honor Society and the American Library Association. Presently, he and his wife Claire live in Henderson, Nevada, with their two French mastiffs. He can be contacted by email at hand.phillip@gmail.com.

www.ingramcontent.com/pod-product-compliance
Lightning Source LLC
Chambersburg PA
CBHW051542250626
47157CB00001B/156